PRAISE FOR ISABELLA MALDONADO

A Killer's Game

"Intense, gripping, and compulsively readable, *A Killer's Game* goes from zero to ninety on page one and never slows down. FBI agent Dani Vega is a heroine to cheer for—tough, inventive, and highly capable. A winner."

—Meg Gardiner, #1 *New York Times* bestselling author

The Falcon

"Another great read from [Isabella Maldonado]! I'm a Nina Guerrera fan, and this book is the best of the series so far. Don't miss it!"

—Steve Netter, Best Thriller Books

A Different Dawn

"A horrifying crime, cat-and-mouse detection, aha moments, and extended suspense . . ."

—*Kirkus Reviews*

"Maldonado expertly ratchets up the tension as the pieces of the puzzle neatly fall into place. Suspense fans will be enthralled from the very first page."

—*Publishers Weekly*

"A thrill ride from the very start. It starts off fast and never lets up. It's one of the best thrillers of the summer."

—*Red Carpet Crash*

D0188009

"*A Different Dawn* is a heart-stopping journey on parallel tracks: police detection and personal . . . Isabella Maldonado has created an unforgettable hero in Nina Guerrera."

—Criminal Element

"A killer of a novel. Fresh, fast, and utterly ingenious."

—Brad Thor, #1 *New York Times* bestselling author

The Cipher

"The survivor of a vicious crime confronts her fears in a hunt for a serial killer . . . forensic analysis, violent action, and a tough heroine who stands up to the last man on earth she wants to see again."

—*Kirkus Reviews*

"[In] this riveting series launch from Maldonado . . . the frequent plot twists will keep readers guessing to the end, and Maldonado draws on her twenty-two years in law enforcement to add realism. Determined to overcome her painful past, the admirable Nina has enough depth to sustain a long-running series."

—*Publishers Weekly*

"*The Cipher* by Isabella Maldonado is a nail-biting race against time."

—POPSUGAR

"Maldonado does a superb job of depicting a woman who's made a strength out of trauma, and an even better job at showing how a monster could use the internet to prey on the vulnerable. Maldonado spent twenty-two years in law enforcement, and her experience shines through in *The Cipher*."

—Amazon Book Review

"A heart-pounding novel from page one, *The Cipher* checks all the boxes for a top-notch thriller: sharp plotting, big stakes, and characters—good and bad and everywhere in between—that are so richly drawn you'll swear you've met them. I read this in one sitting, and I guarantee you will too. Oh, another promise: you'll absolutely love the Warrior Girl!"

—Jeffery Deaver, *New York Times* bestselling author

"Wow! A riveting tale in the hands of a superb storyteller."

—J. A. Jance, *New York Times* bestselling author

"Intense, harrowing, and instantly addictive, *The Cipher* took my breath away. Isabella Maldonado has created an unforgettable heroine in Nina Guerrera, a dedicated FBI agent and trauma survivor with unique insight into the mind of a predator. This riveting story is everything a thriller should be."

—Hilary Davidson, *Washington Post* bestselling author

A KILLER'S GAME

OTHER TITLES BY ISABELLA MALDONADO

FBI Agent Nina Guerrera series

The Cipher

A Different Dawn

The Falcon

Detective Veranda Cruz series

Blood's Echo

Phoenix Burning

Death Blow

A KILLER'S GAME

ISABELLA MALDONADO

THOMAS & MERCER

Published by Thomas & Mercer, Seattle

www.apub.com

Amazon, the Amazon logo, and Thomas & Mercer are trademarks of Amazon.com, Inc., or its affiliates.

ISBN-13: 9781662507830 (paperback)
ISBN-13: 9781662507823 (digital)

Cover design by Shasti O'Leary Soudant
Cover images: © Laurie Allread, © Marie Carr / Arcangel Images
Photo on page 41 courtesy of Library of Congress, Prints & Photographs Division

Printed in the United States of America

*For the Grinnans,
who opened their home and their hearts
to welcome me into their family.*

CHAPTER 1

FBI Special Agent Daniela Vega assessed her environment and calculated her chances. She had less than seven minutes to get to her meeting with the special agent in charge of the New York Counterterrorism Division. A stickler for protocol and punctuality, SAC Steve Wu would not appreciate her showing up late.

She eyed the barista. If he kept up his frenetic pace, she could make it from the packed Lower Manhattan coffee shop to SAC Wu's office on the twenty-third floor of 26 Federal Plaza at a fast walk with sixty seconds to spare.

A woman elbowing her way toward the pickup counter jostled Dani into the man beside her, who was dumping a packet of sugar into his open cup. His piping-hot coffee splashed onto the back of Dani's hand.

"What's the matter with you?" the man snapped at her.

Dani pressed her lips together and shook the steaming droplets from her hand, where an angry splotch had already blossomed. The man placed a lid on his cup, sent her another scowl, and squeezed through the crowd toward the door.

The barista shouted her name above the din. "Dark roast, black with an extra shot," he said, handing the cup to her. "That should jump-start your day."

It would take a lot more than a jolt of caffeine from strong coffee to get her heart pounding. Perhaps searching a building with a hidden IED would move the needle, but those days had ended with her final deployment before she joined the Bureau ten months earlier.

"Breakfast of champions." She lifted the cup in salute, then turned and shouldered her way through the throng to the sidewalk. She was about to take her first sip when buzzing from inside her pocket stopped her.

"Hey," a man sitting on the sidewalk holding a cardboard sign called out to her. "How about some change?"

She slid out the phone with her free hand and lifted it to her ear. "Vega."

"Have a heart, lady," the man continued, shifting his gaze to the cup in her hand. "I bet that coffee tastes good."

SAC Wu's voice carried through the small speaker. "Where are you?"

"Just left the Starbucks at the corner of Lafayette and Worth, sir," she said. "Right across the street from you."

"I'm postponing our meeting," Wu said. "Someone called in a bomb threat at the courthouse. Given the target, this could be terrorist related. Go over there and check it out."

Her eyes traveled across the street to the other side of Thomas Paine Park. "Which courthouse?"

The New York County Supreme Court, Thurgood Marshall US Courthouse, and the US District Court for the Southern District of New York were all past the park on the other side of Centre Street.

"County Supreme Court," Wu said. "And—to make matters worse—there's a group of over a hundred schoolkids touring the building right now."

"On my way." She disconnected and thrust her untouched coffee toward the man on the sidewalk.

"Bless you," he said, taking it from her outstretched hand and clutching it protectively against his chest.

"You're wel—" An angry shout drew her gaze across Lafayette Street to the opposite corner.

"Hey," a man in a business suit called out to a fellow pedestrian who had bumped into him. "Watch where you're going."

It was a common sight in the bustle of early-morning foot traffic, and the special agent in charge had directed her to report to the scene of a bomb threat nearby. She should not have registered the brief interaction.

Yet she did.

Some would call it hypervigilance, but to her it was a combination of experience and situational awareness. She shifted her gaze from the man who had made the remark to the person who had collided with him. She couldn't see his face but took in his short dark hair and billowing tan trench coat. Tall and broad shouldered, he tucked a folded black mini umbrella close to his body, pivoted, and started across Worth Street.

It was late May, and rain was in the forecast, so it wasn't his foul-weather gear that had caught her eye. Instead, she'd noticed the way he carried the umbrella, which was clasped tightly in his right hand. He gripped it in a way she would describe as tactical. His purposeful steps and powerful bearing reinforced the impression.

Commotion pulled her attention back to the businessman, who had collapsed to the ground. She rushed across Lafayette Street. By the time she reached him, he had begun to convulse. Flecks of foam spewed from the corners of his mouth, and his eyes rolled back in his head.

A woman screamed. Several onlookers took out their cell phones. Some called 9-1-1; others began taking videos and narrating the scene.

Dani had witnessed acute toxin poisoning before and recognized its effects. The reason behind the umbrella became apparent. It had been the delivery system. Given the speed of the reaction, she knew she could do nothing for the man in the business suit, now lying motionless on the sidewalk. But she could catch the man with the umbrella, the man who had crossed Worth Street and was heading toward Thomas Paine Park.

She slid out her cell phone and started after him. Aware NYPD dispatchers were already fielding calls from the crowd around the victim, she tapped redial, connecting her directly to the person who had the authority to activate every resource in the city. Responding to the victim had delayed her, and Umbrella Man had a substantial lead.

Wu barely had time to answer before she blurted out her situation, ending with a description of Umbrella Man.

"I'll send agents to your location and request PD assistance," Wu said when she finished. "But they're evacuating the courthouse now. The situation has escalated to a full-scale counterterrorism response."

Dani saw NYPD officers in orange vests stepping onto the roadway to stop traffic on the street. A cabdriver gunned his taxi to get through before the street was closed, nearly clipping her seconds before she reached the other side of Worth, where she broke into a run on the gray octagonal pavers that covered the plaza.

"Subject has picked up the pace," she said into the phone as she watched Umbrella Man moving among the lush trees. "He's inside Thomas Paine Park. I need NYPD to head him off when he comes out the other side to Centre Street. He'll run right into them."

She had defied Wu's original order to report to the scene of a bomb threat in a sensitive location. She didn't know the SAC well and had no idea how he would react, but she figured the threat at the courthouse was contained. This suspect, however, would remain at large if he managed to get away from her.

Wu responded after a moment's pause. "I'm on my way," he said to Dani, apparently reaching the same conclusion. "Keep me updated on your location. I'm already linked to the PD for the bomb threat. The officers on Centre Street have been diverted to stop traffic and evacuate the courthouse. I'll request backup for you, but it will take a few minutes."

"I'm gaining on him," she said. "But he's well inside the park now. There are a lot of trees and—"

"Just keep the subject in sight," Wu said. "And stay on the phone with me."

She could talk without gasping, even at a dead run, and sent silent thanks to the drill instructors who had pushed her to her physical limits while she'd been in the Army. Umbrella Man changed course and broke into a sprint.

"He made me," she said into the phone. "He's heading away from Centre Street now and back toward the fountain in Foley Square."

When she closed in enough for Umbrella Man to hear her, she opted for a direct approach.

"Stop, FBI!" she shouted at his retreating back, making sure Wu heard the command as well.

She did not expect him to halt in his tracks and surrender, but he would know who was running him down. Any force he used against her would constitute a separate criminal act. As she had predicted, he kept barreling ahead, still clutching the foldable umbrella.

"Don't try to make apprehension without backup," Wu said, his voice sharp with concern.

A crowd of what looked like middle schoolers were running across Centre Street and into Foley Square. The horde of students streamed past the fountain, filling the middle of Federal Plaza.

"Who knows how much of that toxin he has?" Wu continued. "He could jab you and—"

"He's headed for a group of schoolkids," Dani said, cutting him off.

Still more than twenty paces ahead of her, Umbrella Man reached the cluster of children and turned to face her. He raised the black umbrella and pointed its tip toward a girl who looked about twelve.

Dani read his intent and came to an abrupt halt. "He's threatening one of the kids," she said into the phone. "I have to stop."

Wu swore. "Are any uniforms with you yet?"

She glanced around. "They're all across the street, redirecting traffic and evacuating the courthouse. See if some of them can respond over here to surround Foley Square while I keep him occupied. Make sure they know about the poison in the umbrella."

She turned back to the suspect as Wu repeated her words to someone else. An instant later, Umbrella Man squeezed into the group and disappeared from her line of sight.

Rushing forward, she wedged her way through the cluster of children and arrived at the subway entrance. There was no trace of him aboveground, so she arrived at the only logical conclusion. "Alert Transit," she said to Wu, referring to the Metropolitan Transit Authority. "He's gone down into the subway."

She started down the concrete stairs, inadvertently pushing people against the metal railing in the middle. Several of them, clearly assuming she was merely late to catch her train, shouted suggestions that she do anatomically impossible things.

She reached the bottom of the stairs and raced to a row of turnstiles with rotating metal partitions that resembled vertical cages. As she pulled out her yellow MetroCard and passed it over the reader, it occurred to her that Umbrella Man must have planned his escape in advance. He had probably figured on walking away rather than being chased, but he had been prepared for any contingency. She pushed through the turnstile, trying to guess his next move.

She turned right and ran down another set of stairs, then pivoted left and sprinted through a long tunnel. The rumble of the trains overhead competed with the hubbub of people striding purposefully along the beige tiled floors.

At the end of the tunnel, she faced another decision. Going straight would take her to the platform for the 4, 5, and 6 trains going uptown and to the Bronx. Another passageway to her right led to the downtown and Brooklyn trains.

Which way had Umbrella Man gone? A thundering clatter told her the downtown train was pulling in. Unwilling to risk missing him, she ran down a short hallway and up to the platform. She arrived in time to hear the two-tone chime sound and see the doors close.

"The number five just pulled away," she said to Wu.

When a long row of silver cars passed, she looked across the tracks at the uptown platform, where another train had pulled in.

"I'd rather not shut down the whole system, Vega," Wu said. "Was he on the five headed downtown?"

A tall man in a trench coat stepped inside the train on the opposite platform. He had a black foldable umbrella in his hand.

"No," she said. "I have eyes on him now. He's on the number six heading uptown."

"Can you get over there?"

She had guessed wrong, and he was about to get away. "I can't," she said. "The train is leaving."

The man looked out the window, and their eyes locked as the doors slid shut.

A slow smile crept across his face as the train whisked Umbrella Man away.

CHAPTER 2

An hour later, Dani peered at SAC Wu through her hazmat suit's face shield. By the time transit police had intercepted the subway train, it had pulled into the Spring Street station two stops up from the Brooklyn Bridge–City Hall stop where she had last seen the suspect. She had responded to help them check each passenger, but none had been Umbrella Man, which meant he must have gotten off at Canal Street, the stop before. She knew the NYPD was reviewing video feeds to confirm this and to figure out which way he'd gone after leaving the platform, but for now he had slipped through her fingers.

Once her eyes were no longer needed in the subway, Wu informed her that no device or suspicious package had been located in the courthouse and directed her to join him at Lafayette and Worth, where the man in the business suit had died on the sidewalk.

Police had cordoned off the area and erected barriers around the crime scene to prevent gawkers, while evidence techs went about their work. Dani and Wu stood at a distance. From her vantage point several yards away, Dani noticed a large carton of Starbucks coffee with a broken spout lying in a puddle of aromatic brown liquid that had pooled on the sidewalk where the victim must have dropped it when he collapsed.

"He must have been on his way to a meeting," she said to Wu. "By now someone's noticed he never showed. Has he been ID'd yet?"

"I'm supposed to hear from the PD shortly." Wu gestured toward the crowd beyond the perimeter tape. "Some people managed to get video before we got the barrier up. It won't be long before his name is common knowledge."

She followed his gaze. "Right now, everyone seems more worried about the hazmat response."

"I know our suits are scaring the public," Wu said to her through his face shield. "But based on your observations and those of other witnesses, we can't take any chances until we know what killed this man."

She had not come into contact with the victim and therefore was spared the necessity of precautionary decontamination procedures and medical screening. The others who had attempted to render first aid were now undergoing a battery of tests in an isolated ward at the hospital.

"Then you agree with me that this was no ordinary mugging and that the bomb threat in the courthouse was a diversion," she said to Wu, baiting the hook. When he nodded, she pressed her advantage. "NYPD has primary jurisdiction on a homicide within city limits, but I think you should push to have this case investigated jointly with them through the JTTF."

She had made her play. The FBI had partnered with the NYPD to create the first Joint Terrorism Task Force in 1980. The group brought in members from local state and federal agencies to combat terrorism. Consisting of investigators, analysts, SWAT experts, intelligence personnel, military liaisons, and others, the model had proved so successful that its mission had spread to include international and domestic terrorism and had been replicated in more than a hundred cities nationwide.

The task force had been her first assignment after leaving the military, the US Army having sharpened her innate talent for pattern recognition to a fine edge, training her in cryptanalysis and international counterintelligence before she had successfully earned a spot in one of its most elite regiments. When she'd ended her tour of service with an honorable discharge, the Bureau had put her hard-won skills to good use.

"You think the murder was terrorism related?" Wu said.

She lifted a shoulder. "We'll know more when we learn who the victim was and what he was up to, but when was the last time you heard of someone being taken out with a toxin concealed in an umbrella?"

Wu's expression darkened. "Sounds like spycraft." He glanced over her shoulder, and she turned to see a tall man in a hazmat suit approaching. "Here comes Flint. He promised to loop me in as soon as he learned something about the victim."

She took in what little of his face she could see, which consisted of penetrating pale-blue eyes under sandy-blond brows. "Who's Flint?" she asked.

"Detective first grade assigned to the Major Case Squad out of One Police Plaza," Wu said. "The NYPD is taking this case damn seriously. Mark Flint is one of their best."

Dani had met only NYPD personnel assigned to the JTTF. Flint worked out of police headquarters, so she was curious to hear that Wu had run across him prior to today's murder case.

Aware of the distinction Flint's rank and assignment conveyed, she respectfully introduced herself when he approached, noting the firm grip of his handshake and the somber expression in his eyes behind the clear shield.

He checked to be sure no one was within earshot before responding. "We got a positive ID on the vic," he said in a heavy Brooklyn accent. "Name's Nathan Costner." He dropped his voice. "Chief of staff for Senator Sledge."

Dani struggled to make sense of the new information. Thomas Sledge was the senior US senator from New York, one of the most powerful elected officials in the country.

"Sledge has several offices around the state," Flint went on. "His Manhattan location is right down Worth Street. Looks like Costner stopped to get coffee for a morning staff meeting on his way in."

Wu blew out a sigh hard enough to fog his face shield. "Senator Sledge's involvement changes everything." He hesitated as if considering his next words. "Such a high-profile target could be part of a larger conspiracy."

Flint crossed his arms. "It's not the senator; it's a staffer," he said. "And we don't know if his job has anything to do with why he was killed. This is just the beginning of the investigation."

Dani lightly tapped her chest with a gloved fingertip. "I was there. He must have jabbed something into him with the umbrella, because Costner went down seconds after he bumped him." She let that sink in before continuing. "I may not be a homicide detective, but I know this was no street crime. It was a hit." She gestured to her supervisor. "I agree with SAC Wu. This was terrorism."

"Which happens to fall under your purview," Flint said, his tone skeptical. "So you'll have to step in and take over the whole—"

"The *J* in JTTF stands for *Joint*," Dani said. "We can investigate together."

Wu gave Flint a calculating look. "You've been assigned to my unit in the past. How would you like a temporary transfer back?"

"That's not up to you to decide," Flint said. "Right now, it's an NYPD case, and I'm the lead detective. The FBI hasn't been invited to assist."

Dani noted that Flint had emphasized the last word. In local homicides, the FBI would *assist* if they had no jurisdiction. And if they were invited.

"Once the identity of the victim hits the news, I'm certain the request will come through channels," Wu said. "Or I can just make some phone calls now and cut through the red tape."

He and Flint eyed each other for a long moment before the detective finally broke the silence.

"I'll notify my chain of command, and you can do the same on your end," he said to Wu. "Between the inevitable media hype, the politics involved, and the department brass demanding answers, this has all the makings of a circus."

"I'm afraid you're right," Wu said to Flint. "I just hope we all don't end up as clowns."

CHAPTER 3

Dani and Wu waited while Flint spent a quarter of an hour on his cell phone outlining the situation to his lieutenant.

"He's on board," Flint told them after disconnecting. "But it still has to go up the chain."

Now it was up to SAC Wu to use his influence to fast-track official approval from the top down in both organizations. Considering the nature of the crime and the identity of the victim, she assumed the NYPD wouldn't mind letting the Bureau into their sandbox.

Wu snatched his buzzing phone from an outer pocket of the hazmat suit. "It's Johnson," he said, referring to his lead analyst. He tapped the screen. "I'm putting you on speaker," he said after a few seconds. "Detective Flint with NYPD Homicide and Agent Vega are with me. They should hear this firsthand."

Another quick tap allowed them to hear Jada Johnson, who had been assigned to the New York JTTF for the past four years. A consummate professional, Johnson unearthed information faster than her colleagues and often anticipated requests before they were made.

Wu had directed the analyst to partner with the NYPD to collect video from the Transit Authority and their own Domain Awareness System, which included a police CCTV system and private security cameras. The network gave them access to more than fifteen thousand cameras in Manhattan, the Bronx, and Brooklyn alone.

"Transit Authority cams got a good visual of him on the platform," Johnson said. "We worked with the NYPD's Facial Identification Section to generate a probe image of his face. Since this investigation involves a serious crime, they're authorized to track his movements in the city. I've reviewed some of the raw feed, but it's still coming in right now."

"Can you send it to my phone so we can see what you've got so far?" Wu asked.

"Texting it to you now, sir," Johnson said.

Dani bent to peer down at the cell phone's rectangular screen. She watched a video of herself sprinting through the throng in the subway and standing on the platform as the train on the opposite side of the tracks left. Her stomach sank again when Umbrella Man's smile blurred as he glided away from her.

"Where did he get out?" Flint said.

"One stop down at Canal Street, like Agent Vega assumed," Johnson said as the image flicked to a man exiting the train. "He didn't stay on long. Probably knew we would stop the train and search the cars."

Which is exactly what had happened. Unfortunately, by the time word spread to the Transit Authority and got to their operators, Umbrella Man had made his escape—without his trench coat. Thousands of passengers had been inconvenienced for nothing. "And he knew enough to change his appearance," Johnson went on. "It took a while to isolate the subway car and go back over each departing passenger."

Dani stifled a groan. Her description had focused heavily on the man's distinctive clothing. She had been able to characterize him as a clean-shaven, tall Latino male in his thirties, with dark-brown hair and an athletic build, but she couldn't say much beyond that besides what he wore. Sophisticated surveillance equipment could locate him, but the beat cops on the street wouldn't have been able to spot him in real time if his outfit was different. The rest of her description fit thousands of passengers.

"Here's the view from inside the car," Johnson said, and the phone's screen flicked to a new feed. "Watch what he does next."

The unknown subject, or "unsub" in FBI-speak, carefully slid the folded compact umbrella into the back pocket of his slacks before taking off his trench coat. He fished into one of its deep pockets with his right hand and pulled out a black leather flatcap. After jamming the hat on, he reached into the sleeve holes and began to tug.

Intrigued, Dani looked on with the others as Umbrella Man pulled the sleeves through the holes. "The raincoat is reversible," she said.

"I'll be damned," was all Wu could manage.

In less than sixty seconds, the distinctive tan trench coat had morphed into a solid black duster. The black cap covered the top of his head, and a quick placement of black-rimmed sunglasses onto his nose completed the transformation. At a glance, he bore little resemblance to the description Dani had provided to responding authorities.

"We've updated the suspect lookout," Johnson said before Wu could ask. "And we've forwarded photos of the new clothing to everyone in law enforcement."

"Didn't he know we would see him alter his appearance?" Wu said.

"It's safe to assume he knew we would review video from security cams and CCTV after the victim on the street was killed," Dani said. "And he figured a change would delay our response long enough for him to get away—which it did."

Johnson switched to a platform feed that showed Umbrella Man exiting the subway car. He glanced around, then casually strolled toward the stairs and up to Canal Street. The video cut to another angle, this time following his progress as he ambled down the sidewalk.

"The time lag for this feed is roughly twenty minutes," Johnson said. "NYPD analysts are compiling and sharing it with us as they go, but we should catch up and have real-time footage soon."

"Are there patrols in the area?" Wu asked. "Can they head in that direction?"

"Dispatch already sent squad cars," Johnson said. "They got the info directly from video forensics through the incident commander, and they're setting up containment."

"Have they been notified that the unsub is in possession of a dangerous toxin?" Dani asked. "They know to use caution?"

"That was the first thing they were told," Johnson assured her.

Dani returned her gaze to the screen and saw Umbrella Man continue to saunter another two blocks, looking relaxed, before turning the corner and ducking under blaze-orange hazmat tape to enter an old building.

"Where's that?" Wu asked. "And can we access all cameras around the perimeter?"

"On it," Johnson responded, keys clacking under her fingers. "NYPD is checking the cams, and I'm researching the location."

"I know that building," Flint said. "It's scheduled for demolition, but it's been closed for asbestos removal first. They've been working on it for over a month."

"Is that him?" Dani said a few minutes later.

A figure had stepped out of the building, wearing white coveralls, a hard hat, and bright-yellow rubber boots. His face was obscured behind a respirator.

"That's a level-C hazmat suit," Flint said. "He's either one of the workers removing the asbestos, or he's the perp."

"There's been enough time for him to have ditched his coat and changed," Dani said.

"Agreed," Wu said. "We need to get over there to check it out."

As he spoke, the man in the hazmat suit retrieved a clipboard hanging from a nail posted outside and went back inside the building.

"Has the video feed caught up yet?" Wu asked.

"Yes, sir," Johnson said. "What you're seeing is in real time."

"The officers will have to get PPEs before entering," Flint said. "It would make more sense for them to order whoever's inside to come out before they search the place."

All first responders had access to PPE, or personal protective equipment, but putting it on would slow them down.

"This has got to be another part of his plan," Dani said. "There's no way he just happened to stroll by this building and decided to pop inside."

"The fact that it was scheduled for demolition and that asbestos had to be removed first would be public information," Johnson said through the phone's tiny speaker, supporting Dani's point. "He would have had plenty of time to make arrangements."

"But how would he know you'd be there to chase him into the subway?" Wu asked Dani. "He couldn't have anticipated that."

Dani had been thinking the same thing and had arrived at the only conclusion that made sense to her. "He knew we would check the city cams after the murder," she said. "So he gave us a trail to follow. He'd intended to leave on that subway car all along. I just made him do it faster."

"You're saying you didn't chase him to the subway?" Flint asked her. "You think he ran there on purpose?"

"He had a reversible trench coat to alter his appearance," she said. "But he knew that would only slow us down briefly because the subway is monitored, so he must have stashed a hazmat suit inside that building ahead of time in order to change into it. He probably intends to blend in with the workers and leave." She pointed at the screen. "Look."

Both men followed her gaze. White-clad figures filed out of the building, heading toward a nearby tent.

"That's the decontamination area," Flint said. "They'll take off their gear and dispose of it or have it cleaned."

Dani turned to the detective. "Can you get a K-9 unit there? Maybe they can—"

"That's a nonstarter," Flint said. "The walls have been opened up, and the building is full of loose asbestos. No way are they going to let their dogs inhale that stuff to pick up a scent."

Had he thought of that as well? Certainly not out of the realm of possibility. This guy was turning out to be two steps ahead of them all the time. She would have to think even farther ahead.

"Where are the police?" Wu asked, frustration sharpening his question.

At that moment, several NYPD squad cars skidded to a stop at the curb. Uniformed officers jumped from the cruisers and ordered the workers to raise their hands.

Dani shook her head. "He's not going to be one of those workers," she muttered.

"How do you know?" Wu asked. "They're covered from head to toe."

"Because he prepared for this too," she said, not sure why, but totally convinced. "This is another delaying tactic. While the PD spins its wheels interrogating this crew, and while their hazmat unit responds to search the building, he's figured another way out."

"I think Agent Vega is right," Johnson said, drawing everyone's attention. "I just heard from the city cam unit. All cameras around the perimeter of the building were disabled prior to the asbestos removal. The only reason we saw him go in was because there happened to be a functioning security camera across the street."

"Tell them to expand the search," Wu said. "Pull back and watch for the unsub in all surrounding blocks. We've mapped his facial features. We can pick him up again."

Dani didn't feel so confident. She didn't say it out loud, but she pictured the man she had chased dramatically altering his appearance or hiding his face and mingling with the throng of pedestrians that crowded the nation's largest city. "He'll have thought of that," was all she said. "He's shown a remarkable ability for strategic planning and countersurveillance. We can keep searching, but we won't find him." At Wu's raised brow, she added, "For now."

"Crime Scene will go through the building," Flint said. "There's bound to be evidence for them to collect. Even if it's microscopic, they'll find it."

"Sir, I just got an urgent notification from our video forensics lab," Johnson said, cutting into their discussion. "While the PD followed the unsub through the city, the JTTF video team isolated his image and ran it through facial recognition."

They crowded in closer to listen as Johnson continued. "We just got a hit," she said. "He's no longer an unknown subject."

CHAPTER 4

"Who is he?" Dani said, anxious to put a name to a man ruthless enough to kill in cold blood and threaten the life of a child to escape.

She was speaking out of turn, but her supervisor didn't seem to notice. Wu merely bent closer to the cell phone's speaker.

"Gustavo Toro," Johnson said, her voice carrying over the traffic noise coming from beyond the perimeter tape. "I'll text his photo to you."

"What do we know about Toro?" Wu asked.

"He has one arrest," Johnson said. "Charged with murder in Maryland twelve years ago but got off on a technicality. He's been keeping a low profile since."

Dani's lips tightened. Toro had killed before, but a glitch somewhere between his apprehension and the court proceedings had allowed him to walk free. Now someone else was dead by his hand.

"That incident looked like a murder for hire too," Johnson continued. "And he never gave up any details about it, so there's precious little to go on."

"How was the last one committed?" Flint asked.

"No poison involved, if that's what you're asking," Johnson said. "He used a knife."

"Quick and quiet for a skilled professional," Dani said. "And no ballistic evidence to leave behind for forensics to collect."

"That was part of the issue in court," Johnson said, fingers tapping the keyboard in the background. "There was a break in the chain of custody with fibers found at the scene."

"Any known association with domestic or international terrorist groups?" Wu asked.

"There's no nexus that I can find with any known cells or organizations," Johnson said. "We also scraped all social media platforms. He doesn't post anything we could link back to him."

Dani wanted to focus on something that would help her put cuffs on Toro faster. "Where does he live?"

"Last known address is here in the city," Johnson responded after a moment. "Texting his license to you now."

Dani stared down at the picture on Toro's New York driver's license. She wasn't sure what she'd been expecting. Maybe horns, fangs, or scales. Some outward indication of the monster that resided within. Instead, she saw regular features that included a square jaw sporting a three-day growth, deep-brown eyes, wavy dark-brown hair, and coppery skin. Some would consider him handsome.

"That address is in Spanish Harlem," Flint said, looking over her shoulder. "Tell NYPD dispatch Detective Flint needs patrol cars to head over there and set up observation," he said to Johnson. "No lights or sirens, but they don't need to hide either."

"Advise them Detective Flint and Agent Vega are on their way," Wu added. "They'll meet up with patrol when they arrive."

Johnson acknowledged and disconnected.

Flint signaled one of the uniformed officers standing nearby. "Agent Vega and I need a ride," he said when the officer walked over. "Let your sergeant know you'll be detailed to us until further notice."

The officer nodded his understanding and trotted back to his idling cruiser.

Flint turned back to Wu. "I'll request tactical support," he said. "We don't have an arrest warrant yet, so we're not going in heavy, but I can justify some serious backup due to the nature of the weapon used and the fact that he's a homicide suspect."

Wu gave him a quick nod. How they apprehended Toro was the NYPD's call, and as lead detective, Flint had the ability to coordinate the immediate response.

"I'm authorized for a knock-and-talk with tac backup," Flint said after disconnecting from a quick phone call to his supervisor. "Let's go."

Without either a search warrant or an arrest warrant in hand, they were limited to only a few constitutional exceptions allowing them the right to look for the suspect in his documented place of residence. Dani agreed their best approach was to knock on the door and listen for any sounds. If Toro tried to jump out the back window, PD would be waiting for him at the bottom of the fire escape. If he barricaded himself inside, they would call out negotiators. If he waited in silence, they would hold their positions while Flint's fellow homicide detectives wrote an affidavit and swore out a warrant. No matter which way he played it, Toro would find himself trapped.

She walked around the back of the squad car and got in beside Flint, who gave the officer the address. He used the lights and siren to get them in the vicinity faster, then shut them off when they neared the closest intersection.

Dani spotted a pair of black-and-whites parked on the two sides of the building visible to her. As they rolled to a stop behind one of them, a SWAT van screeched in beside them, double-parking while its rear door opened, and a row of black-clad tactical officers streamed out.

She was surprised at the speed of the deployment, then recalled how the NYPD's Emergency Service Unit had set up rapid response teams to arrive at an evolving situation in a matter of minutes.

They met with the team leader briefly, outlined the situation, and connected with the ESU's com system. After ensuring every avenue of escape was under observation, they hustled inside the building and climbed the stairs to Toro's apartment on the fourth floor. The tactical operators lined up in formation with Dani and Flint behind them.

The team leader listened at the door. "Someone's talking inside," he whispered into his mic. "Can't tell if it's the TV, though." After another attempt to discern whether he'd heard a show or not, he reached out with a gloved hand and rapped on the apartment door.

The conversation inside abruptly stopped. The door did not open.

Dani's heart thudded. What was Toro doing inside? Had he assumed that since he'd escaped immediate capture he was safe in his residence? Did he have a cache of guns? For that matter, did he have a bunch of blow darts?

"Police," the team leader called out. "Open the door."

Without warning, the door swung inward. From her vantage point at the back of the group, Dani could see a petite, elderly Latina woman put one hand on her chest and cross herself with the other.

The team leader looked past her, scanning what he could see of the apartment's interior. The woman began to tremble, and Dani rushed forward, open credentials in hand.

"I'm Agent Vega with the FBI," she said in her most soothing tone. "We're looking for Gustavo Toro. Does he live here?"

"No hablo inglés," the woman said. *"Pero soy ciudadana."* She straightened. *"Soy boricua."*

Flint raised a questioning brow at Dani.

"She wants to make sure we know she's a US citizen," she said. "She's Puerto Rican."

A couple of the men looked like they could have translated, but perhaps sensing the woman would be more comfortable speaking to a female, they stood back and let her take the lead.

Dani addressed her in polite Spanish. "We're not here to check your immigration status," she said. "We're looking for a man named Gustavo Toro. This apartment is listed as his address. Does he live here?"

The woman shook her head, explaining that her family had moved in more than two months ago and that she had no idea who was living there before that.

"Is there a superintendent or a landlord in the building?" Dani asked.

She pointed down the hall. "Super lives there," she said in heavily accented English before closing the door. She was done talking.

Heavy-booted footfalls trailed Dani as she strode to the door the woman had indicated and knocked. After a full minute of scuffling coming from inside, the door finally creaked open. A pair of red-rimmed blue eyes peered out from beneath scraggly blond brows. The stained undershirt and grungy boxers meant he wasn't expecting company.

Dani took a step back, waving away the marijuana fumes wafting from inside, and held up her creds again. "Special Agent Vega, FBI. We'd like to ask you a few questions."

The super squinted through the haze to study the card. "I got nothing to say to no Feds."

Flint stepped beside her and raised his gold shield. "NYPD," he said. "This property looks poorly maintained." He rested a hand on his hip. "Maybe I should call the Housing Authority." He glanced around. "Might need a full inspection and a tenant survey about how well you respond to their complaints."

The superintendent craned his neck to check out the row of tactical officers lined up behind Dani and Flint. "Is this a bust or something?" He put his hands up in mock surrender. "I just got some weed for . . . uh . . . personal use. I don't sell it or nothing, so I don't need no license."

Since the super seemed more intimidated by the NYPD than the FBI, Dani let Flint ask the questions.

"Now that I have your attention," Flint said. "We're looking for a tenant named Gustavo Toro."

The super scrunched his eyes in concentration. "Oh yeah, he cleared out three months ago."

"His lease was up?" Flint asked.

The super reached under his shirt to scratch his protruding belly. "Can't remember."

"Can we see a copy?" Flint asked.

The super shifted his feet. "I don't think so."

Dani gave him her patented don't-mess-with-me glare and said nothing.

"What are you talking about?" Flint said, jerking a thumb toward the door at the far end of the hall. "That apartment's on his driver's license. He had to prove it was his residence."

The super looked away. "I throw away old records. Don't have room to keep them all."

Dani fought an urge to gather handfuls of his filthy undershirt and shake him. "You can answer our questions here or you can answer them at what we fondly refer to as 'an undisclosed location.'" She waited a beat for his weed-numbed brain to process the threat. "What aren't you telling us about his lease?"

The super jabbed a nicotine-stained finger at her. "There's nothing says I can't rent out an apartment short term if it's vacant."

"Except that you're the super, not the landlord." Flint turned to Dani. "You think the landlord knows his superintendent collects cash under the table from squatters to let them stay in unoccupied apartments without a lease?"

She crossed her arms. "Should we call him and find out?"

A bead of sweat trickled down from beneath the super's matted hair. "You wanted to know about Toro, right?" He glanced from Dani to Flint. "Maybe I can be helpful."

"Do you know where he went?" Flint asked.

"Nah," the super said. "He left the place empty. No forwarding address. Not sure where he went, neither. He's not real talky."

Dani exchanged glances with Flint. Toro had moved out without updating his license, creating another dead end.

"Does he still get mail here?" she asked.

The super frowned. "Do I look like a mail service to you?" He snorted. "Stuff that comes for folks who don't live in the building goes in the trash."

Flint edged closer to him. "You're supposed to return undeliverable mail to the post office. The postal carrier will pick it up."

"That's what I meant to say." The super nodded vigorously, as if that would make his lies more credible. "I give any unclaimed mail back."

"After you've gone through it looking for credit cards, uncashed checks, or gift cards," Dani muttered.

"We're wasting our time here," Flint said under his breath to Dani. "Toro's in the wind, and we've got no trail to follow."

They left the super to enjoy his "personal weed" and gathered on the street below with the tactical team leader. They agreed there was no sense calling out crime scene techs to process Toro's former apartment. The new occupants had lived there for months, thoroughly compromising any trace evidence left behind.

Dani called Wu to report their findings. With no forwarding address to check, Wu told them he would assign Johnson to dig for other residences and ordered Dani and Flint to report to 26 Federal Plaza, known as "26 Fed," where they could begin writing an affidavit for an arrest warrant charging Toro with murder.

"Where is the son of a bitch?" Flint said, sitting beside her in the squad car's back seat on their way back to Lower Manhattan.

Dani felt the same frustration at their lack of ability to lay hands on Toro. "He's out there somewhere, he's dangerous as hell, and he's got no conscience," she said. "I want him too."

"Put yourself in his place," Flint said. "What would you do? Where would you go?"

People usually followed patterns. What were Toro's habits? What routines did he follow when he finished a job?

"I'd go to the one who hired me and collect my money," she said after a moment. "Then I'd get as far away from this city as I could."

She looked out the window at the pedestrians walking by, going about their daily business, unaware of the danger in their midst. Everything about this case was a divergence from the norm. It fit no discernible pattern. That meant the investigation should be undertaken differently as well. She would have to convince her supervisor to handle things in a way that violated standard protocol. At this point, however, the NYPD was still the lead agency. Would Flint agree with her proposal?

CHAPTER 5

SAC Steve Wu sat beside his chief analyst, Jada Johnson, at the long rectangular conference table that took up the middle of the Joint Operations Center. Equal parts situation room, briefing area, and observation point, the hub boasted a perimeter containing moveable cubicles surrounding a central table embedded with visual controls and an intercom system.

He had chosen to use the JOC for this investigation because of its capabilities. In this space, he could speak securely with anyone from the security personnel who guarded the building's entrances to the President of the United States. Right now, the screens displayed a patchwork of video feeds from CCTV cameras across the city as analysts combed through them with sophisticated computer programs in a fruitless hunt for Gustavo Toro.

He glanced up as Agent Vega walked in, Detective Flint in her wake. He didn't waste time with pleasantries. "We're prepping a BOLO for Toro," he told them as they settled at the table. "As soon as you secure a warrant, we'll enter him into NCIC."

Wu was counting on the National Crime Information Center, which was the largest computerized index of criminal justice information in the nation, to snag Toro. Any law enforcement officer who came across him would simply have to run his name to find out he was wanted for murder. Any border he attempted to cross or flight he tried to board would result in immediate detention.

"Do we have any aliases for him?" Flint asked. "Someone in his line of work would probably have a bunch of identities."

"Working on it," Johnson said. "Nothing yet."

"What about a car?" Vega asked.

"Nothing's registered to him, and he hasn't received any tickets driving someone else's vehicle," Johnson said.

Wu hadn't been surprised Toro didn't own a vehicle. Many people who lived in the city didn't bother with the inconvenience and expense when public transportation, taxis, and services like Uber were so readily available, especially if they stayed here only part time.

"We've been trying to find other addresses for him," Wu told them. "There are a lot of men named Gustavo Toro in the world, but we think he has a place in Monaco."

Flint raised his hand. "I volunteer to go check it out."

"Nice try," Wu said. "But we have no indication he's gotten on a plane. We checked international travel manifests and found him on an incoming flight from Charles de Gaulle to JFK four days ago on a one-way ticket." He raised a brow at Flint. "I've already contacted our Paris legat. They'll investigate his overseas address and report back."

The FBI's legal attaché in Paris covered Monaco, and, disappointing though it might be to Flint, an agent could get eyes on Toro's address from there much quicker than anyone flying from New York.

"He must make good money," Vega said. "His place in Spanish Harlem was modest, but the French Riviera can be pricey."

"Does he have a day job?" Flint followed her line of thinking. "Or is murder a full-time gig for him?"

"He hasn't filed any income tax for the past several years," Wu said. "So he's working off the books, or he pays tax overseas." The comment reminded him of another avenue he had begun to pursue. "Speaking of money, we're getting authorization to track his credit cards and cash withdrawals. That should give us an idea where he is."

Toro's life was about to become exponentially more difficult. Wu was satisfied with the plan he'd devised and the traps he'd begun to put in place to catch Toro. It would get increasingly harder for him to operate, and, sooner or later, he would give himself away.

"Could we hold off on the BOLO and NCIC?" Vega asked.

Wu's own bafflement was reflected in everyone else's expressions. Why would she propose taking their best tool for locating Toro off the table?

"I believe we should use a different approach," Vega went on. "From what we can tell, Gustavo Toro is a professional assassin. In this case, the target was very close to one of the most powerful people in the US government. The method of execution—and yes, I'm calling it that—is some sort of toxin delivered through a device that requires a high level of sophistication." She looked around at each of them. "Everything about this was meticulously planned—including his escape. The only way to know who's behind it is to locate and arrest Toro, then get him to talk."

"Which is why we're putting out a BOLO," Flint said. "I don't see the problem with—"

Vega raised a finger to put the detective on hold. "If every law enforcement agency, every media outlet, and therefore every person is looking for him, whoever hired him is going to realize we've identified Toro, and that he's the only one who can lead us to him."

Wu grasped her meaning. "He won't go anywhere near Toro, who becomes a liability."

"We need to move carefully," Vega said. "If we plaster his name and face everywhere, we'll find his body floating in the river."

"A literal dead end for this case," Flint said. "I get it."

"There's another advantage," Vega went on. "If he doesn't know we've made him, he's more likely to either come out of hiding so he can leave town, head to an ATM to get cash, or make some other mistake."

"He'll think he's free to move around," Flint said. "But we've got to be proactive. We can't just hope to stumble across him while the body count goes up."

"I wasn't suggesting that," Vega said, frowning. "I'm saying we wait twenty-four hours to see if we can pick up his scent. We'll continue to use face rec on all city cams. He'll have to make a move soon. Once we catch him, we quietly pull him in and give him a choice." She lifted a shoulder. "Become an informant or rot in prison."

Wu regarded Vega for a long moment. She thought they could turn a hit man into an asset. If they were successful, Toro would tell them about every crime he'd committed, potentially closing many unsolved cases from all over the country and maybe the world. How many people had literally gotten away with murder thanks to Gustavo Toro?

"Why not just bring him in and squeeze him?" Flint asked her. "Either way we get names and dates out of him."

"If Toro does a perp walk, he's burned," Vega said. "He couldn't do a sting."

One of the ways to corroborate any statements Toro made would be to have him contact a former client and record a conversation about their previous arrangements. This technique, called a sting, would support Toro's testimony in court. A highly publicized arrest would mean that everyone who had ever hired Toro would be highly suspicious if he suddenly reached out to them.

Wu leaned back and steepled his fingers, contemplating both Vega and her proposal. She was a new agent, but her background had impressed him. In fact, it was one of the reasons he had specifically requested her for the JTTF. He had expected someone with her elite military experience to be disciplined and tough, but he had not anticipated her unorthodox way of thinking. Was it her experience in the field or her cryptanalysis training that led her to view obstacles as minor hindrances?

He detected no signs of uncertainty in her body language or expression, only quiet confidence. Either her commanding officers would have been supremely capable leaders, or they would have found Vega intimidating.

He recalled the words of the assistant director at his last promotion. *"There's nothing more damaging to an institution than an insecure leader,"* Hargrave had told him. *"You're a rising star in this organization because you're a strong supervisor and mentor. Many eyes are on you, and expectations are high."*

The eyes his boss had alluded to were on him now. He was accustomed to high expectations, which had been drilled into him from the time he was small. Vega did not intimidate him, but the lingering question was whether or not he could trust her judgment. Hargrave was in charge of the New York field office, and he had made Wu directly responsible for all the decisions as well as the outcome of this case, which could have profound implications for the trajectory of his career. The decision was his to make, and he would live with the consequences.

He turned to Flint. "I can get behind Vega's plan if it's only for a day, but will the NYPD go for it? We have to present a united front."

Flint dragged a hand through his thick sandy hair, making it stand on end. "I'll run it up the chain. We'll have to coordinate this from the top down if we're going to keep the senator's nose out of our investigation."

"Explain what we're trying to do," Wu told the detective. "Sell it."

"Might not be able to guarantee you an entire twenty-four hours, but I'll do what I can," Flint said. He stood, pulled out his cell phone, and walked away from the table.

Wu was about to question Vega more about her proposal when Johnson spoke up.

"I have a request for a video link, sir," she said to him. "It's the director of the NYPD crime lab. They've isolated the substance that killed the victim." Johnson paled. "The director says it's something she's never seen before."

CHAPTER 6

Dani leaned forward in her seat, eyes riveted to the screen. The director of the crime lab would not routinely provide an update on a murder case, even a high-profile one, and her comment that she'd never seen anything like this before had everyone on high alert.

The director's timing had worked in Dani's favor by distracting Wu, who was pressing for details about her proposal to turn Toro. She'd have to answer the SAC's questions eventually, but she'd have more time to prepare.

"This is Dr. Letitia Gardner," Johnson said, switching half of the main screen to a secure video link.

A woman in her fifties with salt-and-pepper braids skimming the shoulders of her crisp white lab coat appeared. The closed office door behind her indicated she had sensitive information to report.

"Can I speak freely, SAC Wu?" Dr. Gardner said into the camera.

"Go ahead," he said. "Everyone here has clearance."

Local law enforcement personnel detailed to the task force were deputized as JTTF officers and underwent a background check for a top-secret security clearance so they could share classified information with their federal counterparts. Detective Flint had been detailed to the task force in the past, and his clearance was still valid.

"Did you identify what substance killed Mr. Costner?" Wu asked.

"Tetrodotoxin," Dr. Gardner said. When everyone exchanged glances, she elaborated. "There are several species of animals that make their own poison. The best known is the puffer fish, although the blue-ringed octopus and the rough-skinned newt also have it." She adjusted her silver-rimmed glasses. "But none of those creatures created this particular dose."

Dr. Gardner looked grim. "The toxin that killed this victim was synthesized from a rare species of poisonous frog native to the rain forests of Colombia in South America."

Wu's dark brows drew together. "A frog?"

"Commonly known as the golden poison frog," Dr. Gardner said. "It's also called the golden dart frog because tribal hunters used its secretions to tip their blow darts. Its scientific name is *Phyllobates terribilis*."

Johnson's fingers had been flashing over her keyboard while Dr. Gardner gave her initial statement. An image of a bright-yellow frog materialized on the screen beside the lab director.

"I found some info in one of our databases," Johnson said when Dr. Gardner paused. "It says the golden poison frog may be the most toxic animal in the world."

"It can kill a man?" Dani asked, still wrapping her mind around the incongruity of the deadly-but-cute little amphibian. "How?"

"It produces an alkaloid batrachotoxin in the glands of its skin that acts like a nerve agent," Dr. Gardner explained. "Each frog carries roughly one milligram of toxin, which is enough to kill two full-grown rhinos." She paused to let the information sink in. "Or up to twenty humans."

Dani considered an umbrella with a concealed needle as a delivery mechanism. "Then an intramuscular injection could have transmitted a dose similar to a blow dart."

Dr. Gardner nodded. "This poison was synthesized and carefully preserved. Whoever did it had access to lab equipment and knew what they were doing."

"Who sells these frogs?" Wu asked. "Is there a local distributor here in the city?"

"I checked," Dr. Gardner said. "They're endangered. It's illegal to import them." She raised a finger. "But here's the critical point. They won't make the poison if they aren't in their natural habitat."

"Can you elaborate?" Wu said.

"If you take a golden poison frog and keep it in a terrarium, it will soon become harmless," Dr. Gardner said. "From what biologists can determine, the animal's internal system metabolizes the toxin from its diet, which consists of a wide variety of insect species native to the rain forest." She lifted a shoulder. "It's something that can't be replicated in a lab or mass produced."

"So this toxin came directly from Colombia?" Wu said, then drew the next logical conclusion. "There's a South American connection somewhere."

"Without a doubt," she responded. "This species is only found there, and the animal had to be in the rain forest to produce the poison."

Wu tensed. "Who knows about this?"

"Just me and the forensic analyst who examined the victim's blood sample," Dr. Gardner said.

"Word is bound to leak," Wu said. "But I'd like to delay the inevitable as long as possible. I'll have to brief everyone up the chain all the way to the top. The case has gone international."

Dani agreed. A staffer working for a high-ranking elected official had been assassinated with an exotic poison that could have come only from overseas. There had to be a lot more going on than anyone had bargained for.

She waited until the lab director signed off before addressing Johnson. "When you ran Gustavo Toro, did you find any connection with Colombia?"

The analyst was already bringing up the digital dossier she had prepared on Toro. An instant later, the file appeared on the main screen.

"His passport shows no travel to Colombia," Johnson said. "At least, not under his real name."

"We're lacking key information," Flint said. "We can't tell who he's been associated with."

Wu turned to Johnson. "Do a deep dive on any police interactions in his background, even noncriminal ones." He hesitated. "Don't contact Interpol to request a worldwide criminal history report yet." His gaze flicked to Dani. "I'm liking your idea about capturing Toro and turning him more than ever," he said. "But I'll have to call the US Attorney's Office and run it through the Bureau's hierarchy to get buy-in before we can offer him a deal."

His comment spoke volumes about where the case now stood. The United States Attorney for the Southern District of New York would be directly involved in any federal prosecution and would therefore need to be in on the ground floor for any discussions of plea deals or conditional immunity. His last remark also meant that Wu was preparing to get in front of the NYPD. The implications of the new evidence made the move logical to her, but she didn't know how Flint would take it.

The detective had opened his mouth to speak when Johnson cut in. "We have an urgent request from the security personnel at the front door," she said. "I'm putting the supervisor on-screen."

Without waiting for acknowledgment, she tapped the controls, and a section of the main screen showed a uniformed FBI police sergeant Dani recognized from the screening she had undergone entering 26 Fed earlier.

"We have a situation," the sergeant said without preamble. "You need to send an agent down to the front desk area immediately."

"What's the nature of the problem?" Wu asked.

"Someone is here claiming to be a friend of the man who was killed this morning," the sergeant responded. "You know, the senator's chief of staff?"

Wu straightened in his chair. "What does this person want?"

"He's got an envelope," the sergeant said. "Told us his friend instructed him to bring it straight to the FBI if anything happened to him. We screened him and opened the envelope per protocol. There's a note inside, but it looks like some sort of coded message. I can't make heads or tails of it."

Wu's gaze shifted to her. "Agent Vega will be down immediately."

CHAPTER 7

Dani's foot tapped the elevator's polished floor as she rode down to the building's lobby. Finally in her element, she was anxious to make headway on a case that grew stranger at every turn.

She had always been a voracious reader fascinated by words. Languages came easily to her, as did anagrams, codes, and logic puzzles. She'd gotten a perfect verbal score on her SATs, and when she had also gotten high marks on the Armed Services Vocational Aptitude Battery, she'd found herself being recruited by every branch of the military. When the Army recruiter told her she would be referred to special training for linguists and codebreakers as soon as she completed basic, she negotiated for a shot at the Ranger Assessment and Selection Program to follow in her father's footsteps. The recruiter pushed back, finally admitting that he had washed out from RASP several years earlier. He didn't come out and say that women couldn't pass such a grueling course, but that was what she heard. Rather than dissuade her, his unspoken judgment made her more determined. He finally caved when she threatened to walk down the street to the Navy recruitment office.

After basic, she completed RASP 1, earning her "tab." Weeks later, she went on a classified overseas mission to decipher coded materials in a terrorist stronghold. An IED killed three of the men in her unit. She had channeled her grief into action, returning to Fort Benning to complete RASP 2, becoming one of the few women who had earned a "scroll" and joined the ranks of the Army's elite 75th Ranger Regiment. She pushed the dark thoughts from her mind as she exited the elevator and strode toward the front security area.

"Thank you for coming so quickly, Agent Vega," the sergeant said as she approached. "We put him in a secure area to wait for you." He gestured toward one of the interview rooms along the wall.

As soon as she opened the door, the man inside shot to his feet. Of average height and slender build, he wore a gray suit with a starched white dress shirt that contrasted with his dark skin. Dotted with perspiration, his bald head gleamed under the fluorescent lights in the small room.

"Malcolm Brown," he said, sticking out a trembling hand.

She shook it and gestured for him to resume his seat at the small rectangular table in the center of the space. She noticed the manila envelope Brown clutched in his free hand. The seal had clearly been broken, and the top edge was torn.

"You're an FBI agent?" he asked her.

She showed him her creds. "I'm assisting in the investigation into Nathan Costner's death," she said. "I understand you were friends. I'm sorry for your loss."

Brown held the envelope out to her. "Nate was like a brother to me," he said. "I knew he was upset over the last week or two, but he wouldn't tell me what was wrong."

She took the envelope from him and laid it on the table, keeping her gaze trained on Brown's expressive features. She posed an open-ended question. "What made you think he was upset?"

Brown twisted the gold wedding band around on his finger. "I'm an attorney," he began. "We were in practice together before he went to work for Senator Sledge. Nate was usually pretty easygoing, but he became intense . . . almost paranoid."

"He seemed afraid?" she prompted.

"He asked me over to his apartment last week," Brown said. "Told me he needed my help because something might happen to him. I asked him why he didn't call the police, and he said he couldn't trust the NYPD, or the state police, or any law enforcement other than the FBI." He gave his head a small shake. "He even said he was lucky he was divorced and that his wife and kids were on the other side of the country, because they were out of harm's way."

"He never mentioned anything like this before?"

"Never. He was a solid guy, straightforward and hardworking. He was the last person you'd expect to get mixed up in anything illegal, but when I saw him, he was acting secretive and—there's no other word for it—scared."

"What did he tell you when he gave you the envelope?" she asked. "You must have had questions, and he had to give you some kind of explanation."

Brown shifted in his chair, clearly uncomfortable. "He told me to trust him and not ask questions or call the police."

"After what happened, I think he would want you to tell us everything you could."

"Nate got a phone call a couple of weeks ago," Brown said after a long moment. "There was no caller ID. He said it sounded like an older male with a deep voice he didn't recognize."

Dani felt her brows inch up but made no comment.

"He wouldn't share what the caller said. Told me the less I knew the safer I'd be."

"If the information was so dangerous, did the caller tell Nate why he didn't take it to the authorities?"

"According to Nate, the caller didn't trust anyone in law enforcement." Brown glanced away. "So he told Nate to choose a reporter who would run an exposé. Obviously the caller would assume Nate had a good working relationship with plenty of media representatives, based on his position."

"You're saying the caller wanted Nate to be like Deep Throat?"

"That's what I gather," Brown said. "He was supposed to be an off-the-record source, then produce the proof the caller supplied, along with whatever evidence he found on his own."

"He was supposed to investigate too?"

Brown nodded. "Nate said the caller knew the reporter would want more than one source to corroborate the information. Besides that, he wanted Nate to satisfy himself that this was real."

Dani drummed her fingers on the table. "So Nate did his own research and found something that got him killed."

Brown shifted in his seat. "That's what I think happened," he said quietly. "And that's why he gave me the envelope."

She gentled her tone, trying not to sound accusatory. "And you never tried to open it?"

Security said they had opened the envelope, but she had to find out whether Brown had peeked inside and resealed it before bringing it to 26 Fed.

"He warned me not to, so I didn't," Brown said. "To be honest, it's a relief to hand it over to you."

"Did he give you anything else?" she asked. "Materials, communications, or special instructions?"

"He just told me to get it to you guys. Unlike the caller, Nate trusted the FBI to handle whatever this is."

Dani picked up the envelope. "This could be time sensitive. I'll get started on it right away. Did you give your contact information to the sergeant?"

Brown nodded and handed her a business card. "My cell number's on the back. It's the fastest way to reach me. If I don't answer right away, I'm probably in court."

She took the card and asked him one more time if he had anything else to offer, then escorted him from the building.

She opened the envelope in the elevator and pulled out a single sheet of paper. There were two rows of seemingly random letters at the top of the page. Beneath that was an image that looked like a copy of a vintage late-nineteenth or early-twentieth-century photograph.

SQGFHMYJKJUDSQGNS

UTQPNNWPNE

CHAPTER 8

Dani rushed from the elevator, anxious to get to the Joint Operations Center and start breaking what could only be a cipher.

"We were watching the interview remotely," Wu said as soon as she entered. "What's inside the envelope?"

"It's a coded message," she said, placing the paper on the conference table. "There's no way whoever created this included a picture for decoration. Most codes require a key to solve them." She tapped the image with her finger. "We need to figure out who this man is, because I believe the photograph is the key to deciphering the clue."

"He looks familiar," Flint said, peering over her shoulder. "But I can't place him."

"Can you run him through face rec?" Wu asked Johnson. "His clothing, hairstyle, and that mustache are not from this century, but if he's well known, perhaps he'll show up as a match in a historical database or something."

"I don't need to run this through any databases," Johnson said. "This man is my hero."

Everyone looked at her expectantly.

She stretched out the moment, breaking into a big grin. "He's been known to keep me up at night."

"Want to enlighten us?" Wu finally said.

Johnson sobered. "It's Sir Arthur Conan Doyle."

"The man who created Sherlock Holmes," Wu said. "Seems fitting for a clue."

"Give me every pertinent date in Doyle's life," Dani said to Johnson. "Birth, death, marriage, christening, graduation, and anything else that pops up."

"What are you thinking?" Flint asked while Johnson worked her keyboard.

"This could be what's called a date shift code," she said. "You use a significant date to encrypt a message. It's simple but nearly impossible to break if you don't have the date." She pulled out her pen. "That would explain why whoever wrote this included the photo. The clue is based on a specific date related to Doyle. I think we should try his birth date first, since that's what came first in his life chronologically."

"May twenty-second, eighteen fifty-nine," Johnson said. "I'll put other significant dates on the screen."

"Show me how you figure this out," Wu said, sliding a legal pad in front of her.

"There are different ways to do it, but to get the most variety in the encryption, you would represent the date with a total of eight digits."

She clicked the top of her pen and wrote 0-5-2-2-1-8-5-9 on the pad. She knew dates were configured differently in other countries, but she decided to try the standard American format since the crime had taken place in the US.

"The message begins with the letter *S*," she said to Wu. "So you put the first number in the date, which is a zero, above that." She scribbled the number down quickly. "You continue the same way. The next letter in the clue is *Q*, and the next number is five." She wrote the number five above the *Q*.

"What happens on the ninth letter in the clue?" Flint asked. "There are only eight digits in the key—if it even is a key."

"You just keep repeating the date over and over," she said. "So the ninth letter would go back to having a zero above it."

She finished writing and stood back. "Now for the decryption," she said, the familiar rush of solving a puzzle quickening her words. "Going back to the beginning, the first letter was an *S*, right?" She waited for both men to nod. "Since the first number was a zero, you don't shift the code at all. The first letter in the answer is *S*."

She bent to write an *S* on the bottom of the page. "The next letter is *Q*, and the next number is five, so you shift the alphabet five letters."

"Which direction do you go?" Wu asked.

"Good question," she said, enjoying herself despite the gravity of the situation. "It could go either way, but since English reads from left to right, most people encrypt in that direction."

"Which means you'd go the opposite way to decrypt," Wu said.

"Exactly." She gave Wu a smile. He was every bit as intelligent as she'd heard. "So the *Q* would become an *L*." She jotted the letter down.

"That means the next letter, which is a *G*, would shift two letters and become an *E*," Flint said, proving he was just as quick.

"Let's see what we get when we use Doyle's birth date as the key for the whole thing," she said. "Based on the first three letters, I think that's correct."

A minute later, she straightened. All conversation halted for a moment as everyone took in the revealed message. Dani wrote it on two lines as it appeared in the original version.

SLEDGETAKESBRIBES

PROOFINPIC

"The first part is pretty damned clear," Flint said. "Sledge takes bribes."

"Now we know you were right about the date shift code," Wu said to her. "But I'm not clear on the second line. It looks like it says, 'proof in pic.'" He looked from the notepad to Dani. "Where is it?"

She recalled a photograph of a mountain range her team had taken from an enemy stronghold during her last deployment. After close analysis, they discovered the seemingly innocuous image concealed a map and a list of targets. She met Wu's inquisitive gaze. "Steganography."

"I know you're not talking about a court recorder or a dinosaur." Flint's Brooklyn accent added an extra layer of sarcasm to the remark. "So how about you explain what that is?"

"It's a way to conceal information inside text, sound, images, or objects," she said, trying to explain the concept. "Someone downloaded this photograph from an open source, then digitized it. After that, they could embed all kinds of data into it."

"It's not a digital image now," Wu said. "It's a printed copy. How are we supposed to extract any data hidden inside?"

"As long as the image has sufficient quality, there are computer programs with algorithms designed to do that," she said. "I've used them before." She turned to Johnson, who had abandoned her keyboard to listen in on Dani's explanation. "I need you to scan the photograph of Doyle and send it to cryptanalysis as a digital file. Tell them it's a stego-image. They'll know what to do."

When Johnson crossed the room to retrieve the sheet of paper, Dani touched her forearm to stop her. "Don't upload it to the main server," she told the analyst. "It could contain malware."

"Of course," Johnson said, and Dani couldn't tell whether the sharpness of the response indicated irritation that Dani had thought it necessary to warn her or that she had been about to load the document directly into the FBI's internal server.

The JTTF had several stand-alone computer systems that allowed access to the internet and to an interconnected web between them, but not into the Bureau's system. Digital evidence often came from a variety of sources, some of them definitely shady, and it made sense to open those files only in a walled-off virtual environment.

Wu interrupted Dani's musings with a question. "We haven't found anything in Nathan Costner's background to indicate he has the capability or knowledge to produce this kind of coded message," he said. "Who created this document?"

"His best friend said someone sent him the proof," Dani said. "Costner was supposed to do his own research to corroborate the caller's statements, then take what he found along with the envelope to a reporter."

"How would a reporter decode the message?" Flint asked.

She chewed her lip in thought. "He must have figured Costner would reach out to a highly seasoned investigative reporter at a big news organization. Someone who would have access to plenty of resources."

"The chief of staff couldn't decode the message by himself," Wu said. "And he wouldn't go to the media without making damn sure there was evidence that the senator was corrupt. The scheme puts the entire burden on Nathan Costner to expose Sledge while the caller hides in the shadows and watches the scandal unfold. Brilliant."

"Only Costner didn't have the same distrust of the FBI," Dani said. "He made sure his friend took the evidence directly to us in the event of his death."

"You realize what this means?" Wu said. "The caller must have encrypted the evidence but described the allegations to Costner verbally. As the senator's chief of staff, he was in the best position to corroborate the claims."

Another piece clicked into place. "Sledge must have caught Costner going through his files," she said. "Or maybe Costner confronted him."

"If that's true, the senator is not just corrupt," Flint said. "He's a murderer."

"And a conspirator," Dani added. "He hired Toro."

Wu shook his head. "I've investigated my fair share of powerful people. They don't get their hands dirty, and there is never a direct link to their crimes."

"Okay, so we won't find a check written out to Toro with 'murder for hire' in the memo line," she said. "But maybe we can connect them with phone calls, money transfers, or CCTV footage of a meeting somewhere in the city."

Wu countered the suggestions one at a time. "Burner phones, overseas banks, and intermediaries."

Nailing a high-ranking official wasn't going to be easy. Then again, she wasn't used to easy.

"Then we break the chain at its weakest point," she said. "We find Toro and squeeze him."

"In the meantime, we prepare evidence to use as leverage," Wu said. "A pro like Toro won't talk unless we have him cold."

They all digested this for a moment before Johnson interrupted the silence. "There's something else you all should see."

The main wall screen flashed a vivid blue, then connected with a local news feed.

"Senator Sledge is in town," Johnson said. "And he's holding a live news conference right now."

CHAPTER 9

Dani swiveled her chair at the conference table to get a better view of the live news feed Johnson had transferred to the wall screen. The situation room fell silent as Senator Sledge strode out of the massive early-twentieth-century modernist-classical-style building where he maintained one of several offices spread throughout the state. He walked down a set of stone steps to a lectern bristling with microphones. Dressed in an impeccable blue suit paired with a burgundy silk tie, he raised his hands to bring order to the jostling crowd of reporters before him.

"This is a sad day for everyone who works with me," he began in somber tones. "My chief of staff, Nathan Costner, was murdered today walking down the street. He had just bought coffee for the rest of the staff, something he did every Monday morning to brighten everyone's week. That's the kind of person he was. Always thinking of others. Generous to a fault. And now he's . . . gone." The last word came out as a hoarse croak. Sledge tugged out a handkerchief and dabbed at the corners of his eyes.

Dani had a saying: *They're not crying unless you see real tears and snot.* The senator's performance was impressive, but her bullshit detector was blaring.

Still clutching the handkerchief, Sledge composed himself and continued. "Nate was on his way to a meeting with me. We were going to discuss new legislation I'm proposing." He leveled an intense gaze on his audience. "And I take responsibility for his death."

Dani heard Wu's ceramic coffee mug thud down onto the table but kept her eyes on the screen. What was Sledge up to?

"I have long been at odds with the scourge that is the opioid epidemic in this country and those that feed it," Sledge said. "A steady stream of opiates is manufactured in South America and shipped up here, where it's sold to an increasingly addicted public. Colombia, in particular, is known for growing the products as well as the violence involved in carving out territories and distribution hubs. Over the years, my efforts in supporting law enforcement, levying taxes, and enhancing penalties has had a tremendous impact on drug lords, who have previously enjoyed a great deal of power. Their supply lines are interrupted, and their money is running low. Clearly, they wanted to send a message. They wanted to threaten me. And Nate Costner, my right-hand man, paid the price. He was murdered with a poison that could only have come from one place in the world." He paused for dramatic effect. "Colombia, South America."

As soon as he finished speaking, several reporters began a barrage of questions. Sledge pointed at a well-known national correspondent standing near the front, and the din subsided.

"What kind of poison was it?" the correspondent asked. "And how do you know it could only come from one place?"

"The poison is made by the golden dart frog, and it has to be living in its natural habitat to produce the toxin."

"The chemical components can't be reproduced in a lab?" the correspondent followed up.

"Lab results show it's all natural, and it's definitely from that species of frog. There aren't any other—"

The end of Sledge's sentence was drowned out by Flint, whose obscenities rivaled anything she'd heard in the barracks.

"Have you received any threats?" another reporter asked. "Has anyone claimed responsibility?"

Sledge straightened. "A man in my position—a man who takes on powerful criminals—is always a target. It's part of the job. I'm willing to stand up for our great nation, but I never intended for anyone else to pay the price for my actions. That's why this is doubly tragic, and that's why I feel responsible."

"What's going to happen now?" another reporter chimed in. "Who's investigating?"

"This is clearly a case for the Joint Terrorism Task Force right here in the city," Sledge said without hesitation. "The NYPD began the investigation as a homicide, but now that evidence is leading us to another country, federal partners will get involved. That includes the US Capitol Police, the FBI, Homeland, and even the CIA." He spread his arms in an expansive gesture. "There's no telling how far this reaches and where it will go, but rest assured that I will follow the case every step of the way to ensure Nate Costner's death is thoroughly investigated and that those responsible are brought to justice, no matter where they are."

"He's worming his way in," Wu muttered. "He'll demand constant briefings."

A logical strategy. Sledge had given himself a plausible reason to stay abreast of the investigation. And to cover his tracks before anyone got too close.

Sledge lifted both hands, putting a stop to the incoming questions. "I can't say any more at this time. As you can imagine, the case is sensitive and ongoing. Further information about the progress of the investigation will be released through the JTTF."

Johnson stopped the feed after Sledge climbed back up the steps and disappeared inside the ornate office building.

"He screwed us in every way possible," Wu said. "Someone obviously leaked the information about the golden dart frog to him, which doesn't surprise me. He didn't get where he is without having a ton of contacts in all kinds of strategic positions." He gave his head a disgusted shake. "Then he essentially forces us to devote resources to the overseas angle by making a public announcement about the source of the toxin." He scowled. "If that's not enough, he uses the opportunity to paint himself as some sort of patriotic hero out to save our children from the opioid epidemic."

"And don't forget that he's also put everyone on notice that he fully intends to insert himself into our investigation," Flint said.

"He planned that whole show perfectly," Dani said. "We're in a serious bind."

"I've got an idea," Wu said, getting to his feet. "It's going to take buy-in from Washington."

"What's the plan?" Dani asked him.

"I'll explain if I get approval," he said, crossing the room toward the exit. "If this works, the senator will never see us coming." He opened the operations center door. "If it doesn't, I'll be transferred to an admin assignment somewhere in the bowels of the Hoover building, never to be heard from again."

CHAPTER 10

At an undisclosed location far away, a click of the television's remote ended the live feed of the senator's news conference, but the anger left in its wake did not ebb. The temptation to punch a fist through the drywall or snatch the whiskey decanter from the credenza and hurl it at the screen was nearly overwhelming. Giving in, however, would serve no purpose other than to make another mess to clean up.

Nothing had gone as planned. That fool of a chief of staff had not followed instructions. He must have confronted his boss with the evidence—or he'd gotten caught sniffing around, and now Sledge had silenced him.

An exotic poison that could only be sourced in Colombia had been a masterstroke of misdirection on the senator's part. Sledge had claimed he'd been the real target, providing a motive and pointing the FBI away from Nathan Costner's secrets to another continent to hunt for suspects.

Now the Feds would chase their tails as they always did, getting nothing done while the real criminals got away with murder. Again.

A sickening feeling of déjà vu followed. Sledge was about to slip the net. If he did, all the others involved might do so as well. What had Costner done with the mountains of damning evidence? Had he confided in a reporter as instructed? Unlikely, or he wouldn't be dead.

How would the truth ever come out now? Was it time to go directly to the media? No. Journalists insisted on sources. And corroboration. Just like the FBI. There was no way to come out from the shadows to point a finger at Sledge or the others who had wrought so much damage, ruined so many lives, and ended more than one.

Fortunately, a slight adjustment to the timeline would ensure none of them would escape justice.

Escape.

The word had taken on a special meaning over the years. Starting from a place of darkness, it became a hobby that had morphed into an obsession. Puzzles, riddles, and clues provided mental challenges in virtual escape rooms. What if the room wasn't virtual?

The senator thought he was above the law, but he had no idea that an unknown nemesis was about to hold him accountable for his actions.

Nemesis. The word brought thoughts of vengeance—and a smile. Senator Sledge would go down never knowing who his real nemesis was. Poetic justice for a man who destroyed others without getting blood on his own manicured hands.

The new identity was perfect. *Nemesis* would be the name to use during the next phase of the plan. Unfortunately, Costner's death meant Sledge's retribution would now come after everyone else's, but that didn't matter, because he would be helpless to stop it.

Nemesis would make sure everyone involved would reap exactly what they'd sown.

CHAPTER 11

Wu sat in an overstuffed visitor's chair across from his immediate supervisor, Assistant Director in Charge Scott Hargrave, who ran the FBI's New York field office. Most field offices were headed by special agents in charge like Wu, but the NYFO was one of only three overseen by an ADIC. Consisting of more than two thousand special agents, it was the Bureau's largest in terms of personnel and handled a wide variety of sensitive cases, demanding a higher level of accountability.

After Wu had outlined his plan to deal with Senator Sledge, the assistant director had wasted no time passing the buck. Hargrave's unique position gave him the juice to arrange for an unscheduled video briefing with FBI Director Thomas Franklin, which was how Wu found himself repeating his proposal to Franklin.

The virtual briefing had been every bit the root canal he'd anticipated. Franklin had a reputation as a brusque, no-nonsense leader who did not suffer fools and expected either immediate answers or explanations as to why they were not forthcoming. After Senator Sledge's grandstanding on live television, Wu expected Franklin to be especially sharp with his questions.

The director did not disappoint.

After Wu had responded to each issue, the director gave what appeared to be reluctant approval and disconnected the secure link.

Briefing concluded, Hargrave slipped off his glasses and pinched the bridge of his nose. "That was painful," he said. "But at least he agreed to give your plan a try."

The choice of words was not lost on Wu. This was *his* plan, not Hargrave's. It made no difference that the idea for the first phase of the proposal had come from a subordinate. Once Wu embraced the concept, he owned it. If things went well, Hargrave would be sure to couch the after-action report in terms of his own leadership when he informed the director. If the situation devolved into a shipwreck, Wu would find himself bobbing at sea, clinging to a life preserver. All by his lonesome.

Such was the way of internal politics in the upper ranks of the Bureau.

"Locating Gustavo Toro is our top priority," Wu said. "He's the key. Once we find him, he tells us who hired him, and we follow the trail from there." He paused for emphasis. "Wherever it leads."

"Toro is proving to be hard to find," Hargrave said. "Especially since we haven't put out a BOLO or entered him into NCIC."

Wu countered the criticism underlying the comment. "Even the director agreed the suspect would be more valuable to us if we didn't burn him."

Franklin had initially balked at the idea of hunting Toro down without the benefit of the law enforcement equivalent of a full-court press. After listening to Wu's explanation that a dead suspect would offer far less than a cooperative asset, Franklin had reluctantly agreed. He did, however, limit Wu to twenty-four hours before announcing Toro's name publicly and plastering his face on every available virtual and physical surface. If they captured Toro before that, the second phase of Wu's proposal—which had necessitated the call to Washington—would kick in.

"I'm surprised the director agreed to the rest of your plan," Hargrave said. "I've never known him to hold off on briefing the Senate Majority Leader, especially regarding an accusation involving a fellow senator."

"The investigation will be compromised from the start without the strictest confidence," Wu said. "Sledge is an Independent, so he has no party affiliation, but he's close to the leadership in both houses of Congress. If word about what we're doing leaks out, he'll call in every favor he can to impede us. Franklin understands that, and he's willing to take the blowback when the case is over."

If Hargrave caught the subtle dig about his own lack of willingness to shoulder fallout, he didn't let on.

"Everyone will know you conducted a phony investigation," Hargrave said. "No one likes being tricked, especially not people in power—or the media. It's going to get ugly."

"The secondary investigation isn't fake," Wu said. "But it's not our main focus."

"No, that's just a sitting US senator." Hargrave waved a hand in sarcastic dismissal. "No big deal."

"Senator Sledge is running a false-flag operation with this Colombian angle," Wu said. "He's forcing us to engage in our own deception in response."

His plan had been to split the investigation, running simultaneous but completely separate probes, both reporting to him. Secrecy was key, and only a handful of people would know about the second concurrent investigation.

The first team would openly work the international leads. Fortunately, the JTTF had vast resources already in place to help in that regard. There were members from DHS, CIA, NSA, DEA, ICE, and military intelligence, among others. During his tenure in his current position, Wu had overseen many investigations around the globe. As long as US citizens were affected or threatened in some way, the task force's considerable resources could be brought to bear. Wu knew most people had no idea what really went on within these walls, and they slept a hell of a lot better than he did for it.

He would personally answer any questions from the media or Senator Sledge with heavily redacted information from the international team's progress. He could plausibly claim that much of their work was classified, and that updates would be few and far between. The senator had a security clearance and could demand more information, so reports would have to be carefully prepared for him.

Meanwhile, a second team would conduct a covert inquiry into Senator Sledge. The encrypted message Agent Vega had partially deciphered provided enough evidence to get started, and it appeared one man had already been killed for going down that path. Much would depend on what the rest of the message had to offer, but they could begin with a stealth examination of the contracts he associated himself with and his contacts.

US senators did not personally award government contracts, but the right word here or there could go a long way toward a successful bid. The term "Beltway bandit" had been used for decades to describe the practice. While the low bidder was supposed to prevail, the parameters of a contract could be written in such a way that only one vendor met the requirements.

Such was the way of politics inside the Beltway.

"Who will be at the helm of the international investigation?" Hargrave asked.

Wu had already made up his mind. "Wagner," he said, certain Hargrave wouldn't find any reason to object. Paul Wagner had been with the Department of Homeland Security since its inception. Well respected and capable, he was the perfect choice for the public face of a sensitive international investigation that impacted the highest levels of government.

Hargrave nodded his assent. "In a way, Senator Sledge did us a favor with his little stunt. The NYPD are stepping back and requesting Detective Flint remain with the JTTF in a support role while we take the lead."

Wu had expected that. It had been a calculated risk on Sledge's part. He might hold more sway with the NYPD commissioner than the FBI director, but he had direct access to both. And the ability to throw his weight around.

"The covert investigation is highly sensitive," Hargrave said. "I want you to run point on that personally."

Wu was the special agent in charge of the FBI's New York Counterterrorism Division, which included the largest JTTF in the nation. He supervised more than 450 personnel from sixty-one different law enforcement agencies.

He was not a case agent.

And then realization dawned. This assignment was equal parts plausible deniability for Hargrave and a test for Wu. If the assistant director put a high-ranking official like Wu out in front, he could reasonably claim to have left all major decision-making up to his subordinate. If it all blew up, Hargrave would be clear of the fallout. No one would criticize him for lack of supervision when he had appointed his second-in-command to lead the case.

Wu inclined his head, acknowledging the implications. "And I'll perform my normal duties as well."

"Let me know if you need additional help," Hargrave said, turning back to the papers on his large desk. "You can take your pick."

Understanding himself to be dismissed, Wu got to his feet. He was about to leave when his cell phone buzzed in his pocket. After reflexively pulling it out, he tapped the screen and sucked in a deep breath.

"What's up?" Hargrave asked him.

"I asked Agent Vega to text me if computer forensics and crypto extracted any hidden files from the photograph of Sir Arthur Conan Doyle."

Still holding the phone, he turned it so Hargrave could read the single word glowing on its screen.

JACKPOT.

CHAPTER 12

Dani glanced up as Wu strode into the task force's situation room. The SAC's normally smooth features were drawn, and his jaw was taut. Judging by his demeanor, any forward progress in their investigation would be welcome.

"Senator Sledge is dirty as hell," she said, getting straight to the point.

Wu gave her a curt nod and shifted his gaze to Johnson, who was at her terminal. "Show me what we've got."

Johnson typed in commands that populated the viewing screen with an array of digital files. "It's a treasure trove," she said. "I don't know who got this stuff or how they did it, but the evidence against the senator goes back years."

She began clicking open the files, expanding spreadsheets, correspondence, and wire transfers that mapped out a trail of financial institutions around the world, leading from the United States to a bank account in the Cayman Islands. Other files showed how the offshore account could be linked back to Sledge through a variety of screens.

"Calling it evidence is a bit of a stretch," Wu said after studying the screen for several minutes. "None of this is admissible in court. We need to confirm everything with our own investigation."

The FBI couldn't rely solely on anonymously sourced information to make an arrest, and no US Attorney would use it to prosecute. Dani had been thinking about the challenge this newly obtained data posed while waiting for Wu to return from his meeting with the assistant director.

"We don't know what the anonymous caller said to Nathan Costner," she said. "But my guess is he died trying to corroborate the information we just found. Now it's our job to do it without getting caught."

Detective Flint, who had been silent for the past several minutes, weighed in. "Sledge might have already taken measures to destroy any evidence that would prove what's in these files."

"Whatever steps he took would leave a trail of its own," Wu said. "Making him guilty of obstruction and other crimes."

"Speaking of other crimes," Dani said. "I figured out how he orchestrated the hit on his chief of staff."

Wu took the chair beside hers. "Explain."

"Toro knew this was a high profile hit," she began. "He mapped out an elaborate escape plan complete with backup contingencies in case he was spotted."

Flint nodded. "He also knew the city cams would be able to follow him and planned ahead with a change of clothes."

"And he's probably the one who called in the bomb threat at the courthouse," Wu added. "How does that lead to Sledge?"

"Toro would need a location to lie in wait for Costner," she said. "He needed a choke point, and the senator provided it."

She waited, giving Wu and Flint time to consider the logistics involved. The Army had trained her to be on high alert around any choke points, and she naturally spotted them in this scenario.

She gave them a hint. "Sledge mentioned it during his press conference."

Wu brought his hand down on the table. "The coffee."

"Affirmative," she said. "According to Sledge, Costner always bought coffee for the whole staff on Monday mornings."

"Sledge has offices all over the state," Flint said. "So he must start the week at his Manhattan location. That way, Toro would know exactly when and where his target would be."

She smiled. "Sledge has no idea his comments about Costner's generosity gave us one of the missing pieces as to how he was set up."

"That's excellent circumstantial evidence," Wu said. "But it's not proof." He shifted his gaze to Johnson. "A solid money trail would go a long way toward a conviction in court."

"If the trail hasn't disappeared," Flint said.

"I don't think even a senator could get a foreign country to purge their banking records," Johnson said from her cubicle. "But I'll look into it."

"Be discreet," Wu said. "Let's not set off any alarm bells in the Caymans."

"There's one way to get some solid information," Dani said. "We find Gustavo Toro and make him talk."

Flint nodded. "He's the key to this whole thing. If we get him to turn state's evidence, we can—"

"What judge would sign an affidavit accusing a US senator based on the testimony of a hired assassin?" Wu said, frustration evident in his tone. "For that matter, what jury would believe a killer over someone they probably voted for?"

Dani agreed. "We need more than anonymous documents and the word of a hit man. It's going to be a challenge for him to find usable evidence." Aware of the potential fallout, she chose her next words with care. "Someone will have to infiltrate the senator's staff."

Wu bristled. "Absolutely not."

The conversation ground to a halt. Dani had inadvertently stumbled over a line the SAC was not willing to cross.

Johnson cut through the awkward silence. "The video squad sent me a notification," she said, glancing at her screen. "They got a face rec hit on Toro." Her eyes drifted up to meet with Wu's. "He just walked out of the Golden Chrysanthemum Hotel."

Dani jumped out of her chair. "We can catch him if we hurry."

The hotel was in Chinatown near the intersection of Canal and Mulberry Streets. She could run there in about five minutes.

"Slow down," Wu said, getting to his feet. "Let me get a few agents together so we can take him down without anyone getting hurt."

"NYPD can get to him faster," Flint said, pulling out his phone. "I'll request a black-and-white and give them a description."

"We never put out a BOLO," Dani said. "We're trying to keep the arrest low key so we can take him to one of our off-site facilities for interrogation. That means no patrol units."

Wu addressed Flint. "Ask them to respond to the area. I don't want to use them unless we have to, but I'd like them nearby in case this goes to hell."

"He's on the move," Dani said. "Let me get eyeballs on him so he doesn't vanish. I'll keep him under observation until we can box him in."

"Go." Wu pointed at the conference room door. "And take Flint with you."

She raced into the hallway before he could change his mind.

"I expect constant updates," he called after her.

CHAPTER 13

Minutes later, Dani sprinted across Lafayette Street while Flint's heavy footfalls pounded the pavement a few steps behind her.

"Where the hell are you going, Vega?" he called out. "We should turn right on Walker Street to get to the Chrysanthemum. We'll lose Toro if we stay straight on Lafayette."

She had no intention of allowing Toro to elude her a second time. He was cunning, but she was strategic.

"I've got a plan," she called over her shoulder.

Minutes ago, Wu had cobbled together eight JTTF members to bring Toro in. Breaking up into four teams of two, they kept in constant communication while one pair cut through Columbus Park to approach from Mulberry Street. Another team went down Baxter Street, and a third circled around to cover the far side of Centre Street in case he went west on Canal. Dani and Flint, who had a head start, were supposed to use Walker to pick Toro up as close to the hotel as possible. Each pair would move in closer, incrementally tightening the circle until Toro was trapped.

At least that had been the plan.

"How about you clue me in," Flint said, slightly out of breath. "Because we're not where we're supposed to be."

She slowed enough to let him run beside her. "You requested marked patrol cars to report to the area. Toro will see them and get spooked."

"We've given up our position," Flint said, still panting as he raced to keep up. "Our part of the perimeter is open."

"He'll run," Dani said. "But we'll be waiting for him."

"How the hell do you know that?"

There was no time to explain. Her specialty was recognizing patterns, and she now had a baseline example of his behavior to work from.

"Trust me."

She really hadn't given Flint much choice. He could have stayed where he was, but she knew he would not desert his partner on such a critical operation. She held up her creds and raced across Canal Street, heedless of the screeching tires, blaring horns, and obscene gestures around her. She reached the sidewalk and dodged a woman pushing a stroller, hurdled over a display of knockoff designer handbags, and made a sharp right turn.

Despite his sweat jacket with the hood pulled down low, she spotted Gustavo Toro, legs and arms pumping as he ran into her field of vision from the right. Putting on a final burst of speed, she launched herself at him.

"Stop, FBI!"

Toro's head spun in her direction an instant before he let out a grunt that was equal parts surprise and pain as Dani's shoulder slammed into his, knocking him to the ground. He flailed beneath her, struggling to throw her off.

She latched onto his midsection and withstood desperate punches and kicks, never easing her grasp as he fought to free himself.

Seconds later, she felt the force of another body thudding down on top of them as Flint added his weight to hers.

They each pinned an arm and a leg to the sidewalk, immobilizing him.

While Flint used his free hand to slide out his cell phone and call Wu, Dani slapped cuffs on Toro's wrists. "Do you have any poison on you?" she asked him.

When the investigation began, they had all agreed that anyone taking him into custody would immediately restrain his hands so he couldn't deliver a fatal dose of frog poison.

"What are you talking about?" Toro said through unsteady gasps.

"That's how you want to play this?" she said to him. "Fine."

An oversize black van screeched to a halt by the curb as the other pairs of agents converged on their position. The group surrounded Toro, obscuring his face while they hustled him into the waiting transport vehicle and hopped inside. The driver took off as soon as Flint slammed the side door shut, and Dani was satisfied that the whole operation had been completed with minimum attention. Unfazed by the scuffle, passersby had paid them little attention.

As soon as Wu had agreed to convert Toro into an asset, he had arranged for a driver and a van to stage near 26 Fed. When he sent the teams out to intercept Toro once he'd been spotted leaving the hotel, he had dispatched the driver to circle a five-block radius until the suspect was in custody.

After they finished searching Toro, whose pockets contained only a cell phone and a wallet, Flint looked from her to Toro. "Either one of you injured?"

She shook her head, but Toro seemed to weigh his options. "Don't think so," he finally said.

She'd seen the tactic before. He would wait to hear the evidence against him, then decide his neck hurt and he needed to go to the hospital, where he would either attempt an escape or consult with his attorney before questioning began.

"How did you two find him?" one of the other agents asked.

Flint looked at Dani. "I was wondering the same thing."

"The last time I had the pleasure of an encounter with our friend here," Dani said, gesturing toward their captive. "He bolted for the nearest subway when I chased him. Everything else he'd done had been meticulously planned, so I figured he viewed subways as good escape routes."

Toro gave his head a disgusted shake, as if he couldn't believe he'd allowed himself to become predictable.

"In a panic situation, when there was no time to plan," Dani continued, "Toro reverted to the backup strategy he'd used to escape last time." She shrugged. "I went to the Canal Street station to intercept him before he could hop on a train."

Toro had nearly made it. Dani had juggernauted into him on the sidewalk a few steps away from the descending stairs that led to the platform below.

"Intercept me?" Toro said, his tone filled with indignation. "You hit me like a linebacker." He tipped his head one way and then another. "You could have hurt me."

"Planning to sue the FBI?" Dani said. "I wouldn't count on it." She scooted closer to him. "In fact, I think you're a lucky man. You might be floating in the Hudson right now if we hadn't found you."

Toro gave her a hard stare but said nothing.

"He thinks he's smart," Flint said. "Let's see if he has enough brains to save his own ass."

Toro gave Flint a calculating look. "You've got an NYPD detective shield around your neck, but you're not taking me to the police lockup," he said, then shifted his gaze to Dani. "I'm in federal custody, which means Agent Badass here and her friends think I'm worth talking to."

"Your only value is what's inside your head," she said.

He regarded her a long moment. "Nothing's for free. I hope you're willing to pay my price."

CHAPTER 14

Dani stood outside the door to the off-site interview room with Wu. She raised a brow at him. "You think Toro is the key and I can turn him?"

"Pun intended, I'm sure," Wu said. "He's a vault. I want you to open him up."

Toro was disguised and on a solitary mission, which worked in their favor when they had whisked him away in an unmarked windowless van. The FBI's New York field office was a hive of activity, and they needed the privacy an off-site space would offer. The speed of the takedown was also fortunate. Busy pedestrians rushing to catch trains or taxis had paid little attention, and no one had posted videos of them anywhere the analysts could find online. As far as the world knew, Nathan Costner's killer was still at large. So far the plan was working. Time for the next critical phase.

"Don't get me wrong," she said to Wu. "I'm anxious to get into the room with Toro, but why me?"

As the newest person in the unit, she had assumed Wu would choose a more senior agent to conduct such a sensitive interrogation.

"You're the only one who figured out what he was going to do, and you caught him," Wu said, then dropped his voice. "Let me be blunt. I don't think Toro expected to be outmaneuvered by a woman. If I'm reading his physical cues right, you frustrate and annoy him."

This was the last thing she'd expected to hear. "Then why would he be more cooperative with me?"

"Because you challenge what he views as his superiority, so I'm guessing he'll try to get the better of you in your next encounter."

She rested a hand on her hip. "I don't know whether to be flattered or insulted."

"Neither," he said flatly. "You're the appropriate asset for this assignment."

She was comfortable with that. As in the military, she was a tool to be used as necessary, nothing more. Toro had already been Mirandized, and he'd insisted that he did not want an attorney present.

No doubt he'd already worked out a strategy and believed he had enough valuable intel to buy his freedom. Like so many before him, he thought he was above the law. Thought he could bend the rules to escape accountability for his actions. No way would she let him weasel out of a murder rap, but he might be able to make his situation better.

If he cooperated.

Someone like him should never glimpse sunlight again except through a set of bars. Who knew how many people he'd killed? And he did it for money. Worst of all, he'd never had to answer for his crimes. The one time he'd been arrested, the case had been dismissed on a technicality. Not this time.

Her only challenge would be hiding her contempt for him. She'd interviewed enough people to understand that judgment shut them down. Despite her disdain for the man she was about to deal with, she forced herself to remember that—like her—he was a tool. Her job was to find out who had used that tool to set the chain of events in motion leading to Nathan Costner's death. If she failed, the true perpetrator would escape justice.

Dani gestured toward the closed interview room door. "We can't wait any longer. Whoever hired Toro may be keeping tabs on him. If it's obvious he's missing for long, that would make everything we're trying to accomplish moot."

"We'll all be watching and listening," Wu said. "If you want one of us to come in, ask Toro if he wants a cup of coffee. That will be our cue." He held out a manila folder. "Keep your earpiece in listening mode. I'll let you know if you bump up against any legal guardrails."

She took the folder and waited for Wu to step back out of view before opening the door.

Toro leveled her with a glare. "You."

He managed to infuse the single word with contempt before his lips curved into a slight smile. Someone had come to talk to him, which he no doubt knew strengthened his overall position.

She strode over to take the chair across from Toro, who was now out of his sweat jacket. The hood he'd pulled down to cover half his face had not been enough to hide his identity.

"What's in the folder?" Toro said, tipping his head toward the spot where she had deliberately placed it on the table between them.

She redirected him. "First, tell me who hired you," she said, effectively getting to the point and changing the subject at the same time. "And how they paid you."

A money trail would go a long way toward corroborating anything Toro had to say about who had ordered the hit, while also establishing a timeline.

Toro crossed his arms over his chest. "The only reason I'm not in a cell right now is because you all want something from me, which means I can bargain."

She leaned across the table, invading Toro's space. "We're giving you a chance to have a life. Right now you're looking at spending the rest of your years in a federal penitentiary." She jabbed a finger at him. "And I'll make sure it's the worst hellhole I can find."

Toro uncrossed his arms and angled his body forward in imitation of her posture. "You don't want me. You want the one who sent me." He leaned back in an exaggerated show of complacency. "And I'm the only way for you to get to him, so no, I don't think you'll send me anywhere."

Concerned about overplaying her hand, Dani shifted gears. "I think you should be asking yourself what you can offer us to keep yourself out of prison," she said. "You must realize that your so-called employer will turn on you once you get a life sentence."

The team had put together a dossier on Toro's background. The Paris legal attaché had confirmed the address in Monaco was his primary residence. He would soon find his property seized and his accounts frozen. Other than the Spanish Harlem apartment he'd recently left, they hadn't found much in the US. He appeared to own no property and seemed to prefer a variety of female companions rather than a steady relationship. Johnson had found no evidence of children, so Dani couldn't use his family as leverage.

"Your situation is simple." She placed her hands on the table. "It's you or him. What's it going to be?"

She kept her eyes locked on his. She had cut through an hour's worth of talking and gotten to the heart of the matter. Would Toro spend the rest of his days in a prison cell, or would he turn on his employer? His dark-brown eyes bored into hers, assessing her. She knew the rules. Don't break the silence. Don't look away. Don't fidget.

After an interminable moment, he heaved a sigh. "What you're asking is going to be difficult."

"I said your situation was simple. I never said it was easy."

"I'll cooperate," he said. "After I get full immunity. In writing."

Wu had arranged for an Assistant United States Attorney to be on hand for just this purpose. The office of the Southern District of New York wasn't far from their off-site undisclosed location, streamlining the process. The AUSA had prepared a proffer letter in advance in the hope that, since Toro had no legal counsel, he might accept the terms. Dani opened the manila folder he had been eyeing, pulled out a thin stack of stapled papers, and slid it across the table.

"Before you sign any agreement, you should understand that your cooperation will involve more than just naming names," she told him.

He narrowed his eyes. "What do you have in mind?"

She dropped the bomb with a casual air, as if it weren't important. "We need to get inside."

Toro's brows shot up. "Inside what, exactly?"

"Inside whatever organization is behind the death of Nathan Costner."

He stiffened. "How do you know there's an organization? Why couldn't it be one person?"

"This isn't a mugging or a jealous husband killing off a rival," she said, cutting through his bullshit. "A single person does not assassinate a politically affiliated target using an exotic poison delivered by an umbrella. That's terrorist stuff. There's a group behind this, and you're getting an undercover agent inside."

Toro glared at her in silence for a long moment. The pen in his hand hovered over the paper. "Are there suicidal agents in the FBI? Because what you're asking is—"

"Let us worry about who we're sending in," she said. "Your job is to set it up."

He swore. Wu had been right to send her in. Toro was flustered, something she imagined was unusual for him. She didn't give him a chance to regain his composure.

"What group are you a part of, Toro?" she asked, pressing her advantage. "Because anyone involved is guilty of conspiracy at the bare minimum."

His jaw tightened as he absorbed the information. He remained silent so long she expected him to abruptly end the interview and request an attorney; then he appeared to come to a conclusion. "There is a group," he finally said. "But I want that document signed by everyone involved before I talk about it."

Wu's voice carried through Dani's earpiece. "Tell him to look at the last page," he said to her. "The AUSA is with me in the observation room. It's already signed."

Dani flipped the stapled pages to the last one and pointed to the signature line. "Done."

He scrutinized the document several minutes before initialing various paragraphs and scrawling his name at the bottom.

"I want to hear all about the group," she said, slipping the signed document back into the folder. "But first tell me who hired you."

"He goes by 'the Colonel,'" Toro said. "I'm not sure what his full name is, but a couple of the guys call him 'Colonel X' sometimes. I think his first or last name starts with *X*."

Johnson, who was also listening in, would work with military intelligence analysts assigned to the JTTF to comb through various databases for anyone fitting that description.

Dani tried to help narrow the search. "Is he a real colonel?"

Toro shrugged, palms up. "No idea. He acts like he could be military, though."

"What does he look like?"

"White, in his fifties, gray buzz cut, physically fit, walks like his boxers are starched."

She shifted to an open-ended question to see how forthcoming Toro would be. "Explain what happened when he hired you."

"We all have burner phones," Toro began. "I was . . . out of town."

She crossed her arms. "We know about the place in Monaco." She didn't elaborate. Let him wonder what else they had unearthed.

"The Colonel called me about a week ago," he continued. "Said he had a high-priority assignment for me here in the city. The target was Senator Sledge's chief of staff, and the hit was supposed to take place in a public setting where police would find him fast."

"Why did the Colonel want him found in a public place?" she asked.

"He didn't say." Toro lifted a negligent shoulder. "I didn't ask."

He stopped, so she prompted him. "How were you supposed to do it?"

"The Colonel left an envelope for me at the front desk of the Chrysanthemum Hotel. I checked in four days ago under the name Guillermo Tovar." One corner of his mouth lifted. "Same as my real initials, so it's easy to remember."

She gestured in a circular motion with her hand after he paused to admire his own cleverness.

He took the hint. "There were three darts inside, along with a note containing the target's schedule and personal info."

"What happened to the other two darts?"

"I'm not stupid enough to be caught with incriminating evidence." He gave her an insolent smile. "The umbrella, darts, trench coat, hat, and glasses all ended up in the river along with the hazmat suit I changed into." He put a hand to his mouth in mock embarrassment. "Oops. Was that illegal dumping? I guess I'm really in trouble now."

He had disposed of the murder weapon and his disguise. The ERT would search his hotel room anyway, but he was probably telling the truth.

"You watched him then?" she continued, refusing to let him bait her.

Toro shook his head. "I scoped out my route and made my plans. According to the schedule, the target would buy coffee at the Starbucks on the corner of Lafayette and Worth at eight in the morning. After that, he would walk down Worth Street to the senator's Lower Manhattan office."

He had just confirmed their theory. Only a few people knew Costner's habits. And one of them was Sledge. She would take him through the rest of the plan, then work to tie it back to the senator.

"I took a cab to the corner of Park Row and Worth," Toro continued. "A good distance away from the coffee shop. Once I got out, I started walking toward Lafayette."

"You were coming toward Costner then?" She deliberately used the victim's name, refusing to depersonalize him as Toro did. "What happened next?"

"I had modified a foldable umbrella to hold the dart," Toro said. "All I had to do was wait for the target to walk by."

"Did you know what was in the dart?"

"I was only told that it was highly poisonous and not to let it touch my skin."

"You didn't synthesize the poison yourself then?"

"Not in my wheelhouse," Toro said.

"Who does the Colonel know who could create a poison dart?"

Another long silence followed. She waited him out.

"Had to be Doc Tox," he finally said.

They had crossed another threshold, but she wanted to know how much more he would give up. "Who's Doc Tox?"

"Chemist," Toro said. "Don't know much about his background, but he's the Colonel's go-to guy for biohazardous stuff."

"Name, address, and description?"

"The guy gives me the creeps. I don't hang out with him. Like everyone else, I have no clue what his real name is or where he lives, but he's a white guy in his early forties with curly brown hair. Not sure where he learned chemistry and bioweapons. Maybe he was in the military; maybe he worked for a private lab somewhere; hell, maybe he's a frustrated high school science teacher. Who knows?"

She chose her next words carefully. "Does he have the ability to obtain . . . exotic poisons?"

"Sure. He travels a lot and smuggles stuff into the country. Not sure how he manages it, but I've seen what he can do."

She couldn't waste time on details that could be fleshed out through extended interviews later. The clock was ticking, and this so-called colonel would notice if Toro was out of pocket too long.

"But you knew the dose you placed in the umbrella was lethal?" she asked, documenting his guilt.

"Of course." He looked annoyed. "That's why it's called a hit."

She ignored the sarcasm. Part of her job was tying up legal loose ends in case the information was needed in court. She wanted to get the full extent of the danger he posed to the public on record. "And you pointed the umbrella's tip at a child when I chased you?"

His features darkened. "No one was supposed to notice me. Everyone else stopped to help the target." He met her gaze. "You didn't, though. You ran after me instead."

Had a cold-blooded killer just accused her of insensitivity?

"The girl." She emphasized the words, keeping the blame where it belonged. "The child you were prepared to kill. Was that some sort of backup plan?"

"The backup plan was the bomb threat."

He had just confessed to another felony. "You called it in as a diversion?"

His response oozed sarcasm. "I killed a man in broad daylight in a place filled with cops and Feds," he said. "So, yeah, I needed to keep everyone busy for a few minutes."

He seemed uncomfortable when she mentioned the student he had threatened. "Back to the girl," she said.

His lips flattened into a hard line.

"You've got what we call a 'queen for a day' letter," she said, using the legal vernacular. "Your free pass will expire. Now's the time to talk if you want any kind of immunity at all."

"Yeah," he said quietly. "I would've killed her to get away."

She allowed the revulsion simmering beneath the surface to flicker across her face for the briefest moment before slipping in the most important question, hoping to catch him off guard. "Who does the Colonel work for?" she asked. "And what reason did he give you for targeting Nathan Costner?"

"You don't get it, do you?" Toro let out a humorless laugh. "I get paid *not* to ask questions when people hire me."

"You just murder whoever they tell you to?"

"When we were coming here in the van, I overheard one of the other agents mention that you'd been in the military." He studied her. "Is that true?"

"What's your point?"

"Then you're not so different from me, are you?" he said. "You took orders to kill people you didn't know who had never done anything to you personally."

"That was to defend my country," she said, voice rising. "That was—"

"For money," he cut in. "You got a military salary and benefits, didn't you? That makes you a paid killer too."

She jumped out of her chair and leaned over the table. "You don't get to call me a mercenary," she said, pointing first at him, then at herself. "We are not the same. I had every right to question any orders I thought were illegal. I still do as a federal agent."

No one in the armed services or law enforcement was required to carry out an unlawful order. To the contrary, they were required to refuse.

Wu's voice sounded in her ear. "Back down, Vega. He's jerking your chain."

The smile on Toro's lips told her Wu was right. She sat down again and smoothed her slacks while her supervisor redirected her.

"We have to find out if Senator Sledge got the Colonel to do his dirty work," Wu continued. "And we need solid evidence. Tell Toro he has to get an agent inside."

"You get one of our agents into the group," Dani said to Toro, "or the deal's off."

Toro dragged a hand through his dark, thick hair. "You don't know what you're asking." When she made no response, he elaborated. "We all use code names. I go by *Bull* because my last name is Toro, and I'm not part of the herd. I'm alone, like a bull. Everyone I've worked with knows that about me. To say I'm suddenly partnering up would cause way too much suspicion. My supposed partner and I will both end up with some extra holes in our bodies by the time the first meeting's over." He paused. "Actually, they'd keep the guy alive a lot longer while they interrogated him to find out who he was, who sent him, and why. His death would be slow and painful. I'd go pretty quick."

"It would be up to you to sell it," she said. "We haven't got a choice. No jury is going to believe anything that comes out of your mouth. Not that I blame them. An agent has to corroborate your testimony in court."

"You're not hearing me." Toro was adamant. "I hardly know any of the others in the group, because I work alone. I've only accepted team assignments three times. Every other job has been solo."

She started to speak, but Wu's urgent transmission forestalled her next question. "Don't waste time asking about other contracts right now," he told her. "We'll circle back to that when we have time. Stand by."

A few seconds later, Wu entered the interrogation room and took the chair beside Dani. She had no idea why the SAC had come in unannounced but knew to pretend this was all part of the plan. Toro should think they were all on the same page.

"We need to come up with a reason why you would change how you operate," Wu said to Toro. "And I have an idea."

CHAPTER 15

Wu walked into the interview room and tried to project an air of calm when he scarcely believed what he was about to suggest. From the time the JTTF team began to suspect Toro had been hired by Senator Sledge, the problem had been collecting evidence against a public official with so much power and influence. Wu had gotten authorization for an undercover operation that did not involve infiltrating the senator's office. Then Toro balked at the idea of partnering with an agent, and Wu could feel his plans imploding. When Toro mentioned a shot caller known as "the Colonel," a new strategy immediately began to take shape.

While Vega had been in the interview room locking horns with Toro, Wu had been engaged in his own battle of wills, convincing a reluctant Assistant US Attorney and a downright skeptical assistant director to his way of thinking. In the absence of better options, they had both agreed in the end.

Now he had to get Toro on board, and he would do it personally rather than guide Vega through the process over her earpiece. This was his plan, and he had to be the one to make it work.

"You come in here thinking you got some big idea," Toro said to him. "But nothing's going to convince the others I woke up one day and suddenly changed how I do business."

Wu hadn't shared the underlying reason he thought his unconventional plan would work. If the ADIC and the AUSA knew that particular detail, they would never have given their consent. He regarded Toro for a long moment before he began, trying to determine the best way to broach the subject.

He decided on an indirect approach. "You're not dating anyone right now, are you?" he asked, as if he didn't already know.

"What the hell business is it of yours?" Toro asked.

"We haven't found any evidence of a recent romantic relationship," Wu went on. "But you've had several in the past."

"The FBI is spying on me?" Toro shot to his feet. "You have no right to—"

"Once we ID'd you, we checked every place you might hide out," Wu cut in. "Including friends, lovers, and known associates. It's part of the job."

Toro plopped back down in his chair and said nothing.

"Sir, I must be missing something," Vega said. "What does Toro's love life"—she gave him a quick glance—"or lack thereof, have to do with this investigation?"

Time to drop the bomb. "Toro gets you inside because the two of you are . . . involved." He took advantage of their stunned silence to elaborate and turned back to Toro. "You met Vega at a bar recently when a man started aggressively hitting on her. You were about to intervene when she kicked the crap out of the guy, thoroughly impressing you, and you asked her out." He shifted his gaze to Dani. "Once you two started dating, it didn't take you long to figure out what kind of work he did. You told him you wanted to partner with him because—"

"Bullshit," Toro broke in. "I'd never talk about my work, and I'd never partner with a woman."

Dani showed no reaction, and Wu figured it was not the first sexist comment she'd heard over the years. She ignored Toro and focused an icy stare on him.

Oblivious to the growing tension between Wu and his subordinate, Toro continued his rant. "Do you seriously expect me to introduce her to the Colonel as my date on the next assignment?" He let out a derisive snort. "And even if I did, the Colonel has the resources to check her out. It would take him about ten seconds to find out she was a Fed."

Their time constraint was forcing the words out badly. Wu held up a placating hand and started again, addressing both of them. "The identity we construct for Agent Vega will have a military background similar to the one she has in real life. The fact that she's been in combat situations, knows how to handle weapons, and is well versed in tactics makes it more credible that a man like you would take her up on the offer." He paused. "And it would make her more tempting for the Colonel to put her on his team—or at least try her out. With the background we'll give her, he'll see that she's battle tested. You could also explain that having a woman on his team would create more options and be an asset."

"The Colonel won't just let a newcomer into the group," Toro protested. "He personally recruited each of us."

"How many members are there?" Wu asked.

"Including him," Toro said. "Twelve."

"Vega would make it a baker's dozen then," Wu said.

Toro studied Vega as if seeing her for the first time. Wu didn't care for the hungry expression that settled into the lines of his face as he gave her a slow perusal. He allowed Toro a full minute to consider his options before he pressed the point.

"Or you could spend the rest of your natural life in a cell," he said into the silence.

Toro swore. "This plan is probably going to get us both killed, but it might be the only way."

It sounded as if Toro was coming around to his way of thinking, but Vega's total lack of response did not bode well. She hadn't uttered a word since he had outlined his idea, and her silence spoke volumes.

Too professional to criticize him in front of their prisoner, she clearly had reservations, but if she had known the truth behind his suggestion, she would not have held her tongue.

When he had assured Vega she was the correct person to conduct the interview, he'd referenced the fact that Toro had appeared upset at being bested by a woman. What he didn't share was the litany of observations he'd made watching Toro's body language. Increased respiration, flushed skin, and dilated pupils when he looked at Vega betrayed his attraction to her. Tense muscles and a deep scowl also indicated his feelings were conflicted.

Undercover investigations were among the most dangerous in law enforcement, and Wu was gambling that sending Vega in with someone who viewed her differently than he would a male agent might make Toro hesitate if the Colonel gave the order to harm or kill her. For someone with Vega's training, a moment's hesitation on Toro's part was all the edge she needed.

"There might be an opportunity for me to introduce her," Toro said, cutting into his thoughts. "I'm supposed to meet with the Colonel and the rest of the team tomorrow."

"When were you going to drop this little bomb on us?" Wu said, exasperated. "If that's our timeline, we need to plan. What's this meeting supposed to be about?"

"The Colonel got us a different kind of gig," Toro said. "We're supposed to go through a series of virtual exercises."

Toro was either lying, or he was leaving out important facts. "Explain," Wu said to him.

"All I know is we're headed to a studio that will record everything we do in a VR format." He shrugged. "Maybe someone who makes video games wants to see how real people will react in order to create realistic scenarios." He waved a dismissive hand. "Don't know. Don't care. It pays well. That's what matters."

Wu could hardly believe it. "There won't be any criminal activity involved?"

"The Colonel said it's just an exercise. There won't be any real people there except us."

"Where is this VR exercise going to be?" Vega asked.

"No clue," Toro said. "The Colonel organizes everything. We just show up at the pickup spot with all our gear."

"Where's the pickup spot?" Wu asked.

"Somewhere in the city," Toro said. "He'll text me with the location right before I need to be there."

Classic countersurveillance maneuvers. Perhaps this so-called colonel was the real thing. If he was, Johnson and the military intelligence personnel helping her would put a name to him soon enough.

"Who's the client?" He wanted any drop of information he could squeeze out of Toro. "And how long will it take?"

"Have you been listening to me?" Toro said. "I don't ask questions. The Colonel takes care of logistics. I'm paid to know just enough to get the job done. That's it."

He wondered how Vega was taking the new information. She'd taken an oath to defend her country and the Constitution. She'd risked her life for both. Could she ally herself—even on a temporary basis—with someone who had no loyalty, no allegiance, and no moral compass?

"Agent Vega?" he finally said to her.

"I'll do it," she said quietly. "But let me make one thing crystal clear." She narrowed her eyes on Wu. "Whatever fake military background you construct for me will not include the 75th Ranger Regiment." She crossed her arms. "That's nonnegotiable."

He understood honor. "I have nothing but respect for your service in such an elite position," he said to her without hesitation. "We'll fabricate a history that won't damage the reputation of your former unit."

"If this so-called colonel was ever actually in the military, he would know that no Ranger would ever use their training to become a contract killer." She flicked a hard glare at Toro before turning back to Wu. "We take mental and psychological assessment tests to make sure we're fit for the assignment. We pass background checks and hold security clearances. We're not heartless killing machines released on the battlefield to wreak havoc."

Vega was breathing hard, something he had never seen her do before. Was she trying to convince herself, or everyone else?

"The scrolls are something you earn every day," she continued. "None of us would do anything to dishonor the regiment."

He'd struck a nerve, so he asked her a question to redirect the conversation. "What scrolls are you talking about?"

She looked up as if searching for patience. "Soldiers who complete both parts of the Ranger Assessment and Selection Program and serve in the 75th Ranger Regiment wear a tan beret and a uniform patch with a scroll." She met his gaze. "They're part of the Army's Special Operations Command. It's an honor and a distinction."

"Hold up a second," Toro said, eyeing her again. "I didn't think women could be in special forces."

Vega rounded on him. "Get your knuckles off the ground, Toro. Women have been in the 75th since 2017, and the first female infantry officer led a Ranger platoon into active combat back in 2019."

"Whoa." Toro raised his hands in mock surrender. "Didn't mean to offend."

"I would have to give a shit what you think to find anything you say offensive," Vega shot back, the flush climbing her neck belying the words. "And I don't."

Wu changed the subject again. "When we backstop your cover, I'll make sure it says nothing about special forces," he said to Vega.

"So you're a badass soldier," Toro said to her. "But can you bullshit your way out of a jam?"

"I did undercover work in the military," Vega said. "I can handle myself."

Wu was aware of her brief stint in Signature Reduction, one of the largest covert programs ever devised by the Pentagon. Her work had been classified, but he had the clearance for a briefing on several of her assignments, which was one of many reasons he had requested her for the JTTF.

"Her record speaks for itself," he said as much to Toro as to the unseen audience watching in the conference room. "She's got plenty of UC experience."

Before leaving the Army, Vega had served in their most elite combat unit, where she had smashed through closed doors, glass ceilings, and preconceived notions. Wu had no doubt she was more than qualified for this assignment. Her only challenge would be dealing with Toro, whose loyalty was only to himself.

CHAPTER 16

Dani followed Wu from the interrogation room with every intention of questioning her orders. New agents dreamed of working a high-profile case in an undercover capacity. On the other hand, she was being partnered with someone depraved enough to murder a child to save himself. He would have no issue stabbing her right between the shoulder blades if it meant escape.

Wu had his reasons for selecting her for this mission, and she wanted to know what they were. She waited for him to enter the observation room where he had watched with the Assistant US Attorney before joining the interview. With the AUSA gone and the room empty, she launched into her primary area of concern.

"Sir," she began. "Toro is—"

She stopped when he put his cell phone to his ear. "SAC Wu." His eyes widened. "I'll put you on speaker. Agent Vega should hear this." He held out the phone and tapped an icon.

"We ID'd the Colonel." Jada Johnson's excitement was contagious.

"Who is he?" Wu asked.

"Retired Colonel Xavier Treadway," Johnson said.

"What branch?" Dani asked.

"Served twenty-eight years in the Army. Retired and now represents defense contractors."

Wu's brows shot up. "Represents them how?"

"He's a lobbyist," Johnson said. "Private companies looking to score lucrative DOD contracts hire his firm. He's brokered billion-dollar deals."

"That could be how he knows Senator Sledge," Dani said. "Lobbyists meet with elected officials all the time."

"Access the Congressional Record," Wu said to Johnson. "See if you can find a nexus with the senator and any bills he supported that might benefit a defense contractor that hired Colonel Treadway's firm."

"On it, sir," Johnson said. "I reached out to my counterparts with military intelligence for some more background," she continued. "Treadway was trying for brigadier general but never got that promotion. Instead, the Army quietly forced him to retire."

That got Dani's attention. "Was his last assignment at the Pentagon?"

"How did you know?" Johnson asked.

"It's logical," she said. "He probably knew he wouldn't get promoted and made every contact he could inside the Beltway during his last assignment so he could cash in later."

Wu gave her an appreciative nod. "He set himself up to become an influencer in DC and a conduit for government contractors. After he left, the same generals who had blocked his promotion had to come to him for access."

She had seen the type. There were some who had managed to claw their way into leadership positions who had no business being there. Such people stewed in their resentment when they could climb no higher, determined to make everyone around them pay homage. What she didn't know was exactly when Treadway had sold his soul.

CHAPTER 17

Dani noticed that the set of Wu's shoulders was as tight as his jawline. The SAC had called an obligatory preop meeting before sending her on the undercover assignment. What made the briefing unprecedented was the inclusion of one of the highest-ranking officials in the Bureau and a paid assassin, two individuals she would never have pictured in the same room together.

Dani figured Assistant Director in Charge Scott Hargrave had decided to run the meeting personally because of its implications. The possibility of charging a sitting US senator with fraud, taking bribes, and conspiracy to commit murder took everything they did to a completely different level.

"Take a seat." Hargrave made it a general comment for everyone in the room as he pulled out a chair at the head of the rectangular table.

Wu and Dani sat along one side while Toro lowered himself into the chair across from them. They were still at the off-site secure location, and the digital forensics unit had data-mined every part of Toro's cell phone in what they termed a "phone dump" before implanting listening and tracking devices. Satisfied, they had returned it long enough for him to call the Colonel and report that he was still in the city and actively evading law enforcement—with the help of his girlfriend.

The team had listened in while Toro went on to push their carefully crafted background story about Dani, whose newly created fake identity was Nicola "Nikki" Corazón. In case the man calling himself "the Colonel" was in fact affiliated with the military in some way, the Bureau had gone to the trouble of manufacturing a fictitious military career that had ended with her dishonorable discharge for excessive violence in the field and using unauthorized weapons.

The Colonel agreed to use the VR exercise as a test drive for Nikki. He also promised to check out her background ahead of time but told Toro to bring her with him to the meeting spot on the following day. Nikki would get no pay unless she proved herself worthy. The first hurdle overcome, now she was prepared to hear what else the Bureau had in store for her.

"We're here to establish protocols and ground rules," Assistant Director Hargrave said after everyone settled. "This operation is extremely sensitive, with a high risk of violence or personal injury and required authorization at FBI HQ through the Undercover Review Committee. The FBI director himself and the Assistant Attorney General for the Criminal Division have given their approval and want to be kept apprised."

He paused, letting the gravity of the pronouncement sink in. She had never been involved in an assignment with so much high-level oversight. At least not since she'd left the military.

"That's not going to work," Toro said. "We can't do this by committee. That's no way to catch these guys."

Hargrave narrowed his eyes. "And yet we managed to capture you in less than twenty-four hours," he said. "More to the point, we conduct meticulous and thorough investigations before we bring a charge. That's why we almost never lose a case in court. We're methodical."

Toro held up both hands in mock surrender. "I'm just saying that we're not going to be able to run everything past Agent Vega's chain of command. Things will happen fast."

"Which is the only reason you're here at all. I am going to make it perfectly clear where the lines are and what the penalty is for crossing them. For Agent Vega, it's her career. For you, it's your freedom."

Hargrave's dual-targeted comment put Dani on alert, as she was sure he had intended. The ADIC may have been looking at Toro when he spoke, but his words were clearly directed at her. Ultimately she bore responsibility for Toro's actions as well as her own, and watchful eyes far above her pay grade would scrutinize their every move.

"SAC Wu will outline the ground rules," Hargrave continued. "And they apply to both of you." He looked at each of them in turn before his gaze rested on Wu.

"This is spelled out in the Attorney General's guidelines for our undercover ops," Wu said. "The following acts are prohibited: participation in violence, except in self-defense or preserving the life of another. Initiating criminal acts. Unlawful investigative techniques. Participation in criminal acts, except in emergency situations as set out in section four, subsection H, paragraphs one through five."

Toro narrowed his eyes. "What the hell does that mean?"

Wu sighed. "It means you are authorized to do certain things that would be considered crimes if committed by someone outside of law enforcement."

"Figures," Toro said. "You guys commit crimes that you lock other people up for."

"The rules about this are very clear," Wu said. "You can't just do whatever you want. Agent Vega will make sure you understand your limits."

"Sometimes you have to establish yourself as a criminal," Dani said to Toro. "Sometimes you have to make bribes or purchase contraband." She turned to Wu. "By the way, what's our budget, sir?"

"One million dollars," he said. "Without additional approval."

"Now you're talking," Toro said.

"That's Agent Vega's budget." Hargrave pointed at him. "*You* spend nothing."

"Since we have the protocols in place," Wu said before Toro could make a rude comment, "let's discuss how we're getting Agent Vega inside the group."

This was the part Dani had been dreading. She wondered how far things would have to go and how much time she would have to spend with Toro.

"So, Agent Vega—excuse me—Nikki Corazón and I are a couple," Toro said to the room at large. "Now what?"

"We'll show you the background we've constructed for her," Hargrave said. "Make sure there are no red flags in it." When Toro nodded, he continued. "We've put our best people on it. We scrubbed everything from her real life, including social media, and have given her an entire life story. She was charged with felony assault after knifing a biker in a bar, but got it busted down to a misdemeanor and put on probation. The Colonel can dig all the way back to her kindergarten, where she was noted for her constant disruptive behavior, by the way."

"I'm a bad seed," Dani said. "And I make poor choices."

"You'll have to do something about your look," Toro said. "Right now, you scream government issue."

"You just get me to that meeting tomorrow," Dani said. "I'll be sure to look the part."

"Are you ready?" Wu asked Toro.

"Do I have a choice?" He glanced at Dani. "Either the Colonel will buy this, or we'll both end up with a bullet to the head. The problem is, we won't know which until we get there."

CHAPTER 18

Dani had barely made it into the cramped Bronx apartment before her younger sister ran at her full tilt. Erica's slender form was in stark contrast to Dani's athletic build, and Dani barely had to brace herself for impact.

As Erica squeezed her tight, a rush of self-recrimination surged through Dani. She did not come to visit as often as she should, but the silent reproach that emanated from her *tía* Manuela kept her at bay.

As it was meant to do.

From the day Dani and her younger siblings, Erica and Axel, had come to live with their aunt and uncle nine years ago, *Tía* Manuela had made her feelings clear without uttering a word. Erica and Axel were the good kids. Dani was too much like her mother.

Message received.

She had tried to prove to her aunt—and everyone else—that although she might look like her mother, she was her father's daughter at heart. He had been a Ranger, so that's what she wanted to do, too, even as a young girl.

Her very soul ached at the memory of her father. She recalled how happy she'd been when his last tour of duty ended unexpectedly and he told the family he was coming home for good. In her childlike naivete, she'd thought it was because he wanted to be with them all the time.

That he couldn't stand to be away for months at a time on maneuvers or deployments.

Only later did she learn that he had suffered a traumatic brain injury that left him with debilitating migraines, tinnitus, and vertigo. After his medical discharge, the family had moved back to New York from Georgia so that Dani's mother, who was battling demons of her own, would have help coping with the added burden.

According to whispers Dani overheard from relatives after what they referred to only as "the incident," her mother had always been emotionally fragile. Something had happened in her childhood that no one would talk about. Dani didn't notice anything at the time. Her mother was her mom. That was all.

Then came the morning when twelve-year-old Dani woke up to the sound of her mother screaming. The police and the ambulance had come. Paramedics carried a tiny bundle from the nursery where her baby brother slept. They had used the term "crib death," and Dani found out only later what that meant. For her three older surviving children, it meant devastation. They lost both their little brother and their mother that day. She became an automaton who drifted through each day, completing household chores and other obligatory functions with little awareness of the world around her.

Despite his own struggles, their father did his best to care for the older children, and life began to return to normal as he gradually helped her mother regain her mental footing and recover from the loss.

Things were getting better . . . or so everyone thought, but their chances at a normal life died with their father when Dani was seventeen. Her mother's most powerful tether to reality snapped, and she sank into a mental morass and was never the same after that—and neither were her children.

"You came for Axel's birthday," Erica said, stepping back from their embrace.

"You say that like there was a chance I'd forget," Dani said, lifting the gift bag to show her sister. "Never missed either of your birthdays yet."

A male voice interrupted them from across the room. "Knew you'd come."

They both turned to see Axel sauntering into the tiny family room from the narrow hallway that led to the bedrooms.

"Feliz cumpleaños," Dani said, holding out the gift bag. She knew better than to give him a hug. Axel didn't do hugs.

He grasped the bag's thin ribbon handles and peered inside. "You know me so well," he said, lifting out a box.

She had searched for weeks to find a 3D logic puzzle difficult enough to challenge him. Most would have taken him less than sixty seconds to complete, but this one was designed by a Mensa group, so she figured it would last him a couple of hours. Maybe.

"That should take you a minute," she said. "There's a gift card in there too. Don't spend it all on booze just because you turned twenty-one today."

Axel pulled the plastic card out of the bottom, his eyes widening when he saw the amount printed on the front. "I wouldn't waste this on alcohol, but I might consider using it to buy an NFT."

Dani suppressed an eye roll. Axel was all about cutting-edge technology, including nonfungible tokens and cryptocurrency. They had stayed up late one night arguing when she discovered he was socking every penny he could scrounge into blockchain-based investments. She was afraid he would lose it all, but he was confident about his financial strategy.

Dani's thoughts were interrupted when Manuela walked in from her bedroom. Their eyes locked. Erica and Axel looked from one woman to the other and back again.

"I came to see Axel," Dani said by way of explanation.

"Did you have a good visit?" Manuela asked, emphasizing the past tense.

Dani bristled. "I've only been here five minutes. I was about to—"

"And it's been real nice to see you," Manuela said firmly. "Thanks for coming by."

Dani reminded herself this was her *tía*'s home. Technically she had no right to be here, and neither did her brother and sister, who were of legal age. They had both qualified for scholarships and lived on campus most of the year, but Manuela allowed them to stay with her between semesters and on holidays. The fact that Manuela accepted money from Dani for her niece and nephew's care may have nudged them into land-lord–tenant status, but Dani would never push the issue on their behalf. Regular schools were still open, but universities were already on summer break, and her siblings could be sent out to fend for themselves. Better to bite her tongue and keep the peace than go to war with family.

She had to stop by before she left, despite the pain her visit would cause everyone involved. She knew the rules. Deep undercover meant no outside communication. But she had a favor to ask her sister, and she had to check on her brother.

She swallowed the words trying to force their way out of her mouth and changed tactics. "I also wanted to ask Erica for a favor."

Manuela's eyes narrowed. "What kind of favor?"

"A new hairstyle."

"She doesn't do hair anymore," Manuela said. "She works as a med-ical assistant down the street." She smiled at Erica. "She's going to be a doctor someday."

Erica gave her aunt an apologetic grimace. "I don't mind."

Manuela's gaze—and her scowl—returned to Dani. "Why the sud-den interest in your appearance?" She gave her a critical perusal. "It's not like you've put a lot of effort in before."

Dani felt a hot scald creep up the back of her neck but kept her tone light. "It's time for a change."

"I've got some of my old stuff in the bathroom," Erica said in an obvious attempt to defuse the growing tension. "We can do something with your hair." She grasped Dani's hand and began tugging her toward the hallway. "It'll be fun."

"I'll help," Axel said. "You know, moral support and all."

Dani allowed herself to be led, shooting a glance over her shoulder to see Manuela standing in the family room, hands on hips, glaring at them.

"I wish she would lay off you," Erica said after closing the bathroom door. "She just can't let shit go."

"She'll never be in charge of your fan club," Axel said to her. "But she always manages to cash your checks."

Dani had told her brother and sister about the money she sent every month to make sure her aunt spent it on them. She didn't think Manuela would overtly steal from her own family, but having checks and balances in place avoided temptation and left nothing to chance. It also encouraged Manuela to keep providing a place for them to live until they were ready to strike out on their own.

It couldn't have been easy for Manuela, whose own children were grown and had left the apartment nine years ago, to suddenly find herself responsible for raising her brother's three teenage children. She had always been closer to Erica and Axel, and the preference became more pronounced each day after they moved in. Whenever Dani did something Manuela didn't care for, she would mutter, *"como tu mamá,"* under her breath—but loud enough to be sure Dani knew she was acting like her mom.

After their mother, finally broken, had been committed to the psych ward at Bellevue Hospital, CPS had taken her three children to live with their *tía* Manuela and *tío* Pablo, only a few blocks away. Dani had been seventeen at the time, four years older than Erica and six years older than Axel. CPS workers had been pleased they could each continue to attend their same schools, assuring the judge at the custody hearing that they would get support from their friends.

They had been woefully wrong.

A full change of identity and relocation would have been better for them as far as Dani was concerned. Their friends gossiped about them before finally ghosting them. They had all overheard the whispers in the halls. *"Did you hear what happened? Their mom is loca. That whole family must be messed up."*

On her eighteenth birthday, Dani had followed in her father's footsteps and joined the Army.

Combined with the other benefits, her military paycheck had provided enough extra income to make up for any extra financial burden her younger siblings caused their aunt and uncle. Eventual promotions and hazardous duty pay she'd received on active duty had gone toward a college fund she'd set up for them.

Axel had qualified for a full-ride scholarship to Columbia University, and Erica had done the same at NYU, but they both had plenty of expenses.

"I dropped by to say happy birthday, and to say goodbye for a while," Dani said quietly, aware neither sibling would like what they were about to hear.

"I thought you weren't going on any more secret missions." Erica's tone was only half-kidding. "You promised me you'd turned in your secret decoder ring when you left the Army."

They had all grown up on sanitized and declassified stories about their dad's days in the military, and Erica made it clear she did not want Dani to join the Rangers. Terrified her big sister would be captured or killed, she nearly broke down every time Dani went on a classified mission.

"Something came up," Dani said, trying to sound more casual than evasive. "I need to change my look. Figured you could help."

"What did you have in mind?" Erica asked, suspicious.

"This won't be an ordinary makeover," Dani said. "I'm thinking about something a bit more . . . tactical."

"Tactical?" Erica repeated, crossing her arms. "What's up?"

Axel gave her a knowing look. "She's going on an undercover assignment with the FBI."

"I can neither confirm nor deny your allegation," Dani said, trying to lighten the mood. "All I can tell you is I need to look like someone who would gladly kill you."

"Like one of those female assassins in FPS games?" Axel asked. "I could see that."

He spent every moment not devoted to study playing first-person-shooter video games. Dani kept waiting for him to get bored with his hobby, but he had a YouTube channel where he narrated his virtual exploits and had already gained over ten thousand subscribers.

"Maybe," she said to him.

"Okay, I can work with this," Erica said, pacing.

"Whatever you like." Dani rolled her eyes. "Just make me look deadly. Can you do that?"

She pretended not to see their curious gazes. No way would she admit she was about to team up with Gustavo Toro, a man whose callous disregard for life defined him. A man she was depending on for her very survival.

She did it in the hope Toro would lead her to the person ulti-mately responsible for Nathan Costner's murder. She did it because no one should escape justice—even the rich and the powerful. She did it because it was her job.

A part of her hoped her brother and sister would never understand what it felt like to be her.

CHAPTER 19

The next morning Dani stood in front of SAC Wu, whose frank appraisal unsettled her.

"This is your best approximation of a female assassin?" he asked her.

She looked down at her recently acquired wardrobe. "I figured black goes with everything," she said. "And it's suitable for all occasions."

"I like it," Toro said. "You don't look like a Fed now."

Which had been the whole point.

"The hair is a bit much," Wu said. "It's going to take a while to grow it all back."

Her sister had shaved both sides of Dani's head, leaving a thick mane covering a wide swath down the middle dyed jet black and plaited into a braid beginning at her forehead and continuing halfway down her back.

"At least it stays out of my face," Dani said. She decided not to tell them about the special barrette she'd put in her hair. She hadn't worn it since her last classified military op.

"Now you're Nikki Corazón for sure," Toro said. "You look like you could hold your own in a bar brawl."

She shot him a look. "I'll try not to disappoint."

Everyone turned at the sound of the door opening.

"Excuse me, sir," a slender woman in her forties with a decidedly bookish air said to Wu. "I've made the adjustments. Are you ready?"

Wu nodded. "Come in, Sandra." He turned to Toro and Dani. "This is Sandra Feehan. She designed your wearables."

Sandra lifted a box that looked like it could have held cigars and opened the lid. She reached inside, took out a man's smart watch, and handed it to Toro. "This contains a tracking device." She waited for him to take it and continued. "I've also tapped into the health-monitoring features so they relay information about your pulse rate, stress level, and sleep to a dedicated system."

"But will you know if I get my ten thousand steps in?" Toro said. "Because that shit's important."

Sandra ignored the question and turned to Dani. "I had to modify this for your wrist," she said, holding out a heavy black leather cuff bracelet. "This was originally meant for . . . uh . . ."

Dani could practically hear the unspoken words as Sandra trailed off. Their time had been short, and everyone had assumed a male agent would go undercover with Toro.

She took the bracelet, which felt heavy. Uncomfortable with the reminder that she was no one's first pick to go on this assignment, she covered her awkwardness with a question.

"Does this have a tracker as well?"

Sandra smiled. "Of course. And both of your cell phones will too." She pointed at what appeared to be three decorative silver coins set into the leather. "This coin provides the same data as the watch."

"No hidden weapons in these things?" Toro said after Sandra left the room. "I was expecting one of the watch's dials to release knockout gas when you turn it." He shook his head. "I didn't even get an exploding pen."

"This is the FBI," Dani said. "We're also not getting a briefcase that turns into a parachute or a shoe phone."

"You'll get your gun back when you and Agent Vega leave for the meeting," Wu said. "I'm not wild about it, but everyone knows what you carry, and it would be suspicious if you had something different or went unarmed."

"I never go anywhere without my piece," Toro said.

The comment reminded her of an earlier conversation with Wu. "Did you get what I requested?" she asked him.

Her supervisor opened a lunch box–size case. Dani reached inside and reverently lifted the matte black Sig Sauer P220 semiautomatic nested in foam packing.

"Tell me this isn't straight from the factory," she said.

"Give me some credit, Vega," Wu said. "There was no time for you to go to the range, but I had the range masters put a couple hundred rounds through it."

She sniffed, catching the scent of gun oil, then thumbed the release and pulled back the slide to work the action. "Chamber's empty," she said.

Wu handed her two full magazines.

She took them both and seated one with a satisfying snap. She stashed the extra in the upper left pocket of her leather jacket, then grasped the slide and racked it back with a jerk of her hand to chamber a round.

"I need it to go bang when I pull the trigger," she said by way of response to Wu's raised brow.

"Do I get extra ammo?" Toro asked, watching her slip the Sig into a holster attached to her black webbed belt.

"You get exactly what you came here with," Wu said to him. "No more."

Toro motioned to Dani. "Except a partner in crime."

Dani took advantage of the opening to ask a question that had been on her mind since they had learned about the Colonel.

She looked at Toro. "What would make a retired military officer go rogue? Did he say anything to you about his background?"

"He made it a point *not* to reveal anything about himself," Toro said. "I never even knew his name, much less whether he was actually a colonel. He certainly never talked about his business dealings or his contacts."

She turned back to Wu, who had reviewed the dossier prepared by Johnson and her military intelligence cohorts. "Did the analysts uncover anything we can use for leverage?"

"Treadway is divorced," Wu said. "Kids are grown. No grandkids. He's fifty years old and in excellent health."

"He's a ranking officer, so he's a trained tactician," she said, thinking out loud. "I just don't get how he would sink to this."

"You have no idea how low he can go," Toro said quietly. "You'd better hope your cover is never blown."

CHAPTER 20

Dani stood beside Toro at the mouth of a nearly deserted alley and checked her watch. Two minutes past the meeting time.

Toro jerked his chin in the direction of a rapidly approaching black panel van. "That's them. We won't know for sure whether it worked or not right away," Toro said as the van slowed. "The Colonel is strategic. He might give us some rope to see if we hang ourselves before he orders the rest of the group to jump us." The creases around his mouth tightened. "Problem is, we won't know until it's too late . . . which is the point."

As the van pulled to the curb and glided to a stop, Dani felt the familiar tightening of her stomach before she went into an unknown situation. There was no time for her to respond, but she had been forewarned.

The vehicle's side door slid open, and two men beckoned to them. Dani hauled herself inside after Toro, noting that the rear compartment was sealed off from the front, separating the driver from the passengers.

"You've got a strange idea of a date," the taller of the two men said to Toro. "We've never had a couple on the team before."

"Nice to see you again, too, Chopper," Toro said, reaching around her to slide the door shut.

The one called Chopper eyed her with suspicion. For the hundredth time, she entertained doubts about her cover, but Toro had concurred with Wu that no other agent had a prayer of getting inside the Colonel's group.

The shorter man directed a sneer at her. "I don't like working with women."

"The Colonel is okay with it," Toro said. "That should be good enough for you." He gestured toward Dani. "She goes by Nikki."

Dani knew better than to smile or make small talk and kept silent as the van began to move.

"This is Jock," Toro said to Dani, tipping his head toward the shorter man. "He competes in iron man events in his spare time." He turned to the man who had greeted them. "And this is Chopper."

Chopper's lips twisted into a grim smile. "Not because I like to ride custom bikes."

"He has an affinity for edged weapons," Toro said by way of explanation.

So far her new cohorts consisted of a muscular misogynist and a knife-wielding mutilator. Lovely.

They rode in silence for an hour before Dani felt the van angle downward and make several turns as if they had gone into a multi-level subterranean parking garage. She couldn't recall any structures fitting that description in Manhattan. Had they gone into New Jersey? Wherever they were, the surveillance teams would have had a tough time maintaining a tail over such a long distance. At least they still had their concealed tracking devices.

When the van came to an abrupt halt, Chopper slid the door open and hopped out. The pungent stench of urine hit her before she clambered from the vehicle to find that she'd been correct about the underground garage, but she couldn't pinpoint her location. The gray concrete walls and floor could have been anywhere, and the fact that the space was only half-filled with cars told her they had likely descended to the lowest level.

Two more men were waiting when they got out. One could have been a heavyweight boxer, with bulging muscles and a misshapen nose that looked fresh out of the ring. He stepped forward, holding a metal-detecting wand.

"This is Guapo," Toro told her. "He's got security duty today."

Dani figured the code name was ironic, because the man before her would hardly be anyone's description of handsome. His face had been fractured in many places, and deeply scarred as well.

When Chopper, Jock, and Toro stood with their arms and legs spread, she followed suit, wondering what they would do with her weapons and bracelet cuff.

The wand emitted a high-pitched tone, prompting Chopper to remove first a compact pistol, then a shiny butterfly knife. He placed them inside a duffel bag clutched in Guapo's free hand.

"Well isn't this cute?" Guapo said, smirking at the gun that fit in the palm of his beefy hand.

"That's a Glock Model 30, asshole," Chopper said. "There are ten .45-caliber rounds in the magazine, and one of them could be for you."

"Do we all need to drop our pants and get out a ruler?" Toro said. "Or can we get on with this?"

As Guapo moved on to Jock, Chopper stepped over to the next man, who held something that resembled a bright-yellow plastic flashlight with coiled wires where the bulb should have been.

"What's that?" Chopper asked the man.

"Extra security," he responded, pointing the end with the coils at Chopper. "Hold still a sec."

Chopper frowned. "I'd like to know what you—"

"Done," the man said after pressing a red button on top of the device. "Didn't hurt at all, did it?"

Chopper grumbled and stepped aside.

Dani figured the thing must be some sort of scanner, but her mind was on a more pressing matter as she saw Jock drop a .357 Magnum revolver and a switchblade into Guapo's duffel. What would she do when he finished with Toro and came to her? The rule book said she should not give up her weapons, but she was certain her undercover assignment would end here and now if she refused to turn them over.

Toro bent to place his gun and knife in the bag, and Guapo stepped in front of her. He looked down at her with interest as he passed the wand over her. The first beep sounded at the top of her head.

She pointed at her hair. "Just a metal hair clip," she said.

Guapo grunted and kept going. He did not seem to care about her bracelet, either, for which she was grateful. She might be unarmed, but at least she could still be tracked.

As expected, the device beeped again when he passed it over her chest. He rested the duffel bag on the floor and reached out to her with his free hand, eyes alight with lascivious interest.

"Back off." She reached inside her upper pocket and pulled out the extra magazine, then dropped it into the bag.

A second pass of the wand confirmed there was nothing else in that spot. He muttered something crude under his breath and went about his business, scanning her body until another tone sounded at the small of her back.

"Nice piece," Guapo said, admiring the Sig Sauer she had pulled out. "Good stopping power."

"When I shoot something," she said, "I want it to stay down."

Guapo jerked his chin toward the duffel, and she hesitantly placed the pistol inside.

"We'll be getting these back, right?" she asked him.

"Absolutely." He continued to scan, stopping at the top of her boot and waiting while she slid out a black tactical folding knife and tossed it into the bag, where it landed among the other weapons with a metallic clatter.

Before she had a chance to see what he was doing, the man with the yellow flashlight-looking device had already pointed it at her and pressed the red button.

Based on his evasive comment toward Chopper, she decided not to press him for details about what kind of scanner it was.

After stooping to pick up the duffel, Guapo sauntered over to the black van they had arrived in and gave the side panel two thumps with his fist. The van sped away, heading in the direction of the ramps that led up to the street-level exit.

There were only two reasons to dismiss their transportation. One was because they were all about to be killed where they were. The other was to switch vehicles and evade a tail. Neither option boded well. Guapo continued walking until he came to a charcoal-gray Suburban with windows tinted so dark it was impossible to see inside.

He motioned them in, and Dani joined the others climbing into various seats. The driver faced forward, avoiding eye contact with his passengers. As soon as they were all inside, he drove smoothly upward and out of the garage.

Finally able to see her surroundings, she made out a sign confirming that they had traveled into the Garden State. The nearby waterfront and surrounding buildings told her she was in Jersey City.

The vehicle switch had been an unexpected tactic, telling her more about the group's sophistication and expertise than anything Toro could have said. Fortunately for her, the FBI would be able to track their hidden transmitters despite the vehicle transfer.

"By the way," Toro said to the second man, his tone casual. "What was that thing you zapped us with? I mean, I'm still going to be able to father children someday, right?"

A slow smile split the man's face. "You're still fine," he said. "But your electronics—not so much."

Dani concealed her alarm. "What do you mean?"

He turned to her. "That was a handheld EMP device. You may as well toss your cell phones. They're paperweights now."

She made an effort to control her expression. An electromagnetic pulse generator that size would fry any electronic device within a yard.

In retrospect, that explained why they had been standing away from other cars in the parking garage. They hadn't gone to the Suburban until after the EMP had been put away. Why hadn't Toro warned them about this?

She cut her eyes to see him glance at his smart watch and curse. As she had feared, his watch and her hidden tracker had been rendered useless along with their cell phones. She doubted Wu and the others were aware of the vehicle switch, which had taken place deep underground.

In less than an hour, she and Toro had been disarmed, surrounded, and left completely on their own.

CHAPTER 21

Wu sat with the others in the JOC, looking at the series of wall-mounted monitors that formed two rows of streamed images. He focused on the center screen, which displayed the satellite feed.

"What's that garage he's driving into?" he said to Johnson, stationed at the computer terminal closest to him.

She typed rapidly before directing Wu's attention to a different screen. "It's a public self-park in Jersey City on Washington Boulevard," Johnson said. "There are levels above and below ground."

Wu shifted his attention to Flint. "Tell the alpha team to go in after them."

Flint tapped the screen of his cell phone and put it to his ear. "Wait sixty seconds and follow them in," he said. "But make sure you stay well back. If the van is parked, find a space where you can keep an eye on it, but do not approach unless it's an emergency."

"Depending on how many levels that garage has, they'll have to use the radio to get back in touch with us," Wu said, watching one of the teams they had tailing Vega and Toro make its way around the block before pulling inside the garage.

Detective Flint broke the silence a minute later. "The van's coming out."

Wu switched his gaze back to the satellite feed. Sure enough, the same black van was leaving the parking garage, where it made a quick right turn to merge with traffic.

"Must have picked up more passengers in the garage," Wu said. "Tell the beta team to pick up the tail."

Flint spoke into his phone in an urgent undertone while Wu watched the alpha team emerge from the garage. To his relief, they turned left, having gotten the message to leave the other teams to follow the van.

"The alpha team never caught sight of the van inside the garage," Flint said, then disconnected and addressed Johnson. "Can you contact whoever manages that self-park to see if they have security cams on all the decks?"

"On it," she said, tilting her head back down to her computer screen.

Wu appreciated Flint's levelheaded reassessment of the evolving situation. He hoped they would eventually be able to get footage of whoever had been picked up or dropped off underground. In the meantime, they would follow the van's progress.

"Excuse me, sir," Johnson said, alarmed.

"What's wrong?"

"I'm not sure how it happened, but we've lost all four tracking signals." At his raised brow, she elaborated. "The ones in their cell phones and on their person." The color drained from her face. "They all went dark."

"I refuse to believe all the devices had a technical glitch at the same time," Flint said.

"Try a total system reboot and see if you can reestablish the signal," Wu said to Johnson. "Get Sandra Feehan to help you."

Johnson got up to speak to another analyst at the far end of the room.

"Now more than ever, we'd better not lose that damned van," Flint said.

"No chance of that," Wu said, not sure whether he was trying to convince himself or the others in the room.

He watched the van while he waited for a report from Johnson. The van meandered through traffic until it made a quick turn and entered a parking garage on Hudson Street in Hoboken.

"Now what?" Flint said.

Wu voiced a nagging doubt that had begun to form in the back of his mind. "It's as if they know they're under surveillance and are using countermeasures. We've got aerial, ground, and electronic surveillance, and they're trying to defeat them all."

"It's what I would do," Flint said.

"Which means they've probably anticipated the tails we've put on them as well," Wu said. "Have the beta team follow them into the garage. Make sure the gamma team is ready to pick the van up when it leaves, and have the delta team on standby."

He had arranged for a total of six vehicles to trail the van from a distance, rotating out so the driver would never see one car behind him consistently. The satellite had been an added reassurance, affording them the ability to continue in the event the van traveled a longer distance outside the city, where cars would be more noticeable.

"The van stopped three levels down," Flint said, phone to his ear. "Beta team says the driver got out, walked around the outside of the vehicle, then got back in and is now driving toward the exit."

"He's looking to see who's after him," Wu said. "Tell beta to stay put and have gamma pick him up when he leaves."

Wu watched the screen as the van made its way back onto the street. Within moments, the gamma team was trailing him from a discreet distance.

"This guy either has some training, or someone gave him damned good instructions," he muttered under his breath.

"Sir," Johnson said, drawing his attention from the screen. "I contacted the management company. It's an older facility, and their cameras have been broken for months. They haven't gotten around to repairing them yet." She grimaced. "Budget cuts."

"Don't bother with the second garage," Wu said. "We had eyes on him the whole time. We know what he was doing."

"Yes, sir." She shifted her feet, clearly uncomfortable. "We did a system reboot. There is still no signal from any of the tracking devices."

He nodded absently, determined to figure out what the Colonel was up to. Had they underestimated him so badly?

Flint cursed, interrupting his thoughts. "He's driving deeper into Hoboken. Should we intercept?"

This was the question Wu had been wrestling with. So far the only thing that had gone wrong was a failure of the tracking devices. They still had Vega and Toro's transport vehicle in sight. There was no reason to believe they were in danger, and the countersurveillance measures led him to believe they were on the way to see the Colonel. Interrupting the operation now would leave them no better off than before.

"Not yet," Wu said.

He looked on, mounting frustration warring with concern as he tried to anticipate the driver's next move and—more importantly—the strategy behind it. No one spoke. All eyes were riveted to the screen, following the van as it made a series of turns.

"He's driving in circles," Flint said. "Probably checking his rearview."

"Have the delta team take over," Wu said.

The van headed north on Washington Street, turned right onto Third, then left on Court Street before it maneuvered into a cobblestone alley and pulled to the curb.

The driver got out and leaned back inside the open front window, reaching for something. With a bird's-eye view from the satellite, it was impossible to see what he was doing. The delta team had stopped outside the alley and couldn't possibly get a good look from their vantage point.

He found himself holding his breath as the driver lifted out what looked like a bright-red three-gallon container and closed the door.

"What the hell is he . . ." Flint trailed off.

They all watched in dawning horror as the driver began splashing clear liquid from the container all over the van.

"He's going to set it on fire," Wu said to Flint. "Tell everyone to move in."

He shot to his feet while Flint barked into his phone, drawing closer to the screen as if he could somehow put a stop to the nightmare.

Two agents from the zeta team rushed in from the alley's entrance, but not before the driver lit a match and tossed it into the liquid pooled beside the van's tire. Within seconds, a wall of flame erupted to engulf the vehicle.

Johnson clapped a hand to her mouth and spoke through her fingers. "They're trapped in the back." She turned horrified eyes to Wu. "They'll be burned alive."

CHAPTER 22

Dani sat beside Toro in the back row of the Suburban's seats, looking out the darkly tinted windows. It was difficult to make out details of the passing scenery, but she could tell they were headed west, going deeper into New Jersey.

The men around her did not have much to say, everyone apparently content to keep their own counsel, Toro included. She figured they had been on the road for about an hour when the driver slowed to turn onto a smaller roadway. They passed a line of trees that opened into a wide expanse with long bands of asphalt.

Toro bent to whisper in her ear. "This is Lincoln Park Airport."

She had heard of the privately owned airfield but hadn't been there before. "Does the Colonel have a plane?"

"Not that I know of."

Another fifteen minutes took them well past the airport to what looked like an aircraft repair facility.

The SUV ground to a halt, and Chopper was the first one to open his door and leap out. No one spoke as they all clambered from the vehicle and stretched their cramped muscles. Two hangars dwarfed the smaller building where Guapo was leading them. Dani noted that the driver got out and joined them, bringing the total in their group to seven.

Guapo typed a combination into a keypad on a reinforced metal door, and the latch released. He pushed it open and walked through, everyone else in his wake.

Dani saw five other men inside the building. Everyone stood quietly, as if waiting for orders. She stuck close to Toro, figuring that's what his actual girlfriend would do in these circumstances.

Toro nudged her. "The one on the far right is Doc Tox," he whispered in her ear.

She flicked a glance at a middle-aged man with curly brown hair, taking care not to study him overtly. Toro had been right when he'd guessed who had concocted the poison. She would make it a point to stay as far away from him as possible.

Moments later, a tall man who appeared to be in his fifties strode out from the shadows. His close-cropped salt-and-pepper hair added a distinguished look to his gray camo outfit. Even if she hadn't seen his picture in the dossier prepared by Johnson, Dani would have known this was Colonel Xavier Treadway.

"Now that everyone is here, we can get to our first order of business," he said in a deep baritone. His brown eyes swept the room, coming to rest on her. "Which is our visitor."

She felt everyone's gaze turn to her and made it a point to stand erect, looking the Colonel directly in the eyes with enough intensity to transmit confidence without overt challenge.

He ambled toward her, the others moving to make way for him. He came to a stop directly in front of her.

"Nicola Corazón?"

She gave him a curt nod.

"I call her Nikki," Toro said, finally speaking.

The Colonel made no response as he walked in a circle around her. "I see the report of your military experience is accurate."

She had instinctively come to attention under his scrutiny. Eyes forward, spine stiff, hands tight to her sides, her demeanor bore out her backstory. She had subconsciously responded to something in the Colonel's bearing that marked him as a commanding officer. With that level of training and discipline, he would be a formidable adversary should she ever need to face him. She also couldn't help but wonder if he still had access to military records. And if the fabricated history the FBI had constructed would withstand digging if he was able to call in any favors from active-duty personnel.

The Colonel, apparently satisfied for the moment, moved away to face the group. "I'm sure you all are wondering what the nature of this assignment is." He paced in front of them as he spoke. "It's a critical contract, and I have been requested to personally lead the group."

Judging by the looks they all gave each other, she assumed the Colonel's personal participation was a rarity.

"This mission requires twelve people"—the Colonel flicked a glance her way—"but we have thirteen."

Dani felt the tension in the room go up a notch.

"I cleared it with the client," the Colonel continued. "And no one's pay will be affected except Toro's, so I'm fine with having a former soldier among us—even if her discharge wasn't exactly . . . honorable."

The background had held up so far, and the men seemed to be recalibrating their opinion of her.

"An extra body won't hurt, because the nature of this new contract will prove challenging," the Colonel went on. Once he had recaptured everyone's attention, he came to a stop and faced them. "We are going to help create a virtual training program. We are playing the roles of insurgents in an urban-combat scenario. There will be booby traps, barricades, and other obstacles. We may be required to split into teams or work alone at various points."

"Who's putting on the training?" Toro asked. "No one's supposed to know who we are."

"Your identities will be concealed at all times," the Colonel responded. "We'll all be wearing specially constructed suits that will render avatars with no resemblance to your appearance. Your actions will be recorded so they can be converted into a training scenario with options for whoever is going through it."

This reminded Dani of similar exercises she had undergone in the military. Given what she'd learned about the Colonel, she assumed this was part of a private company's attempt to develop interactive training for the military. She wondered how much the Colonel would get as a kickback when the contract sold.

"We're the rats in the maze," Chopper said. "What's the cheese?"

"Double your normal fee," the Colonel said. "And a bonus for the one who finishes first."

"Nice," Guapo said. "I could use the money."

"Yeah right," one of the men who had been waiting in the hangar said to him. "Like it's going to be you."

The usual smack talk followed, with most of the group insulting one another's tactical prowess. Dani and the Colonel regarded each other in silence. She could feel him taking her measure and let him know she was doing the same to him.

He may have been a colonel at one point, but as far as she was concerned, he'd given up the right to the respect his rank demanded when he retained a team of killers to do his bidding. He had clearly been seduced by money and power, forsaking his oath. She had not forsaken hers, and he would soon discover that money and power would do him no good when justice caught up to him.

CHAPTER 23

Dani contemplated how to get incriminating information out of the Colonel.

"It's time to go," the Colonel said to the team. "Our transportation is waiting."

He hadn't mentioned where they were going, and no one else did either. Dani had been on missions where they were not told their destination until their arrival at a strategic location. She had never expected such tactics from a loosely knit group of contract killers. As the Colonel turned to walk outside the building, she felt that she was slipping into uncharted territory.

Toro caught her eye and raised a questioning brow. Certain he was wondering what their next move should be, she gave him a slight nod and fell in line with the others.

She considered her options. If she tried to take them all into custody now, she would end up dead. Her fighting skills were sound, but even if Toro joined her, they would be fighting eleven experienced assassins. And she noticed that the Colonel had a sidearm in his holster.

She could feign a sudden illness and say she couldn't go with them, but what would Toro do? Would he take the opportunity to leave her behind and make a bid for freedom? Twelve against one left her in no position to stop him if he did.

The Colonel would be highly suspicious of her sudden illness and might not allow her to simply leave.

She was hamstrung by circumstance, and any choice she made could end badly. Her best course of action was to go along with the plan until she could gather hard evidence and contact the JTTF.

Despite her close proximity to Toro, she was unable to speak without risking others overhearing or without drawing suspicion by whispering. She kept her silence as the group walked around to the far side of one of the two hangars. The massive bay door was open, and a private jet was sitting at the beginning of a runway.

This was more than she had anticipated. She exchanged a quick glance with Toro, whose expression told her he had been caught off guard as well. Either the others took the fact that they could be headed anywhere in stride, or they already knew where they were going and weren't sharing the information with Toro or the outsider they had come to know as Nikki.

Fully committed now, she climbed the lowered stairs leading into the passenger compartment and took a seat beside Toro with a sudden surge of hope. The pilot would have to file a flight plan with the FAA. Her JTTF team would at least know where she had taken off and landed. The momentary hope faded as she realized that the Bureau would have no way of knowing she was even on a plane at all. They would have no reason to check what would appear to be test flights out of an airplane-maintenance-and-repair facility in another state. She wasn't even sure aircraft being flown for diagnostics and repair purposes were required to file a flight plan. It seemed their mysterious client—and the Colonel—had thought of everything.

The Colonel addressed them as the engines powered up. "You all are damned lucky the client provided this jet, because it's going to be a long flight."

The repair facility probably belonged to the client too. It clearly had no affiliation with the nearby airport, but it had a runway. Flying across the country under the pretext of checking mechanical work done on the craft was against FAA regulations, but no client of the Colonel's was likely to care. The more she thought about everything that had led her up to this point, the less it played like a training exercise.

"Where are we going?" Chopper asked, buckling into his seat.

Dani read the genuine curiosity that prompted his question. Maybe the others really didn't know any more than she and Toro did. If so, they were accustomed to following orders without question. This made them both dangerous and vulnerable.

"Close your windows," the Colonel said in response. "You'll see where we are when we land, which is also when you'll get your weapons back."

Everyone sitting beside a window reached up to slide it shut. They were all now in a tube, totally cut off from the outside world.

Takeoff was smooth, and Dani resigned herself to a quiet trip. At least the cabin was well appointed and comfortable. Unable to talk to Toro, make plans for her arrival, or even see where she was going, she decided to get some rest while she could. Previous deployments had conditioned her to sleep in nearly any situation or position in order to preserve strength and prepare for whatever lay ahead.

She had the sense that several hours had passed when the plane's descent awakened her with popping ears. She longed to slide the window cover open, but no one in the cabin had disobeyed orders. Even a sliver of light at the bottom of the window would have drawn attention.

She barely felt the wheels contact the runway, and the jet taxied to a stop a couple of minutes later. Everyone seemed anxious to get out of the semidark tube, and she felt a sense of relief when they all began to climb down the stairs.

She glanced around, squinting in the late-afternoon glare. They must have flown into a different time zone, which was definitely west of where they had been. She took in a small private airstrip surrounded by a wide expanse of flat, dusty ground. They seemed to be in the middle of nowhere. She could not determine what state they were in, assuming they were still on US soil.

A shuttle bus idled nearby, and the Colonel made his way to its door, which opened with a hiss. The front compartment was totally separate from the passenger area of the bus, and Dani could not get a good look at the driver through the reflective windows.

It seemed the client was determined to keep the group separated from his employees as much as possible. Given the fact that they were all supposed to be nameless and faceless, Dani assumed the Colonel had made the arrangements as part of the contract.

She followed the others once again, taking what had become her customary seat beside Toro near the back. The bus roared off, jolting along increasingly narrower and bumpier roads. Dani peered out at the bleak deserted country going by. She could not make out any landmarks in the featureless terrain.

After what felt like the better part of an hour, they bumped to a stop. The Colonel led the way off the bus, with the others falling in line. Looking around, Dani had the impression they had been dropped off in the middle of a barren patch of earth. There was nothing around except a rectangular cement structure about eight feet tall jutting straight up from the ground like a modern monolith. Senses on high alert, she began to suspect her cover may not have survived scrutiny after all. Were the others about to attack? The Colonel had not returned their weapons as promised.

Before she could form a question, the Colonel led them around the structure, revealing a metal door set into its opposite side. She watched as he punched a code into a keypad above the handle. After a loud metallic click, he pulled it open. When he entered and began to walk down, she realized it had to be some sort of underground facility.

Guapo trailed behind her, making sure she fell in with the others. She hesitated at the entrance and looked down into the gloom lit only by a flickering bare bulb. Her boots thudded on concrete stairs as she descended. She turned to see Guapo pull the door shut after he entered. The metallic clanging had the ominous finality of prison gates closing. A loud electronic *click* followed by a *ka-thunk* told her the reinforced door had been remotely locked.

She was well and truly trapped.

CHAPTER 24

After a hair-raising drive through the Holland Tunnel with lights and siren blaring, Wu stood on the uneven cobblestones in the Court Street alley beside one of the Bureau's Ford Econoline vans. This one had been outfitted for prisoner transport with a stripped-down interior that consisted of two long benches with chains attached to bolts on the floor.

"You want me to take the lead?" Detective Flint asked him.

They had been finalizing how they would interview Kurt Guthry, who waited inside, handcuffed. The two agents on the delta team of the surveillance detail had raced down the alley to catch Guthry before he could escape. They had been driving the transport van, which also served as an operational vehicle.

Hoboken police officers cordoned off either end of the alley to keep spectators away until Wu and Flint arrived. He had wanted to interview Guthry personally, and the vehicle provided the ideal mobile interrogation room.

Flint's patrol contacts had told them Guthry was a well-known local street hood who had only enough ambition to get up in the morning to score dope. If times were desperate, he'd been known to burglarize an apartment or hold up a liquor store. Hardly the kind of trained mercenary the Colonel was known to recruit.

"You go ahead," Wu said, coming to a decision. "I want to focus on his body language. I'll jump in at the appropriate times."

"Yeah, like maybe if I get my hands around this moron's neck and start squeezing."

Wu didn't blame Flint. First, they had thought Agent Vega and their asset had gone up in flames in the back of the van. When the fire department reported the vehicle was empty, they realized they had a new problem on their hands. What had happened to Vega and Toro?

"Time's wasting," Flint said. "We need to find out what Guthry knows." At Wu's nod, he slid open the FBI van's side door and hauled himself inside.

Wu followed, shutting the door with a deliberate bang, hoping to bring the sound of a slamming cell door to Guthry's drug-addled mind.

Watching the prisoner while Flint Mirandized him, Wu detected plenty of nervousness. As he had expected, Guthry waived his rights, anxious to talk. The man was either arrogant or had no information to bargain with. The former would make him a pain in the ass, the latter a complete waste of time.

"I got nothing to hide," Guthry said, the telltale cocaine sniffle putting the lie to his words. "Didn't do nothing wrong."

"You set fire to a vehicle in an alley," Flint said. "That's a felony."

"I was paid to do that."

Now they were getting somewhere.

"Who paid you?" Flint asked. "And what did he tell you to do?"

Guthry struggled to get his synapses firing. "I never seen the dude before. He offered me a grand to use his van to drive some people to an underground parking garage on Washington Boulevard in Jersey City."

If Guthry was telling the truth about his instructions, it would say a lot about their adversary.

"What happened when you drove into the garage?" Flint asked, cutting to the most critical point of the interview.

"I heard people get out of the van. There was some talking. Then someone banged on the back of the van twice. That was my signal to go, so I took off. Never looked back."

"Who got out of the van?" Flint pressed. "How many people, and what did they look like?"

"There was a divider between me and whoever was in the back. Never saw them. The guy gave me the cash and walked away." He shrugged. "Didn't ask no questions. Didn't talk to nobody else."

"They switched vehicles," Wu said to Flint.

"We put all our attention on that damned van," Flint said. "And the whole time they were driving away."

Wu slid the side door open and jumped down to the pavement, leaving Flint to wring whatever details he could out of Guthry.

He pulled out his cell and tapped the speed dial.

"Johnson here." The analyst's tone was crisp and efficient.

He wasted no time with pleasantries. "Get with the New Jersey State PD. Find out if there are any traffic cams around either of the two parking garages the van entered. Pull any footage you can find beginning right after Vega went in." He heard a keyboard clacking in the background. "Send me a spreadsheet detailing every single car that went out of there."

"Yes, sir," Johnson said. "I'll start the observation window fifteen minutes before she entered and capture every vehicle for an hour after she left."

He disconnected. There would likely be hundreds of license plates to run down. Somewhere in that group would be the vehicle that had spirited away Vega and Toro.

A police officer tapped his elbow, interrupting his thoughts. He turned to her.

"We got a hit on the VIN," she said.

Once the fire department had put out the blaze, police had been able to find a vehicle identification number stamped onto the engine block. He had asked them to run it.

"Who's it registered to?" he asked.

She tore a sheet from a notepad and held it out to him. "Here's the name and address of the owner, but don't get your hopes up." She pursed her lips. "The van was reported stolen two hours ago."

Another dead end.

Self-recrimination settled in. He was in charge of the operation. Vega and Toro were his responsibility, and they had gone missing on his watch. He had underestimated the Colonel, a mistake he would not repeat.

CHAPTER 25

Dani stood beside the others under the dim glow of the lone overhead bulb. She was waiting for the next instructions when the light suddenly went out, plunging them all into darkness.

Nerves stretched tight, she heard the men shuffling around as if trying to get their bearings.

"Settle down," the Colonel's voice echoed through the small chamber. "I've got night-vision equipment. Form a line and put your hand on the shoulder of the person in front of you. I'll lead you to your starting point."

The Colonel had known they would be operating in the dark and came prepared, but he hadn't shared that fact with his group. A leader who didn't look out for his troops was no one she cared to follow.

"Why can't we see where the hell we're going?" one of the men called out.

"Because you're supposed to be in a totally unfamiliar environment," the Colonel said, not troubling to hide his irritation. "That's the whole point of this exercise. You'll all start in a separate location and will have to deal with whatever comes up."

She felt Toro's heavy hand on her right shoulder and groped in the darkness with her left hand until she grasped a beefy shoulder in front of her. Unlike Toro, she chose to keep her dominant hand free.

"What's our objective?" she said into the darkness.

The Colonel answered with a single word that was nearly a grunt. "Survive."

As they made their way through what seemed like a maze of corridors, she considered what they'd been told so far, which didn't add up. She kept circling back to the question of why a team of assassins had been hired for this assignment. Mercenaries would act unpredictably, so having them play the roles of the first-person-shooter point of view seemed odd when this was billed as training.

They trudged down a series of stairs, then another, before the line finally stopped. "This is you, Chopper," the Colonel said.

She heard shuffling sounds and assumed he had detached Chopper from the procession and was leading him somewhere close by.

"This is a nylon spandex suit," the Colonel's voice went on. "Strip to your skivvies and put it on. There's built-in tech that will allow the VR system to create an avatar for you."

"What about my face?" Chopper asked in a strained voice. Apparently, the disorientation of total blindness and now isolation in a subterranean structure had him spooked.

"There are optical generators built into the neckline of the suit that will project an image completely covering your head," the Colonel said. "I've seen the prototype, and it's impressive."

She waited another few seconds while the Colonel made final arrangements with Chopper.

"Stay right here," the Colonel said to him. "Remote-controlled bars will rise from the floor, creating a cell. Once everyone is situated, the lights will come on, and the scenario will begin."

The sound of grinding metal told her the bars were locking into place around Chopper. Dani walked on with the others, going down more sets of stairs before they were detached and deposited into separate cells as they went. When it was her turn, Toro gave her shoulder a slight squeeze she interpreted as a sign of reassurance before releasing his grip. The whole experience was disorienting, as she was sure it was meant to be.

Her prior training prepared her to face the unknown, the unexpected, and the unpredictable. She composed herself and allowed the Colonel to grasp her elbow and lead her forward.

"Here's your suit." He pressed slippery fabric into her outstretched hands. "Fold your clothes and leave them here. Wear your boots."

He hadn't said anything about her wrist cuff, and even though it didn't transmit, she'd wear it. She heard the now-familiar grinding noise moments after she sensed the Colonel retreating and put out a hand to feel thick metal bars surrounding her.

"Now's not the time for modesty, soldier," the Colonel called out to her. "Get into that suit, or we all stay in the dark until you do."

He was deliberately reminding her of time spent in the military, where privacy was considered a trivial matter. The success of the mission was above all personal concerns. Aware he was watching her—and that she might also be visible on whatever cameras had been installed in this underground facility—she stripped down to her bra and panties.

The nylon spandex suit slid on easily, clinging to her form like a second skin. She pulled her socks and tactical boots back on and folded her street clothes in a neat pile beside her. She felt completely alone in the oppressive darkness. No sound reached her ears. Had she failed the initial test? Had her cover been blown? Was this all an elaborate ruse to get her alone to interrogate her and kill her as Toro had promised would be her fate if the FBI did not construct a watertight background for her?

She turned her attention to her surroundings. No one within earshot was talking, moving, or breathing. Sounded like she was alone. When she'd stepped out of her boots, the floor beneath her feet was cold and hard. Her fingertips registered what felt like poured concrete.

Overhead lights blazed on, and she squinted against the sudden glare. After several seconds, she opened her eyes a fraction wider to see iron bars across the front of what appeared to be bare gray walls. A prison cell.

Detecting no immediate threat, she contemplated her predicament. If the Colonel was telling the truth, everyone in the group—including himself—had been separated into individual cells. She paced the length of the enclosure, which was completely empty.

She examined the bars and could find no locking mechanism or way to open them. Allowing her gaze to rove over the entirety of the cell, a blinking red light near the ceiling caught her eye.

She moved closer, tilting her head back to study the area around it. As she had suspected, a small circular lens was mounted to the ceiling.

Someone was watching her.

Dani barely had time to process her discovery before an announcement sounded through a hidden speaker.

"Welcome to your trial by combat," the voice said. "Where only one of you gets out alive."

CHAPTER 26

Dani considered the ominous words. Was this part of the scenario? Was this a mind game? It sounded as though something else was going on, but what?

Lacking enough data to draw a conclusion, she turned her attention to the person who had made the announcement. She did not recognize the voice, which was American with no discernible regional accent. The timbre sounded deep, definitely masculine.

"You are all in different parts of this structure," the voice continued. "Your mission has changed. You are not here to create interactive training videos. You are here to fight for your lives. There is nothing virtual about the reality you are in right now."

Somehow, hearing the pronouncement from a disembodied voice made it more sinister.

"There is only one way out," their unseen host said after a brief pause. "Only one of you will be allowed to escape. Everyone else will die."

Dani tried to figure out the endgame as she listened in growing disbelief.

"Some of you may still think this is part of the scenario you were hired to participate in," the voice went on, echoing Dani's thoughts. "Here's a demonstration."

A square patch of light appeared on the wall, and Dani could see the projected image of twelve cells, each containing a member of the group she had arrived with. She assumed the others could see her and not themselves.

"Your first challenge," the voice said as a panel set into the wall to Dani's right slid open. "Type in the correct combination to open the safe. There's something you need inside."

Dani noticed all the others moving toward panels that had opened in their cells as well. She walked to the wall and found a keypad that looked like the buttons on an old-school telephone.

"You have sixty seconds to open the safe," the voice said. "The clock starts ticking after I give you the clue." After a moment's pause, a single question emanated from the speaker. "What is the world's most populous city?"

A small screen above the keypad began a countdown in glowing red numbers.

00:59

Dani's mind began to whir. Her extensive travels had taken her to many large cities. For either personal or professional reasons, she'd been to Mexico City, Delhi, Cairo, Shanghai, and São Paulo.

00:52

She also currently lived in New York, the largest city in the US, but not the world. Probably Asia had the most populated cities, but where in Asia?

00:48

A hissing noise distracted her, and she glanced up to see a row of tubes pumping something that looked like red smoke into the cell. A quick check of the screen told her that everyone else's enclosure also had some kind of red gas streaming in.

00:41

She turned her attention back to the keypad and steadied herself. Panic would not help her think. She pulled her mind back to her previous thought. Asian cities. She recalled Delhi with its sea of humanity, and Shanghai with its massive crowds. Maybe a different city. Someplace she'd never been.

00:35

The cloud of red haze began to float down from overhead, and she instinctively crouched. Once she came up with an answer, she would have to stand to punch in the code, but for now she would stay as far away from the fumes as possible in case they were toxic.

00:29

What features would make a city denser? A thriving economy. Infrastructure. Land. She turned the thought over. The red smoke thickened, descending lower.

00:22

A scream ripped through the air, and she turned to see one of the Colonel's men claw at his throat. He was standing with his head in what looked like a plume of crimson fog, desperately bashing the keypad with his fists. That was the test. Think under pressure. The more stress a human being underwent, the more difficult it was to access advanced cognitive abilities. Even simple things could become hard to recall in a life-or-death situation.

00:18

She lowered herself all the way to the ground and used breathing techniques she'd been taught in Ranger school to bring down her heart rate and calm her nerves.

00:11

She had been thinking about land. A requirement for a large city. But not necessarily for a populous one. What if a city was incredibly dense because land was at a premium? The answer that would have come much quicker if not for the circumstances popped into her head.

00:09

She sucked in a deep breath, scrambled to her feet, and began punching numbers on the keypad. Eyes stinging and watering from the gas, she had to blink several times to be sure she didn't accidentally fat-finger the buttons.

8-6-5-9-6

The safe door opened. She snatched the gas mask lying inside and flung herself back onto the floor, where the air was still breathable, grateful she'd figured out Tokyo was the biggest city on earth. She went through the process of pulling on, tightening, and clearing the mask before attempting a breath.

00:04

The face shield covered her stinging eyes, providing blessed relief, and she could breathe without any discomfort. She swiveled her head to see how the others were doing. Toro was just pulling his mask on, and the Colonel and several others were doing the same. She counted three of their group who did not. They were standing in front of the keypads, frantically pushing buttons.

Another thought occurred to her. Why the countdown? The gas would surely poison anyone who didn't punch in the answer quickly enough. And then the reason came to her in a sickening flash of insight.

00:01

She bellowed a warning. "Hit the deck!"

They either couldn't hear the words through her mask or didn't react.

00:00

A fusillade of shrapnel burst out from the keypads that hadn't been opened. The explosion sent chunks of metal directly into the bodies of the three men who had been standing in front of their respective panels.

They collapsed to the ground, blood, flesh, and bone spewed everywhere. Dani was forcibly reminded of the aftermath of an IED that had claimed the lives of some of her fellow soldiers.

Judging by the rumble in the walls around and above her, as well as the dust fluttering to the ground, she concluded the cells where the detonations had occurred were everywhere except below her. She had gone down several flights of stairs during her walk in the dark. Perhaps she was on the lowest level.

"You bastard!" one of the men shouted at the overhead camera in his cell.

The red gas around them was dissipating quickly, and Dani heard an HVAC system thundering at full capacity.

The man who had yelled at the speaker lurched forward, screaming a stream of obscenities. He reached out and wrapped his hands around the bars. At first Dani thought he was shaking them like an inmate in a prison movie. She could see the muscles in his formfitted black nylon spandex suit flex as the cage around him rattled.

With dawning horror, she realized he was being electrocuted. Teeth gnashed, eyes bugged out, hair on end, he was welded to the metal that was killing him. A few seconds later, his hair began to smoke. Then his suit.

"Stop it!" the Colonel shouted.

But it did not stop. Not for three full minutes. Finally, the smoking husk that had been one of their group slumped to the ground in a smoldering heap.

While the man had been dying, Dani had taken renewed stock of her situation. Four of their number were now dead. Their demise had been brutal and grisly. She shifted her gaze to glance at the Colonel on the monitor. He stood in stoic resolve, but the color had drained from his face. This had not been part of his plan. She felt certain he was equally trapped.

She recalled touching the metal bars of her cell shortly after they rose up from the floor, and nothing had happened to her. The current had been cut off at a certain point, allowing the man who had been electrocuted to fall to the ground, which meant whoever was in control had the ability to electrify the bars at will. It would be wise to assume other things could be electrified as well. Then there was the matter of the gas. Noxious fumes could be introduced into their environment and then cleared using a remote system. Lights had also been extinguished and switched back on.

She concluded that her undercover assignment with the FBI had radically shifted. She was now in a combat situation. The enemy had total control of the battle space, which put her at a severe disadvantage. Unlike in her military deployments, she was not with a trusted team of elite soldiers who would work as a well-trained unit. Instead, she was with a group of homicidal mercenaries who would gladly kill her if they knew her true identity. Maybe even if they didn't. They had worked together before, but she was an outsider. She still had to abide by the rules set out for her, but no one else would operate under the same constraints. How long would it be until she was forced to decide between her oath of office and her life?

"Now you all understand that I'm serious," the voice said into the silence that followed as they all stared at the group video feed. "I have hidden clues for you to solve in order to locate the exit."

Dani pictured all of them scurrying through a maze, looking for crumbs. Their captor was terrorizing and degrading them at every turn.

"Some clues lead to food, water, weapons, and a map. Things you will need to survive . . . because there are many ways to die."

What kind of sick game was this? Dani had received instruction in psychology as part of her military and law enforcement training, but this level of thinking was beyond anything she had encountered in the field or the classroom.

"Finding a clue or supplies gets you closer to escape but also makes you a target. Only one person leaves alive. That person will have to outmaneuver, torture, and kill your former partners to get all the clues needed to escape."

Dani considered the rules of engagement. Whoever was behind this wanted them to spill each other's blood. What if they all chose to cooperate instead? They could search for clues, pool information, and unlock the exit. Someone with enough time and resources to orchestrate the capture of twelve trained assassins would have planned for that possibility. The voice had promised only the first person out would live, guaranteeing that her fellow captives would play for keeps.

"You are all paid killers," the voice said, echoing her thoughts. "Like all animals, you only care about survival, but only one of you will have it. Are you smart enough? Strong enough? Ruthless enough?"

This comment told Dani her cover was still intact. Whoever was behind this believed she was Nicola Corazón, disgraced Army veteran and now one of the Colonel's assassins. Should she mention her true identity now? Would their captor make a different decision, knowing that a federal agent was in the mix? Based on what he had already disclosed, Dani assumed anyone who would make such elaborate plans to watch brutality and death wouldn't have an attack of conscience upon learning an innocent person was present. In fact, that revelation might put her in everyone's crosshairs.

"Your cage will open in sixty seconds. At that point, the search will begin. You will hunt for clues, you will hunt for supplies, but most of all, you will hunt each other. Remember, every kill gets you one step closer to freedom." After a brief pause, the voice went on. "You are not allowed to take anything from your cell. Leave your street clothes, the gas mask, and the night-vision equipment behind."

There was more going on than whoever was behind this was telling them, and the instructions about the night vision applied only to the Colonel, supporting her assumption that he had made a powerful enemy. If it was simply about dealing out justice to people who had committed heinous crimes, their captor had the resources to simply have them all killed one at a time. This scenario had been devised to force them to brutalize each other. Why?

Thoughts of the group brought Toro to mind. He was the only one who knew her true identity. After this morning's meeting, he also understood that she would be operating under the FBI's policies and directives. Even though she now considered herself a combatant, unlike the others, she would be limited in her actions. Toro was supposed to be doing the same, but would he in a life-or-death situation?

If he helped her, he could expect more leniency, but if he killed her, he could escape and disappear permanently. No one would ever know what had happened to her. They would both eventually be presumed dead, and he would be free to live overseas in a country with no extradition to the US. This could be Toro's best and last chance at freedom.

"Call me Nemesis," the speaker's disembodied voice said, interrupting her thoughts. "I am your judge, jury, and executioner. Remember that I am always watching."

With an electronic buzz, the bars around her began to descend into the floor. Even if she had considered hiding inside the cell until the killing stopped, that possibility disappeared along with her cage. As she watched her enclosure sink down, she realized she would have to engage. Eventually, she would find Toro.

And he would either be her greatest ally or her worst enemy.

CHAPTER 27

Dani made an instant shift from strategic to tactical mode. Rather than concern herself with the big picture behind her current situation, she had to focus on her immediate survival.

She performed a quick assessment of her physical state. Other than thirst, she felt well. She had no weapons but still had her tactical hair clip and combat boots, which could prove useful.

The area was lit by a series of bare bulbs with wrought metal covers. She explored, skimming her fingertips along the sides of her cell to feel its surface. The walls, ceiling, and floor appeared to be made of poured concrete. She took a few more steps to examine the open door in the center of one wall. It was metal and painted battleship gray, giving the space the feel of a submarine.

She used both hands to grasp the wheel in the middle of the exit door, thinking to close off the room and stay inside. The latch was locked in the open position. Their captor—Nemesis—must be able to open and close all internal doors remotely, and he wasn't going to let any of them avoid confrontation.

She refused to simply hunker down and wait for someone to find and kill her. Without any alliances except her tenuous one with Toro—which might not even exist—she would have to rely on herself. Time to Ranger up and get on with the mission.

During RASP, each trainee had been dropped alone into forests or mountains and forced to find their way out. To pass, she had to prioritize survival while making her escape. This situation was different in that she had no sense of direction, time of day, or distance. Also, there was the added fun of having a bunch of people actively trying to kill her.

The first order of business was a weapon to defend herself. While she searched for that, she would look for water. She could survive weeks without food but would become dangerously dehydrated in days. Next she had to make a note of any safe places to rest if this scenario went on for a long time. She knew that staying awake for days on end would lead to slower reaction times, then hallucinations, and eventually death. In Ranger school, she had learned to get by on as little as one or two hours, sleeping in almost any position.

After that, whatever tools or first aid their captor had hidden would be a logical target. In an environment that was completely under his control, anything could be valuable. Nemesis had mentioned a map, which would provide critical intel about the surroundings. She would be able to guess where others might be hiding or where she might find the exit. In the meantime, she would create a mental map to orient herself.

This so-called trial by combat would test their survival, adaptive, cognitive, and fighting skills while under pressure. Thanks to Uncle Sam, she had extensive training in each of these areas under highly stressful conditions. Except for Toro and the Colonel, she knew next to nothing about the rest of them. She decided to leverage the one component of the equation she could control.

Herself.

She took up a position beside the door and peeked around the opening. The gray corridor was empty in both directions and eerily quiet. What should she do the first time she ran across one of the other captives?

If possible, she would try talking first. See if they would be willing to form an alliance. This approach would serve to either garner a partner or inform her about her prospects going forward. If they attacked, she would defend herself, using the least amount of force necessary to incapacitate them, then leave them behind. This put her at an extreme disadvantage. She would fight with the intention not to cause grievous bodily injury or death, while they would do everything in their power to disable or to kill her.

What if she saw Toro? Under these circumstances, was he a friendly or a hostile? Without any clue, she opted to treat him the same as the others until she got a read on him.

Plan in place, she headed through the open doorway and confronted her first decision. Did she go right or left? Without warning, the lights in the corridor to her left went out.

Nemesis was obviously watching and had made it clear he wanted her to take the right corridor. She was tempted to defy him and go left, but walking into total darkness without night-vision equipment or a flashlight would be suicidal. Besides, he might punish her for her defiance, and she wouldn't see it coming if she was stumbling in the dark.

With the sense that she was being herded like cattle toward a slaughterhouse, she began making her way down the corridor to the right.

CHAPTER 28

Nemesis turned to the bank of video monitors mounted to the wall. Six rows of five screens displayed thirty separate video feeds. Every nook and cranny of the subterranean structure and an acre of ground above it was under constant surveillance. There was no place for anyone to hide.

Nemesis had not built the facility, which dated back to the mid-twentieth century. After being abandoned for decades, the long-forgotten structure had proved to be the perfect place to retrofit to create a realistic virtual training space for a potential DOD contract.

Total climate control had been part of the facility's original design. Rooms and corridors were sealed off with reinforced blast doors. Lighted signs and an intercom system were built in, as was the observation system from the control room near the surface.

After the site had been purchased, an overhaul and upgrade of the interior had taken three years. Certain employees and subcontractors, each with ironclad nondisclosure agreements, had worked on various components of the facility. None of them had seen the entire setup or knew of its full capabilities. The cutting-edge technology contained inside was a closely guarded secret. Corporate espionage always loomed as a threat, and this facility could revolutionize the way troops were trained. An exclusive defense contract could garner as much as a billion dollars.

Renovations had included pipes in the vents designed to deliver colored smoke for gas-mask training. Adding a component that enabled military commanders to alter scenarios in real time in response to the actions of combatants had finally come online in the past six months. The new capabilities allowed leaders to test both teamwork and individual performance by requiring combatants to solve problems in the field, working separately or in groups.

All systems were go, and it had been time to prepare a demonstration that would make everyone in the Pentagon salivate. Remote virtual training let soldiers guide avatars through endless variations of scenarios from any military base equipped with the technology to connect to this facility. Personnel could also learn by watching highly trained soldiers go through scenarios as avatars wearing the newly redesigned suits.

No more massive field exercises. No more wasting time, money, and other precious resources. This was a new way to train tens of thousands of personnel with zero downtime, zero injuries, and the ability to adapt to any environment or circumstance in a matter of minutes.

But two months ago, Nemesis had been blindsided by a discovery that changed everything, including the intended purpose behind the virtual training facility. Now the confidentiality involved in its creation had made the space perfect for an entirely different audience and a new plan.

A plan of revenge.

Nemesis had to act quickly and had managed to adjust the facility, converting the scenarios from nonlethal to fully lethal. The first test had been designed to release colored vapor unless the correct answer was entered on the keypad. Mixing in poisonous gas had been easy, considering the HVAC system had originally been created to prevent and disperse leaked airborne pollutants. The keypad had been rigged to spray paint balls. Substituting shrapnel had been a fast process, but some of the other obstacles had proved to be more challenging to convert, especially those that involved biohazardous chemicals. The Colonel, who had been more than accommodating in providing access to these items, had no idea he was bringing about his own demise when he delivered them to the facility over a month ago. Nemesis had found that people who had gotten used to operating above the law thought they were untouchable. The Colonel and his cronies were about to learn that no one was untouchable.

A final check indicated all systems functioned perfectly, including the recently upgraded video capabilities. Each combatant's avatar functioned seamlessly, with no way for anyone watching on the dark web to find out there was an actual human being behind the projected image.

If you could call them human beings.

The addition of a thirteenth captive had required some last-minute scrambling, but the overall effect made a nice visual differentiation from the rest, who were all men. Her name was Nicola Corazón, but Gustavo Toro had called her Nikki. A deep dive into various databases had revealed she had been deemed unfit for duty and booted out of the Army. Her violent nature made her a liability as a soldier but a skilled killer.

Nemesis had decided not to hide Nikki's gender, leaning into it instead. A female warrior would provide contrast with the others, and a little eye candy for the audience never hurt. The character depicted by the avatar was a lot to live up to for someone like Nikki Corazón, but the visual was stunning and fit the theme perfectly.

Everything would be recorded, edited for audio and video, then uploaded to an encrypted cloud-based server on the dark web. Subscribers had already signed up to participate in what they believed was a beta test of a new online interactive video game. If the next few hours went according to plan, subscribers would receive a notification with a password allowing them to log in and watch. The next phase would roll out tomorrow, and they could vote for their favorite combatants or place bets on the outcome of the game.

Nemesis figured it might be possible to add an extra layer of participation for premium subscribers, giving them the ability to influence certain parts of the environment. Much would depend on how the beta testing went.

For the audience, it was about world building and creating an immersive experience. For the combatants, it was about survival and outwitting opponents. For Nemesis, the game would serve many purposes.

First, the data collected would be invaluable. Game developers created artificial environments in which players interacted with preprogrammed actors. No matter how much research went into development, nothing could substitute for real human beings making life-or-death decisions.

Nikki's progress down the corridor was a prime example. Even if a background check hadn't brought it to light, it was clear the woman had military training. She moved with tactical precision, checking each opening she passed, making sure no one could sneak up behind her.

At first Nemesis had contemplated eliminating Nikki immediately but was now glad to have her in the game. A female former soldier might prove entertaining. Besides, she was as much of a degenerate as the rest of them and deserved whatever the Fates dealt her.

Thoughts of fate brought an interesting idea to mind. Coming to a decision, Nemesis typed in a few commands, shutting the lights off in all but one direction around Toro, forcing him into a room Nikki was fast approaching.

It would be interesting to see what happened when the two lovers met.

CHAPTER 29

Dani approached the next doorway, preparing to clear the room inside. The lights in the corridor suddenly went out, and the only source of illumination came from inside the room she had been about to check. Nemesis was not subtle.

She flattened her back against the wall beside the open doorway and leaned forward just enough to see about a quarter of the room before straightening again.

Empty.

That left 75 percent of the interior space unknown. Nemesis was forcing her to go in, which meant she would encounter a threat inside. The room's entrance was a choke point, and she would be momentarily exposed when she went through it.

She waited and listened. No sounds of footsteps came from within, indicating the room was either completely empty, and this was Nemesis playing head games, or someone was waiting in silence to ambush her.

What would Nemesis find most interesting? Probably a pair of lovers in a deadly showdown. Since her cover appeared to be intact, Nemesis would wonder if Nikki and Toro would kill each other on sight or form an alliance and betray one another later.

Dani had wondered the same thing. If her guess was correct, Toro would be inside the room, but how could she be sure without risking the fatal funnel created by the doorway?

She could call out to him, but if it wasn't Toro, she'd be giving her position away, making her vulnerable to attack. Whoever was inside would know it was her because she was the only female in the game, and she doubted she could pass her voice off for a man's.

The thought echoed in her mind. *She was the only female in the game.* If Toro was inside, she could signal her presence without a word by using something unique to her.

She reached up and snatched the tactical hair clip, then tossed it inside the room and took several paces back from the opening. The tinkling metallic clatter echoed through the space.

Toro's voice finally broke the silence that followed. "Nikki?"

None of the men wore a barrette. She had counted on him realizing it had to come from her. If someone besides Toro was in the room, she hoped the sound would draw them out, giving her a chance to respond.

When she heard Toro's voice, she knew her assumption that Nemesis would bring them together had been correct. She had gained valuable insight into their captor and a potential ally at the same time.

Unless Toro decided to kill her. Then things were about to get ugly. Again.

"You alone?" she whispered.

"Yeah."

Now for the tricky part. If he invited her in, was he luring her into a trap?

She tried a preemptive maneuver. "Why don't you come out here?"

"It's dark out there," he said. "We can't see who's sneaking up on us. You need to get in here with me."

What he said made sense, but she still didn't trust him. He had everything to gain and nothing to lose by getting rid of her here and now.

"Listen to me, Nikki," he continued when she made no response. "My feelings about you haven't changed. I don't care about this bullshit game. You're still my *mujer*."

She was still his woman. While maintaining their cover as a couple, Toro was trying to communicate that he was abiding by their agreement. She recalled the words of one of her tactical instructors during training. *"When you run across an unknown, be polite and professional, but the whole time be planning how to kill them if you have to."* This was how she would deal with Toro.

She bent at the knees, lowering her center of gravity, and slipped quickly through the door without announcing herself.

He took a startled step back upon seeing her. "Damn. That was total stealth. Didn't hear you at all."

She scanned the room, making sure they were alone despite what he'd told her, before her gaze settled on him. "Wasn't sure what kind of reception I'd get."

"You've got serious trust issues." He spread his arms wide. "A love like ours is . . . special."

Aware Nemesis watched their every move, she suppressed an eye roll and worded her response carefully, speaking on two levels, as he had. "You've had problems with commitment in the past. You can be fickle."

She assumed he would understand that she wanted to know if he was still committed to the plan.

"Yeah, but you're different," he said. "You're that perfect mix of badass and hot that makes me go all tingly." He grinned. "We'll always be partners in crime."

She stooped to pick up her hair clip. "Right," she said, sliding it back into place. "The couple that slays together stays together."

"Exactly. We make a good team . . . as long as you don't change your mind about me."

Perhaps she had kept the tone of their exchange a bit too light. Toro clearly harbored doubts of his own and wanted reassurance. She looked him straight in the eye and made the most solemn vow she knew. "I will never leave a fallen comrade to fall into the hands of the enemy."

"Well, isn't that sweet?" a male voice said from behind them, interrupting their exchange. "I'm all choked up."

They both turned to see Chopper standing in the doorway, holding a butterfly knife.

CHAPTER 30

Dani used her strategy of opening a dialogue while preparing for a fight. She spun to face Chopper and shifted into a fighting stance, eyeing the knife he had managed to find.

Once it became obvious Dani and Toro weren't going to murder each other, Nemesis must have made sure Chopper located a weapon before herding him in their direction.

"You want to join us?" she said to Chopper. "We can pool our resources."

He advanced, flicking his gaze from Toro to her. "Sounds like a good way to get yourself killed. You heard what the dude said. Only one of us gets out alive."

Clearly Chopper had totally bought into the game, but she didn't trust anyone who would kidnap people and force them to battle to the death.

"What makes you think Nemesis will keep his word?" she said. "If he kills the last survivor, there are no loose ends."

"I don't care what you think," he said, pointing the blade's tip in their direction. "I'm stuck in this fucking game, and I'm playing to win."

"You were never big on following rules," Toro said, edging backward. "Why start now?"

Chopper struck without warning, lunging toward Dani, blade slashing directly at her. She had seen his muscles bunch a moment before he moved and was able to sidestep what would have been a deadly attack.

He had no intention of partnering with them. Or talking. Or anything other than killing them. So be it.

She let the momentum of her evasive maneuver carry her around in a semicircle, spinning away only to double back behind Chopper. She had neatly put him between herself and Toro. Belatedly realizing his mistake, Chopper swiveled his head to one side, then the other, swinging the knife toward each of them in turn.

The next sixty seconds would reveal Toro's true intentions. If they worked together, they could take Chopper, even though he was armed and they weren't. If Toro wasn't on her side, he could let her fight it out with Chopper, waiting for an opportunity to attack her from behind while she was distracted. As a third option, he could stand back and watch.

In the past, she had known those beside her, whether in law enforcement or the military, had her six. Now someone who claimed to be her partner could stab her in the very back he was supposed to be watching. Only one way to find out what would happen. She put her theory to the test, drawing Chopper's attention.

"You good with a knife?" she asked him. "That why they call you Chopper? Because I think your edged-weapon skills suck."

The barb had the desired effect, and he charged at her. This time, instead of pivoting out of the way, she grasped his outstretched forearm and launched herself in the opposite direction. His momentum and body weight carried him forward while his arm twisted back, wrenching his shoulder until she heard a loud popping sound. His howl of agony confirmed that his shoulder had been dislocated.

The knife fell to the floor. Busy holding Chopper, she was unable to snatch it up before Toro did. Chopper staggered, using his good hand to grasp his injured shoulder. Without a moment's hesitation, Toro drove the knife into the side of Chopper's neck, yanked it back out, then plunged it in a second time, giving it a sharp twist before pulling it away.

Blood sprayed in rhythmic spurts as Chopper sank to his knees, then flopped facedown on the cold floor.

She looked at Toro. "What the hell was that?"

"It's called survival," Toro said. "That bastard was going to kill us." He wiped the dripping blade clean against his sleeve. "Now he won't."

Dani wasn't sure how to communicate to Toro that this was way beyond the bounds of their instructions. Those protocols and policies, however, had never been meant for a situation like this.

"You've got to put all that good-soldier, team-player shit behind you," he went on. "There is no honor in here. You've got to lie, cheat, steal, maim, and kill. Do whatever it takes to survive. You understand me?"

He was resetting the parameters under which they would operate going forward. Partnering with him had its benefits, but this was one of the drawbacks. Unlike her, Toro would not follow the rules they had both been given.

He reached out to grasp her shoulder, forcing her eyes to his. "You've got to learn to be heartless, or you'll get us both killed, Corazón."

She nearly scoffed. Her *tía* Manuela would have set him straight, explaining that Dani's heart was physically strong like her father's but emotionally stunted like her mother's. She had demonstrated her ability to kill many times over. Saving people seemed to be her biggest challenge.

"Roger that," she said after a long moment. Toro's actions had demonstrated that, so far, he was with her. Their partnership would make them stronger than any individual. They could watch out for each other and work as a team.

Toro spun the butterfly knife with an expert flick of the wrist, folding it back into its split handle. Dani had seen the damage such a deadly weapon could do to a human body, but he treated it like any other piece of equipment. To him, it was simply a tool of the trade. How many people had he dispatched with the same careless efficiency? He'd admitted he had no honor and warned her to forget hers.

In that moment, she knew she'd made a deal with the devil.

CHAPTER 31

Wu glanced up when Jada Johnson rushed into the JOC.

"I've isolated the time window you requested at the public self-park on Washington Boulevard, sir," she said to him. "I found six possible matches for the kind of vehicle you described."

He had directed Johnson to focus on vehicles within the window that were large enough to carry multiple people and that had left the garage driving carefully, without speeding or violating any traffic laws.

"Get them up on the screen," he said, swiveling his chair to face the wall-size monitor.

Johnson picked up the remote and navigated the cursor on the screen to her saved file. Six videos ran simultaneously, showing three SUVs, a stretch limo, and two vans leaving the garage with different time stamps.

"Eliminate the limo," Wu told her. "Too flashy."

She deleted the feed.

"Ditto the last two SUVs," he said. "They both have vanity plates."

He stood and walked to the screen to study the two remaining vans and a charcoal-gray Suburban with tinted windows all around. "Do you have a better angle?"

Johnson clicked open another file that showed all three vehicles from a street-level view.

"That one." He pointed at the Suburban. "It's riding low to the ground." He turned to Johnson. "There's extra weight inside. Could be from several passengers."

"I'll track it, sir." She turned off the feed and slipped out moments before the door opened again. Assistant Director Hargrave walked in with Detective Flint on his heels.

"Status?" Hargrave said, not bothering with pleasantries.

The ADIC wasn't known for his chattiness under normal circumstances, and these were far from that.

Wu answered in kind. "Possible suspect vehicle left the garage approximately ten minutes after the van that brought them in exited. We're tracking its progress now."

"You need eyes from above?"

Hargrave was referring to the various satellite feeds the FBI could access. Wu didn't hesitate. "We have a missing agent in a case that involves a US senator. I want full access to every resource we've got."

"I'll make it happen," Hargrave said. "Have you assigned a team to the Colonel?"

"We've got agents on Colonel Treadway's Battery Park City address," Wu said. "He divides his time between two apartments, one here and the other in DC. I've got a crew from the WFO watching that one."

Wu had contacted the Washington field office to request surveillance but emphasized that no contact should be made without his authorization. Without a search warrant in hand, they might spook their best lead.

"Detective Flint can help one of the JTTF agents write up search warrants for both locations," Wu continued. "But the Colonel's a ghost."

"Does he know we're onto him?" Flint asked. "Is he actively fleeing or just unaccounted for?"

"No one's seen him," Wu said. "There's no banking or credit card activity, and he hasn't left the country or made any travel arrangements we can find. His vehicle is parked in its assigned space at his garage.

He's divorced and lives alone. We gather he hasn't spoken to his wife since their youngest turned eighteen. I seriously doubt she knows where he is."

"I understand we don't have any charges against Colonel Treadway at this time, so our options with him are limited." Hargrave paused as if choosing his words. "But have you reconsidered putting out a BOLO for Toro? You could alert law enforcement that we have a missing agent at the same time."

Wu had been wrestling with the conundrum for the past hour. If he posted a nationwide notice to all law enforcement to be on the lookout for Vega and Toro, they would expand the net exponentially. On the other hand, if Vega had successfully infiltrated the group, announcing that she was a federal agent would put her—and Toro—in jeopardy.

"I vote no," Flint said before he could respond. "Just because we don't have eyes on her doesn't mean she's in trouble. Not only would we blow the whole undercover operation, but we might very well get her killed."

"It's the reason I've been holding off," Wu said. "But we can't wait forever."

"What about Toro?" Hargrave said. "If we put out a bulletin for him, it shouldn't raise anyone's suspicions inside the group."

"They still don't know we've ID'd him," Flint countered. "Like we all concluded before, if they learned we knew who he was, that could make him a liability."

"We'll prepare a BOLO for Toro but won't release it until we have to," Wu said, coming to a decision. "He'll be classified as a person of interest who may have information about yesterday's murder."

"I see where you're going," Flint said. "We make it look like we only want to talk to him about how the toxin was sourced and smuggled in from South America, not that we like him for the hit."

Hargrave frowned. "You're gambling that the Colonel will be upset but won't see a need to eliminate Toro."

"Precisely," Wu said.

Hargrave's frown deepened. "You're also betting Toro and Vega will be together, so finding him will lead us to her."

"That's another problem," Wu admitted. "The longer those two are out of contact, the more I'm beginning to think Toro may have rejoined his group and gone to ground."

"Meaning he got rid of Vega," Flint said, voicing Wu's worst fear.

"We could swear out a murder warrant for him for Nathan Costner's death," Hargrave said. "That way, we could freeze his assets, put him on a no-fly list, and monitor his communications. Hell, you've already put surveillance on his known associates and his listed residences right now."

Wu shook his head. "I've reviewed the op. He was supposed to take her to the meeting, and we were going to get pictures and identify everyone involved in the group so we could start the investigation. Then she would be off to a training exercise. We had GPS trackers on both of them. The plan was simple." He dragged a hand through his thick black hair. "What the hell went wrong?"

"OPR will conduct a thorough investigation to find the answer to that question," Hargrave said. "And your role in the communications breakdown that led to the loss of contact."

A fine time to tell him the Department of Justice's Office of Professional Responsibility was going to open up a case on him. The higher-ups were looking for a scapegoat in the event things went badly, and they'd apparently found him.

"You're still in charge of the investigation," Hargrave went on. "There's no time to assign a new SAC and get them up to speed. Right now we need to get our agent and our asset back in one piece."

He didn't trust himself to respond, so he held his tongue. The only positive thing he could say about Hargrave was that he would always stab you in the chest rather than the back.

CHAPTER 32

Dani helped Toro roll Chopper's body over. The man's deadweight made the maneuver awkward.

"At least there's no IED on him," she muttered.

Toro gave a last shove, and Chopper's limp form flopped over. "What are you talking about?"

"On one of my deployments, sometimes bodies were left behind . . . with hidden surprises for whoever might touch them. Learned to leave them alone."

His expression was sardonic. "You've had an interesting career, soldier."

They had already searched Chopper's upper body; now they checked his legs and feet for any other weapons or useful supplies.

"Most of it I can't talk about," she said, gently squeezing the tops of his boots to determine whether anything was hidden inside. Experience had taught her never to plunge her hand inside anyone's clothing without feeling the outside first. People hid razor blades, needles, and other nasties in strange places.

"Lookee here," Toro said, holding up a folded scrap of paper he had tugged from the boot on Chopper's other foot.

She watched as he unfolded it and laid it down flat. Two of its edges were torn.

Toro tilted his head and peered down. "It's part of a diagram."

"It's a schematic of where we are." She pointed. "That looks like the corridor where I came from."

"How can you tell?" Toro said. "All these damn rooms and hallways look alike."

"Not if you pay close attention," she said, sliding a finger across the sheet. "I passed that box on the wall on the way here. It was made to hold a fire extinguisher, but the box was empty. I'm sure it's that one, because it was six feet from that door."

"Okay, so if we turn it this way, we can see where we are," Toro said. "And it looks like we're on the bottom floor of a seven-level structure."

"When we went down the stairs after we first got here, I couldn't tell how many floors there were," she said. "This place is a lot bigger than I thought."

"Where do you think the exit is?"

"We're underground, so that means the exit has to be on the highest level," she said.

"And we have to go up to get to it," Toro said. "Through multiple levels full of people trying to kill us and whatever surprises Nemesis has planned for us."

As if on cue, the room went dark. Their only source of light was a rectangular shaft from the corridor outside.

"Looks like we're done in here," Toro said.

"We've gotten everything we can from this room," she said. "Now we're supposed to leave."

She could see Toro silhouetted in the light from the hallway, folding the piece of paper they'd found on Chopper before bending to stuff it into the top of his boot. The nylon spandex suit offered few other options.

"Stay behind me," she said to him. "Watch how I move and do the same."

She had neither the time nor the inclination to teach him advanced tactical skills, but she would show him enough of the basics to keep both of them alive.

As soon as they made their way into the corridor, the lights to the left shut off, leaving them only one way forward. Toro's curses behind her echoed her own feelings. After turning another corner, the lights all around them went out, with a sole beam of illumination coming from above.

She tilted her head back. "There's a round hatch in the ceiling."

"And a ladder on the wall," Toro said. "We're obviously supposed to climb up."

Before she could stop him, Toro reached out and grabbed the closest rung.

An image of the man who had grabbed the bars in his cell came to her. "That could have been electrified."

"Nemesis is directing us to go up," he said. "Why would he fry us when we're doing what he wants?"

He climbed to the top of the ladder without waiting for an answer. The circular latch moved easily when he pulled it, and he pushed the metal hatch open. She followed him to the brightly lit room above, which was empty. Toro had been right. Their captor wanted them on the next level.

She resented being shepherded from one place to the next and made a silent promise to find a way to turn the tables on their captor. She was not a sheep and refused to be treated as one, but she'd bide her time and take action when it would do the most good.

This was something she'd learned at Survival, Evasion, Resistance, and Escape training in the Army. The SERE program had taught her how to respond when being held as a POW in a combat situation. Strategies differed depending on specific circumstances, but hers was to lull Nemesis into a false sense of security and act defeated, then rain holy hell down on him at the first opportunity. Because there would be only one.

Questions assailed her in a rapid-fire barrage. How could she communicate her plans to Toro when they were under constant surveillance? She assumed none of the men trapped inside the game with her were the type to cooperate. What were the rest of them planning? If they all managed to put aside their personal objectives long enough to band together, what would their captor do?

There was only one logical answer. Nemesis had spent a great deal of time and money creating this scenario and would not permit them to change the rules of the game. He would start picking them off one by one until they fell in line.

CHAPTER 33

Dani reached out to clutch Toro's arm, bringing him to an abrupt halt.

He lifted a questioning brow. "What's up?"

"Thought I heard something in that room ahead," she whispered.

He lowered his voice. "More than one person?"

"I couldn't tell if it was a person, but it was some kind of movement."

They flattened themselves against the wall and edged closer to the open hatch. Dani missed working with trained law enforcement and military personnel. Under those circumstances, she would have given a silent signal, and her partner would have known to buttonhole their way in, with her taking point.

She caught Toro's eye and gestured to him, then toward the doorway. Next she jerked a thumb at herself and then pointed toward the lower portion of the entrance. Finally she made a hooking motion with her hand.

He considered the silent communication for a moment, then nodded. She could only hope he'd understood. They couldn't risk a whispered exchange now that they were this close to the open hatch.

She held up three fingers. When he gave her a quick nod, she lowered one, then the next, then the third.

They both rushed inside. He hooked around to his right while she went low and to her left. It took only a second to see no one else was inside.

But the room wasn't empty.

"What the hell is that?" Toro said.

She had also noticed a quilted blue blanket draped over a box sitting on a stand in the center of the room.

"I'm guessing we're supposed to see what's under the blanket," she said. "And I'm betting we won't like what we find."

"I wouldn't take that bet."

She took several tentative steps closer. The concealed box resting on the four-legged metal stand was the size and shape of her Army footlocker. Would it explode if they got closer? A vision surfaced of the men who had failed to solve the first clue and had been shredded by shrapnel.

"Safe to assume it's some sort of trap," she said over her shoulder. "Remember what Nemesis said, though. We're in a game. A competition. I don't believe he would design a challenge that didn't have a solution. He's testing us, and there's no fun in creating an IED that simply detonates."

"You're saying he wants to give us a chance to figure out his sick game," Toro said. "He gets off on outsmarting us, and he can't do that without giving us a puzzle to solve."

"That's how I see it." She reached out and grasped the corner of the dense blanket. "Stand back. If it blows, only one of us will get caught in the explosion."

She waited for him to take several steps back, noting the surprise in his expression. He had a lot to learn about self-sacrifice and teamwork. While she didn't trust him in the slightest, she would damn well work with him, and that meant leading by example.

As soon as he was clear, she yanked the blanket off and took a step back, stunned at what lay hidden underneath.

A plexiglass terrarium was perched on the stand. Inside was a massive, lethal-looking king cobra coiled in multilayered rings. Its forked tongue flicked out, lifting up and down before slipping back inside its fanged mouth. She was no herpetologist but knew enough about snakes to understand that it was gathering information about them.

"There's a lid on the tank," she said to Toro. "It's latched shut so the cobra can't escape. Let's check it out."

"Go ahead." He paled. "I'll stay right here."

She shot him a look before bending to examine the terrarium.

"There's an envelope inside with the snake," she called out to Toro. "Another clue, no doubt."

"Fine," Toro said. "We'll leave it for someone else. Let's go."

She rested a hand on her hip. "Scared of snakes?"

"Rattler bit me when I was a teenager. The pain was mind blowing." He shuddered. "Nearly died before they got me to the hospital. I've had nightmares ever since."

Dani gave her head a small shake. She had given Toro the opportunity to bluff his way out of the situation, but instead he'd admitted a weakness that the enemy could overhear. She didn't bother to point out his tactical error now that the damage was done.

"We may not get another chance," she said to him, changing the subject. "I'm going to figure out a way to get that envelope."

"I'd give you the knife." He glanced down at the boot that held the knife they had taken from Chopper. "But I can't see how it will do you much good."

"It won't." She waved the suggestion away as if she didn't care. "I'll think of something else."

She filed the comment away. Toro claimed to be her ally, yet he was hesitant to relinquish control of their only weapon. Was he waiting for the right moment to sink the blade between her shoulder blades? She almost smiled. Let him try.

Turning her attention back to the immediate problem, she examined the tank from all angles. The cobra turned its hooded head to follow her progress as she circled the terrarium. She had been around snakes from all over the world and had developed a working knowledge of their capabilities. Occasionally one of her fellow Rangers had been bitten, but she'd never experienced that particular pleasure.

"The cobra views me as a threat," she muttered to herself. "How can I convince him I'm not?" She paused. "Better yet, how can I lure him out of the tank to get what's inside?"

Toro's response bordered on panic. "Don't let that damned thing out."

Ignoring him, she studied the snake more closely. "I can't tell if it's a spitting cobra."

"What difference does it make?" Toro asked her. "It's poisonous. It'll kill you."

"Spitting cobras can spew a stream of venom from as much as six feet away." She threw him a look. "They aim for your eyes, and the toxin can cause permanent blindness."

"Well isn't that just the pickle on top of this turd sandwich?"

She strolled around the tank again, thinking. Snakes could not hear, but they keyed in on movement, and their sight was good. An idea occurred to her.

She stooped to pick up the blanket. "This wasn't just left here to hide the tank. It's part of the solution to the problem."

"What the hell are you going to—"

"I need something to catch him."

"Exactly how are you going to get him to—"

"Leave it to me." She lifted the blanket. "I'm going to unlatch the lid and open the terrarium while you keep the snake distracted."

"Are you *loca*?"

"You need to stand in front of the tank and make a lot of big movements. You need to be close enough for the snake to view you as a threat, but not so close he can lunge out and bite you."

"You said he could spit venom and blind me. I'm not getting near that thing."

"I said *maybe* he was a spitting cobra. I don't know. If you're concerned about it, just keep a hand over your eyes. That's where he'll aim."

"How long have you been doing hard drugs, because you're high if you think I'm going along with this suicidal plan."

"You know, I think it's a good idea for you to cover your eyes. That way you won't see what's going on. It'll help you stay calm."

"Let me get this straight. I'm going to scare the snake so you can do . . . what?"

"Sneak up behind it and throw the blanket over its head. Once I do that, I'll have to move quickly. The blanket's thick, so that helps. I'll pin his head down to the bottom of the tank and you reach in and grab the envelope."

"No. Fucking. Way."

"If anyone's going to get bitten, it's me." She moved to the back of the tank and put her hand on the latch. "Besides, if he does spit, he won't be able to do it once I drop the blanket on his head."

"You're going to do this, aren't you?"

"The top is coming off. Are you with me or not?"

Cursing, he moved closer to the glass case. The cobra swiveled its head to look at him, apparently not sure who presented the greater threat.

"Get his attention," she said to Toro. "Wave your arm and move your body."

Toro lifted a hand to cover his eyes and began sweeping his other hand back and forth. The snake hissed, flared its hood wider, and moved with him.

"Good," she said, gradually lifting the lid. "He's following your hand. Keep it up."

The snake rose from its coil, head swaying as its reptilian eyes stayed locked on Toro's quivering hand. She bent to place the lid on the floor, then chose her moment and flung the blanket onto the snake.

"Got him." She forced its head down as its body uncoiled, writhing beneath both her hands. The cobra was stronger than she had anticipated. "Hurry up and grab that damned envelope," she said to Toro, who had dropped his hands to his sides and appeared rooted to the spot. "I can't hold him much longer."

Her comment seemed to break the spell, and he reached in beside her to grasp a corner of the envelope, sliding it out as the snake thrashed.

"Now what are you going to do?" he asked her.

Good question. "Get the lid and put it back on when I say."

"You're nuts."

"Do it!"

He bent and snatched up the lid, then stood beside her.

"When I say go, I'll pull back. It will take him a second or two to get out from under the blanket. That will give us enough time to get the lid back on before he can strike or spit."

She waited a beat for him to steel himself. "Go."

She released her hold on the viper, pulling back out of the way as Toro slammed the lid down on top of the terrarium and latched it shut. The cobra flailed a moment longer; then its hooded head shot out from under the blanket. It reared back and struck at the glass in a frenzy of fear, rage, or both.

"Glad that's over," a deep male voice said from the doorway behind them. "Now you can hand that envelope over to me."

They both spun to see Doc Tox holding a semiautomatic pistol.

CHAPTER 34

Wu sat in the front passenger seat of the black Tahoe while Flint maneuvered through the heavy Queens traffic. It had taken forty-five minutes to make it from Manhattan by way of the Queens–Midtown Tunnel. Judging by Flint's gritted teeth and liberal use of profanity, he was every bit as frustrated with their tedious progress.

Johnson and her fellow analysts had used every resource at their disposal. A combination of satellite feeds and city cams had enabled them to follow the suspect vehicle's movements through the city. One of the traffic cameras had gotten a clear shot of the license plate, which turned out to be a temporary tag issued by a used-car dealer in Queens.

The charcoal-gray Suburban had traveled deeper into New Jersey after leaving the underground parking garage, which had no functioning security cameras. He agreed with the others that this was no coincidence.

This level of planning and sophistication indicated a large-scale effort with plenty of misdirection. Grudging appreciation for the Colonel's countersurveillance skills made Wu one part leery and five parts pissed off.

The SUV had continued along the turnpike until it disappeared under the dense canopy of trees that shrouded the Pine Barrens. They had contacted the New Jersey State Police with a request to search for the vehicle, but the Pine Barrens constituted over seventeen hundred square miles of mostly rural land, with plenty of dirt roads. Local legend had it that no one would ever know how many bodies were buried within the vast forest that took up nearly a quarter of the state. The SUV could have been ditched in a spot so remote it might take years to locate.

After the dead end with the Suburban, the driver was their best lead, so Wu and Flint were on their way to interview the used-car dealer who had sold it. They would be able to learn the buyer's name, address, and perhaps a lot more.

"Finally made it," Flint said, pulling into the dealership.

Wu's hopes dimmed as he took in the weeded lot surrounded by a rusty chain-link fence. When a heavyset man with a bad comb-over left the small building to greet them, he grew still more pessimistic. This seemed like the kind of place that might sell a car for cash—no questions asked.

Wu got out first, and before he could say a word, the salesperson greeted them.

"You two looking for a car?" He gestured toward the lot behind him. "I've got plenty. All of them in good condition too." He gave them an oily smile. "I'm Brad."

Wu held up his creds. "Agent Wu, FBI." He tipped his head toward Flint. "This is Detective Flint with the NYPD. We want information about a Chevy Suburban you sold recently."

The date on the temporary tag had been the day before yesterday, but Wu held that detail back, interested to see how forthcoming the interviewee would be.

Brad's face fell. "Only sold one Suburban this month."

"Was it dark gray?" Flint asked.

Brad nodded.

"Could you show us the paperwork?" Wu finally said when Brad offered no other information.

Brad looked away. "I've got a bill of sale inside. Come with me."

They followed him into a building that looked even more dilapidated than the car lot. Trailing him into a tiny office with threadbare carpet, they stood in silence while he sat at his desk in front of a large monitor.

"You guys don't need my computer, do you?" he asked, reddening as he made a series of clicks with the mouse.

Flint hooked a thumb into his belt loop. "We don't care about your internet porn addiction," he said. "As long as the stuff you're watching is legal."

Brad's face flushed a deeper shade. "It is."

They waited another moment until he finally glanced up. "I'll print it out for you." He swiveled in his chair to snatch the single sheet sliding out of the printer and passed it to Wu.

"This is it?" Wu said, incredulous. "One page?"

Brad straightened his tie. "It was a cash deal. No need to run a credit check or anything." He held up his hands. "Hey, my job is to make sure we don't buy or sell any stolen cars. That SUV was not stolen. That's the extent of my responsibility."

Flint leaned in close, towering over Brad, who was still seated. "Did he drive it from the lot?"

Brad swallowed audibly. "Yeah."

"Then you had to make sure he had a valid driver's license, didn't you?"

"He showed me a license. It looked okay."

"Did you make a copy?"

"Yeah." Brad hunched over his keyboard again. They heard more clicking; then another sheet of paper glided from the printer.

Wu glanced down at a color copy of a New York driver's license. "Why did you make us work for this?"

Brad blinked. "Huh?"

"Never mind." Wu hated wasting time. Brad could have told them about the ID right away. Instead, he had seemed to wait for them to ask for it specifically. Was he stupid, crooked, nervous, or just antipolice? Unable to decide which, he pressed for more. "Did the driver match the photo?"

Brad nodded. "That's what he looked like."

After a few more responses that were less than illuminating, Wu took Brad's business card and contact information before they made their way back to the Tahoe.

He closed the doors so they wouldn't be overheard, then pulled out his cell, snapped a picture of the license, and sent it to Johnson. Twenty seconds later, his phone buzzed.

"Got the pic, sir." Johnson's tone was crisp and professional, as usual. He'd been damn lucky the day she had been assigned to his unit.

He put her on speaker. "I need everything you can find on Thomas Kinchloe."

"Stand by. I can do a preliminary search right now." A few moments later, she came back online. "There's no record of that license."

Flint leaned over to speak directly to the analyst. "What do you mean?"

"I've accessed the New York Division of Motor Vehicles database," Johnson said. "I pulled the image. The Thomas Kinchloe who had that license died two years ago."

Wu looked at the picture of the blond man with pale skin and blue eyes who graced the copy of the license in his hand. "So this isn't our suspect."

"That would be my guess, sir. Someone probably stole the license from the real Kinchloe."

"Run the picture through face rec," he told her, moving on to the next course of action. "Maybe the suspect substituted his real picture for Kinchloe's."

"On it." This time she disconnected.

Johnson called back less than five minutes later. "More bad news, sir."

"Why should our luck change now?"

"I confirmed that the face on the license belongs to the real Kinchloe. Date of death, last November third."

Flint's brows furrowed. "So whoever bought the Suburban did not substitute his own picture for the one on the license?"

"But our pal Brad confirmed that he looked like the photo," Wu said.

"Do you really put a lot of faith in Brad?" Flint let out a derisive snort. "Because I don't. He was so anxious to sell that vehicle, he probably barely looked at the guy's ID. Once he saw cash, it was a done deal as far as he was concerned."

"Whoever did this is clever," Wu said. "My guess is he lifts wallets from men who resemble him. He holds on to their licenses, using them when he needs to."

"Another dead end," Flint said on a sigh.

The SUV had disappeared into the Pine Barrens, probably never to be seen again. The driver could have easily hitched a ride back to the city or had another car waiting. If they told New Jersey police to be on the lookout for a man generally matching the car buyer's description, he could easily put on a ball cap and frustrate the search. Besides, they had no charges to hold him on at this point.

"Dammit." Flint slammed his fist against the steering wheel, interrupting Wu's thoughts. "We have to go back to the JOC and look at more video. We need to see if the Suburban was riding as low to the ground when it left the other garage. There could have been more switches, and we'll have to track down more vehicles."

"Or they could have split them up into separate cars," Wu said. "As long as the windows were dark, or if they put them in the trunk, we'd never know."

"What if the Suburban was still heavy going to Jersey?" Flint said. "That would mean they were still inside the whole time."

"Then we have an even bigger problem," Wu said. "Searching the Pine Barrens." He didn't add that they would likely be on a recovery operation rather than a rescue mission if that were the case.

"Do you think that's where they are?"

"I sure as hell hope not," Wu said. "We may never find them in that forest."

CHAPTER 35

Dani assessed her situation, making several observations at once. Doc Tox was alone and had not fired on them despite having the perfect opportunity while she and Toro wrestled with the cobra. Clearly he wanted something from them besides whatever was in the envelope.

Doc had a white-knuckled grip on the pistol, obviously more comfortable with poisons than firearms. Dani recognized the weapon's compact, boxy shape as the Glock Model 30 that Chopper had originally brought with him. If Doc was foolish enough to let his guard down, she would have it out of his hand before he could pull the trigger.

"Why don't we all see what's in the envelope together?" she said to him. "Then no one feels left out."

Doc swung his gaze, and the muzzle of his gun, from Toro to Dani. "How about if both of you are dead and I take what I want?"

Dani had already formed a plan, but would Toro pick up on it? She edged away from Doc, making an exaggerated show of raising her hands. "I don't want any trouble. You can have the envelope."

"He'll shoot us anyway," Toro said.

She took the opportunity to convey her strategy. "Then we should treat him exactly like that snake."

"I hear you," Toro said, giving her a knowing look before goading Doc. "I saved his life once, and this is the thanks I get."

Doc frowned at Toro. "You never saved my life. What the hell are you talking about?"

Dani took full advantage, inching sideways. While the two men argued over a past assignment they had been on together, she managed to circle around behind Doc.

Just like they had done with the cobra. Toro had understood her.

She would have only one chance to strike. Lowering her body, she planted her left leg and lashed out with her right foot, connecting with the back of Doc's knees, buckling them. She knew his natural impulse would be to raise his arms to steady himself, which is what he did. For a split second the muzzle of the gun pointed straight up. She used that moment to drive her shoulder into his back, pitching him forward.

Toro grabbed for the gun, but Doc was too fast. He got off a shot that went wide, but Dani was on him before he could pull the trigger again. With practiced efficiency, she proceeded to deliver a barrage of knee and elbow strikes to every part of his body within reach.

Toro drove his fist to Doc's face, briefly disorienting him. Dani wrapped her hands around the pistol's slide, preventing it from firing, and hung on tight.

Doc's hand was firmly wrapped around the grip. Unfortunately for him, his index finger was still on the trigger, pulling it frantically in a fruitless attempt to fire the weapon.

She had one play, and she made it, wrenching the pistol to the side with all the force she could muster.

Doc shrieked in pain when his wrist bent at an unnatural angle, crushing his finger in the trigger guard. Dani gave another ruthless twist, yanking the gun in the opposite direction.

Doc's howl resounded through the room, echoing off the concrete walls. Like a wounded beast, he channeled his anguish and rage into renewed strength. He kicked her thigh, and pain shot like an electric current along the femoral nerve in her quadriceps.

Toro dove onto Doc's back, taking them all to the ground. Doc landed on top of her, with the pistol trapped between them.

The impact of two men crashing down onto her squeezed the breath from Dani's lungs. Darkness crept in around the edges of her vision. She knew she had only seconds to act.

The pistol's slide began to slip through her sweaty fingers while Doc angled the muzzle toward her stomach. Getting gutshot in the middle of this deadly game would spell her death. She kept one hand where it was and moved the other to pry Doc's finger from the trigger, resulting in another shriek of pain. He would have already shot her if she hadn't injured his trigger finger and grasped the slide.

Toro smashed his fist into Doc's temple, stunning him for an instant. Taking full advantage of his momentary disorientation, she wrapped her hand around Doc's. Grunting with the effort, she rotated the barrel in the opposite direction and laid her index finger on top of his.

"Stop," she said through gritted teeth, giving him one last chance. If he didn't take it, this would only end with one of them dead.

His response was to push the muzzle back toward her abdomen. Before he could maneuver the weapon into position, she squeezed Doc's index finger—still caught under hers—and pulled the trigger.

She felt the vibration from the explosion through her sternum. The gun was still trapped between their bodies, muffling its report. Doc stiffened, his eyes widening in shock; then he slumped onto her.

Deadweight.

She had not taken a life since leaving the Army. The possibility of deadly force always lurked in the background in her new career, but it was not the unseen ever-present companion it had been before. Nemesis had forced her into a position where she would dredge up all her previous training. Was Toro right? She had already lied and killed. Would she have to cheat and steal as the game progressed?

Toro heaved Doc's limp form off Dani. "Son of a bitch fought like hell."

She didn't bother to point out that Doc had been fighting for his life. Instead, she shoved the gun into the top of her boot and bent to lay two fingers on the side of Doc's neck. "Nothing."

"Quit worrying about saving people," Toro said. "Or we'll never get out of here."

She glanced up at him. "Spoiler alert. No one's getting out of here alive." She looked back at Doc. "That's the whole point."

"How can you be so sure?"

"Remember what Nemesis said during the little intro speech?" she asked him. "We're all a bunch of killers. We're expendable. He views us as gladiators fighting to the death for his amusement." She looked at him. "We're killing each other because he tells us to."

"You mean like being a gun for hire?" Toro said, indignant. "Like what I do for a living?"

He had almost blown her cover with that comment. "What we do to earn money isn't the issue," she said quickly, trying to repair any potential damage. "Now isn't the time for this discussion anyway," she added.

Perhaps the stress of the game had gotten to him, or maybe he'd been friends with Doc, but he had taken her remark as a personal insult and was lashing out in response.

"Like I told you before, you killed plenty of people in the military," Toro said. "People you never met. And you did it on someone else's orders for money, only you call it a salary." He gestured back and forth between them. "We're no different."

She got to her feet. "We could not be more different."

He took a step closer. "You think you're special because you were a Ranger? You—"

She drove her knuckles into his throat, cutting off his air and ending his words.

He sank to his knees, coughing and sputtering.

"I told you that was a pickup line," she said, trying to play it off. "For some stupid reason, I was trying to impress you."

He continued to clutch his throat as the color drained from his face. "Sorry, honey," he finally managed, voice rasping.

She summed up the situation in one word. "Shit."

CHAPTER 36

Nemesis sped the video feed backward a few seconds, then played it again.

"You think you're special because you were a Ranger? You—"

Then the throat punch. The look they exchanged followed by her lame attempt to gloss over his comment. There was no doubt about it. They were hiding something.

Nemesis had learned the hard way about secrets. They ruined lives, destroyed fortunes, and got people killed. After all, they were the reason behind the game.

Toro had called her a ranger. Did he mean a Texas Ranger? A forest ranger? Nikki Corazón had claimed she was trying to impress him. She was a soldier, so being part of an elite Army unit would be impressive.

But there weren't any female Army Rangers. The training was too physically and mentally demanding. On the other hand, if a woman did somehow manage to succeed, that would be newsworthy, right?

Nemesis rolled the black leather swivel chair to the main computer and typed FEMALE ARMY RANGERS into a search engine. Several stories popped up. The first women completed Ranger training in 2015. After that, a handful had gone on to join the 75th Ranger Regiment, one even leading an infantry platoon in combat.

None of the stories featured Nicola Corazón. Maybe she had been bragging to pick up Toro at a bar. Official government archives had already revealed Corazón's military career. She had been regular Army. No special forces. No commendations. Nothing unusual except the dishonorable discharge that cut her service short.

Law enforcement agencies weren't the only ones with facial recognition technology. Nemesis digitized and uploaded Corazón's face to conduct a full-spectrum sweep of all available media sources.

Hundreds of pictures populated the screen, including everything from school yearbook pictures going back to kindergarten to social media fluff. A few commands narrowed the search to anything containing the term *ranger*.

A feature story in a neighborhood newspaper with limited distribution in the Bronx popped up. The headline read LOCAL TRAILBLAZER OVERCOMES TRAGIC PAST. Squinting at the photo of a newly minted Ranger beneath the banner, Nemesis looked past the shaved head and camos to pick out the recognizable features of Nikki Corazón's face. Only the news story identified her as Daniela Vega.

Damn.

Who was Daniela Vega? According to the story, she was a Puerto Rican girl from the Bronx who had made her community proud by being among the first women to become a Ranger in the 75th Regiment out of Fort Benning, Georgia.

The articles mentioned a trauma in Vega's past. Fingers jabbing the keyboard with unnecessary force, Nemesis went through layer after layer in a search for anything from the Bronx involving a family named Vega. It didn't take long to spot a headline dating back nine years.

BRONX WOMAN MURDERS HUSBAND

The victim was identified as disabled Army veteran Sergio Vega, forty, and the suspect was his wife, Camila Vega, thirty-seven. They lived in an apartment building on Benedict Avenue in the Castle Hill neighborhood, had been married nineteen years, and had three children.

Several weeks of reporting followed before the story faded from public interest. Camila had been found kneeling by her husband's body, holding the bloody knife used to stab him. Police had taken her into custody but determined she was unable to answer questions due to her mental state. She was eventually found unfit to stand trial by reason of insanity and remanded to the psych ward at Bellevue for treatment until deemed sufficiently recovered to answer for her crime. Further online searches revealed no change in Camila Vega's circumstances.

Could these two have been Daniela Vega's parents? A closer examination of the news articles about Daniela's military success revealed that she had been twenty-two years old when she graduated from the second part of Ranger school, which would make her twenty-six years old now.

Daniela's father had also been an Army Ranger and was wounded in action, receiving a Purple Heart, a Silver Star, and a medical discharge.

After leaving the Army, he must have returned to his old neighborhood with his wife and their three children. A few years later, Daniela's mother had killed her father and was now in a mental institution. Daniela would have been seventeen at the time of the murder nine years ago. She had enlisted the following year, probably to escape her past.

Very few organizations could create such an elaborate fake history. The educational, social media, and military records had been thorough and convincing. Only a multilevel detailed search with specialty software uncovered the truth.

Who had the ability to scrub every image that did not align with the Corazón persona? Just as important, who would go to all the trouble?

Only three types of people created a false identity going back to early childhood: criminals, spies, and undercover cops.

Working on defense contracts required limited access to certain government databases. Using access gained from those contracts in the past allowed Nemesis to create a back door into the federal employee database.

Less than five minutes later, the answer popped onto the screen. Nikki Corazón, paid assassin, was actually FBI Agent Daniela Vega. As Nemesis suspected, no one had purged the file from what they would consider a secure internal system.

What about Gustavo Toro? He'd been involved in the operation that had changed everything ten years ago. He had also murdered Nathan Costner. He couldn't be an agent.

So why were they posing as a couple? Only one logical reason. Vega was working undercover, and he was helping her infiltrate the Colonel's group. The Feds must have caught Toro, and he'd snitched on the others to save himself.

Nemesis sat back in the overstuffed black leather chair, fingers steepled. This new development needed careful consideration. And a tweak to the plan. The first order of business was to delete Toro's comment about Vega being a Ranger before uploading that camera's footage to the dedicated server. The FBI would be looking for their missing agent by now, and the remark could attract their attention.

Had the Feds already connected the dots that would lead them here? No. The Colonel had been ordered to take every precaution, and he might be a soulless killer, but he knew tactics. He would have made sure no one followed them.

Did the Colonel know Vega was FBI? Again, no. He had called to say Toro wanted to bring Nikki Corazón with him at no extra charge. She had military experience, and the DOD types might like a female in the training scenario. Of course, that was when the Colonel thought this was all about getting a defense contract.

Before he learned the truth of his situation.

The FBI presented a new problem. Could they track Vega down?

Not likely. The pilot who flew the team here, well paid and always discreet, had been the one to suggest the repair hangar in New Jersey to get a small aircraft up without filing a flight plan. Their current location was so remote that any approaching vehicles could be detected miles away.

A review of current news stories revealed nothing about a search for a missing agent. The FBI must be hesitant to reveal her status as one of theirs and blow her cover. A peek into what must be a desperate but quiet hunt for Vega would offer a warning if they were getting close. Unlike accessing the federal employee database, hacking into the FBI's secure server to gather information about the investigation was too risky. The Feds had firewalls and traps specifically designed to catch and trace virtual intruders. A softer target would make a better choice, but who? Where would the FBI share information outside of their own ranks?

Nemesis crossed the room and poured two fingers of scotch, using the time to contemplate the problem. This was yet another puzzle to solve. The answer presented itself after a few sips. Vega's family would notice her missing and start asking questions. The Feds wouldn't want that because she was undercover. They would have to share a certain amount of information about her disappearance and what they were doing to find her. They were bound to reveal more to the family than the public—if they ever even acknowledged what had occurred.

A specially designed Trojan horse virus could create a back door into a computer belonging to one of her closest relatives. Once inside the system, controlling the camera and microphone would make it possible to spy on them, providing all the information the family knew in real time. Strategic problems solved, Nemesis swirled the liquid in the glass, considering the ramifications of Vega's presence in the game. Everything had been planned to punish those who had been involved in the fiasco ten years ago. When Nikki Corazón had wanted in, Nemesis had allowed her into the game, under the impression that the female assassin had as much blood on her hands as the others, just not the same blood. Now Nikki turned out to be Special Agent Daniela Vega. How did that change things?

Draining the glass, Nemesis concluded that it didn't.

If the vaunted FBI had done their job ten years ago, none of this would be happening. First, they never detected years of criminal behavior. Next, they failed to figure out who was behind the crime once it came to their attention. Finally, after it was over, they never investigated enough to learn the truth. Killers had gotten away with murder, and they could have stopped it, but they didn't.

Nemesis had discovered the truth. Not the damned FBI.

Agent Vega was too young to have been involved back then, but she was guilty by association. Fate had brought her here to answer for her agency's incompetence. Her presence would make the retribution complete.

A new idea began to take root, bringing satisfaction with it. The undercover spy was about to get a surprise.

CHAPTER 37

After a nerve-racking drive from the used-car lot in Queens to the Bronx, Wu climbed to the top floor of a five-story walkup on Benedict Avenue. The century-old building wasn't built with heavy vehicle traffic in mind and had no dedicated parking. Flint had spent twenty minutes of their lives they would never get back circling the block before finally throwing an NYPD placard on his dashboard and double-parking.

An urgent phone call had brought them here to speak with Agent Vega's family. Vega had an apartment in Brooklyn, but Wu had just learned her younger sister and brother lived with her aunt and uncle when university wasn't in session. Her younger brother, Axel, had called the main JTTF number, asking for the special agent in charge. When pressed, he claimed to have information about his sister that he could share only in person.

Wu had put off discussing Vega's status with her family, but now her brother was forcing his hand. Vega had mentioned visiting her younger siblings before the undercover assignment. Without divulging details, she must have told them she'd be unavailable for a while.

He would have to walk a fine line, learning what Axel had discovered that had prompted him to call the JTTF while not letting on that she was MIA.

Unless her brother had already figured that out.

Wu had worked out what he wanted to say in case the family had questions about her situation on the drive over, but his carefully worded reassurances were bound to fall short. How could he explain losing someone he was responsible for?

Flint had offered to make the notification, but Wu wouldn't weasel out of his responsibility. Vega had gone missing on his watch. He would take the brunt of whatever shitstorm was coming—from the Bureau and from the family.

He also hoped a preemptive strike would discourage the family from going to the media, giving him the opportunity to emphasize that their continued silence was the best way to keep Vega safe while they followed up on whatever Axel had to share.

The apartment door creaked open at Wu's knock. A woman in her fifties stood at the threshold, eyeing them with a healthy dose of suspicion. Johnson had texted basic info from Vega's personnel file to Wu on the drive over. The woman matched the photo of Vega's aunt taken when the background investigators had come to interview the family for her top-secret security clearance.

He held up his creds. "Special Agent in Charge Steve Wu, FBI. Is Axel Vega here?"

Her gaze shifted to Flint, who showed her his gold shield. "Detective Mark Flint, NYPD."

Her dark eyes narrowed. "What do you want with Axel?"

Before they could respond, a young face that resembled Vega's appeared over the woman's shoulder. "Did you say something about Axel, Aunt Manuela?" she asked, eyes widening when she saw their IDs.

"Can we come in?" Wu made a point of glancing up and down the narrow hallway. "We should talk in private."

The young woman who had to be Vega's younger sister, Erica, put a hand to her chest and rushed toward the back of the apartment. "I'll go get Axel."

Manuela blew out a sigh. "I don't want any more questions from nosy neighbors. I had enough of that for a lifetime." She stepped back from the door and motioned them inside.

Aware she was referring to the local scandal about her brother's murder nine years earlier, Wu made no comment.

Manuela turned and strode through the cramped foyer into a tidy living room. Despite four adults living in such close quarters, the space was organized and uncluttered.

The young woman returned with a young man Wu also recognized from Vega's file in tow.

"I'm Erica and this is Axel," she said. "Why are you looking for him?"

Axel's face flushed. "Because I asked them to come here."

Axel hadn't told his family he'd called the FBI. That meant he hadn't shared whatever he'd learned about Vega.

Wu broke the awkward silence that followed. "Perhaps we should speak to Axel alone before we—"

"Not happening," Erica said, turning to her brother. "I want to know what's going on."

"It's okay if my family hears," Axel said. "But before I explain, there's something I need to know." He hesitated before directing his gaze at Wu. "Where is Dani?"

Wu didn't like where this was going, and it was just getting started.

"Why don't we sit down?" he said, glancing at a grouping of mismatched furniture. "I'd like to—"

"I don't want to sit," Erica said. "I want you to tell us where Dani is. Now."

Wu made an effort to keep his features neutral. "That's the problem, Miss Vega. We aren't sure where she is at the moment." He gestured to Axel. "Your brother says he has information about—"

Erica cut him off. "You can lose car keys." She gave him an incredulous look. "How the hell do you lose a person?"

"Dani told us she was doing an undercover assignment," Axel said quietly. "But she wouldn't say more. If you can at least confirm that much, I might be able to help you."

Now that he'd shown his hand, Wu plowed ahead, spending the next several minutes providing a bare-bones overview of Vega's disappearance. He kept the details generic, not sharing the nature of the case she was working on and specifically leaving out any mention of Senator Sledge, his chief of staff, or an asset she would be working with.

He watched their body language as he spoke. Their aunt Manuela wore a closed expression, while Axel studied his shoes. By the time he finished, Erica seemed close to the boiling point.

"That's it?" Erica said. "That's all you can tell us?"

"Her assignment is classified, Miss Vega." He used his most soothing tone. "I can't give you more information, but your brother has promised to share what he knows."

All eyes turned to him.

"Have you heard from your sister?" Wu asked, curious to hear what had prompted such an obviously shy young man to speak up in front of strangers who were also authority figures.

"I was checking my social media last night," he said, eyes still trained on the floor. "And someone DM'd me a link with malware."

Wu was familiar with the tactics employed by both private and state-managed parties that disseminated viruses by tricking unsuspecting recipients into clicking a direct message link containing malicious code.

"What does that have to do with Agent Vega?" Flint asked, speaking for the first time since entering the apartment.

"It was spyware," Axel said, finally looking up. "It was supposed to be a free download for a computer game, but it looked sketchy. I'm developing anti-hacking software for an extra-credit summer project." He shrugged. "Figured I would test it out because whoever sent the link wouldn't give up. I kept getting message requests on social media to friend or follow them and open the link."

Wu shared Flint's frustration but framed his question more gently than the detective had. "I'm not following. Can you explain the connection with your sister's disappearance?"

"Might be better if I show you," Axel said. "Be right back."

Erica watched him leave the room before turning to Wu. "He's on a full-ride scholarship to Columbia," she said, as if the comment needed no explanation.

And it didn't. Wu was a Columbia graduate himself, honoring his family by earning a degree from one of the finest universities in the nation. Anyone who gained admittance had to be an exceptional student. Scholarships were granted based on financial need, which meant Axel had managed to qualify without the advantages of private schools, tutors, or a family legacy of Ivy League education that had benefited many of his peers. Wu had done the same many years earlier.

Axel returned carrying an open laptop, set it down on the coffee table in the center of the room, and kneeled beside it. "My program is still in development, but it's designed to be more than just anti-hacking software."

"What else will it do?" Wu asked, intrigued despite the circumstances of their visit.

"Obviously there's a firewall to block any virus from getting in," Axel said. "But I've written code that will infect the malware with its own virus and travel back to its source."

Wu resigned himself to the tech speak, trusting that Axel would not waste their time when his sister could be in danger.

"Last night I activated my program before clicking on the link," Axel continued. "The filter immediately detected and contained the spyware, then latched onto the source code. I followed the breadcrumbs to the dark web through a series of proxy servers." He glanced around at them, excitement animating his features. "Here's what I found at the end of the trail."

Wu and the others dragged chairs over to sit behind Axel, who angled the laptop to give them a better view. After an agonizing minute, a website appeared on the screen. The site looked unremarkable, a black background with the word NEMESIS in a bold font. Beneath the words were buttons labeled WATCH, VOTE, and PARTICIPATE.

"This is the portal to enter an online game that's going viral across the dark web," Axel said. "At first I just thought it was a scam to spread a virus, but I got curious and decided to check it out. It won't let you past this page without joining, so I created a fake account. Once I got in, I saw that it looked like a virtual escape room game with multiple levels. Avatars of Greek gods were moving through the different rooms."

Wu still wasn't sure what was going on, but he started to get an unsettled feeling in the pit of his stomach.

Axel clicked on the WATCH button, followed by a username and password. A portal opened, and a seven-level structure appeared on the screen. Eight avatars moved around in different levels.

Axel swore under his breath.

"What's wrong?" Wu asked.

Axel moved the cursor to one of the rooms. "Another player went down." Reading their confusion, he elaborated. "There were originally thirteen avatars in separate cages. There was a clue they had to solve. Three of them didn't get the answer fast enough and blew up. After that, one of them got mad and grabbed the bars of his cage. The instant he touched the metal, he was electrocuted. That's when I saw the glitch."

"What glitch?"

"When the guy was frying, there was an instant where the skin on the avatar fragged a bit. It looked like a real person. I screen-grabbed the image before it repaired itself." He opened another window and typed in commands. "Look at this."

Flint leaned in to study the freeze-frame closer. "That does look like a real person."

"Can you expand the face?" Wu asked, thinking he could get Johnson to run it through face rec.

Axel used his thumb and index finger to zoom in. "It's kind of pixilated," he said. "But you should be able to isolate the image and clean it up."

Axel had instinctively grasped what he wanted. The kid was smart.

"I think the power surge from the electrical charge might have overloaded the circuits and caused the glitch," Axel went on. "Once that happened, I figured since the electricity was real, maybe these people were real. I mean, why would you create an avatar and then cover it with another avatar on top of the first image?" He shrugged. "Makes no sense—and it's a huge waste of time and effort."

"But why live subjects?" Wu asked.

"Don't know," Axel said. "But look at this." He moved his cursor again, this time indicating another avatar lying on the floor in the lowest level of the structure. "This guy wasn't dead last time I checked." He glanced at his watch. "About half an hour ago. This isn't in real time. This stuff is edited before it goes out."

"Looks like he got stabbed in the neck and bled out," Flint said. "The spatter pattern looks like it came from an arterial bleed."

"This game needs investigating," Wu said. "Is that why you're bringing it to our attention?"

"Watch these two," Axel said, clicking the captured still image closed and directing their attention to a pair of avatars moving along the bottom floor.

Wu watched the image of a woman clad in ancient armor with gold breastplates and a matching helmet make her way down a corridor, leading a large creature with the body of a man and the head of a bull.

"If I remember my ancient Greek mythology," Wu said, taking in the massive pair of horns sprouting from the avatar's head and the silver ring in its broad nose, "the one in the back is a Minotaur, and the one in front is Athena."

"The Minotaur is obvious," Flint said. "But how can you tell about the woman?"

"There's an owl perched on her helmet," Wu said, recalling a classical studies course at Columbia. "Athena was the goddess of war and wisdom. She was often shown with an owl. The armor is also a dead giveaway."

"You can zero in on certain rooms and characters," Axel said. "And you can go back to catch what you missed." He hit a button, and the images zoomed in reverse. "Listen to what Athena says here."

The feed started forward at normal speed. Athena was speaking to the Minotaur in an electronically altered feminine voice. "I will never leave a fallen comrade to fall into the hands of the enemy."

Axel stabbed his keyboard, freezing the scene. "Did you hear that?"

Wu looked at Flint, who seemed equally baffled, then back at Axel. "Perhaps you should explain."

"When Dani became a Ranger, she had to recite their creed," Axel said. "I helped her memorize it." His eyes widened. "That line is taken verbatim from the Ranger Creed." Realization hit Wu with the force of a physical blow. Now he knew why Axel had shared the video with them.

Axel sped up the feed again before resuming normal speed. "Watch Athena move," he said.

The goddess avatar made her way down the corridor in a way that made Wu think of the tactical training he had received at Quantico. She cleared rooms methodically and seemed to be in charge, directing the Minotaur, who remained behind her. When she gestured with her left hand, he noticed what looked like a thick band wrapped around her wrist.

"Is that a cuff bracelet on her wrist?" Flint said, apparently spotting the same thing.

"Could be," Axel said. "Can't be sure because it's not part of the avatar's suit, so it shows up like an extra-thick layer." He frowned. "That's not important, though. She used to teach me military stuff for fun. I know how my own sister moves, and this is pure Dani." He paused. "I also researched the avatar and came to the same conclusion you did. Athena is the goddess of war, and Dani was a soldier."

Wu shifted his gaze back to the Minotaur, certain Axel was right. "Half-man, half-bull," he murmured, then repeated the key word. "Bull."

He looked at Flint, unable to say more in the presence of civilians. No one here knew—or could know—about the exact nature of Dani's assignment and who she was with.

Flint nodded his understanding.

Toro was the Spanish word for bull, and it was also Gustavo Toro's code name. Axel was thinking about his sister's real military background, unaware that she had gone undercover as Nikki Corazón, also a soldier. Either way, it made sense that she would be portrayed as a goddess of war. Unfortunately, he couldn't tell whether her cover had been blown or not, but he did know that avatars in what was supposed to be a virtual world were dying in real life. Flint had no doubt arrived at the same inescapable conclusion he had.

Agent Vega and Gustavo Toro were trapped inside a killer's game.

CHAPTER 38

Dani gazed at her grotesquely misshapen face. The fun house mirrors covering the walls of the room made her feel like she'd been sucked into a nightmarish version of a Salvador Dalí painting. The mirror reflected what she felt inside rather than a physically accurate image, contributing to the surreal effect.

She had just killed a man. And not for the first time.

As in combat, she'd done what was necessary to survive, but this time felt different. At eighteen, she had told everyone she was joining the Army to honor the memory of her father but never admitted—even to herself—that she was also running from the legacy of her mother.

Toro had called her a killer, and she had responded with all the righteous indignation of the guilty. Now she looked at her distorted reflection and saw all the way into her soul. She could no longer deny the truth of who and what she was.

"We're in the right place," Toro said, tapping the handwritten message scrawled on the back of the envelope. "Let's open it."

The instructions had directed them to the next room, where they would find a wall of mirrors before breaking the envelope's seal.

"I haven't had a chance to check this yet," she said, holding up the compact pistol she'd taken from Doc Tox.

She would never carry a weapon into battle without knowing whether it was loaded and functional. A firefight was not the place to find out whether the gun would go bang when she pulled the trigger.

"Watch my back," she said to Toro as she released the magazine, dropping it into her hand. She had noticed that the weapon felt a bit light and wasn't surprised to find the magazine empty except for one .45-caliber round at the top.

Cursing, she pulled back the slide to see a single round in the chamber.

"We've got two shots," she said.

"So there were only four bullets in there to begin with," he said. "I'm sure that's not how Chopper kept his gun, so that means Nemesis is screwing with us. Again."

She seated the magazine back in place. "Maybe there's a cache of ammo hidden somewhere." Grateful for its compact size, she tucked the gun into the top of her boot and straightened. "Let's have a look at the clue."

As if by tacit agreement, neither of them had mentioned Toro's blurted comment since leaving the cobra room. She had to assume Nemesis had heard the remark. The FBI had scrubbed as many photographs of her from news stories when she graduated Ranger school as possible, but someone with the kind of resources Nemesis had at his disposal could go far deeper than a Google search. What were the odds that every last image of her face anywhere on the web over the past four years had been expunged?

Operating on the assumption that her plans had gone to shit—always a prudent position—that meant any hope that Nemesis would stop the game had died as surely as Doc Tox. Despite his speech about how they were all a bunch of soulless mercenaries, Nemesis clearly didn't care who Dani was or what she did.

So be it.

Toro tore open the seal and pulled out the folded paper inside. She glanced around his shoulder to read a printed message.

BREAK THE RULES, MIRROR IMAGES ABOUND, BESIDE YOURSELF ANGRY, DOOR TO FREEDOM

They looked at each other. Dani read it out loud, still unable to make sense of it.

"This is bullshit," Toro said. "How the hell are we supposed to figure out what it means? It's nothing but a jumble of words."

"A word jumble," she said to him. "What if that's exactly what this is?"

Toro simply looked at her.

"This is written as groups of three words separated by a comma." She tapped the page. "What if the words are out of order? Or what if the letters are scrambled?"

Toro's eyes widened. "We have to unscramble all these letters? That would take forever without a computer."

"You're not wrong." She turned her attention back to the printed lines. "Still, we should stop trying to make sense of the words as a whole and look at them as separate pieces of information. Think of them as data points."

She couldn't explain to Toro that breaking down configurations— whether in language, numbers, or visual images—was her superpower. She had always had a gift for pattern recognition, and the Army had refined it. Her assignments with the Rangers had also given her the ability to discern and solve codes in life-and-death circumstances.

Like those they were in now.

"Why would there be commas after every third word?" she muttered to herself after a few moments. She started to get a sense of something floating just out of reach. "What if the phrases make no sense because they're not supposed to?"

"That would mean somehow the words do," Toro said.

And then it hit her. "Every third word is followed by a comma," she said, her excitement growing.

"Rules abound angry freedom," Toro said, reading from the paper. "I don't follow."

"Look at the first word in each phrase," she said.

Toro bent his head down again. "Break mirror beside door."

She grinned at him. "Now that makes sense, doesn't it?"

He nodded appreciatively. "Yes, it does."

She strode to the open doorway and peered outside, checking the corridor in both directions. "Don't want anyone sneaking up on us again."

She had allowed the cobra and the envelope to distract her long enough for Doc to get the drop on her. Never again.

Toro joined her, laying a palm against the warped surface of the mirrored panel adjacent to the doorway. "I can't feel a latch." He pushed against the perimeter of the panel. "It doesn't open when it's pressed either."

"The note said to break it."

"If that's what it meant."

She gave him a look.

He sighed. "All right. That has to be what it meant."

"We could shoot it, but I'd rather not announce our location."

Toro reached into his boot and slid out the butterfly knife. "When this thing is closed, the handle makes a decent hammer. I could smash it. But it's still going to make noise."

"Less than a gunshot," she said. "Go ahead and try with the knife."

Toro wrapped his hand around the handle and pulled his arm back.

"Wait," she said. "Make sure you only hit it with the metal. Keep your palm as far from the striking end as possible."

"You're worried about me." He lifted a brow. "You still love me after all."

He was trying to keep up the pretense in case Nemesis wasn't onto her, but Dani didn't see much point. "I just don't want you to get cut," she said. "We've got no first aid, and you're zero help to me if I have to carry your ass through this maze."

"Fine." He adjusted his grip and brought the end of the knife down hard against the center of the mirror, smashing a hole straight through.

They both peered inside.

"Can't see anything in there," Dani said. "Break out the rest of the panel."

They both turned their heads away to avoid flying shards as Toro punched repeatedly. When he stopped, a large section of the mirror was missing, with jagged pieces around its edges and more scattered on the floor.

Dani poked her head through the entry door to see if anyone was coming to investigate the source of the noise. Satisfied they were still alone for the time being, she watched Toro reach in and yank at a wrapped parcel duct-taped to the wall behind the spot where the mirror had been.

He wrenched it free and held it up to her. "Think it's a bomb?"

She rolled her eyes. "Don't give Nemesis any ideas." Then she answered his question. "If it is, we're already screwed. I'm no bomb tech, but I've probably had more experience with IEDs than you." She held out her hand. "I'll open it. You can wait outside the room if you're worried."

"And miss the potential for a grisly death?" He passed her the parcel. "No way."

He watched in silence as she began to unwrap the package.

"Attention, everyone." The baritone voice Dani had come to despise echoed through the space.

She and Toro froze, staring at each other.

"I have an announcement," Nemesis continued. "Two traitors are among you. The woman in the game with you is a spy. Because the bull brought her with him, I am putting a million-dollar bounty on both their heads. Of course, you have to survive and escape to collect." After a brief pause, the transmission ended with a parting shot. "Happy hunting, everyone."

"Obviously, Nemesis overheard your comment," Dani said, voicing her earlier conclusion. "And he doesn't care who dies."

"I fucked up," Toro said, dragging a hand through his hair.

Dani interrupted the apology that followed, which would serve no purpose in the battles to come and wasted valuable time. "You know the Colonel's crew," she said. "Is there any chance of reasoning with any of them about this?"

"Anyone with a gun will shoot us on sight," he said without hesitation. "If they don't have a weapon, they'll find another way to kill us."

She smiled. Nemesis had overplayed his hand. Toro—whatever his original intentions had been—was now fully committed to work with her thanks to the bounty. She did not share the thought with him, nor did she express her firm belief that Nemesis would live up to his name, creating more hazards and obstacles for them than anyone else. They both had targets on their backs, and an attack could come from any direction at any time.

"Something was odd about the announcement," she said to him. "Did you notice that Nemesis didn't use either of our names?"

He nodded but offered no thoughts on the matter.

"You were 'the bull,' and I was either 'the woman' or 'the spy,'" she said, pressing her point. "It's like he didn't want to identify us. There must be a reason, but I can't figure it out."

Toro shrugged. "We all go by nicknames or code names. Everyone knows who he was talking about. Makes no difference what we're called, does it?"

"Wait a minute," she said. "How would he know your code name?"

Toro blinked. "No clue."

"This is about your group." She thought back to the first announcement. "Remember when he said we were all killers?" At Toro's nod, she continued. "He knows exactly who you all are and what you do. I was an acceptable addition because he thought I was the same."

"Your point?"

"I want to know who Nemesis is and what's behind all this."

"That's a luxury we don't have at the moment," Toro said. "We can figure it out in our spare time if we ever find a way out of here. Right now I'm focused on surviving, and I suggest you do the same."

"I can multitask," she said. "Besides, I think learning what's really going on can only help us survive."

"Suit yourself," he said. "But you can't understand the mind of a madman."

Still bothered by the enigma that was Nemesis, she tipped her head toward the package still clutched in her hand. "Better find out what's inside before someone tries to claim the bounty."

CHAPTER 39

Wu sat beside Assistant Director Hargrave in the JOC at 26 Fed. Before leaving the Bronx, he had called his top cybercrimes specialist to get him up to speed on the new development, while Flint scheduled a briefing for everyone involved in the investigation.

Mouth open and eyes fixed on the wall screen, Hargrave slowly placed his mug of coffee on the conference table. "Did you see the size of that fucking snake?" he said into the silence that pervaded the room.

In all the years they'd worked together, Wu had never heard his supervisor utter an obscenity. That more than anything else he could have said betrayed the turmoil brewing underneath his tightly controlled exterior.

"At first I wasn't sure the avatars were Agent Vega and Gustavo Toro," Hargrave said. "But if anyone could handle a king cobra, it would be a former Ranger." He gave his head a disbelieving shake. "She was fearless."

"Unlike Toro," Flint said. "He did everything short of running out the door, screaming."

"Can't blame him," Hargrave said. "I don't like snakes, either, and that one was a monster."

"Well Toro sure as hell didn't run from the guy with the knife," Wu said before turning to Sanjeev Patel, the cybercrimes expert he'd connected with Axel Vega. Patel had followed Axel's instructions, using a computer unconnected to the FBI's secure server to access the game on the dark web.

"Can you show the assistant director the feed from earlier?" Wu asked him.

Patel, who had set up camp in the ops center, was positioned at the laptop he'd linked to the wall-mounted display they'd been watching. The oversize screen was also separate from any computer equipment other than the laptop.

"I managed to capture everything that happened from the very beginning," Patel said. "Looks like the game went live fairly recently, so I'm caught up." He reversed the recording at high speed, stopping at Wu's instruction.

"Vega and Toro were in one of the rooms, talking," Wu explained for Hargrave's benefit. "Then someone came in with a knife."

They all watched the scenario play out in silence. On the screen, it looked like Athena and the Minotaur were having a discussion when they were interrupted by a muscular man with a beard. His short tunic had an anvil on the front, and he carried a butterfly knife.

The encounter was brutal and short. Hargrave flinched when the Minotaur slammed the knife into the other avatar's throat twice.

"The son of a bitch didn't waste any time," Flint said.

"He did what he had to," Wu said. "It's hard to second-guess their decisions when we're out here."

The remark had been directed as much to Hargrave as to Flint. Everyone at the highest levels of law enforcement would scrutinize everything Vega and Toro did, and he wanted to plant the seed that they were operating under unprecedented circumstances right from the start.

He turned to Patel. "Make this a dedicated screen and link the feed directly to it. We need to have eyes on this twenty-four seven."

"Who's the guy with the knife supposed to be?" Hargrave asked. "The avatar looks familiar, but it's been a long time since I studied mythology."

"That's Hephaestus, sir." Analyst Jada Johnson spoke up for the first time since the meeting began. "God of fire and metalworking, among other things. He forged weapons for the gods."

Wu had tasked her with going through the various feeds to isolate each avatar and research the images to find the best match. All eyes shifted to the main wall screen, where she pulled up a series of pictures. Most of them showed a bearded man with heavily muscled arms, working at a forge.

"The picture of an anvil on his tunic clued me in," Johnson said.

"What's the point of avatars from mythology?" Hargrave posed the question to the room at large. "Why not just hide their identities with generic faceless figures?"

"You don't know much about gaming, do you?" Patel said, then quickly added, "Sir."

Wu took pity on the cybercrime specialist, who spent more time with computers than people. "Gamers are drawn to visually appealing characters with backstories of their own in a challenging environment," he said by way of explanation.

Patel nodded. "There's an aesthetic. The game has to be challenging, but it should look good too."

"So using characters from an existing universe makes them visually appealing and also gives them a recognizable history," Hargrave said, then gestured toward the screen. "Who is the one who got shot?"

Johnson spoke up again. "Thanatos," she said. "The personification of death. His black wings were the giveaway."

The figure lying on the floor looked like a Greek warrior with enormous, crumpled ebony feathers sticking out from under his still form. Johnson switched to an image of Thanatos.

Flint narrowed his eyes. "Hold on a sec. The caption says Thanatos was the god of nonviolent death. That doesn't sound right if he's supposed to be a killer."

An explanation occurred to Wu. "Unless he uses poisons rather than guns."

Flint turned to him. "You mean the one Toro called Doc Tox?"

Wu nodded. "Some toxins are really nasty, but others basically put their victims into a permanent sleep."

"You think the people trapped inside the game are all part of the Colonel's crew?" Hargrave asked.

"We haven't finished our analysis," Wu said. "Vega and Toro's avatars have a special meaning. The others might, too, and that could help us ID them."

"And maybe if we knew why the person behind this is fascinated by Greek mythology, that would help us ID the perpetrator," Hargrave said.

"Or perpetrators," Flint said. "It probably took a team of people to pull off something on this scale."

Wu disagreed. "It may have taken a group to retrofit the facility to support an interactive virtual arena, but how many people would be on board with creating a game where real people actually die?" He shook his head. "I'm sensing a deeply disturbed individual behind this."

"That's a lot of people for one person to control," Flint said. "And a lot of space."

"The Colonel and his team were lured into a trap," Wu persisted. "They walked right into the spider's web on their own. Once they were inside, one person could manipulate the environment using technology already in place."

Patel weighed in. "The tech is cutting edge. The avatars are being generated in a real environment, and the way they're done is beyond advanced. It's next-level stuff. The control system would be optimized as well. One person could do it, especially since there are downtimes for editing and uploading the feeds."

Wu got to the point that concerned him most. "If this is real, Vega and Toro are in constant danger."

"If it's real," Hargrave added, "they've both already killed people and will have to keep doing it."

"Every piece of data we've been able to gather points in the same direction," Flint said. "This shit is happening."

Wu agreed. They were watching it all play out, and there was nothing anyone could do to stop it. He had all the resources of the FBI at his disposal, yet he had never felt so powerless.

CHAPTER 40

Dani gently pulled back a corner of thick silver tape, gradually releasing its hold from the brown paper that covered an object roughly the size and shape of a brick. The wrapping fell open, revealing a box made of black plastic.

"It's got a small latch on the side," she said, flicking it open with her finger as the brown paper dropped to the floor. She held the box in the palm of one hand and lifted the lid with the other.

"It's a bottle of water," she said, reaching in to grasp it. "But there's something underneath."

"What's this thing?" Toro said, pulling the other item from where it had been tucked under the water, then holding it up as he frowned.

She recognized the cutting-edge technology instantly. "It's a new kind of gas mask."

Her unit had been issued similar masks on her last deployment. They were a fraction of the size of conventional ones and had highly sophisticated filters. The Army had been field-testing prototypes, which had proven successful. But how had Nemesis gotten his hands on one?

"There was a mask for each of us during the first clue, but we were forced to leave them behind." He glanced at her. "Now we get one back. Why?"

Dani read the dawning comprehension on his expressive face before sharing her own conclusion. "I'm seeing another round of airborne poison in our future."

She did not bother to point out that Nemesis was living up to his name. The first sign of smoke would pit her against Toro in a battle for the only means of survival.

She noticed him tuck the compact mask into the top of his boot without comment, a silent act that spoke volumes.

She looked away, annoyed with him for making the move so nonchalantly, and stooped to pick up the discarded wrapping paper. "Something's written on this."

Toro crowded close to her, anxious to see the printed words that had been concealed on the inside of the brown paper. She considered holding out on him, forcing them to confront the issue of the gas mask before moving forward, but decided to let it go.

For now.

She held the sheet in both hands, allowing him to get a good look. Sure enough, there was another clue.

GO THROUGH THE PORTAL THAT OPENS FOR YOU.

They had no sooner finished reading the words than a metallic clicking sound was followed by a section of the wall sliding to the side, revealing an entrance to another room. She hadn't realized it was a hidden door when she'd initially scanned the area.

Toro gave her a sardonic look. "Ladies first."

"So considerate of you."

"I know, right?" he said. "I'm such a fucking gentleman."

She steeled herself for surprises and made her way through the open hatch with Toro close on her heels. As soon as they both crossed the threshold, the door clanged shut behind them, locking them inside.

"I've never been claustrophobic," Toro said. "But this whole game thing makes me feel trapped and suffocated."

Part of their captor's tactics, no doubt. She felt the same oppressive sense of confinement Toro did but willed herself to remain focused on the task at hand. "Look at that wall." She pointed to the opposite side of the room and crossed the floor to get as close as she dared.

A row of seven small round hatches the size of dinner plates, each a different color, were set into the wall. A mounted screen above them glowed to life.

YOU ARE SEALED INSIDE THIS ROOM. YOU HAVE THREE MINUTES TO SOLVE THIS PUZZLE. IF YOU FAIL, YOU WILL DIE IMMEDIATELY OR REMAIN TRAPPED IN THIS ROOM. IF YOU CHOOSE TO DO NOTHING, POISON GAS WILL BE DISPERSED INTO THIS ROOM.

She caught Toro glancing down at his boot, no doubt checking to be sure the gas mask was still there. At least one of them might survive if they chose not to play.

"So we've got three minutes to solve this," she said. "We should assume the clock has already started ticking."

"I'm looking at seven round hatches," Toro said, standing beside her. "I'm assuming we open them."

"It would never be that easy," she said dryly. "There's bound to be a—"

Before she could finish the thought, new words appeared on the screen.

YOU MAY OPEN ONLY ONE OF THE HATCHES.
WHEN YOU DO, YOU WILL SEE A RED BUTTON
THAT YOU MUST PUSH. TWO OF THE RED
BUTTONS WILL DETONATE A BOMB. TWO OF
THEM WILL SHOOT POISON DARTS. TWO OF
THEM WILL PROVIDE FOOD, BUT LEAVE YOU
TRAPPED IN THIS ROOM. ONLY ONE WILL
UNLOCK THE EXIT AND ALLOW YOU TO LEAVE
UNHARMED.

She turned to Toro. "These hatches are painted all the colors of the rainbow. I wonder if that's how we're supposed to figure out which one to open."

Toro studied them. "You'd think we'd have more to go on."

"You see how it's set up so you have to stand within arm's reach to push a button?" she said. "Puts you square in the line of fire for either the darts or the bomb. Like the first devices after that little welcoming speech. It's damned clever—and efficient."

The screen changed again.

HERE IS YOUR CLUE:

CERTAIN DEATH LIES TO THE IMMEDIATE LEFT
OF THE FOOD. RED AND VIOLET HIDE IDENTICAL
THINGS. THE SAME IS TRUE FOR ORANGE AND
INDIGO. WHEN YOU'RE NOT SURE, THE BEST
CHOICE IS TO IGNORE CAUTION, AND GO.

A digital clock appeared above the words. It began at 3:00, then quickly showed 2:59, then 2:58.

"Three minutes," Toro said. "What the hell?"

"Shut up and let me think," she said. "This is a logic puzzle. We're supposed to use all the clues in those lines to figure out which hatch to open."

"And if we get it wrong, we'll get poisoned or blown up."

She began to pace, the movement helping her sort through possibilities. "Let's start with the constants and work toward the variables."

"The constants are the knowns?"

"Exactly. The red and violet hatches are on either end of the row, and they are alike. That means they both hide something deadly, or they both hide food. The same is true for orange and indigo, which are the next ones in. According to the first sentence, the two circles that cover the food have something deadly to the left of them." She turned to face the row of round hatches. "I'm going to assume that refers to our left as we stand in front of them."

"How can you be sure?"

"I can't," she said flatly. "But I've got to start somewhere, and we're running out of time." She recognized the signs of panic in Toro's demeanor. This is where her training and background worked in her favor. She had to get him to help her or, if he couldn't, then to be quiet. "Toro, I've had to figure things out while bullets have literally been flying all around me. I'm asking you to lead, follow, or get out of the way."

He crossed his arms and glared at her. So be it.

She turned back to the puzzle and began to mentally slot her conclusions into place. If she put the bombs on either end behind the red and violet hatches, that would satisfy the clue, because they would both kill her. If she placed the food behind the orange and indigo circles, that would work, too, because they could each have something deadly to their left. Assuming she was correct, only the yellow and green circles remained as the unknowns.

"We've got thirty seconds left," Toro said, apparently unable to hold his tongue any longer.

She held up two fingers. "I've got it down to the yellow and green hatches," she said. "But I can't go any further."

"Have you used all the clues?" he asked her.

Good point. She had not taken the last sentence into account. "When you're not sure, the best choice is to ignore caution and go," she muttered to herself.

Something nagged at the back of her mind. What was she missing? She had to be decisive, to ignore caution.

Caution.

She canted her head to one side. The yellow and green circles lined up like the lights on a traffic signal.

Yellow meant caution.

Green meant go.

"That's it," she called out to Toro.

"What's it?" He sounded equal parts leery and desperate.

"When you're not sure, the best choice is to ignore caution and go," she repeated for his benefit. "When you're driving, a round yellow light means caution. Green means go." She stepped in front of the green hatch. "The clue says to ignore caution and go."

Toro moved to lay a restraining hand on her arm. "What are you doing?"

"I'm going to open this hatch and push the button," she said calmly.

"If you're wrong—"

"Then you can haunt me in the afterlife." She tipped her head toward the clock. "We've got less than ten seconds. Do you have a better option?"

He dropped his hand and took a step back. "Go ahead."

He didn't duck down or distance himself from her. He was remaining in the kill zone beside her for a second time. Interesting.

She opened the green hatch, saw a bright-red button mounted into the wall, and pressed it without hesitation.

A moment passed.

Another heartbeat later, the exit door unlatched and slid open.

A disembodied voice emanated from above them. "I'm impressed."

They both glanced up to find the source of the sound, which was an overhead speaker. Dani noticed that this time she could not hear the words echoing down the halls. It appeared Nemesis was speaking to them privately.

"Impressed enough to make an offer," Nemesis continued. "But only to the Minotaur."

Dani saw her confusion reflected in Toro's face when she glanced his way. Apparently he believed the comment referred to him, but he didn't know why Nemesis had referred to him as a mythological creature.

She thought back to a course on mythology from her sophomore year, recalling that the Minotaur was imprisoned in a labyrinth because he had killed too many people. Since *toro* meant bull, and his profession involved murder, and he was currently trapped in a mazelike structure, the name was fitting.

For whatever reason, Nemesis was about to make an offer that excluded her. With a growing sense of dread, she concluded the announcement had something to do with the recent revelation of her true status as an undercover agent.

"I am prepared to cancel the bounty on your head if you kill your partner," Nemesis said. "I will explain to the rest of your group that she tricked you and that you had no idea she was a spy—which we both know isn't true—but they won't think you turned on them anymore. As a bonus, I will direct you to the closest location where another weapon, food, and more water are located. She's not going to get out of here alive. Why share her fate? Especially when you can be a free man. A very wealthy free man."

In the silence that followed the announcement, Toro slowly turned toward Dani, his gaze decidedly calculating.

CHAPTER 41

Wu braced himself for the next onslaught of questions from the assistant director. The JOC had become claustrophobic, and he longed to get out in the field and take action. Promotion demanded sacrifice, and the higher one went in the bureaucracy, the less hands-on investigation one did. Instead of finding his missing agent, he was directing others to do it.

And defending himself in the process.

"They've clearly been captured," Assistant Director Hargrave said. "But where are they being held?" He narrowed his eyes. "We've got to source the game, even if it is on the dark web."

Wu gestured to his cybercrime specialist. "We're going through the game to find where it's being hosted."

"The website is only accessible when the system is on, so that limits me to following cyber footprints while the game's being streamed," Patel said. "I put a system in place to record everything so we can retrieve it in case the files are deleted, but that doesn't help with tracking."

"What are you doing to hack into the game then?" Hargrave asked.

"I'm putting together a team of my best people," Patel said. "We'll monitor the site around the clock and write code to exploit any vulnerabilities and find a back door in, but we haven't had any success yet. Whoever is behind this knows what they're doing."

"What about proactive intervention?" Wu asked.

"We'll access the site and become subscribers, using some of the fake profiles we've set up. After we're in, we'll try to initiate a dialogue with the game's developer. At the very least, we'll sprinkle some fairy dust."

"Come again?" Hargrave said.

Wu, accustomed to Patel-isms, translated for the assistant director. "He means they'll seed the target server with tracking malware. If it works, they can use it to locate the originating IP address and follow other subscribers."

"Do we have a warrant for this?" Hargrave asked.

"Affirmative," Patel said. "And the AUSA is on board."

Wu had made sure Patel collaborated with the Assistant US Attorney's office. He'd also secured an agreement to temporarily seal the warrant to prevent the senator or anyone else from learning about it and taking steps to hide evidence. Even in exigent circumstances, Wu made sure they had followed the law.

Flint had been listening to the exchange. "You said the creator is sophisticated," he said to Patel. "How do you know he won't figure out the Bureau is behind those fake profiles?"

"To access the site, we'll use an anonymous browser that routes us through a series of proxy servers run by thousands of random individuals around the world." Patel lifted a shoulder. "Our IP address will be totally unidentifiable and untraceable."

"But you're going to infect the game with our own virus, right?" Hargrave asked. "Then you can shut it down so there's no audience."

Wu cut in before Patel had a chance to respond. "Even if we could, I'd argue against it. First, the game is our only way of knowing the status of our agent and our asset. Without it, we're completely in the dark. Second, we can keep trying to locate the game developer as long as we can access the site, and third, if we make the game useless, all the players might become useless."

No need to spell it out. Everyone understood the potential ramifications.

Hargrave blew out a frustrated sigh and turned to Patel. "You told us the feed is never livestreamed. What's the time delay?"

Patel shook his head. "Can't be sure." He gestured toward the screen. "Did you notice that sometimes you can see the whole structure, and other times it zooms in to cover the action in a given room?" He demonstrated with a few seconds of recorded video before continuing. "That's editing, but I can't be sure how long the gap is between when things happen and when we see them."

"Let's table the cyber search for a moment." Hargrave turned to Wu. "What else have you been doing to find Vega and Toro?"

Wu understood the subtext. He was in charge of the operation, and their safety was his responsibility. He had already failed once and needed to redeem himself. He'd been authorized to allocate any of the FBI's resources toward finding their missing personnel, and the assistant director wanted to evaluate how he was conducting the effort.

"Satellite images revealed no new data," Wu began. "The team of agents I sent to New Jersey combed the Pine Barrens, searching for the Suburban, and came up empty. Another team followed up with the used-car dealer, who was no more helpful after a search warrant than he was when Detective Flint and I paid him a visit."

"What about the cars coming from area garages?" Hargrave asked.

"I have Jada Johnson overseeing a group of analysts collecting and reviewing video feeds from cameras outside the parking structures," Wu said. "There are still hundreds of license plates to run through and cross match with various databases. It's a time-consuming process, and we'll follow up on any leads."

Hargrave frowned. "What else have you got for me?" he asked. "I'm jumping on a video call with Washington as soon as we're done here."

Hargrave would brief everyone up his chain of command all the way to the top, and he wanted to be prepared. Nothing would be more embarrassing than having Director Franklin or one of his deputy directors ask questions to which he had no answers.

"There are three options when you first access the site," Wu said, then waited for Patel to bring up the opening screen with buttons for PLAY, VOTE, and CONTRIBUTE. "Watching the game is free, but any other involvement is pay to play. I want Patel and his team to participate on all levels."

Hargrave's brows shot up. "You want us to transfer funds to the suspect's site?"

"It will provide another avenue for investigation," Wu said. "We can follow the money, especially if the payment is in some sort of cryptocurrency that can be transferred with a digital signature."

"That doesn't always work," Hargrave said. "I don't want us inadvertently funding a criminal enterprise."

Wu had anticipated pushback. There had been tragic instances in the past where the FBI and other law enforcement agencies had allowed money to "walk" by purchasing contraband, and the cash had disappeared into a black-market vortex. Although rare, these incidents grabbed headlines when they inevitably came to light, causing public scandal and internal investigations that had torpedoed promising careers.

He lifted his chin. "It's a risk I'm willing to take."

"How much?"

Wu gave Patel a significant look.

"I can't be sure until we access that part of the site," Patel said, taking the cue. "But from what I've seen so far, it looks like you can pay to vote for a specific avatar. The ones with the least votes face more challenges."

"It's a popularity contest?" Flint said.

"Sort of," Patel said. "Subscribers upvote and downvote. From what I can tell, it looks like avatars that are downvoted get punished in the game."

Flint paled. "Punished?"

"Everything's still in beta mode," Patel said. "Looks like the developer is attempting to gauge audience participation for now."

"It galls me to send money," Hargrave said, echoing Wu's own feelings. "But I agree we need to give Vega and Toro an edge while we figure out where they are."

"Speaking of which," Wu said, moving on to his next objective. "We're scouring the videos for clues in the background." He signaled Patel to pull up a freeze-frame of some avatars in one of the rooms.

"How do you know the environment is not a hologram projected on a blank background?" Hargrave asked.

"Because of the way the avatars interact with the space," Patel said. "The snake and the glass tank were both real; the guy getting electrocuted when he grabbed the metal bars was real, and so was the knife used to stab the other guy to death. Some of the stuff might be projected, but everything that requires physical contact is there."

Hargrave looked skeptical. "How can you be sure? I've seen movies and TV shows where—"

"Because of the glitch." Patel navigated to the point of the electrocution and zoomed in. "When that happened, more than just part of the human body under the avatar got exposed. You can also see the flooring and background for a split second. The physical space is a perfect match of what's represented in the game. It hasn't been visually modified like the players inside the game have."

Hargrave squinted at the screen. "Why didn't the developer edit this out?"

"He's had to review a lot of footage and might not have noticed." Patel shrugged. "Or maybe thought it was only for a second and it wouldn't matter, or maybe he figured no one was recording the video to go back and examine it closely."

A speck of yellow interrupting the gray background caught Wu's eye. "Can you expand the area in the upper right corner of the glitched space?"

Patel typed a series of commands into his computer, zooming in on the quadrant. The speck became a square with yellow and black.

Wu pressed him. "Can you make it bigger?"

"I'll expand it as much as I can," Patel said. "Any closer and the image will be pixilated."

Everyone leaned in close to study the yellow-and-black image that filled the screen moments later.

"That looks like the corner of a sign," Flint said. "But I can't make it out."

Wu thought about what kinds of signs might be posted. An idea began to take shape, bringing a fresh wave of dread in its wake.

He crossed the room to tap the screen. "This looks like the bottom of a capital letter, and this part of the image could be the edge of a trefoil."

"What's a trefoil?" Flint asked.

Instead of answering, Wu turned to Patel. "Split the screen and put a radiation hazard symbol on the other side."

In less than thirty seconds, Patel posted an image with three rings in a bright magenta design.

"Colors and design aren't right," Wu said. "Let's see an earlier version."

A rectangular sign with what looked like a three-bladed black propeller on a yellow background replaced the first image.

"I'll superimpose the radiation symbol over the video," Patel said, excited.

The room fell silent as he dragged the trefoil to overlay it on the corner of the captured video feed.

"It's close," Hargrave said. "But not perfect."

"Wait a second," Flint said. "My grandad lives upstate. He built a fallout shelter in the sixties. He hung a sign with a symbol that looked sort of like that."

"Here's a fallout-shelter sign," Patel said after a quick search.

This time there were three yellow triangles, their points touching in the center of a black circle.

"Same color scheme, same era," Wu said. "Unfortunately, there's not enough of the letter in the video feed to tell whether the sign says 'caution,' 'radiation,' or 'shelter.'"

"What are you saying?" Hargrave asked.

"The floors look like concrete, and the walls seem to be a combination of concrete and metal painted battleship gray, with some exposed pipes attached. There's no natural light coming into the frame, and the cage around the bare light bulb on the wall looks like something straight out of the Cold War era."

"So our current working theory is that they are in an underground space?" Patel said. "Like a midcentury nuclear facility or fallout shelter?"

"Even decommissioned nuclear facilities are strictly controlled." Hargrave looked dubious. "And a shelter would have to be massive to have that many rooms and corridors."

"It's the only actionable intelligence we have at the moment," Wu said, undeterred. He shifted his gaze to Johnson, who had been quietly working at her terminal during the briefing. "Can you get a list of fallout shelters built by the government during the forties through the eighties?"

"Why built by the government?" she asked.

"I can't imagine any private citizen or group with enough money to create an underground facility this big. It would take permits, engineers, heavy equipment, and hundreds of people to accomplish. That would add up to millions even back then."

"On it, sir." She bent back to her computer.

Hargrave gave him an appreciative nod. "I see your point. Keep me apprised of any developments."

Wu watched the assistant director leave, aware that he would be on a conference call to Washington within minutes. How would those among the highest echelon of law enforcement accept the knowledge that an FBI agent and the civilian she was responsible for were combatants in a deadly game? A contest watched by people on the dark web around the world, people whose votes sealed the fates of real human beings they believed to be virtual. What would happen if they discovered they were unwitting participants in a modern-day blood sport where real gladiators died?

Wu considered the gladiators who had fought in ancient Roman amphitheaters for the entertainment of crowds that gathered to watch. They were usually slaves, prisoners of war, or people condemned for committing crimes. The game's developer was making sure a crowd was watching, but Vega and Toro were not slaves or POWs, so what crime did he believe they had committed to earn a place in his coliseum?

CHAPTER 42

Dani turned to face Toro, prepared for an attack. She looked into his inscrutable dark eyes, unable to read his expression. She viewed the situation from his perspective and could see how a chance at freedom and a million dollars might make him reconsider their alliance. Time to set him straight.

"Thinking about taking Nemesis up on the offer?" she asked him. "Because you won't live to collect the bounty if you try."

"Got to admit," Toro said. "He made it tempting."

She gave him a mock pout. "And here I thought we were friends."

He visibly relaxed. "I'm not going to kill you," he said quietly.

"At least not yet." She made the statement lightly but wanted him to know she hadn't let her guard down despite his attempt at reassurance.

"You're right," he said. "Not yet."

"You suck, Toro."

"Back at you."

That settled, they made their way down the corridor, carefully checking each open door they passed. As soon as they turned the corner and started down another hall, metal bars slammed down behind them.

"What now?" Toro said, echoing her thoughts.

The walls around them slid down into the floor, disappearing to reveal a vast room.

And five other people split into two groups lining opposite walls.

Dani recognized Guapo, Jock, the Colonel, and two more of his men she'd seen at the hangar in New Jersey. She reflexively bent to pull the gun from the top of her boot, hiding it behind her back until she knew how the others would react. Based on the glares directed at her, she concluded none of the others had a gun, or they would have shot her where she stood.

She thought back to the announcement Nemesis had made to the others. He'd described her as a spy and condemned Toro for bringing her to their doorstep but never mentioned her affiliation with law enforcement.

Why not? What was he hiding?

She pushed aside thoughts of their captor's motives and scanned the area. They were divided into three groups, each on a different side of a much larger room. There was a metal ladder bolted to the wall on the fourth side, where no one was located. A bottle of water sat on the floor at the foot of the ladder, which led up to a balcony circling the perimeter of the room above them. She could also make an educated guess about the patchwork of metal squares covering every inch of the floor except the outer perimeter, where they were all standing.

Apparently their captor had herded them toward this spot for a confrontation. Coming from different directions, they were prevented from direct physical contact by the squares, which no one seemed willing to step on.

The voice Dani had come to dread reverberated through the space around them. "When the game began, there were thirteen," Nemesis said. "You are the only survivors. We'll see how many of you are left after the next challenge."

Dani looked around at the others and read her own apprehension in their grim expressions. Some of them would not leave this space alive.

"Your objective is to get across the room in one piece," Nemesis said, allowing a moment for them to absorb the implied threat before continuing. "As you may have guessed, the floor is covered in pressure plates. If you step on the correct squares, you can cross safely. Your reward is the water, but you have to get to it first. Once you do that, you can climb up the ladder to get to the next level. As you can see, there's no going back."

All paths of retreat had been blocked by bars. They were trapped together in a cage, forced to use their wits and cunning to escape the room or die trying.

"Your clue is on the message board," Nemesis said.

Words glowed on a rectangular sign beside the exit door.

IF YOU FOLLOW THE SEQUENCE OF THE SQUARES RATIONALLY, YOU'RE GOLDEN. IF YOU DON'T, YOU'RE TOAST.

Dani waited for more, but Nemesis had stopped talking. The oddly worded phrase must have some significance beyond the literal meaning.

"I can't believe we have to figure out another damned clue," Toro muttered to her, then called out to the others. "Why don't we work together for a change? We could all get across the squares and share the water after we get out of the room."

A derisive combination of laughter, obscenities, and rude gestures met his suggestion.

"You gave it a try," she said to him. "Can't say I'm surprised at their reaction. You and I are at the top of their hit list after Nemesis called me a spy."

She took advantage of her first opportunity to see the others in action. Their response to this situation would give her valuable intel about their capabilities and limitations. She and Toro occupied the side directly across from the ladder. The two men whose code names she didn't know were on the side to her left, while Guapo, Jock, and the Colonel lined the wall to her right.

Raised voices drew her attention. The two men on the left were shouting and pointing at each other.

"Guess they're having a difference of opinion about how to proceed," Toro said to her. "We're all used to working independently. When we're together, the Colonel's in charge."

"Only this time, the Colonel isn't on their team," she observed.

As a Ranger, she'd been trained to follow orders but also to lead others and to operate independently when necessary. These two knew little about teamwork and were rudderless without a leader.

She glanced at the Colonel, who watched the argument in silence, flanked by Guapo and Jock. His gaze shifted to her, and she sensed the frank appraisal in his hard expression. He seemed to view her as more of a threat than the others. If he knew her true background, he would have been even more concerned.

Before she could dwell on the Colonel any further, the squabble between the two men on the left escalated. Without warning, one of them planted his hands on the other's chest and shoved. The second man screamed, arms windmilling as he keeled over backward.

The instant his body touched the pressure plates, the air sizzled and crackled with high-voltage electricity. His entire body spasmed and jerked until the current stopped, apparently switched off from a control room somewhere in the facility. They all stared as smoke curled up from the man's inert form.

If she had known their argument would go this far, she would have pointed her gun at the men and ordered them to stand down. Now the man who had pushed his cohort was alone, and there was nothing to be gained by revealing that she had a weapon, a trump card she would keep up her sleeve as long as possible.

"Like I said"—the cold, flat voice of Nemesis filled the room again—"if you fail, you're toast."

The sound of Jock's retching—and the scent of charred flesh—permeated the space.

"The pressure plates around the body reset automatically," Nemesis said as a final warning.

"And then there were six," Guapo said loudly enough for everyone to hear.

His exaggerated air of casual indifference to the carnage did not fool Dani, who detected an underlying note of strain. As much death as the man might have caused or witnessed over the years, she doubted he had ever seen anything like this. On the other hand, her background had given her a front-row seat to some of the most despicable violence human beings could visit upon each other, and she kept her composure.

To her, the way to survive both the game and the immediate problem was to stay calm enough to use logic. Panic reduced the ability to think, especially in abstract ways. An accelerated heart rate and rapid breathing disengaged higher mental processes in favor of basic survival instincts. This particular puzzle called for more advanced problem-solving.

The others must have come to the same conclusion. The Colonel had beckoned to Guapo and Jock, calling them into a huddle to strategize. They kept their distance from each other, though, unwilling to gather close enough to risk being shoved onto the plates.

She felt the corner of her mouth lift in an ironic smile as the Colonel frowned at his men. They were members of the same group, but they were not a team. They had no trust, no allegiance, no loyalty.

She turned to Toro. "When Nemesis said we'd be toast, he meant it literally."

He nodded. "You think the rest of the clue is literal too?"

"I've noticed a pattern," she said. "Nemesis chooses words that can be interpreted different ways."

"If you follow the sequence of the squares, you're golden," he repeated from the clue.

"If you follow the sequence of the squares *rationally*," Dani corrected. "That must mean there's a logical order to the arrangement of the pressure plates."

She let her conscious mind recede, allowing individual words to stand out.

"A logical order is a progression," she muttered. "And golden. Another odd word choice."

"It's a common enough expression," Toro said. "When you're golden, you're good to go. You can cross safely."

"There's another thing," she went on, disregarding Toro's comment, sinking deeper into her own thoughts. "Nemesis said to follow the *sequence* of the squares, not the placement or the pattern."

A distant memory that had been floating in her subconscious broke through to the surface. After their father died, she and her siblings had moved in with their aunt and uncle. Axel became distraught. Therapists did their best, but Dani was often the only one who could soothe him. She understood him in a way others didn't.

Even as a young boy, Axel loved math. Dani instinctively sensed that rational equations gave him a feeling of control in a world that had become chaotic. Math problems could be solved. They made sense, while feelings often did not.

When he was at his worst, Dani would sit with him and take him through mathematical progressions, which calmed him and refocused his attention. His favorite was the Fibonacci sequence, which was both easy to grasp and complex to calculate in his head. Its simple elegance was also beautiful when graphed out on a chart.

She turned to Toro. "The Fibonacci sequence." She could not mention anything about her brother while Nemesis was listening. The less he knew about her family, the safer they would be.

Toro lifted a quizzical brow. "The what?"

She dropped her voice. "The Fibonacci sequence is closely related to the golden ratio." She waited for him to appreciate the significance of the words. "It's a mathematical progression. Basically, you start with zero and one; after that, you add the two numbers to get the next one in the series."

"I don't follow."

"Zero plus one equals one," she said. "Now you have three numbers: zero, one, and one. You add both ones to make two. Then you add the last two numbers, which are one and two, that makes three. Again, you add the most recent two numbers, which are two and three, and that gives you five."

Toro's face showed comprehension. "Then you add three and five to get eight." When she nodded, he smiled. "You think that's the pattern of the squares?"

"I do," she said. "The only problem is to figure out where to start counting them."

They both looked at the rows of pressure plates.

"There's nothing else in the clue," Toro said. "Maybe there's something different about one of these plates."

"We're looking for zero," she said, casting her gaze across the floor. A single polished metal plate stood out from the rest, which were all brushed steel.

She pointed it out to Toro. "The shiny one over there," she whispered.

He followed her gaze. "If that's zero, how do we jump to it? It's too far away."

"Remember how we were wondering where to start?" she said. "This room is laid out as a rectangle. Now that we know where point zero is, we can use the Fibonacci sequence to chart a spiral using the squares. There will be a point at which a part of the spiral will intersect with each edge. That's the place where we take our first step. It's ingenious, because it doesn't matter which side of the rectangle we're on, we can all follow the equation to travel to any other side."

"Maybe you'd better do the math," Toro said. "You've done it before."

She focused on the shiny square and began her count. She had charted many beautiful symmetrical spirals with her brother. This would be no different. Taking her time, keeping her breathing steady, she kept count until she reached the point of intersection.

"This is the plate," she said to Toro.

"Let's just make sure," he said, taking off his boot. He dropped it onto the plate. Nothing happened.

The intercom above them crackled to life. "The plates are only activated with at least a hundred pounds of pressure," Nemesis said. "You cannot cheat by dropping an object on them to test them."

Guapo, who had been about to copy Toro's move, cursed and pulled his own boot back on. They all should have known Nemesis would thwart any attempt to defeat his carefully laid trap. He wanted to see them suffer and die, and his bloodlust wouldn't be satisfied with anything less.

Toro looked at Dani. She noticed the others watching her as well. They could not have overheard the whispered conversation she had shared with Toro, but they realized Dani had a theory and was about to put it to the test.

This was her idea, and she would be the one to try it. She surreptitiously tucked the gun back into her boot to free her hands, making it easier to balance, then double-checked her previous count and came to the same point of intersection. She would be proved right or wrong. She braced herself and placed her foot firmly on the pressure plate.

Nothing happened.

Toro exhaled a noisy breath he'd probably been holding since she had started to take the first step. "You must be right," he said to her. "I can follow in your footsteps."

"What about us?" Guapo called out to her. "Are you going to leave the rest of us here?"

Her spiraling path along the pressure plates would take her to a contact point with each of the other sides. She would soon be within their grasp.

Or within shoving distance.

Toro's eyes traveled to her boot, then back up to her face. He raised an inquiring brow. His suggestion was clear. Why not use her gun to hold them all at bay while the two of them crossed the room?

She had already decided to use that tactic as a last resort. There was only one round left in the magazine and one in the chamber. She couldn't take them all out. Once she fired twice, everyone would see the slide lock open after the second shot and know the gun was empty, ending her ability to bluff her way out. She had to save ammo in case of a firefight later.

If she could gain their cooperation, she wouldn't have to give up the element of surprise that came with her tactical advantage. Never let the enemy know your full capabilities. Let him believe he has the advantage . . . until it's too late. She would outmaneuver the others, and they would never know it.

It would do her no good to solve the problem only to have one of the others topple her onto the plates to fry like the first man. This required cooperation. Not trusting them in the slightest, she used her only leverage.

"I've figured out a solution," she announced. "But none of you will ever leave this room unless you follow in my footsteps, which means you have to let us go first." She gestured to Toro and then to herself. "When we make it to the other side, we'll take the water and leave."

"No deal," the Colonel said. "According to Nemesis, you're a spy."

"You're taking the word of someone capable of all this?" She swept a hand out to encompass their surroundings. "I thought you were smarter than that."

He glowered at her. "I'm smart enough to know not to give the enemy an unfair advantage."

Toro leaned close to her and dropped his voice. "I think we should tell them."

Toro wanted to reveal that she was an undercover FBI agent. Nemesis already knew that fact but hadn't told the others, which meant he didn't want them to know. Was he afraid they would side with her? Protect her? Not hardly. These were hardened criminals. Mortal enemies to law enforcement.

So why hide her status?

Dani considered whether doing the opposite of whatever Nemesis wanted might improve her situation—or at least thwart his plans. Up to this point, she'd been in reactive mode, forced to deal with each threat as it came. Time to go on the offensive.

"That's a big gamble," she whispered to Toro. "It could backfire."

He had suggested the move, but she felt the need to warn him anyway. There was no going back from this decision.

"Everything and everyone in this place is actively trying to kill us." Toro rested a hand on his hip. "How exactly is our situation going to get any worse?"

Point taken.

For the first time, her position as a law enforcement officer could work in her favor. Unlike the rest of them, she had rules to follow. Rules that prohibited her from killing in cold blood. They would instantly understand her limitations.

"I'm not a spy," Dani said. "I'm an FBI agent." She allowed a moment for them to digest the information before elaborating. "Nemesis found out a while ago but didn't want you to know."

The Colonel narrowed his eyes on Toro. "You sold us out to the Feds?"

She found it interesting that he didn't question her claim. He was ready to believe it without proof. The others would likely follow his lead.

"You would have cut bait if you knew I'd gotten caught," Toro said to the Colonel. "Like everyone down here in this hellhole right now, I did what I had to."

"Maybe we wouldn't be here if it weren't for you," the Colonel shot back.

Now they were getting somewhere.

"What if it's your fault?" she said to him. "Maybe you and your band of merry men took out the wrong person. Ever stop to think that's why you're here?"

The Colonel crossed his arms. "Of course I have."

She pushed harder. "Only you have too much blood on your hands to know which assignment—"

"I know which assignment," he said, then seemed to recall himself and snapped his mouth shut. "For all the good it does us."

So Nemesis hadn't targeted them because they were paid assassins. The Colonel had just admitted that this was retribution for a specific case. Perhaps determining what case that was would lead her to learning the identity of their captor, and that knowledge might help her escape. Or not.

"Maybe we can figure out the pressure plates on our own," Jock called out to her. "Then we don't need you or your fucking badge."

"You don't have a chance." She let out a derisive snort. "You'll die trying."

Everyone remained in a silent standoff for a long moment as they recalibrated their options based on the new information. That, and they were each trying to figure out a way to double-cross her after she led them safely to the other side.

"Deal," the Colonel finally said.

One by one, the others echoed his agreement. She waited until each one of them made eye contact with her and acknowledged them in turn. Aware this was a temporary cease-fire rather than an alliance, she proceeded to the next plate.

Slowly she made her way to the side that connected with the Colonel, Guapo, and Jock, who fell into line behind Toro. Her balance and coordination were excellent, and she was pleased to see the others had no trouble trailing her. She reached the side with the man who had pushed his comrade to his death, and he joined the growing line after Jock.

They were nearly to the exit side. This would be the most dangerous point of the crossing. Dani jumped over the last plate to get to the bare cement floor, rushed to the ladder, and spun to face the others, who were leaping one by one onto the floor close by.

The man who had pushed his partner was the last to step onto the closest plate. He had started to make the jump when Guapo turned and lashed out with his booted foot, kicking the man's chest. The look of shock and dismay at the betrayal was the last thing Dani saw before he flew backward, landing on the squares behind him.

"That's enough," Dani shouted over the crackle of forking electrical currents doing their work. She bent to pull her gun out and leveled the sites on Guapo. "One more move and you'll join him." She made the rules clear. "Stopping you from killing others qualifies as justified deadly force."

Guapo raised his hands in mock surrender. "Just thinning the herd a bit. The guy was an asshole anyway."

The cold brutality of his comment disgusted her, as did the certainty that Nemesis had enjoyed the show. Two more of their number were dead, and the air was redolent with the scent of charred flesh. To make matters worse, she had showed her hand to the Colonel, who now knew she had a sidearm.

"Toro and I are leaving," she announced, covering the others with her weapon. "Give us a sixty-second head start before you leave this room. While you wait, you can decide whether you're going to kill each other."

There would probably be more of what Guapo called "thinning the herd" after she left, but there was nothing she could do about that. If they had no honor, she could not force it on them.

She turned to Toro. "Let's get out of here."

They had both defied Nemesis. First, Toro chose not to take him up on the offer of a bounty to kill her. Next, she had revealed a secret about herself that he had kept hidden. The question in her mind wasn't whether they would be punished, but when and how.

CHAPTER 43

Wu saw the same exhaustion he felt reflected in Patel's features. Normally smooth, the cybercrime specialist's youthful face bore lines of fatigue. Apparently Wu wasn't the only one who had spent the night at his desk.

"Give me your report and then go home and get some rest," he said to Patel. "You're dead on your feet."

Wu had called another "all hands on deck" meeting at the JOC, anxious for updates from agents assigned to run down leads. He wanted to hear from Patel first because the cybercrimes team had been watching Vega and Toro in the game, upvoting both at every opportunity, using numerous fake profiles designed to look like they originated from different countries.

Patel began with the most critical information. "So far Vega and Toro are okay," he said. "But remember that the game isn't being livestreamed. We can't tell what's going on at any given moment."

"So we don't really know anything about their status," Flint said, turning toward Wu. "It's like you said before: we see what he wants us to see and hear what he wants us to hear."

There were times the avatars must have been speaking to each other, but their faces didn't move and there was no sound. They must have been saying something the game's developer did not want the audience to hear. At other times, everything the characters said could be heard, but through a synthesizer that altered the voices beyond recognition.

"We've made progress." Patel's air was defensive. "Have a look."

They all turned to the wall screen, which flipped to display footage captured from the game.

Three men dressed in armor straight out of ancient Sparta strode down a corridor.

"The one in the center is Ares," Patel said.

Wu had no trouble recognizing one of the most famous Olympians. "The god of war."

"We did some digging," Patel said. "You remember that Vega's avatar is Athena?" At Wu's nod, he continued. "There's an important distinction between the two. Athena is the goddess of war and wisdom. She is an expert strategist and leader. Ares, on the other hand, represents the sheer violence and brutality of war. She's all about discipline, and he's all about bloodlust."

"I wonder if the game's creator knew how close he was to the truth about Vega," Flint said to no one in particular.

"What about the two avatars with him?" Wu asked. "They're identical except for the color of the crest on their helmets."

The pair of soldiers flanking Ares had similar armor, complete with breastplates and metal head coverings obscuring all but their eyes and mouth. The top of their helmets had a spiked row of dyed horsehair down the middle. One of the soldier's crests was solid black, the other red, and Ares's crest was striped red and black.

"That's one of the reasons we're sure this is Ares," Patel said. "He's often shown with his twin sons, Deimos and Phobos. Deimos is the god of terror, and Phobos is the god of panic. When they march into battle with their father, the enemy breaks ranks and runs."

"Who are these guys in real life?" Flint asked.

Wu had his suspicions. "Let's start with Ares," he said. "The war god would represent someone brutal and violent. A man with plenty of blood on his hands on and off the battlefield. A man with subordinates who create fear while he inspires bloodlust."

Patel met his gaze, and understanding passed between them. "The Colonel."

Wu inclined his head in acknowledgment. "The teams of agents at his apartments in DC and Manhattan haven't seen any sign of him. He's MIA."

"Then the others in the game are his crew," Flint said. "Which means this has something to do with Nathan Costner's murder."

Wu wasn't ready to follow him down that path without more evidence. "We know the Colonel and Toro were involved in the murder," he said. "And Toro believes an operative called Doc Tox synthesized the poison used. Beyond those three, we can't prove anyone else was in on the conspiracy."

He had been struggling with the complexities of the investigation all night after a midnight call on a secure satellite phone with Paul Wagner, the DHS agent overseeing the Colombian angle. Wagner wasn't making much headway, and they both agreed it was because Senator Sledge's insistence that cartels were behind the hit was pure misdirection.

"We can't rule out coincidence," he said. "What if Costner had a business on the dark web, and he ripped off the wrong people? Whoever is behind the game took his revenge, and now he's cleaning house."

Flint frowned. "He's killing off the people he hired so they can't ID him?"

"But why that bizarre hit on Costner?" Patel said. "An exotic toxin that can only come from Colombia?" He shook his head. "Just kill him and be done with it. Better yet, bump him off and make it look like an accident. If it works, there's no investigation to contend with."

"Nothing about what this guy does is simple." Wu pointed at the screen. "Look how elaborate the game is. He could put a bullet in each of their brains, but instead we get a multiple kidnapping and a sadistic game."

The room grew quiet as everyone contemplated the dilemma.

"You know what this feels like?" Wu decided to share his conclusion after a night of careful consideration. "Revenge. At the bottom of all this is a personal grudge. We'll find out who's behind it by digging into the private lives of every player we've identified so far."

"We've already done that," Flint said.

"Then dig harder," Wu said. "Something connects these people, probably a past crime."

Patel's dark brows drew together. "If the original crime went unsolved, we'll never find the link."

Wu refused to give up. "If that's what happened, then we'll have to solve the old case and the new one at the same time."

"Without knowing where to look?" Flint said.

"Start with Colonel Treadway," Wu said. "It's time to execute that sealed search warrant we've been keeping in our back pocket."

"You want this on the down low?" Flint asked.

The FBI had teams trained to gather evidence without leaving any sign that a search had been conducted. Evidence Recovery Team members would defeat security measures, unlock doors, and take dozens of photos of the space before touching anything. The search itself would be meticulous, with each item replaced in its exact position to match the pictures.

Wu nodded. "I'm sending in the special ERT. Don't want Senator Sledge to know we're getting close to him yet."

A man with the kind of power and influence Sledge had could make trouble for their investigation. In fact, he already had. Right now he believed the FBI was partnering with DHS and the DEA, chasing down the story he was pushing about Colombian cartels. When he found out his closest allies were under a spotlight, Sledge would know they were circling around him.

Like a cornered rat, he would lash out in every direction, and Wu was certain to be in his crosshairs, professionally and perhaps literally, judging by what had happened to the senator's chief of staff.

CHAPTER 44

Dani checked both ways before entering the narrow corridor after climbing the ladder to the next level up. Toro raced ahead, apparently anxious to put distance between themselves and the others. They turned a corner and quickly scaled a flight of cement steps. The metal door at the top swung open, surprising her.

"This is almost too easy," she said to Toro. "After forcing us together, Nemesis is letting us spread out again for some reason."

"Maybe he knows if we all stay together, the game will be over quicker," Toro said. "Can't stop all the fun too soon."

That could explain their situation, but she still sensed a trap. Her instincts had saved her life in the past, so she chose to heed her blaring internal warning system.

She noticed tiny red lights at regular intervals above them.

"Look at this," Toro said, pointing his chin at the metal rungs of another ladder, this one leading up to a closed hatch in the ceiling. "We'll never get out of here if we don't keep going up."

"I'll check it out," Dani said, pulling out her tactical hair clip and tossing it against the metal to see if it was electrified. When nothing happened, she picked up the clip and shoved it back in her hair before wrapping a hand around one of the rungs.

Toro stayed below, watching her scale the ladder. When she got to the top, she reached up to grasp the latch.

"It's locked," she called down to him.

"You sure?" he said. "Try pushing harder or see if there's a second release."

She climbed back down and gave him a look. "Have you been paying attention?" She gestured around. "This whole thing is about solving puzzles and fighting to survive while trying to escape."

"You're saying we'll have to solve a clue to unlock the hatch." He made it a statement.

She glanced around the corridor. "First we have to locate the clue."

They both walked down the passageway, looking high and low. There was a metal pipe attached to the wall with brackets above their heads. She hadn't paid much attention to it before but now saw three black plastic buttons in a row above a section of pipe, almost blocked from view. Each button had a cartoon drawing of a monkey etched in white.

Toro came up behind her and studied the buttons. "What do you think happens when you press them?"

"Something unpleasant . . . or they could unlock the hatch," she said. "But it won't be anything straightforward." She turned to him. "Give me a boost. I'm going to get a closer look before we touch anything."

He interlaced his fingers and held out his hands. She put a booted foot onto his palms and steadied herself against the wall as he heaved her upward.

"You look lean," he said, grunting. "But you must be solid muscle."

"Suck it up, Toro. If you drop me, I'll get up and kick your ass."

"Yes, ma'am."

She focused on the buttons and saw nothing distinguishing about them except the monkeys. The first monkey was covering its mouth with its hands, the second covered its eyes, and the third covered its ears.

She felt along the pipe. The edge of her palm hit something, dislodging it.

"Something fell," Toro said. "Looks like a folded piece of paper." She hopped down and stooped to pick it up. "This will be a clue."

FOLLOW THE ANCIENT JAPANESE PROVERB. MIZARU, KIKAZARU, AND FINALLY IWAZARU WILL GUIDE YOU. OUT OF ORDER, THE MONKEYS BRING YOUR RECKONING, FOR YOU HAVE COMMITTED ALL MANNER OF EVIL.

"Looks like Nemesis is still dishing out retribution," Dani said. "We only get one chance to push the buttons in the right order."

"This is the whole 'see no evil, hear no evil' thing," Toro said. "I never knew it came from an old Japanese proverb."

"Neither did I," she said. "And I didn't know the monkeys had names. How are we supposed to tell Mizaru from Iwazaru?"

"If I had my cell phone, I could answer that question in about ten seconds," Toro said. "But there's no way to look it up. Maybe we're supposed to guess."

"So far Nemesis has been all about logic and deductive reasoning," she said. "Let's try that before we start pushing random buttons."

"Are they always shown the same way?" Toro asked. "Because I don't recall what order they're normally in."

"How about the order of how much most people use each of their senses?" Dani asked, thinking out loud. "People who have use of their vision tend to rely on it most, so it would be first."

"Working that way, hearing would be next," Toro said. "Then talking."

"That's not the way the monkeys over the buttons are lined up," she said. "Which makes me think we're onto something. Nemesis wouldn't put them in the correct order."

"Unless he was using reverse psychology."

"I don't think so," she said.

Toro's brows went up. "Are you willing to bet both of our lives on that?"

"This may be the only way up to the next level," she said. "Which means we've got to deal with it sooner or later. I vote for sooner." She raised her hand to the buttons and paused to give him the same opportunity she had before. "I understand if you want to go down the hall and wait to see what happens. At least one of us should survive. There's nothing keeping you here."

The offer was genuine, but she also meant it as a test to find out if his loyalties had changed after their last deadly encounter.

"I'll stay," he said quietly.

She reached out and pressed the button in the middle first, then the third button, and finally the first.

She let out a long, slow breath as a loud electronic click sounded, and the bolt slid back from its place in the hatch.

"Let's go," she said to Toro. "It may lock again soon."

He followed her up the ladder. This time, the hatch opened easily. Instead of swinging open, the round metal covering slid sideways, recessing into a slot in the ceiling. Facing another tactical problem, she pulled the pistol from her boot. Poking her head up through the open hole would make her vulnerable to anyone waiting above to ambush her.

She reached down to Toro with her free hand. "Hand me the knife."

"What do you need with—"

"Just do it." She wiggled her fingers impatiently.

The closed butterfly knife slapped into her palm, and she brought it up. A quick flick of her wrist opened the grip, exposing the polished metal of the blade. She raised her hand up through the opening. Using the reflective metal surface like a mirror, she rotated the knife around. The room above them looked like the rest, with the exception of a rectangular work bench situated in the center.

Taking no chances, she climbed out quickly and did a better threat assessment. Toro was already making his way onto the floor beside her when she finished and put the pistol away.

"Looks like a dead end," she said, handing him back the knife. "There's no exit. We'll have to go back down and find another way up to the next level."

Before she took two steps, a loud clank stopped her in her tracks. The hatch they had just climbed through had sealed itself shut.

"It's probably resetting," Toro said. "So no one gets inside without solving the clue."

"I still have the piece of paper in my pocket," she said. "It'll be pretty damned hard unless the clue is replaced, or if there's another copy hidden somewhere else in the passageway." A sense of foreboding stole through her. "Or what if no one else is supposed to make it in here because this room is a trap?"

Toro started to respond, then froze.

She heard it too. The steady hiss of gas. She looked around and saw plumes of grayish-white mist rolling toward them in waves across the floor.

"Get up on that bench," she said to Toro, flinging her body onto a metal stand in the middle of the room. Staying away from the fumes may only buy them a few seconds, but it was all they had.

Toro landed beside her, and they both got to their feet to keep their heads as far away from the surging vapor as possible. He bent to pat the side of his boot with urgent fingers. When he straightened, he held the gas mask they had found in the mirror room earlier. Their eyes met.

There was only one mask.

CHAPTER 45

SAC Wu leaned back in his swivel chair and stroked his jaw, giving his full attention to the woman sitting in one of the two chairs in front of his desk. He had widened the circle of people involved in the investigation to include Dr. Portia Cattrall, who headed a contingent of the Behavioral Analysis Unit assigned to the New York field office.

Dr. Cattrall had spent the past several hours reviewing video captured by Patel's team, as well as background on Toro and Vega. She had also gone over information the task force had unearthed about Colonel Treadway and Senator Sledge.

"In my opinion, whoever created the game is not psychotic," she said. "There are other mental health issues at play, but he's in full control of his faculties."

Cattrall had sifted through all available reports, deriving conclusions in preparation for the briefing Wu had requested. She'd made it clear her findings could not be definitive at this point but that she would provide whatever assistance she could.

"You believe one person is behind this?" Wu asked, interested to hear confirmation of his own assumption.

"I do," she said. "The person behind this was traumatized at a critical phase in his youth. I get a sense of arrested development."

He fished for actionable information. "What kind of trauma?"

"Hard to say," she hedged. "But computer games are more than mere entertainment for him. He's both merged and submerged in a world of his own creation. A world where he is in charge."

"Then why not just kill his enemies outright?" Wu asked.

"That's the whole point of the Greek-mythology angle. The gods toyed with humans. They usually didn't kill them outright, often manipulating them toward their own demise using their character weaknesses."

"Those inside the game lived by the sword, so they are forced to die by the sword," Wu said, considering her words. "But this feels very targeted. Very personal. What if one or all of them killed the wrong person? Someone the game developer loved?"

"I came to the same conclusion," she said. "Going to these lengths has all the earmarks of revenge. The Colonel and his group were lured there for a reason. Whoever is behind this did not simply abduct random people off the street."

"That means he would have to know the Colonel somehow," Wu said. "Treadway is the link that connects this whole chain. He has worked with Senator Sledge; it's his crew that was captured. We're still going through everything that was confiscated during the searches of both his residences, but the early report from the ERT doesn't reveal anything of value so far. They're compiling a list of everyone he's had dealings with."

"I'll help analyze whatever you come up with."

"What's your assessment of the Colonel?"

"The dossier from military intelligence was interesting," she said. "He was trying for brigadier general but never got that promotion. Instead, the Army quietly forced him to retire."

Wu had read the report too. The Army had used its policy requiring personnel to promote to stay in. Combined with limits on the percentage of officers who can serve above the rank of captain, the cards were stacked against Treadway when he was poorly rated by those serving both above and below him.

"I think he used the contacts he had gained during his last assignment at the Pentagon to gain money and power denied to him in his military career," Cattrall added.

He had certainly succeeded. He'd spent several years becoming an influencer in DC and a conduit for government contractors. Now those who had blocked his promotion had to come to him for access.

"His military history and reports helped to build a psych profile for the Colonel," she continued. "One of the reasons he was not promoted to general was his willingness to do anything to win." She paused for emphasis. "Human rights and the health of his troops took a back seat to his need to come out ahead."

"He was an overbearing asshole," Wu summarized. He had his own experience with such leaders, referred to in the Bureau as "blue flamers."

She gave him a sardonic smile. "Precisely. He was feared but not respected."

"It's safe to assume the Colonel would be her biggest threat inside the game," Wu said, thinking out loud.

"Or Toro, if he double-crossed her."

Wu grimaced. "We've all been concerned about that, but I'm hoping he won't because . . ." He trailed off, unsure whether to voice his suspicions.

"Because he's attracted to Agent Vega," Cattrall finished for him.

He should have known a psychologist would read the signs, but he was surprised she'd been able to do it without the benefit of close observation that he'd had when they first arrested Toro.

"I saw clear signs in the video from inside the game," she went on. "He talks a lot of smack, but he stands by her when it counts. When their lives are on the line."

"So she only has all the other homicidal maniacs out to get her," Wu said. "I almost feel sorry for them."

Thoughts of Vega's physical prowess and intelligence reminded him of the other reason he had sought out Cattrall's input.

"When an opening came up in the JTTF, I requested Vega to fill the vacancy," he said. "At the time I was focused on her background in special forces and code breaking and didn't go too deep into her personal life. Now I'm concerned about the toll all this will take, considering what happened to her."

"I was wondering when you'd get around to that," Cattrall said with a knowing look. "I reviewed the police report, and it was far worse than what came out in the news."

"Vega was only seventeen at the time," Wu said. "The police withheld a lot from the media to protect her and the other children. Everyone knew her mother killed her father, but they didn't know Vega had walked into the middle of it."

The NYPD report indicated young Dani Vega had walked home from Bronx Compass High School in the afternoon and entered her family's apartment on Benedict Avenue to discover her father lying on the living room floor. Her mother had been kneeling over him, clutching a bloody butcher's knife later determined to be from their kitchen.

Dani had rushed to disarm her mother, who collapsed in hysterics, and tried to resuscitate her father. She had called 9-1-1, and the call taker had talked her through CPR while dispatching first responders. Police and EMTs had arrived to find Dani trying to save her father, and her mother catatonic.

"I spoke with her mother's treating psychiatrist at Bellevue this morning," Cattrall said. "Camila Vega is beginning to show signs of improvement, but she's still not communicative. Her IQ tests out in the top two percent, but she has a history of being emotionally unstable. He has gathered from Camila's family that she was abused as a child in some way. No one will talk about it."

"Their three kids were sent to live with their aunt and uncle," Wu said. "They have an apartment on a different floor in the same building." He recalled the meeting with Erica and Axel that had cracked the case wide open. "I met her aunt, who I gather was not fond of Dani."

"The aunt is her father's sister," Cattrall said. "She told the psychiatrist she never liked Camila. She obviously transferred her resentment onto the only target at hand . . . the daughter who reminded her of the sister-in-law who murdered her brother."

Wu didn't waste his breath pointing out that it wasn't fair, instead focusing on how this could impact his agent. "I can see why she joined the Army at eighteen."

"She seems to have idolized her father and wanted to follow in his footsteps," Cattrall said. "Pushing herself to attain the same elite status he did tells me she wanted to prove she was her father's daughter—not her mother's."

Wu understood more than he was willing to share. Constantly in the shadow of his older brother, he was on his own relentless campaign to prove himself to his family.

"But things went to hell overseas," Cattrall continued.

According to military records, Vega was deployed to assist a Ranger unit tasked with disrupting an overseas terrorist cell. After enemy combatants were taken into custody, she deciphered coded messages written on scraps of paper in their compound. Unfortunately for everyone involved, she did not decode the materials fast enough.

Within minutes, explosives detonated in the room where two members of the team were guarding the prisoners, killing all of them. Vega, who was among those injured in the ensuing collapse of the building, told her FBI applicant investigator she held herself responsible. One of the scraps she was examining contained coded information about remotely detonated devices placed in the building. If she could have deciphered the information faster, she could have evacuated the building.

Wu thought Vega was being hard on herself, but the mission had resulted in her return to the States for a lengthy recovery, during which she completed her bachelor's degree in an accelerated program. She healed fully during that time, returning to Fort Benning to earn her scroll, becoming one of a small contingent of women to earn the distinction. She was assigned to the 75th Ranger Regiment, where she served honorably until her tour of duty ended.

He posed the question that had been nagging at him since he'd delved deeper into her files. "How would someone with Vega's history react under these circumstances?"

"Our applicant psych eval detected evidence of PTSD, but not substantial enough to prevent her from executing her duties as a federal agent," Cattrall said. "Of course, her current case is not anything close to a typical assignment."

A monumental understatement. Vega was trapped in a closed environment, thrust back into a combat situation where she was forced to kill others and witness their grisly deaths, knowing all the while she could be next. What would that do to the psyche of a combat veteran?

Wu's admiration for her only grew as he learned more about her. The fact that she had gone through as much as she had in her life spoke to an enormous inner reserve of strength, but everyone had a breaking point. Would Vega reach hers in the confines of a brutal game?

"I'm also concerned about you," Cattrall said to him. "You're showing signs of stress and fatigue. When is the last time you slept?"

Her observation disturbed him. "I'm fine, Doctor. I'll sleep when my agent and our asset are safe."

She gave him a long look, letting the silence stretch between them. "You may outrank nearly everyone in this building," she said. "But I can go to Assistant Director Hargrave and let him know your judgment may be compromised by extreme exhaustion."

"You can't do that."

"I can and I will if you don't level with me."

He blew out a frustrated sigh. "I haven't been sleeping much, but I catch quick naps in here when I can."

"You're working around the clock because you hold yourself responsible for their capture." She made it a statement rather than a question.

His shoulders slumped a fraction. "It's on me," he said quietly. "All of it."

He would face a formal inquiry from the Office of Professional Responsibility. They would find him responsible, and he would accept whatever discipline came his way. His only shot at redemption—from the Bureau as well as from his own conscience—was to get Vega and Toro back safely.

CHAPTER 46

Dani considered their predicament. Toro had the mask and the knife, but she had the gun. They were both standing on a bench that formed an island surrounded by a sea of thickening haze that continued to rise. Soon the room would be filled with whatever toxic gas Nemesis had released.

She flipped through a mental catalog of various gases described in her training and immediately thought of several that were lighter than air and would therefore rise in a confined space. None of this gave her confidence, and she shut down that avenue of thought. It did not serve either of them.

"Looks like only one of us gets out of this alive," Toro said, apparently coming to his own conclusions on their dilemma.

As they locked gazes, she ran through every conceivable scenario, discarding one idea after another. They could not share the mask, which had to be properly sealed to remain effective. If her guess about the gas was correct, it was an extreme irritant to the eyes and sinuses as well as the throat and lungs. The mask would become contaminated if exposed to the airborne particles, rendering it useless to both of them if they tried to swap it back and forth.

She had spent thousands of hours learning how to adapt and overcome in the most dangerous circumstances. Survival, the most primal instinct, screamed for dominance.

But she was more than her primal instincts. She was Daniela Vega, FBI agent and former soldier.

She was also the daughter of a murderer. She had been forced to kill many times and had just done so again mere hours ago.

Recalling her earlier conversation with Toro, she considered what made her different from him. And then she knew.

She lived by a code.

Part Ranger, part FBI, part personal, she had developed her own core values. When she had accepted this assignment, that included responsibility for Toro. She had to answer for his actions, and she also had to ensure his safety to the best of her ability while they worked undercover together.

Nemesis wanted to demean and demoralize them, watch them scratch and claw like animals in a pit. She refused to debase herself for someone else's amusement.

She finally broke the silence. "I'm not going to shoot you and take the mask, if that's what you're asking, Toro."

"Didn't think you would." His gaze shifted away, putting the lie to his words. He stared at the mask in his hands without putting it on.

"It's not going to do you any good unless it's on your face," she said. "And it has to stay tightly sealed."

He still didn't move. The gas crept higher, spreading across the room. He seemed to be having some sort of inner battle.

He held the mask out to her. "Put it on."

She stared at him, stunned. "I told you I wouldn't take it from you."

"And I would have fought you if you tried," he said. "But you didn't. So now I'm giving it to you."

She found herself in a quandary as the mist reached their knees. It went against her training, her core beliefs, and everything she stood for to save herself and watch someone else die in her place. Even if that person made his living as a hired gun.

He thrust the mask into her hands. "Take it, dammit. I've been a shit my whole life. Never believed in anything other than money. Never had any regrets . . . until now."

She sensed his resolve but couldn't understand it. "Are you sure?"

"You already have honor. Give me the chance to do one honorable thing before I die." He hesitated. "Just do me a favor."

She closed her hands over the mask. "What's that?"

"Find Nemesis and stop him. Lock him away forever, or, better yet, kill the son of a bitch."

He had given her a mission. A mission greater than herself that demanded her survival. He must have figured it was the only way she would do something so antithetical to all her beliefs. And he'd figured right.

She lifted the mask to her face. "He won't get away with this," she said, pulling it over her head and tightening the straps. "I promise."

The gas rose to their chests, then above their heads. She grasped Toro's hands, which were trembling. There was nothing more to be said.

Watching him closely, she wondered what his first reaction to the gas would be. Would he convulse and fall from the bench into the fog that now covered the entire floor like a thick blanket? Would he retch? Would he . . .

She kept watching and saw no sign of distress. "Are you okay?" she asked, her voice muffled by the mask.

"Other than needing a fresh pair of boxers, I'm all right," Toro said.

She gave it some thought, then reached behind her head and loosened the straps.

"What the hell are you doing?" Toro shouted.

She slid the mask off. "I was just thinking the gray mist was covering the floor like a thick layer of fog when it came to me." She gestured around. "This is water vapor. It's harmless."

"What?"

"Nemesis likes to play mind games," she said. "Torment us into choosing who will live and who will die."

"He forced us to say goodbye to each other," Toro said, breathing hard. "For his fucking entertainment."

Right on cue, the latch opened with a clang that reverberated through the room. Nemesis was watching and listening.

Dani cut through Toro's colorful stream of expletives, redirecting him to focus on the mission. "We have to go back down through the hatch, and you need your head in the game. I have a feeling the next surprise won't be harmless."

CHAPTER 47

Nemesis paced across the control room, teeth grinding. A quick check of the video feed revealed that Daniela Vega was a problem. The woman was changing the dynamics of the game. Her growing legions of fans were skewing the data.

Toro had looked at Vega with something more than admiration. They had pretended to be a couple. Were they starting to fall in love for real? Maybe that was why they were both getting so many upvotes.

Star-crossed lovers. Pathetic.

Some women flirted and strutted, manipulating men at every turn, but Vega seemed to have no clue she was beautiful. The spandex suit clung to her athletic feminine form, and even though the viewers couldn't see her body through the avatar, Toro certainly could.

And Vega's avatar had turned out to be strangely accurate. Athena, goddess of wisdom and war, of strategy and logic, was among the most popular in the Greek pantheon. Her persona in the game was proving to be just as charismatic.

Vega was winning the competition and gaining more fans in the bargain. Nemesis had no military background, but the Colonel and Vega were demonstrating what that kind of training and discipline could do. Everyone inside had blood on their hands. They all knew how to kill. But only two of them were battle tested. They were the most dangerous.

Orchestrating a meeting between them would make for a great show. Then it would be simpler to deal with whoever survived that encounter.

Hopefully it would be the Colonel. He deserved special retribution for what he had done. After all this time, no earthly court would convict him, so trial by combat would give him what he deserved. Treadway should die alone, broken, and humiliated, exactly the way he had made others feel.

If it came down to Vega and Toro instead, they would find themselves on the receiving end of another dilemma, and this time one of them would die.

CHAPTER 48

Dani watched the vapor in the room dissipate. Nemesis had finished toying with them for the moment. Now that she literally and figuratively had a moment to breathe, Dani paused to consider the driving force behind the torment. This went beyond revenge. It was obsession.

If she could understand how this all began, perhaps she might figure out who Nemesis was. Calling him out by name might put a stop to his plans. At the very least, if she knew who she was dealing with, she could personalize everyone involved. Nemesis could no longer hide behind an invisible voice, unseen and untouched, and manipulate them like toy soldiers. He would come out from behind the facade and become a real person, which meant they would be real people as well.

Worth a shot.

How could she put a name to the creepy voice that had set her teeth on edge every time she heard it? It dawned on her that cracking the case was like cracking a code. Begin with the known, and work toward the unknown. What did she know?

To put it in military terms, she was collateral damage, not the primary objective. The Colonel and his group had been the targets.

She glanced at Toro. "How many assignments did all twelve of your group go on together?"

"You think you can figure out who Nemesis is," he said. "I've already thought of that, and it's a dead end."

"Humor me."

He frowned in concentration. "I remember three missions with the whole team."

"Describe them."

"The first one involved getting technology from a rival developer."

"Corporate espionage," she said, refusing to gloss over the crime. "What tech did you steal?"

"You make it sound so ugly," he said with mock indignation. "A firm in Silicon Valley was working on new software for a cloaking device. We were hired to find out how far they'd gotten along. The turnaround was short, so we had no time to get someone on the inside. We had to break into their off-site lab. Very labor intensive."

"Who hired you?"

"Only the Colonel knows the identity of the client," he said. "But it turned out the company that hired us was actually ahead of them, so technically we didn't steal anything."

"Which company did you break into?"

"Quasardyne Enterprises. They went out of business a few years later. They were gambling their whole future on getting that DOD contract."

"What were the other two jobs all of you had as a team?"

"One was a sabotage operation. We introduced malware into the operating system of a company called Zetaform. They're out of business now too."

"Why did that take the whole group?"

"They had tons of security and on-site secure servers unconnected to anything online. We had to get into their physical premises to upload the virus."

"I guess when there are millions at stake, there's no low you won't sink to." She shook her head. "What was the third contract?"

"Kidnapping."

"Who the hell did you kidnap?"

"You've heard of Oscar Brinkley?"

She nodded. "Tech billionaire." Images of news headlines flooded back to her. "Were you guys behind that fiasco?"

"*Fiasco* is the right word," he said, glancing down. "It was supposed to be a ransom job, but it turned into a murder."

"His wife was killed, and his daughter was returned unharmed— physically anyway," she said. "But the case went cold."

"They were both supposed to be returned for ten million each."

"What happened?"

"When Brinkley didn't cough up the ransom right away, the Colonel shot the mother," he said in a neutral tone, as if there had been a slight hiccup in an ordinary business transaction. "After that, he paid up to get his daughter back." He stopped, eyes widening. "Brinkley called in the FBI."

A sense of growing momentum rushed through her as connections began to click into place. "What did the Bureau do?"

"They fucked everything up," he said. "Tried to track the wire money transfer. We figured that out pretty damned fast. In fact, that's when it happened."

"When the Colonel shot Brinkley's wife?"

Toro gave her a quick nod. "I was standing in the room when the Colonel came in. He didn't say a word, just walked over and drilled a round right into her forehead."

Dani felt her lip curl. "I would call him an animal, but that's an insult to animals."

She slotted this detail in with the other information. She had never read the FBI files on the case, so she was working from memories of media reports.

"I'm assuming you don't know who the client was?" she asked Toro.

"Like I told you before. It's our job not to know."

"Even when it involves an innocent woman and her child?" She glared at him. "But why should I be surprised when you were willing to kill a girl to get away from me?"

He held up a hand. "No one was supposed to get killed during the kidnapping. It was strictly a financial transaction. That's why we all needed to be involved. It takes a lot of people to abduct two people and control them for days on end." He dragged a hand through his hair. "Then we had to return them, only that changed into returning only one of them."

"This had to be more than just a money grab," Dani said. "Was Brinkley's company about to secure a government contract?"

If a rival corporation was competing against him, disrupting his personal life with a ransom demand would be a way to throw him off his game and make a profit in the bargain.

"No idea," Toro said.

She was missing key information. "There must be more, can you—"

A blast of sound cut off her words. After a long, loud tone Dani recognized as an emergency alert signal, a bulb mounted to the ceiling and resembling the cherry light on an ambulance began to rotate. She felt Toro move close to her as the room filled with an eerie red glow. Putting her back to his to cover the space, she scanned the area. A small rectangular screen high on the wall's digital display went from 00:10 to 00:09.

"Countdown clock," she said.

Toro turned to follow her gaze. "What the hell happens when it gets to zero?" he said, looking for threats.

"We're not staying to find out," she said, moving toward the hatch set into the floor. It had unlocked moments ago, and she hadn't heard it reset. Nemesis obviously didn't like where their conversation was going. Dani took that as a sign they were getting close to something, but whatever they were on the verge of figuring out would have to wait.

00:07

"It's unlocked," she said, trying the handle.

A bright circle of fluorescent light from below appeared when she yanked open the round door.

"Follow me." Holding her gun in the low ready position, she began to climb down the metal ladder. "I'll clear the area."

She didn't want Toro to believe she was evacuating herself from danger first. Fully aware of their predicament, she suspected Nemesis might have guided the other captives toward them before flushing them from their concealed position. She was exposed going down the ladder, and there was no way to take the time necessary to proceed safely. The damned clock was forcing her to choose which risk she thought was worse.

00:04

"Clear," she called out to him. "Get down onto the ladder and close the hatch behind you."

Whether it was more poisonous gas, an explosive device, or another dangerous creature about to be set loose, they would be better off with a metal door separating them from whatever Nemesis was about to unleash.

00:02

Toro's booted feet appeared as he climbed down the ladder. She kept her back to him, continuously scanning for threats. Overhead, the hatch clanged shut, cutting off any retreat.

"What the hell was that about?" he said, sucking wind.

"Another head game? A real threat? Who knows?" she said. "Either way, it was our cue to leave." She glanced at him. "Let's find another way up to the next level."

Ultimately they all had to get to the surface. The space was vast, but there could be only a limited number of ways to do that. She gave Toro a hand signal, and they went down the hall back to back, watching out for each other.

They walked past a pair of corridors, one branching off on either side, after peeking around the corners first to make sure they were empty. Dani was just thinking that two people were less than ideal for clearing a large building when a dark figure stepped out from around the corner ahead of her.

In less than a second her sights were leveled directly on the Colonel's chest.

He had managed to find a gun, and it was trained on her. "This has been a long time coming," he said, smiling.

CHAPTER 49

Dani faced the Colonel, each in a tactical stance, pistols aimed directly at the other. A classic standoff. She hadn't known he'd located a firearm, and then recognized it as the Sig Sauer she had brought with her. She had to assume it was loaded.

The weapons they were finding in the game had been planted by Nemesis after he confiscated them. Now a pistol she was responsible for was about to be turned against her.

Unless she could stop it.

According to protocol, she was supposed to identify herself as a federal agent and give the suspect a chance to surrender. She'd already taken care of the first requirement, but the second could get her killed. She stalled for time to come up with a plan.

"You've got twenty years on me," she said to him. "My reaction time is faster than yours."

"I've got twenty years more experience," he corrected. "And action is always faster than reaction."

He was threatening to shoot first. If he did, he would likely hit her before she could move. Her best option would be to shoot from a stable position an instant before diving to one side. Despite what action heroes did in the movies, she knew that trying to hit her target while in the process of jumping out of the way would likely result in a missed shot, and she had only two rounds.

The Colonel moved a step closer.

She heard Toro, who was beside her, take a step back.

The Colonel was a tactician. He threatened to fire on her but hadn't done it yet. She could think of only one reason why.

"Where are Guapo and Jock?" she asked, refusing to address him by his former military rank or call him "sir." He deserved no such respect.

"We parted company." He edged closer. "Decided to split up after we found a cache of weapons and ammo."

Toro backed up again, instinctively retreating.

She held her ground, certain the Colonel was advancing on their position to maneuver them into an ambush. There were countermeasures she could take, but how could she warn Toro without giving up the element of surprise?

She took one step back, careful not to let Toro get too far away from her to hear her whispered command, then spoke in her softest tone. "Stop."

Toro froze.

The Colonel flicked a glance in his direction. "What's this?" he asked Toro. "Taking orders from your girlfriend now?" He paused a beat before continuing. "Or should I say your handler?" Accusation sharpened his words. "You know what happens to snitches, don't you?"

If he was telling the truth and they were all armed, the Colonel would have sent Guapo and Jock down the other two corridors they had passed. While he distracted her, his men could approach unseen from either side, trapping them in a pincer movement.

She had no doubt the Colonel had employed the classic military tactic in the past, but always with troops who had drilled in the technique. Guapo and Jock were lone operators. If she played this right, she could use their lack of training to her advantage and lure them into a cross fire. Since she didn't have enough ammunition to take them all out individually, subterfuge was her only option.

She and Toro would be exposed to gunfire as well, but her plan was their best option under the circumstances. She had a split second to decide whether to follow standard FBI protocol or act according to her military training and neutralize the threat immediately. Taking out the leader might temporarily disorient the men who had looked to him for guidance.

She processed multiple factors at the same time, and a part of her understood that Nemesis had created a grand finale by directing the Colonel to their location after making sure his group found weapons.

This was not entertainment. People's lives were at stake. Toro had shown himself to be loyal. He had been willing to sacrifice himself for her. She could do no less for him.

That included taking a bullet if necessary.

Toro was the only one without a firearm. He would have to follow her instructions without hesitation, or he would die. Whatever trust they had built would be critical in the next few seconds.

"Back up slowly," she said to Toro, then dropped her voice to a whisper. "Be ready."

While she held her position, Toro crept backward. The Colonel's grin confirmed her suspicions. He believed they were falling into his trap. She sold the deception by keeping her sights trained on the Colonel, who would assume she was covering their retreat.

She made out the faint shuffling of boots from the corridors behind Toro. She adjusted her earlier plan, realizing she would need to move while firing after all.

The unmistakable *snick* of a safety being released was her cue. One of the men hiding in the corridor behind her was preparing to shoot.

"Get down!" she called out to Toro as she launched herself toward the ground and squeezed the trigger, praying that thousands of hours of repetitive firing drills had honed her skills enough for the nearly impossible shot.

The Colonel staggered backward. The round had hit him square in the chest. As he began to crumple, his hand reflexively clenched with his index finger on his trigger. The cacophonous boom of the gun's report in the empty space rivaled the noise of the weapon she had just fired.

Everything seemed to happen in slow motion as she hit the floor on her stomach and rolled onto her back, weapon now aimed in the opposite direction toward Guapo and Jock, who had emerged from the corridors behind them in a sneak attack.

Jock was already down, motionless. As she had hoped, they had all gotten caught in a cross fire. The Colonel had shot his own man, and she wasted no time acquiring her next target, ending Guapo's wild shooting with a single round to his forehead.

The haze of smoke curling from her Glock's muzzle cleared enough for her to see Toro, who was off to her right, double over and collapse. She jumped to her feet and rushed to neutralize all threats before aiding her fallen partner.

She secured each weapon as she went to check on the Colonel, Jock, and Guapo, finding each man lying motionless in a widening pool of blood.

She ran back and fell to her knees beside Toro. A hole in his upper abdomen oozed crimson.

His eyes fluttered open when she pressed her hand against the open wound. "No good." The words came out in a hoarse rasp.

She had experience with field dressings but had no med kit handy. She picked up his hand and placed it where hers had been.

"Press hard," she commanded.

She fished the butterfly knife from his boot and cut a section of spandex from his sleeve into a long strip, then shoved it under his hand, stanching the flow.

"I'm a lost cause," he said on a groan. "Remember what I said before?" When she didn't answer, he grabbed her arm with his free hand. "Find Nemesis. Take the bastard down."

She could tell by the red bubbles frothing at the corners of his mouth that the bullet had perforated a lung. The hollow-point round would have expanded to ping-pong around inside his body, causing massive internal damage. The rounds had been designed for law enforcement to avoid the bullet passing through the intended target and striking innocent bystanders.

"Promise me," Toro said. "Now."

His gaze locked on hers. She knew what would happen if she agreed. But she did it anyway.

"I promise," she said quietly.

He coughed up a thin trickle of blood. "There's something you should know." His eyes drifted closed.

"What is it?"

This time, his eyes opened only halfway. "That kid in front of the subway," he said. "I was bluffing. There was only one dose in the umbrella."

She recalled chasing him through Federal Plaza, when he had pointed the end of his folded umbrella at a young girl standing in front of the subway entrance. After he'd been caught, he had claimed the umbrella was loaded with three lethal doses of frog poison.

In his final moments, Toro wanted her to know he was not the monster she had thought him. For whatever reason, he could no longer bear the idea that she would think of him as someone who would take the life of an innocent child. Why did he care what she thought?

His mouth worked, forming words she could not hear. She bent down closer and turned her ear toward his lips.

"I wish . . ." He coughed again. "Wish I was different. Maybe we could have . . ."

She felt him squeeze her arm one more time before it dropped to his side. Throat tightening with emotion, she laid two fingers across his neck and found no pulse. His heart had stopped pumping.

The heart that had finally come to terms with everything he had done, everything he had been, everything he had given and taken in this life. He had declared himself ready to die earlier, and she had believed he cheated death. But death had merely been waiting for the moment when neither of them was prepared.

She wanted to scream, wanted to shout at the uncaring walls around her. Instead, she forced herself to her feet.

She had a promise to keep.

CHAPTER 50

Wu continued to watch the wall screen, unable to tear his eyes from the spectacle playing out before him. They had all watched Athena lead the Minotaur, followed by Ares, Deimos, Phobos, and another mythological figure Johnson had identified as Hermes around a minefield of electrified pressure plates, and then around the body of Zelos, whom Hermes had killed at the beginning of the scene. After Phobos pushed Hermes to his death, the field of avatars in the game had dwindled to five.

Vega had been brilliant, and his admiration for her had grown with each obstacle she overcame. He could not step inside the game and help her, but he could damn well make sure he did everything possible to find her.

"Where the hell is Johnson with that report?" he asked Patel, who was hunched over his computer at the far end of the table.

Patel's head popped up. "She went to the bathroom, sir."

Wu turned away, unwilling to let others see how annoyed he was becoming with himself. People had to go to the bathroom now and then. It wouldn't help for him to snap at his team because of his own frustration at their lack of progress.

They had researched scores of fallout shelters going back decades, but none had panned out. Doubt had crept in, and he was concerned they were spinning their wheels while Vega battled for her life.

Meanwhile Patel and his team had chased the cyber bread crumbs down too many false trails to count. The money they had spent upvoting Vega had disappeared into a black hole, never to be seen again. They had not been able to bait the game's creator into a dialogue, and the so-called fairy dust Patel had attempted to sprinkle had vanished.

"It happened again," Patel said, cutting into his thoughts.

Wu picked up on a note of excitement he hadn't heard in a long time in the cybercrime specialist's voice. "What happened?"

"More glitches." Patel froze an image on the secondary screen that linked directly to the dedicated laptop he used to access the game on the dark web. "Each time someone fell onto the pressure plates, it must have overloaded the system for a split second. You can't see it with the naked eye, but I had a hunch based on last time, so I went back through the recorded video of that scenario frame by frame. Took me an hour, but this is what I found."

Wu leaned forward. "Expand it."

Patel zoomed in on the section with pixilated edges around a clear section of background. The undisguised space was far larger than the first portion he had found.

"Right there," Wu said, leaping to his feet to rush toward the monitor mounted to the wall. "Make this part as big as you can without distorting it." He tapped the screen with his index finger.

When Patel expanded the rift, a wide section of one concrete wall filled most of the viewing area. "See that in the corner?" he said.

Wu saw it too. "The same black-and-yellow trefoil," he said. "Only this time there's enough to know what it is."

Now he knew why they hadn't had any luck chasing down fallout shelters.

Flint, who had been on the phone with the ERT leader at the scene of Colonel Treadway's DC apartment, muttered something and disconnected. "That looks like a symbol for nukes," he said. "And you can see the last three letters of the word above it are I-O-N."

"It's a radiation warning symbol," Wu said. "And you're right . . . it's used at nuclear sites. The I-O-N could be the end of either 'radiation' or 'caution.' Both have been used on signs like these in the past."

"Then it wouldn't be at a fallout shelter," Flint said.

Wu shook his head. "Just the opposite. A shelter is the last place you'd see a warning sign like that. They're designed to keep radiation out."

Johnson, who had come back from the bathroom during the discussion, weighed in. "You said nuclear sites were heavily regulated, so I excluded them from my search parameters." She wore a pained expression. "We've been looking at the wrong set of data."

He didn't need the reminder that his remark—although well intentioned and accurate—had delayed their progress. "That was my call," he told her. "And we still can't be sure that sign is anything other than decoration."

"I don't think so," Patel said. "Why decorate something you plan to cover up with a computer-generated background?"

Wu heaved a sigh. "You wouldn't." Before he gave a new order, he scanned the screen again, looking for more information. He revisited his earlier thoughts about who would build such an elaborate structure. The space was massive, yet paradoxically confined and claustrophobic.

"You think if you stare at it long enough something will click?" Flint asked him.

"None of it makes sense," he admitted. "This must have cost millions to build, especially when you consider the electricity, climate control, and security features."

"I've never seen anything like it," Flint said.

Something caught Wu's eye. "What's that set into the wall on the left edge of the screen?"

Patel panned to the left and enlarged a different portion of the image.

Flint followed his gaze. "Looks like part of an air lock."

Wu turned to Johnson. "What kinds of buildings have air locks?"

Johnson's fingers flew across the keyboard. "Space stations, underwater research centers, clean rooms, hyperbaric chambers . . ." She glanced up. "Anything that needs to be pressurized or restrict the flow of air." She lifted a shoulder. "Some newer office buildings are installing them to reduce their carbon footprint. It's easier to keep heating and cooling costs down with an airtight vestibule at the entrance."

"I think it's safe to eliminate space stations," Flint said, deadpan.

Wu knew he was on to something, but it was just out of reach. "The facility they're in doesn't have windows. The walls, ceilings, and floors are made of cement. This is no modern office building."

"That danger sign looks antique," Flint said. "Like something from an old James Bond movie."

"You're right," Wu said, getting to his feet. "In fact, everything we've seen in the background could have been teleported from the Cold War era." He studied the screen for a long moment as realization slowly dawned. "I've got an idea."

He had to test his hypothesis before taking his theory to the assistant director. He wasn't concerned about further damage to his career, but he didn't want to waste more precious time running down a lead that went nowhere.

He checked to see if the team would arrive at the same conclusion he had. "What kind of facility was built in the fifties and sixties, mostly of concrete, with air locks, had its own power and water source, and would be nearly invisible to satellites or air reconnaissance?" He paused. "A place that would have held radioactive components at one time, but those components are now gone?"

The irony of the situation was not lost on him. Just like Vega, they were trying to solve a puzzle with limited clues in a race to save lives.

No one answered for a full minute; then Patel's eyes widened in sudden comprehension. "A missile silo."

Wu pointed at Patel in silent acknowledgment before shifting his gaze to Johnson. "Get me a list of every decommissioned missile silo in the US."

Johnson rushed back to her seat, Patel on her heels. He sat beside her, and the two began collaborating.

"There are Nike, Titan, Atlas, and Minuteman sites sprinkled throughout the country," Johnson said. "The Nikes were surface-to-air, so they were partially aboveground."

"Eliminate those," Wu said. "This is a total stealth operation. If I'm right, this entire complex is subterranean."

"It's a fairly extensive list," she said. "I'll put it up on the wall screen."

Perusing the rows of data, Wu instantly saw the problem. "This list is historical and all inclusive. I'm looking for silos that have been sold to private individuals or organizations."

Rows of sites disappeared from the screen.

"That only leaves about forty total," she said.

"Give me the names of the purchasers," Wu said. "Something's bound to pop."

The door to the JOC opened and Assistant Director Hargrave walked in. "Washington is asking for a progress report," he said to Wu.

He had hoped to delay sharing the new theory until he had something solid to go on. "We're running down a potential connection."

He went on to explain his idea as Hargrave looked increasingly skeptical.

"You think someone bought an abandoned missile silo and converted it into their own personal underground coliseum?"

"In a word, yes," Wu said.

Before he could argue his point further, Johnson spoke up. "I have the names and addresses of the buyers."

Bless her timing.

"Put it on the screen," Wu said, then scanned the fresh data. "Run those names through all databases and see if anyone has a criminal record."

"There's no need," Hargrave said, following his gaze. "I recognize the name of the person who purchased the Titan II silo outside Tucson, Arizona." He turned to Wu. "And you should too."

Wu looked again. Then he saw it. "Oscar Brinkley."

He felt the visceral snap of a missing piece fitting into place. Brinkley had been through a terrible ordeal ten years earlier. He had suffered the kind of trauma that could break a man's spirit. Or twist his mind.

"You mean Oscar Brinkley, the tech billionaire?" Flint asked.

Wu nodded. "Brinkley's company holds government contracts," he said. "Which could be the key to how this whole situation started." When the others merely looked at him, he went back to the beginning. "Before Senator Sledge's chief of staff was killed, Nathan Costner left a coded message with his best friend accusing the senator of taking bribes. What if Brinkley found out his competitors had paid the senator kickbacks to influence the DOD to award contracts to them?"

"You think Brinkley was the one who sent the coded message to Costner?" Hargrave said.

"He would have the technology to digitize the evidence and hide it in the photograph of Sir Arthur Conan Doyle," Wu said. "And he wouldn't want to publicly point the finger at Sledge, because he still deals with other elected officials."

"Suppose you're right," Flint said. "What does this have to do with the Colonel and his crew stuck in a death match?"

"The Colonel facilitated DOD contracts," Wu said, excitement building as he fleshed out his thoughts. "Maybe Brinkley discovered he also facilitated the bribes?"

"Colonel Treadway was the bagman who got the money into the senator's accounts in the Cayman Islands?" Flint asked.

Wu nodded. "When Costner failed to expose the senator, Brinkley captured the Colonel and his crew."

Patel's dark brows furrowed. "Why would he bother with the team of assassins?" he asked.

"I have a theory about that too," Wu said. "But I need one more piece of information to be sure I'm on the right track." He reached over to tap the com button on the table.

A gruff male voice responded to the call. "Major Edwin Caparaz."

"Major Caparaz," Wu said, addressing the JTTF's military intelligence liaison. "Could you find out if Oscar Brinkley or any of his subsidiary companies have any contracts with the DOD?" Another thought occurred to him. "Or if he lost out on any bids?"

"How soon do you need it?" Caparaz asked.

"How soon can you get it?" Wu responded without missing a beat.

"Understood," the major said and disconnected.

Wu had jumped several steps ahead without explaining himself. He would soon be proved right, or he would look like a fool. Worse yet, he could be running headlong into another dead end while Agent Vega and Toro did the same.

CHAPTER 51

Wu paced across the JOC, struggling to bring order to his racing thoughts.

"You suspect Oscar Brinkley is the one behind this game?" Hargrave asked him.

Wu nodded distractedly, still thinking. "His company is one of many with government contracts, but the coincidence that he owns a decommissioned missile silo is too much to ignore." He turned to Johnson, who was still at her terminal. "When did Brinkley buy the site?"

"More than five years ago, sir," she said after glancing at her screen. "But why use it for this game? It makes no sense."

"Something happened to his family ten years ago," Wu said. "You and Patel would have been in high school at the time, so you might not remember the headlines."

Johnson shook her head. "Sorry, sir. I know who Brinkley is, of course, but not what happened to his family."

"Oscar Brinkley's wife and young daughter were kidnapped and held for ransom," Wu began. "He paid the money, but only his daughter came home alive."

"I was an investigating agent on the case back then," Hargrave added. "Despite our best efforts, the crime is still unsolved to this day."

Wu had been assigned to the Atlanta field office on the other side of the country and hadn't had any direct involvement in the investigation. Interested to hear the perspective of someone who did, he turned to his supervisor.

"Care to share?" he said to Hargrave.

"I was working out of the San Francisco field office," Hargrave began, taking a seat at the head of the conference table. "We got a call from the Santa Clara Police Department requesting our assistance in the investigation of a double kidnapping. The captors left a ransom note demanding ten million each for their safe return. The SCPD wanted to keep it out of the news."

They hadn't succeeded in holding the press at bay for long. The crime had become fodder for armchair detectives and media pundits around the world due to Brinkley's fame. Wu recalled the story playing out for several weeks before fading from public awareness.

"The wife, Sylvia Brinkley, and their teenage daughter, Megan, were abducted in a parking garage at a shopping mall," Hargrave continued. "From what we could tell, it looked like people had been following them and found an opportunity to snatch and stuff them into a waiting van."

Wu stopped pacing when a minor but critical detail came back to him. "A van in a parking garage, right?"

Hargrave met his gaze. "Seems like more than mere coincidence that we're dealing with some of the same elements now."

"This has to mean something," Patel said. "What happened next?"

Hargrave's expression darkened. "Brinkley wired ten million to an offshore account listed in the note."

Johnson put her fingertips to her lips. "But the demand was for double that amount."

"He acted against our instructions," Hargrave sighed. "Brinkley reasoned that he should give them half up front and half when the two were safely returned. Otherwise they would have no reason to let them go at all."

"That didn't work out well," Wu said.

"No, it did not," Hargrave agreed. "The kidnappers must have assumed Brinkley would not complete the transaction if they gave up their hostages, which is what we told him they would think." He closed his eyes and heaved a sigh. "Brinkley received an email with a picture of his wife with what the forensic analysts estimated to be a nine-millimeter bullet hole in the center of her forehead and the back of her head blown out," he went on. "She was clearly dead."

"That's when the story leaked," Wu said. "I remember national headlines about her murder."

"Everything became monumentally more challenging after that," Hargrave said. "The kidnappers reiterated their demand for another ten million to release the daughter."

"This time he paid, right?" Johnson said through fingers still resting against her lips.

"He wired the funds immediately. We tried everything we could to track down the money transfers, which went through several financial institutions, but some of the countries involved did not have agreements with US law enforcement at the time, and we couldn't follow the trail all the way to the end."

"No back channels?" Wu asked. "Unofficial ones?"

"Not this time," Hargrave said. "We even tried to electronically tag the deposit, but it didn't last through multiple transfers. We interviewed people in the banking industry in the various countries involved, but everyone we dealt with was either well paid or thoroughly scared into silence. Even off the record."

"You told us the girl was released," Patel said. "Was she okay?"

"She walked into a convenience store in Santa Clara about an hour after the money was sent," Hargrave said. "She was disoriented. Told us she had been dropped off at a nearby corner by some men in a van. Her captors had covered her head in a pillowcase during the drive."

"Did she describe them?" Wu asked.

"They wore masks whenever they dealt with her while she was in their custody," Hargrave said. "She could only say they were males with average builds and no distinguishing accents. Based on her statement, about a dozen men were involved."

"What did Brinkley do?" Johnson asked.

"He was furious with us," Hargrave said. "Blamed the Bureau for getting his wife killed, because we didn't find the kidnappers and rescue them right away." He shook his head. "I get that he was distraught, and that he's a business mogul used to doing things his way and thinking he's the smartest person in the room, but this was our area of expertise. When he sent the final payment, he didn't even tell us before he did it. We had planned additional tracking technology for the transfer, but he told us after the fact that he'd been worried they would find out and kill his daughter too."

"What about the investigation into the abduction after the daughter was returned?" Wu asked.

"We did extensive testing on the daughter's clothing and skin," Hargrave said. "Took her through the story multiple times, looking for the tiniest detail. But every lead petered out."

"How did Brinkley react?" Wu asked.

"Called us incompetent," Hargrave said. "A couple of months later, Brinkley stopped cooperating. Said his daughter had been traumatized enough by the men who took her, and he didn't want us poking and prodding her anymore. He basically shut us down. We still investigated, but after months without progress, the case went cold."

"A distraught parent can be unreasonable," Johnson said. "His daughter probably told him she didn't want to talk to the FBI anymore and he was protecting her. I don't know how I would act under the same circumstances."

Wu caught the glow of the com light near the center of the conference table and reached out to tap it. "SAC Wu."

"Major Caparaz," the responding voice said, filling the room. "I have the information you requested."

Wu leaned forward. "What did you find out?"

"Oscar Brinkley's main company has had several contracts with the DOD over the years. Currently he's bidding for funding to develop virtual training."

Wu exchanged a glance with Hargrave before prompting Caparaz. "What's the nature of the training?"

"According to the proposal, it involves designing a completely interactive scenario-based virtual reality system. A soldier in training would wear a special suit and interact with computer-generated characters as well as other real troops. Commanding officers could use a control panel to manipulate the environment in real time according to how their personnel reacts to a given situation."

Wu's mouth went dry. "Where was this system supposed to be developed?"

"It's only described as a highly secure facility," Caparaz said. "He would allow Pentagon officials to tour the site if he became one of the finalists in the bidding process."

The color had drained from Hargrave's face. "Did Brinkley include a sample? Anything that might involve a way for us to access his system remotely?"

"Negative," Caparaz said. "The process was in the first stage. He promised more if he made it to the second stage. Sounds like he was concerned about his intellectual property getting stolen."

"Send a copy of the proposal to the JOC," Wu said. "I need everything you've got on this VR training, especially if it involves how it works."

"Roger that," Caparaz said and disconnected.

"This answers our original question," Wu said. "Brinkley bought the most secure facility he could find, which was a decommissioned missile silo in Arizona, and retrofitted it over the past five years to design a space for his VR training."

"Holy shit," Patel said. "The military could train all its personnel using this technology. They could change the environment inside for any terrain." He spread his arms wide in an expansive gesture. "Newly promoted officers could be trained at the same time by manipulating the controls to see what happened. An opposing AI army could be programmed to react in real time. All without having to leave the base."

"That could be worth a billion dollars to the Pentagon," Hargrave said. "It wouldn't eliminate the need for physical drilling, but it could cut back on expenses and injuries dramatically."

Wu posed the question that had been nagging him most. "Why did Brinkley convert the operating system for what would have been a lucrative defense contract into the VR game we see now with Greek gods killing each other?"

The room grew quiet.

"The only way this makes sense is if Brinkley somehow found out the Colonel and his crew were behind the kidnapping and murder ten years ago," Flint said. "He must have believed one of his competitors not only bribed the senator, but also hired the Colonel to sideline him with a personal crisis that would have demanded all his time and attention."

"For that kind of money," Patel said, "it wouldn't be a stretch. They could get a payday out of the job at the same time."

"Knowing Brinkley, retaliation would be more important to him than money," Hargrave said. "If this was about revenge, he certainly had the means and the motive to carry it out."

"Once Brinkley was convinced the Colonel was responsible for his wife's death, he did not take the evidence to the FBI, because he thought we were incompetent," Wu said. "He didn't trust the criminal justice system and didn't want to risk losing the case in court, so instead he creates his own 'trial by combat.'" He air quoted the words. "A phrase the game's developer used more than once."

"Is he capable of that level of violence?" Flint asked, directing the question at Hargrave, the only one who had dealt with him personally.

"He's an unusual person, to say the least," Hargrave responded after a moment's thought. "Reclusive. Competitive. Secretive."

"All traits that landed him in the top tier of tech entrepreneurs in the world," Patel said. "He pioneered some of the most innovative software out there. I've read that he's described as driven and intense."

"Sounds ruthless," Flint said.

"Tech development is a bare-knuckled sport," Patel said. "You don't get to Brinkley's level without sharp elbows."

Wu glanced at Hargrave. "We already have enough to interview him, but I don't think that's our best move."

He had been considering the problem during their discussion. Now convinced that Brinkley was behind the game, he laid out his strategy.

"Brinkley is a billionaire," he began. "How would he travel from Santa Clara, California, to a remote location outside of Tucson, Arizona?"

"He'd fly in his private helicopter," Flint said without hesitation. "There wouldn't be a landing strip for his private jet."

"Exactly," Wu said, then turned to Johnson. "Can you check the FAA for any flight plans filed in the past week that match those criteria?" She bent to her keyboard, and another thought occurred to him. "While you're at it, check to see if any private aircraft belonging to Brinkley flew from New Jersey to Arizona since Vega and Toro disappeared. They might have driven across the country, but air travel would be faster."

"They could have flown under the radar," Flint said. "Literally."

"How?" Wu asked.

"My brother is a pilot," Flint said. "I consulted with him about a smuggling operation a few years ago. He said you don't have to file a flight plan if you fly under 250 knots while you're below ten thousand feet. If you keep the plane beneath a ceiling of eighteen thousand feet the whole trip, you could fly using visual flight rules, so air traffic control wouldn't monitor you."

Wu struggled to keep up. "But there would be some record of the flight, right?"

"Yeah, but in the case we were investigating, the pilot dropped below the radar threshold, then changed directions before landing. We had no idea where he went for quite a while."

This was going to be more difficult than Wu had anticipated. "If we manage to get confirmation that Brinkley or one of his aircraft went anywhere near Tucson, we'll have enough for a search warrant."

"We already have enough to try," Hargrave said. "Let's see if we can get paper for all his properties."

Wu was glad the assistant director was on board, because he was about to make a big ask.

"I propose we call out our HRT and fly out there immediately," he said. "It will take hours to write the affidavit and get a judge to sign the warrant, but it will also take hours to fly from here to Tucson."

"What if we can't get a judge to sign?" Hargrave said. "You want to fly clear across the country and back for nothing?"

"If we're successful, we'll have boots on the ground at the premises without any delay," he countered, then held up his hand to forestall Hargrave's next objection. "I know the Phoenix field office has their own on-site HRT, but Director Franklin ordered us to keep this investigation to the absolute minimum number of people possible. Besides, we've been in on this from the beginning, and we know every detail of the case. In the time it takes to get the search warrants, we can be at the scene."

Hargrave steepled his fingers, regarding him for a long moment before he spoke. "Agreed. You can make the arrangements with HRT and oversee the paperwork."

The assistant director expected him to remain in his office in a supervisory capacity. He reflected on his position as a special agent in charge. He had loved being a field agent when he first joined the FBI. The thrill of the chase, going after bad guys, and rushing into danger had driven him.

Nowadays he sat in his comfy chair in the corner office and sent others into harm's way. He'd learned that it was exponentially harder to order someone else into a deadly situation than to go in himself.

He felt the full weight of responsibility for Vega's current predicament. He'd come up with the idea to send her in undercover because he suspected Toro had feelings for her, which he had believed would give her an edge. Technically she had agreed to go, but he had known someone with her background would never refuse a call to action. It was not in her DNA, and he had taken advantage of that. She was every bit the goddess of war and wisdom her avatar represented, and he would never forgive himself if he could not get her back safely.

And then it hit him all at once. He was done following protocol. Done sitting behind a desk. Done sending others into danger. From now on, he wasn't just in charge of the investigation, he was running point.

"I'm going to get Agent Vega back," he said to Hargrave. "Personally."

CHAPTER 52

Dani folded Toro's lifeless hands across his chest and got to her feet. She pushed down her emotions and oriented herself to the mission at hand. This was war, and she had transitioned her mindset fully from federal agent to military mode. Her objective was no longer arrest and apprehension. It was search and destroy. Whoever Nemesis was, he was about to learn the consequences of fucking with an Army Ranger. The final words of the Ranger's creed came to her. *Readily will I display the intestinal fortitude required to fight on to the Ranger objective and complete the mission, though I be the lone survivor.*

"Game's over," she called out into the silence surrounding her. "I'm the last one standing. According to your rules of engagement, I go free."

She expected no response but made the declaration anyway. She was supposed to die but had had the audacity to survive, ruining her captor's carefully laid plans. He'd better get ready, because she was about to ruin a hell of a lot more than his plans. Now that she didn't have a pack of killers on her heels and Toro's safety to worry about, she was free to take any risks she chose. And that meant going on the offensive.

Circling back, she bent to search the Colonel and his two men. As she had hoped, the Colonel was carrying a clue tucked in his boot.

She unfolded the paper and laid it beside the one they had pulled from Chopper's boot. Another section of the map was revealed. Enough for her to see that the only way up was through another hatch at the end of the corridor to her left.

She paused, studying the hand-drawn diagram and pinpointing her location on the fourth level down from the top. Why would the underground structure they were in have seven levels going straight into the earth and nothing on the surface? This section of the diagram also showed a tube-shaped passageway at a ninety-degree angle to the main structure two levels above her current position. It seemed to lead to a completely separate room. Was that the control area where Nemesis sat at a bank of computers, tormenting them all?

Before they entered the facility, she had seen nothing but featureless terrain on the surface, stretching out for miles around. It looked like the Desert Southwest, but she couldn't tell what state she was in.

If the seven-level structure was vertical, and the horizontal tube leading to the separate control room was attached to the second level down, that would indicate that the whole complex was subterranean. Why make all parts of the facility—even the control center—underground?

The FBI would not be able to locate her using satellites. The tracking devices she and Toro had received had been rendered useless by an EMP device. The plane they had flown in had taken off from a repair hangar rather than a standard airfield with a control tower, so there would be no record of the flight. No one was coming. She had to find a way out or die down here like the others, because Nemesis would never set her free.

Her best chance of escape was determining what kind of structure she was trapped in. The place looked old but freshly renovated. Perhaps the original infrastructure could provide a way to strike at the unseen enemy. Nemesis would be watching, but he could not read her thoughts.

As long as he was secured in his control room, she could not put a stop to his game. She would have to draw him out, but how? On the battlefield, the most common strategy called for surrounding the enemy, cutting off their supplies, and waiting them out. This was not an option for her.

She was alone, and Nemesis had total control. Or did he? The Army had taught her how to kill people and break things for tactical advantage, which was especially effective in asymmetrical warfare. Her current situation was about as asymmetrical as it got.

She glanced up at the pipes that ran along the walls and ceiling. Some must have supplied toxic gas to various rooms, but others probably housed electrical wiring. If she damaged the wires, she could prevent Nemesis from controlling certain aspects of the facility. On the other hand, she might inadvertently shut off all the power, including the lights, but it was a risk she was willing to take. She shifted her gaze to the cameras mounted to the ceiling throughout the space, their tiny red lights glowing at regular intervals. What if she blinded Nemesis?

She formed a plan of action and set out to locate the hatch leading to the next level. Minutes later, she climbed up another ladder and pulled at the hatch's lever, which was unlocked.

Interesting. Nemesis wanted her to go up.

Alert for traps, she went through an open doorway leading to another corridor and continued along the narrow passage until she found what she was looking for.

The hatch leading her up to the second level where she could access the horizontal tube that led to what she assumed was the control center. Now was the time to implement what she had come to think of as Operation FU. She pulled out one of the three guns she had seized and calmly shot out the cameras in the ceiling.

Nemesis reacted immediately. "Stop what you're doing."

Unfortunately her ears were ringing, and she could barely make out the words. She used the situation to her advantage.

"What?" she called out. "I can't hear you. Speak up."

The voice boomed louder. "Stop shooting."

The second transmission enabled her to locate the hidden speaker. She made a statement designed to elicit a particular response. "I'm going after the pipes next," she called out. "You won't be able to pump in gas anymore. Once I find the electrical cords, you'll lose all control over this space."

She raised her gun and put four rounds into the nearest pipe, tearing it loose from the bracket that held it bolted to the wall. A cluster of multicolored wires dangled from the broken tube. Now frayed and blackened, the wires sparked with ominous arcs of electricity. The lights flickered briefly but stayed on.

"If you do not stop right now—"

Dani shot out the intercom that had been well concealed amid the pipes in the open ceiling.

The speaker crackled, emitted a loud buzz, and died.

Now that Nemesis was blind, deaf, and mute, Dani turned her attention to the door. She expected her enemy to either deploy a lethal counterattack or send someone out to engage with her, which was what she wanted. As soon as the door opened, she would have a chance to get through.

To do that, she had to survive whatever countermeasure Nemesis threw at her, and she had no doubt his retaliation would be both swift and brutal. She braced herself.

Bring it on.

CHAPTER 53

Nemesis hit the master switch, sending the entire complex into utter darkness. The control room was the only place with light, and no one could get inside.

Until it was time.

Agent Vega's movements would slow to a crawl. With no option other than to fumble around in the dark, she wouldn't get far.

Fortunately night-vision cameras would allow the audience to see Athena's progress once she entered a space with functioning equipment again. And Nemesis would be watching, too, between editing and uploading the big finale to the game.

There were thousands of viewers now, many placing side bets on the outcome. A quick review of the chat rooms around the game had revealed that the odds on Athena had been long. Some people were about to make a lot of money. This merited consideration going forward. When the game moved from beta testing on the dark web to a final version using computer-generated avatars, perhaps there could be a way to tap into the speculation.

The decommissioned silo had been a bargain five years ago, and several years of renovation had totally reformed it to create the perfect arena for virtual training. Newly designed software connected to a completely dedicated server guaranteed protection from corporate espionage and hacks. Everything was moving along smoothly. And then disaster had struck.

Proof that Colonel Treadway and his team of operatives had been the ones behind the kidnapping surfaced. The next challenge had been to determine who had hired them and—most importantly—why. The final pieces fell into place quickly. The FBI had nearly a decade and couldn't figure it out. Turning the evidence over to them would guarantee another miscarriage of justice.

This game would correct all that. It had been easy to reconfigure the systems in the silo to render avatars that had nothing to do with the military, preventing any connection to a defense contract that could arouse suspicion.

But first, loose ends needed trimming.

Senator Sledge should have been indicted by now, or at least be the subject of a growing public scandal. Circling back to him would have to wait until the current situation was resolved, which should take only a few more hours. Enjoyable as the game was, it was good to end it before the FBI caught on. There was no way to tell what the Feds were up to without risking another Trojan horse virus or a cyber honeypot designed to trap and trace a hacker.

Everyone directly involved in the kidnapping and murder was now dead, but a federal agent was still alive. Colonel Treadway was supposed to be the last man standing. He had been the trigger man, and his punishment was to watch everything he had worked for implode, knowing he would die in disgrace, and that he would be reviled in death.

Agent Vega had ruined those plans, and now she would suffer the consequences. The FBI would finally pay for their incompetence ten years earlier. They would learn what it was like to lose someone you care about when it could have been prevented if they had done a better job.

CHAPTER 54

Six hours after his conversation with Assistant Director Hargrave, Wu sat in the back of the bus provided by the FBI's Tucson Resident Agency, bumping along increasingly desolate desert roads. The team had landed thirty minutes earlier, and their fellow agents had been waiting for them with transportation.

With no direct flights available from New York to Tucson International Airport, Hargrave had arranged to borrow one of the FBI's leased Gulfstream jets. A flight that would have eaten up most of the day with a layover and connections had been reduced to under five hours. In addition, they were able to continue their work, which would not have been possible on a crowded commercial flight.

The highlight of the trip came when Johnson called to advise them she'd heard back from the FAA, who had uncovered evidence that Brinkley's private jet may have flown from New Jersey to Arizona the day Vega went missing. They also confirmed that his helicopter pilot filed a flight plan from his home in Santa Clara to the coordinates of the missile silo a week earlier, removing all doubt about Brinkley's involvement.

"Can't be much longer now," Flint said, checking his watch.

Wu had considered ordering the detective to remain at the JTTF, but Flint had been determined to go, insisting he could write the affidavit just as well in the air as he could on the ground. He'd been correct, and the Assistant US Attorney had conferenced them in with a judge using a secure satellite video link. Half an hour before landing, he had used the onboard printer to make sure they had warrants in hand.

"We should be there in about fifteen minutes," Wu told the team. "There's no downtime in this op. We hit it as soon as we get to the scene."

Other technology made their travel even more productive. Patel had provided regular updates during the flight as he and the other cybercrime specialists continued to try to hack into the game. They no longer needed to locate where it was occurring, but any evidence they could glean would help in court when they hauled Brinkley in front of a judge.

"Anything new show up with the drone pass?" Flint asked, interrupting his thoughts again.

Wu had requested aerial drone surveillance and satellite images of the area around the silo. He and the HRT had pored over dozens of digitized photos while on the flight to Tucson. They had originally been looking for a large building and nearly missed the entrance when scanning great swathes of scrub-covered desert foothills. Finally Wu had spotted a solitary concrete structure, just big enough to hold a reinforced metal door. With nothing else around, it looked like the door led to nowhere, but it clearly opened to a set of stairs descending straight into the earth.

He had expected massive bay doors designed to slide open when the missile launched. Instead, there was an enormous hatch, built to withstand a nuclear strike, that had been sealed by the government when the site was decommissioned. So much for opening the top to gain access.

"No vehicles anywhere in the vicinity," he said to Flint. "According to the flight plan, the chopper dropped Brinkley off and returned to base. Assuming he prepared in advance, he might not need supplies for a while."

The silo had its own air, water, plumbing, and power from an attached generator, but whoever was there would need food eventually. Rations could have been stockpiled long ago, and the people inside could live underground for years without having to surface. A miserable existence, but feasible.

They had risked a couple of drone flyovers in the past fifteen minutes to get a closer look and were able to make out the remnants of rotor wash from a helicopter in the dusty ground, but not much more.

Flint went back to studying the schematic of the underground facility they had obtained from records of the sale.

According to the listing, as well as archived information Johnson had unearthed, Brinkley had purchased a Titan II nuclear missile complex about half an hour south of Tucson. The government had decommissioned all Titan sites and sold off many of them over the years. Most were in disrepair after decades of neglect, but Brinkley had the funds to renovate and repurpose this one.

They had reviewed the photographs and blueprints. The place had been designed to withstand a nuclear attack. The only weakness was the ventilation system, which offered the possibility of literally smoking them out, but Wu had dismissed that idea out of hand. The chance of casualties or other unintended consequences was too great.

His cell phone buzzed in his pocket. He slid it out and put it to his ear. "Wu here."

Patel sounded frantic. "Are you watching the game right now?"

Patel had given him a laptop with a secure connection to the dark web so he and the others could monitor the situation in case anything changed before their arrival. He had slipped the computer into his duffel after they landed and had been about to have a last look at the game before they arrived at the site.

"Checking it now," he said, propping it open on his knees while Flint craned his neck to peer at the screen.

Wu thought he'd nailed everything down. He had even dared to hope they might get to Vega and Toro in time. Now he stared at the laptop in disbelief.

When Flint swore, the others gradually left their seats to cluster around him and watch Ares, Deimos, and Phobos all perish in a gunfight with Athena and the Minotaur. Wu registered the appreciative comments from the HRT members around him as Vega drew two of her adversaries into a cross fire before finishing the Colonel with a shot only an expert marksman could manage.

He watched Athena drop to her knees to cradle the Minotaur's head as he drew his last shuddering breaths, amazed at both her tactical prowess and her compassion. The screen reverted to the main page. Show over.

"Everyone else is dead." He heard the hollowness in his own voice as he spoke. "It's down to her now."

He hadn't been surprised Vega won the so-called game, but he'd hoped it would last long enough for them to get inside the silo. He had no idea when the competition had actually ended, and the bus wouldn't get to the site for another ten minutes. As with all the other videos, the feed had been edited. Were they already too late?

"No way is Brinkley going to let her go," Flint said.

Wu pushed the thought from his mind. Negative thinking brought negative results. He would deal with what they found when they got there. This new development meant they might catch Brinkley leaving—or that he might have already gone.

"Check the satellite feeds," he said to Patel, who was still on the phone. "And send up another drone."

When he disconnected, Special Agent Jamar Benton, Hostage Rescue Team leader for the JTTF, turned in his seat to face Wu. "We've turned on the jammers," he said.

Benton had brought lots of toys, including frequency jammers designed to prevent Brinkley from detecting their approach using surveillance cameras or perimeter alarms.

"He's bound to suspect something's up," Wu said, "if he's monitoring his equipment and it all suddenly goes haywire at the same time."

Benton lifted both burly arms, palms up. "Better to suspect than to know for sure. Also, he won't know exactly what we're bringing to his door."

He agreed with the logic but kept coming back to his chief objective. "What do you have that can get us inside the silo?"

Benton rubbed a palm over his bald scalp. "Det cord, breaching tool, and C-4 if we get desperate."

Flint frowned. "Our only real hope is that there's a cipher lock on the door. That thing is built to withstand a direct nuclear strike."

Benton jerked his chin toward the front of the bus. "Gizmo is ready to go."

When they had discussed the problem earlier while studying schematics of the silo, Benton had assured them their main breacher, nicknamed Gizmo, had never failed at getting through a door. He had electronic equipment that could decode and open a blast-proof bank vault and had done so last year when hostages were locked inside.

Wu kept his reservations to himself. Even if they managed to get in, the process would be slow, giving Brinkley time to arm booby traps and other surprises for them. Like Vega, they would all be heading into his world, a space he had renovated to include deadly obstacles at every turn. Benton and his team were outstanding at what they did, but none of them had dealt with anything like this.

"We're five minutes out," the driver announced.

Wu had been waiting for the last possible minute to bring up a deviation from the agreed-upon plan. "Assuming we get in," he said to Benton, "I'm coming with."

"No, sir," Benton said without hesitation.

He outranked Benton, but the HRT leader had tactical control over the operation. Anticipating the response, Wu had prepared his argument in advance.

"I was on the HRT in the Atlanta field office," he began. "I know what to do . . . and I'll make entry with—"

"You haven't trained with us," Benton cut in. "And it's been years since you kicked down a door."

"Riding a bicycle," Wu said. "Put me in the middle of the line."

"Not just no," Benton said. "But hell no." He paused. "Sir."

Flint spoke up. "How about if the SAC and I come in after you start clearing the place? We won't go anywhere your team hasn't secured. I've done it with ESU, and there's never been a problem."

The NYPD's Emergency Service Unit was analogous to the FBI's HRT and often trained together. It was a smart argument on Flint's part because Benton would be familiar with and respectful of his PD counterparts.

Wu hadn't expected Flint to elbow his way in, but if the price of admission included the detective, he was happy to pay it. Both men looked at Benton expectantly.

"You two only come into areas we have advised you are clear," he said, pointing at each of them in turn. "Got it?"

They both nodded their agreement.

Wu dropped his voice and leaned in close to Flint. "I wasn't expecting you to go in with the team."

Flint raised a sardonic brow. "You aren't the only one who wants Vega back."

CHAPTER 55

Dani crept forward in total darkness, right hand gripping her pistol, left hand in front of her, fingers splayed wide. After she had blinded Nemesis by shooting out the overhead camera, he had taken an eye for an eye, cutting the lights to deprive her of sight.

The only interruption in the profound blackness surrounding her as she inched along was the barely perceptible glow of tiny red lights in the ceiling. She had considered shooting them all out but opted to save her ammo for immediate threats. She had performed a thorough check of the weapons she'd confiscated and counted twenty-one rounds between the four pistols. There were no extra magazines. With no expectation of finding more, what she had would have to see her through.

She slid one booted foot ahead of her without lifting the sole from the floor, shifted her weight, then dragged her back foot forward until her feet were together. The technique made for slow, halting progress, but it was the only way to be sure she wouldn't trip on something and fall headlong into a deadly trap or injure herself. Time had lost all meaning, and it felt like hours had passed since her last communication with Nemesis.

The silence held its own form of torment. What was he planning? The game had ended, but he wasn't finished with her yet.

The side of her palm bumped against something cold and metallic. She withdrew her hand quickly, staring at the space in front of her in search of a telltale arc of electricity. Nothing lit up, and she felt no pain. Probably not electrified then. Gingerly gliding her fingertips along the smooth surface, she felt the cylindrical shape of wrought iron rungs. This was the ladder she had seen leading to a round hatch in the ceiling. If she could make it one level up, she would be able to find the tube that accessed the control room.

She climbed up and felt the same kind of latch she and Toro had encountered before. She tried the lever.

Locked.

She waited to see if a display screen might provide a clue to open the hatch.

Nothing.

She climbed back down and considered the situation. Nemesis did not want her moving up to the next level. He was keeping her contained, trapping her below until he made his next move. She had decided to go on the offensive after Toro died but now had to recalibrate her approach based on her new circumstances.

Her captor had access to night-vision equipment, which put her at an extreme disadvantage if he decided to engage her. She would have to rely on her hearing to warn her and provide an idea of where her target was.

A high-pitched sound echoed through the corridor. Her body tensed as she strained to identify the source. Had Nemesis figured out that he could cover his approach with noise? That would mean he was making his move. She pulled a second pistol from her boot and held one in each hand, pointing them in different directions.

The sound grew louder, as if it was getting closer. She tilted her head, trying to get a bead on where it was coming from. The noise died out and then began again, piercing and ominous. She had heard it before but couldn't place it. Why did it make the hair on the back of her neck stand on end?

And then she recognized the hiss of the king cobra that was apparently no longer contained in its tank.

CHAPTER 56

Wu stood between HRT Leader Jamar Benton and Flint. The team had cleared the surface area around the door to the silo. After detecting no sign of land mines or other hazards, Benton had beckoned them over to join the team.

"Just got a report from Patel," Wu said to Benton. "He reviewed the new aerial surveillance. No vehicles have been anywhere near this location. Johnson heard back from the FAA. The flight plan taking Brinkley back to his house is still on file but not active."

"So he's still here," Benton said.

"Has to be," Wu said, then shifted his attention to the silo's entrance. "Will you be able to open the door?"

While his fellow operators stood in a protective circle facing outward to watch for threats, the breacher Benton had referred to as Gizmo crouched in front of the door.

"Halligan tool won't even scratch this thing," Gizmo said over his shoulder. "But there's a cipher lock with a keypad next to the latch." He glanced up at them. "Lucky I came prepared."

He unzipped a black nylon duffel, fished out a device the size of an eraser, and held it close to the metal door. An instant later, the interior magnet pulled it flush against the hard surface with a snap.

Benton gave his head a small shake. "This is why we call him Gizmo," he said to Wu. "It was either that or Inspector Gadget."

While Gizmo finished wiring the device and running it through the decryption program, Benton and his team reviewed the entry plan they had developed on the flight over.

"We've jammed his signal," Benton said. "But we still have to assume he knows we're here."

"What are your protocols when you get in?" Flint asked. "Is this a stealth op?"

He had discussed the logistics with Benton on the flight. FBI agents were required to announce themselves and give suspects an opportunity to surrender before using lethal force, but this situation was so far from the norm that it required a different approach.

"We can't go in guns blazing," Benton said to Flint.

"If you announce, this becomes an instant hostage situation," Flint responded. "Every inch of this place is under Brinkley's control, and he's got Vega."

Wu cut the discussion short, outlining his decision. "HRT will go in quiet and establish control over the exit. They will advance in stealth mode but verbally challenge anyone they encounter."

It had been the best compromise he could come up with.

"Not perfect," he said to Flint. "But it's the best we can do under the circumstances."

"Got it," Gizmo called out, getting to his feet. "It's unlocked. Let me know when you're ready to make entry."

Benton addressed his team. "Line up."

Wordlessly, the tactical operators formed a queue. Gizmo took point by the door while one of his teammates shouldered a rifle.

Abiding by their earlier agreement, Wu and Flint stood back.

Benton raised a gloved hand and silently counted down, lowering one finger at a time. When all he had left was a closed fist, Gizmo grasped the handle, turned it, and flung the door open.

CHAPTER 57

Dani stood in the inky blackness, rooted to the spot, as the hissing grew louder. Her time in the field had familiarized her with various types of snakes, but she was no expert. She racked her brain for information. Could they see in the dark? Scent their prey? Feel the vibration of footsteps through their bellies when they slithered close?

What was her best option? Any move she made might result in stepping on the cobra. Standing still allowed more time for it to zero in on her location. Her boots would probably withstand a bite, but they reached only midway up her calf. Every other part of her body was vulnerable to venomous fangs.

If bitten, her death would be painful and inevitable without antivenom. What if she survived every trap, overcame every obstacle, outwitted every attacker, only to be killed by a creature who operated on pure instinct?

Instinct.

The snake would attack if it felt threatened or sensed prey. What could she do to eliminate that possibility? Put distance between herself and the cobra. The only way to do that safely was to use her acute hearing to figure out where the snake was.

She angled her head to one side, then the other. The hiss filled the space, echoing off the walls. To be so loud, it must be right beside her.

A steadying breath calmed her frayed nerves and beat back the wave of panic that threatened to swamp her. Centering herself allowed the pulse that pounded in her ears to subside, improving her hearing. And then she realized the sound was coming from above her.

Last she checked, snakes couldn't fly.

Which meant the sound was being piped in through the speaker in the ceiling.

"You'll have to do better than that, asshole," she called out into the darkness, deliberately baiting her captor.

The hissing ceased and the lights popped on, stinging her eyes. Blinking, she fought to recover her vision. Nemesis would be aware that sudden light would disorient her. What was he planning?

A resonant *thunk* sounded above her. She turned watering eyes up to the ceiling to see that the locking mechanism on the round hatch was now in the open position.

Nemesis had held her trapped for hours and now wanted her to move up to the next level. Two things were certain. First, her captor had taken the time to engineer a trap of some sort. Second, she could not escape her prison unless she made her way up to the surface.

Lacking any good option, she chose to go back on the offensive.

She tucked one pistol back into her boot and climbed the ladder, still holding the other gun. Once at the top, she hooked her elbow around the highest rung and used her free hand to open the hatch.

She bobbed her head up for a quick scan. The room was empty. Two doors on opposite walls stood open. She climbed up and kept her back to the wall, circumnavigating the room to peek through the doorway on the left. A short hallway containing no visible threats led to a bend. Unable to see around the corner, she moved to the second doorway to investigate.

She was surprised to see a tube rather than the square corridors she'd been used to. The pieces of the map she had seen indicated that the control room was connected to the rest of the structure by a wide cylindrical passageway.

This whole game had been set up as a series of quandaries and impossible choices, and another one confronted her now. Which path should she choose?

The recent reminder of her encounter with the cobra brought the words of her regiment commander back to her. *"When you cut off a snake's head, the tail dies."* He had been referring to taking out the enemy's leadership and communications, but she would adapt the concept to her current situation. With her weapon in low ready position, she edged into the tube that led to what she believed was the brain that made the whole operating system function. Nemesis would not be able to hide behind electronics any longer.

He was permitting her to come after him, which led to a disturbing question. Why does your adversary give up the high ground? You've been fighting for days to take the hill only to find that the other side has relinquished it without a fight. In her experience, that meant the enemy had retreated to a more fortified position to renew the attack at a time of his choosing. Maybe Nemesis had set something in motion that would kill her and destroy all evidence of what had happened before fleeing the scene. Whatever his intentions, standing still would literally get her nowhere. Time to break inside the control room.

Time to soldier on.

CHAPTER 58

Wu made his way through the corridors a few paces behind the HRT. So far there had been no unexpected obstacles to contend with. He found the lack of response from Brinkley disturbing. Aware the facility was filled with surveillance cameras and listening devices, he couldn't discuss options with the team leader. Benton had charted their course of action, and they were moving forward.

They had considered taking a frequency jammer down with them but decided it might interfere with their own com system. If Brinkley hadn't seen them coming before, he knew they were here now.

The team was heading for the control center for two reasons. First, taking over the facility's operating system would effectively prevent Brinkley from using his traps or deploying weapons against them. Second, the schematics they had studied showed that the control center was connected by two tubes large enough to walk through on opposite ends. One tube went to the main silo, where the game had been played—and presumably—where Vega was still trapped. The other tube connected to a hallway with stairs that led up to the surface.

They could not complete their mission without going through the control center, but both of its doors were equipped with a pressure lock.

"Decoding now," Benton said over the com system.

The team must have reached the control room door, and Gizmo was using his device to get through another cipher lock. Brinkley had retrofitted the main doors with coded locks.

Benton's voice carried through Wu's earpiece. "Only one number left," he said in an undertone. "Stand by."

The HRT would unlock the door within seconds. If any traps were set, they would be inside.

Even though he was behind the team, Wu had his sidearm in low ready position. If a gunfight broke out, he would be ready.

The overhead bulbs went out, and they were swallowed in darkness.

"Night vision," Benton said.

Even before he heard the command, Wu had reached up to flip the unit mounted on the front of his tactical helmet down over his eyes.

Instantly he could see the space around him. Brinkley was aware of their approach, but if he thought this would slow them down, he was mistaken.

A few seconds later, the lights flicked back on, blaring through the lenses. Before he could readjust, the lights began to flick on and off at high speed.

The curses around him told Wu the others were equally disoriented by the strobing lights, which had rendered their night-vision equipment useless.

Bam!

A shot rang out, and one of the bulbs exploded in a shower of falling shards.

Another volley of shots destroyed the rest of the lights, and darkness settled around them again.

Brinkley was more resourceful than he had suspected. Strobing the lights was an ingenious way to neutralize their advantage until they destroyed the flashing bulbs. What would they find when they entered the control room?

"Deploying FLIR," Benton said, his voice barely audible over the ringing in Wu's ears.

The team had taken forward-looking infrared thermal-imaging equipment to scan rooms inside the structure prior to making entry. The command indicated Gizmo had unlocked the door and the team was ready to move in.

"Heat signature detected," Benton said. "One adult."

Brinkley was in the control room, doubtless preparing more surprises for them. Benton gave a hand signal, and the team lined up in dynamic entry formation. Wu had done the same many times and knew what would happen next. He would rather have led the charge into the room but had to content himself with rising up on his toes to watch from close behind them.

Benton's silent count ended, and the breacher opened the heavy door as the second operator barged through, shouting commands at the person inside. Strobing lights flickered inside the control room, turning the space into a disorienting spectacle.

The entire line surged in, their figures visible only in fractional freeze-frame increments. Gunshots rang out, the echoes making it impossible to tell who had fired first.

Less than ten seconds later, the shooting stopped.

"One subject down," Benton said through the com system. "Confirmed deceased."

Breaking his promise to wait for the all-clear, Wu rushed into the control room to see who the HRT had killed.

CHAPTER 59

Dani heard shouts and gunshots coming from the other side of the control room door. Thick blast-proof walls and a reinforced door prevented her from making out any words, but it sounded like several male voices and a collection of thudding boots.

Was Nemesis shooting at someone? Everyone else in the game was dead, but had he captured a fresh group of people to force into another round of competition?

A tiny spark of hope flared. Maybe the FBI had figured out where she was and had sent the HRT to attempt a rescue. If she called out, they might be able to hear her through the dense walls. Failing that, she could pound on the door to draw their attention.

But what if it wasn't the HRT? Now that he knew her capabilities, Nemesis could have hired a team of mercenaries to hunt her down. Either way, making noise would give her position away to people who were armed.

Whoever they were, they had command of the control center and would open the door in front of her soon. What option would give her the best tactical advantage? Coming to a rapid decision, she began moving backward through the tube. Within seconds, she had descended back down to the lower level through the open hatch in the floor.

Glancing around, she took up a position of cover behind the nearest corner. The men would have to come through the hatch one at a time, climbing down the ladder feetfirst. From this vantage point, she could pick off an entire platoon one by one as long as her ammo lasted.

If they tossed down a grenade or a smoke bomb, she was already around the corner and could easily retreat to another location to reengage in an ambush attack.

If these men turned out to be mercenaries, they would not find her to be easy prey. She would use every kind of guerrilla tactic at her disposal. And she knew plenty.

She crouched down and laid her spare guns in a neat row in front of her, where she could grab them quickly. She raised her primary pistol up and trained her sights on the hatch in the ceiling when she heard a strange sound.

She whipped her head around but saw nothing. Listening closer, she made out a muffled cry for help coming from the far end of the corridor behind her.

CHAPTER 60

Wu rushed in, the strobing lights disorienting him as he glanced around the control room to find Benton.

"Is anyone from your team hurt?" he asked when he spotted the HRT's team leader.

"Negative," Benton said, then followed up with a sharp question. "Why are you in here? We haven't cleared—"

"Where's the body?" Wu cut in. "Who did you shoot?"

The team had seen only a heat signature before coming in, and he could not fight the sickening dread that they had surprised Vega, who wouldn't have been able to make out the team in the chaos of a dynamic tactical entry combined with strobing lights. She might have fired on them, prompting them to return fire.

Benton gestured toward the ground behind the control panel, and Wu walked around to see the crumpled form of a man lying in a pool of blood. He blinked in the flickering lights and bent close enough to examine the face.

A relieved sigh escaped his lips when he recognized Oscar Brinkley. A semiautomatic pistol lay on the floor nearby, where it had been kicked by one of the tactical operators.

"We returned fire," Benton said. "He got off one round right when we came in and another one after we hit him the first time."

Wu's next order of business was to stop the flashing lights and locate Vega. He stood and turned around to study the array of buttons, switches, and dials covering the control panel. Leaning closer, he spotted a cluster of switches under an image of a bulb. He pressed the farthest one to the left, hoping he didn't inadvertently activate something that might hurt Vega.

The room went dark.

"What the fuck?" one of the men closest to him said.

Ignoring him, Wu pulled down his night-vision equipment and pressed the next button in line. The lights popped back on, and more curses went through the room as everyone flipped their night vision back up on their helmets.

"At least the damned lights stopped," Benton said. "Was getting a headache."

Now able to see properly for the first time, Wu took in the damage done to the control panel during the shootout. It looked like Brinkley had ducked behind it, and the team had blasted several rounds through it while trying to neutralize the threat.

Flint, who had entered the room behind Wu, crossed his arms as he gazed down at the panel. "You guys shot the shit out of that thing," he said.

Some of the holes were large enough to expose wires and microchips. Hopefully they could still communicate with Vega and get her out.

Wu looked up at six rows of monitors that filled the far wall in front of him. He spotted the room where Vega and Toro had confronted the cobra and realized that each row corresponded to a level of the main structure, the bottom row being the lowest level. The video system was orderly, so the rest would be as well.

All he had to do was find the correct controls, and he would be able to unlock the door leading outside this room so Benton and his team could find her. Before that, however, he had to locate Vega and let her know they were coming to avoid the friendly-fire situation he had been concerned about since the moment they had arrived at the silo.

He caught movement on the third level, which was one level down from where the tube connected the silo to the control room.

Relief flowed through him. "There she is."

Benton and Flint gathered behind him.

"She's locked and loaded," Benton said. "She's kept all the guns she recovered from those other assholes in the game." He paused. "I didn't know you could stuff that many weapons into a pair of tactical boots."

"What's she doing?" Flint said.

Vega had reached the end of a corridor and was turning the handle on a door that was apparently locked. She stepped back and seemed to say something.

"I'll try to locate the intercom," Wu said, glancing at the controls again. "We can tell her we're here and ask her what's going on."

He found a tab with an image of an old-fashioned radio microphone and turned the dial up.

"—back from the door," Vega was saying. "If I can't break the knob, I'll shoot the lock."

Wu exchanged glances with Benton. "Someone else is trapped inside the silo," he said, then pressed the button below the dial. "Agent Vega, this is SAC Wu. Can you hear me?"

Vega continued to study the doorknob.

He pressed another button. "Agent Vega?"

She turned the pistol around in her hand, gripping the barrel.

He pressed every button in the cluster below the microphone image and repeated the announcement.

She pulled her arm back and brought the gun's grip down on the knob.

"She can't hear us," Flint said. "But at least we can hear her."

Another smash with the butt of the gun broke the knob completely off the door. Vega opened it and bent down.

"It's okay," she said in a gentle tone. "I've got you."

Vega stood, then slowly backed up as she guided a frightened young woman out from what looked like a storage closet.

The woman appeared to be in her twenties, with long brown hair in a ponytail. Her mouth was gagged with a blue bandanna tied around her head. Her slender wrists were zip-tied together in front of her.

"Who the hell is that?" Flint said, echoing Wu's thoughts.

Wu took in her green T-shirt and blue jeans. "She's not wearing a spandex suit like Vega's," he said. "So she wasn't involved in the virtual game."

"Is it okay if I take this off of you?" Vega asked her.

Wu recognized the technique. Vega was handling her as a victim, asking permission before physical contact to give the young woman a sense of autonomy back.

At her nod of assent, Vega reached behind her head and grasped the knot, then slid the bandanna off. "Who are you?" she asked her.

"M-Megan Brinkley," the woman said, her voice raspy as if she hadn't spoken in a while. "We've got to get out of here. My father built this place, and he's insane. He's had me locked in this closet for days."

"Let's see if I can get that zip tie off you," Vega said, reaching down to pull the butterfly knife from her boot. She opened it with a flick of her wrist and moved Megan's hands into position. "Be very still."

A flashing light pulled Wu's gaze from the monitor. He looked at the panel to see a pulsating red light below the image of a flame.

"There's a fire on the second level of the silo," Benton said, pointing at a three-dimensional schematic of the entire complex.

Wu stood and walked over to get a closer look. Glowing red dots had flicked on, beginning near the entrance to the connecting tube. Every few seconds, another dot lit up.

"The whole second level is catching fire," Flint said. "Is there a fire-suppression system?"

Wu raced back to the panel but saw nothing that looked promising. "Call the fire department," he said to Benton. "And what kind of equipment does your team have handy?"

"We've got extinguishers with foam," he said. "Gizmo's already making contact with the nearest FD, but they're not close. I'll get one of my operators up to the surface to grab the extinguishers." He cut his eyes back to the schematic. "The way that's spreading, I don't think handheld fire extinguishers are going to help."

Wu fought back a wave of panic. "Maybe we can seal the doors and prevent the flames from spreading to other levels."

"Try that one," Flint said, pointing at an array of buttons with rectangles and circles above them. "I'm guessing the rectangles are doors and the circles are hatches."

Wu used the blade of his hand to press all the buttons at once.

Nothing happened.

Flint reached out and mashed the next row of buttons.

Still nothing.

"I believe I've identified the source of the problem," Benton said, lifting a cluster of wires from the back of the panel. Several of them were blackened and shredded by rounds from the tactical team. "We need to get down there before the fire gets worse."

Wu pointed at the screen. "It started just outside the connecting tube leading to the silo," he said to Benton. "The room on the other side is completely engulfed. Your team can't make it to the hatch leading to the lower level without getting barbecued."

He deliberately mentioned Benton's team, making it clear that he would be sacrificing those under his supervision in a futile act of desperation if he commanded them to go in. As a supervisor himself, he understood the responsibility of ordering others into danger and knew the team leader would not send his men to their deaths for no reason.

"Then we're screwed," Benton said in a strained voice. "I cannot accept that we just have to stand by and watch her die."

Wu cursed. Vega and an innocent civilian had no idea they were trapped beneath a growing wall of fire. The only way out was now blocked, and he had no way of telling them what their situation was. After everything she had been through, everything she had survived, she had no way out. Brinkley was dead, but his building might still kill her.

CHAPTER 61

Dani flicked a surreptitious glance at Megan Brinkley before deftly sliding the knife's sharp blade underneath the zip tie.

After Toro told her about the botched kidnapping for ransom, Dani had assumed Oscar Brinkley was Nemesis. Megan appeared to be in her midtwenties, putting her at the right age to be his daughter.

"Thank you," Megan said, rubbing her wrists after the thick plastic tie fell to the floor. "For rescuing me too." She looked her up and down. "Why are you wearing one of my father's VR projection suits?"

Dani looked down at herself. She had become so used to the form-fitting garment she'd forgotten about it. "Long story. Right now I have some questions for you. You said your father owns this place. Where is he now?"

Megan shook her head. "No idea. He locked me in there, and I haven't seen him for a long time . . . I think it's been days."

Was her father watching them now?

She settled for a more basic question. "Your father is Oscar Brinkley?"

Megan's wide blue eyes brimmed with tears. "Yes."

While the response explained the high-tech capabilities behind the game, it also left Dani with more questions. Why would a tech billionaire force people into a deadly showdown? Sensing Megan had limited knowledge, she kept her questions pertinent to her.

"Why did your father take you prisoner?"

"I've worked with him over the years," Megan said. "I'm good at computer-generated imaging, so he pays me to enhance his VR. A few months ago, he told me he was close to nabbing a contract for virtual military training. Said he wanted my help to make it more realistic." She looked down. "He's, um . . . got some issues. I thought he had everything under control, but I think he got off his meds."

Dani felt her brows go up. "Medication for what?"

"You must have seen the news stories about the kidnapping." When Dani nodded, Megan's voice dropped to a whisper. "When I got back, he wasn't the same. Kinda paranoid. We both went to see shrinks." She shook her head. "Looking back on it, I think he finally snapped a couple of months ago."

Megan had to deal with the violent death of her mother and now a father who was criminally insane. Dani's heart went out to her in shared grief. In her case, it was her father who had been murdered and her mother who was mentally unbalanced. She resisted the urge to hug Megan and focused on their immediate survival.

"You said we had to get out of here." She touched Megan's chin, forcing her head up to meet her eyes. "Where are we, and how do we escape?"

"We're in a missile silo outside of Tucson," she said. "We're on the third level down, and there's only one exit." She pointed at the ceiling. "We have to go up, but Dad will find ways to stop us."

A missile silo made total sense. She had wondered why there was only a door on the surface with no building around it. Now that she understood where they were, she appreciated their predicament on a whole new level, and she was all too familiar with the many ways Nemesis had of stopping them from leaving.

An overriding question remained. "Does your father know people who . . ." She hesitated, not sure how to phrase the question so Megan would understand. "People who would be willing to commit crimes for him?"

She had not referred to hired killers, mercenaries, or thugs. Whatever Nemesis had done, he was still her father, and she did not want to risk alienating the only person who knew the complex.

"I don't think so," Megan said, clearly hedging. "Then again, he's been acting strange for a while."

Aware Nemesis was likely listening in on their conversation, she got to the point. "I heard what sounded like a group of men storming the facility. I'm an FBI agent. They could be here to rescue us, or it could be a crew hired by your father to hunt us down."

Megan's pale hand flew to her mouth. "We've got to hide until we know who's in here."

"Is there a place we can go where the cameras can't see us?"

"Let me think." Megan looked up at the ceiling, then stilled, nose wrinkling. "Do you smell smoke?"

Dani had noticed the pungent fumes at the same instant. "I do."

Her heart sank. She hoped like hell the odor was not coming from above, because if a fire had broken out in a vertical structure with only one exit and they were trapped below it, there was no way out.

CHAPTER 62

Dani considered the possibilities. Had the men she had heard on the other side of the door deployed smoke canisters to flush her out, or was there an actual fire in the silo? The answer could mean the difference between life and death.

She looked at Megan. "There are boxes for fire extinguishers in the facility. I've seen some of them, but they were all empty."

"Wouldn't make a difference if they were there," Megan said. "If this place is burning, we have a major problem."

Judging by the color draining from Megan's face, Dani knew she wouldn't like the answer, but asked the question anyway. "What's that?"

"The silo has seven levels. There's a huge diesel fuel tank on the fifth level down. If it ignites, we'll get blown sky-high."

Yep. She definitely did not like the answer. "Why is there a fuel tank in here?"

Megan gestured around. "To generate power. This silo was built to be off the grid."

Made sense. Back in the Cold War days, the military couldn't afford to have its main defense taken out if the electrical grid went down.

"I thought diesel wasn't as flammable as gasoline," she said to Megan, thinking back to her experience with military convoys.

"That's true until the diesel fuel is heated," she said. "Once it reaches a flash point, it'll give off heated fumes that will ignite on contact with flames." When Dani stared at her, she added, "My father taught me safety measures."

"Safety measures," Dani repeated, thinking fast. "Is there a fireproof room in the silo? Someplace where workers could have gone if things went wrong?"

"No," Megan said without any trace of doubt. "And it already feels hot."

Dani felt it, too, but hadn't said anything, not wanting to alarm Megan. She had to keep her calm and mine her for useful information. "I'm feeling the heat from above us. Is there a way to send for help?"

Megan was already shaking her head before Dani finished. "If the fire is above us, we're screwed." She began to shake. "And if the electrical system catches, it'll spread through the whole complex . . . except the control center. That's walled off with a fireproof door."

"Can we get to the control room?"

"The access tube is above us. We're stuck down here. Totally cut off." Her voice rose in panic. "Some of the wiring in this place is original. My dad incorporated it with the new stuff."

"What are you getting at?" Dani asked.

Megan's pallid cheeks were suddenly suffused with a flush creeping up her neck. "Shooting the wires caused a short," she said, breathing hard.

Despite the growing heat, Dani's insides froze. "If you've been locked inside a closet for days, how would you know the wiring was shot?"

Megan stared back at her, making no response.

Dani took a step toward her. "Only Nemesis would know that."

Megan spun and darted back inside the storage closet, pulling the door shut behind her.

Dani grasped the broken knob and yanked the door open again. She rushed inside to find the cramped room empty and dark except for the light from the corridor. Dani groped along the wall until she found a latch. She tugged it, and a panel slid open, revealing hidden stairs.

She barreled down two flights, coming out in another corridor, unsure where she was. Whoever the woman who called herself Megan Brinkley really was, and whatever she had to do with this, Dani had to find her.

CHAPTER 63

Wu turned away from the video feed where he had watched the exchange between the two women. "If Megan Brinkley was watching Vega, she had to be in the control room," he said to Flint. "Not locked inside a closet."

"Then Megan is involved," Flint said. "But is she helping her father, or is she responsible for the whole thing?"

Wu wanted to throw something but kept his anger in check. If Megan Brinkley had been behind it all, had they just killed an innocent man? Worse, how was Vega going to survive?

"Who the hell is this Nemesis Vega was talking about?" Flint asked.

Wu offered the only explanation that occurred to him. "Must be something that was edited out of the feed from the game." He would figure out that detail later. "Contact Patel and Johnson," he said to Flint. "I want everything they can find on Megan Brinkley, Nemesis, and putting out a fire in a missile silo." Another thought occurred to him. "And see if you can get a secure link to the JTTF."

Flint pulled his phone out, and Wu shifted his gaze to Benton. "What's the status on the fire department?"

"Still fifteen minutes out," Benton said.

Every red light on the second floor was glowing, and new ones were blinking to life on the level below. Fortunately Vega had chased Megan down two levels and was now on the fifth level underground. She was safe for the time being, but that wouldn't last long.

"The fire department won't make it in time," Benton said. "And even if they were here now, they might not go in because of the diesel tank."

Wu had checked. The schematic revealed Megan had been telling the truth. There was a large tank filled with diesel fuel on the fifth level down, where Vega was right now.

"I'm not going to give up on her," he said.

"Neither will I," Benton said. "I still want to go down after her."

Wu regarded him for a long moment. "Maybe the sensors are damaged. Take a small team and check the tube leading to the silo. Keep your com link on."

Benton signaled three operators, who followed him to the door opposite the one they had used to come into the control room. They had already determined the door was unlocked. As soon as Benton opened it, a wave of heat flowed into the control room.

The sensors had not malfunctioned.

Benton and his contingent went into the tube. Wu was about to call them back when Flint tapped his shoulder.

"Patel established a secure link on the laptop he gave you," Flint said. "I brought everyone up to speed, and they're already working on the problem."

The problem.

Such a mundane way to describe their current nightmare. A few minutes ago, he had been convinced they had neutralized the imminent threat and were on the verge of rescuing Vega. Instead, he may have overseen the death of an innocent man, and one of his agents was about to die. If that weren't bad enough, a contingent from the HRT was about to sacrifice themselves trying to do the impossible. Finally, if he handled this wrong, everyone involved would end up blown to bits.

Unless his last-ditch plan worked.

He booted up the laptop and accessed the link. "We're running out of time," he said as soon as Patel's face appeared on the screen.

"Understood," Patel said. "How can I help?"

"If I connect this laptop to the control panel, can you hack in?"

Wu waited for what seemed like an eternity while Patel considered his idea.

"Is there a port?" he finally said.

"There are three," Wu said. "And I have a connector cable."

"Plug me in," Patel said.

Wu connected the laptop, hoping the link would not be destroyed by malware or blocked by an elaborate firewall. While Patel hunched over his keyboard, Wu turned to the sound of Benton and his team coming back through the control room door.

"We got the door on the other end of the tube open," he said to Wu. "But we were nearly flambéed."

Gizmo stepped in after Benton. "That whole section is on fire," he said. "The flames beat us back every time we tried to get through. Our fire extinguishers didn't help either."

Benton met his gaze. "If that fuel ignites, it will create a fireball that will blow up the whole complex."

"Correction," Wu said, hating himself for what he was about to say next. "It will blow up the silo—not us. We're in the control room. There's a pressure lock on the door, and it's blast proof. If we seal it, the fire can't get in here."

The room went completely silent. Everyone understood the implication. They could be assured of their safety if they were willing to cut off Vega's only avenue of escape. All eyes were on him. As the ranking official, the call was his to make.

He glanced back to the laptop. "Are you in, Patel?"

Patel's head popped up. "I found a back door, but I'll have limited capabilities. I can't control the functions that are damaged."

"It'll have to do. There could be a way to isolate the fire and deprive it of oxygen, or maybe there's another way to put it out. We won't know until we get into the controls."

"We have to seal this room off while we're in here," Benton said. "Or we go up when this place does."

Wu directed his next words to Benton, but they were meant for everyone. "Leave the door to the control room open, and do not activate the pressure lock. All nonessential personnel are to evacuate to the surface and clear the immediate area. If Agent Vega is going to get out of here, her only chance is for someone to stay and maintain the computer link." He paused to make sure everyone understood. "That someone will be me."

CHAPTER 64

Dani would never have guessed there was a hidden passage between a storage closet and stairs going down two levels. Megan clearly knew a lot about the silo. Information Dani would force her to share once she caught her.

And she would catch her.

She burst through the lower door and raced down the corridor at a dead sprint. Megan was just turning the corner at the far end, and Dani slowed briefly to check rather than running recklessly around the bend. She had believed Megan's father was Nemesis, but it could be Megan or the two of them working together. Either way, Megan had lied to her, and this entire space was her domain. Was she leading Dani into a trap?

Megan had disappeared into a room off to the side, and Dani carefully followed her inside.

As soon as she entered, Dani stopped short. Megan sat perched on a metal railing, facing an opening to the floor below. She seemed to be contemplating leaping down to escape.

"Don't come any closer," Megan said to her. "Or I'll jump."

The drop couldn't be more than twelve feet—totally survivable and unlikely to cause injury—so why the hesitation? She leaned forward, craning her neck to see over the railing, and got her answer.

They were on the balcony level above the floor covered in electrified pressure plates. Judging by Megan's behavior, the plates were still live.

"It doesn't have to end like this, Megan," she said, deliberately personalizing the remark by using her first name. "Why don't you and I work together to find a way out of here and—"

"I'll tell you something useful," Megan said. "But you'll have to go over to the other side of the balcony before I'll talk."

Leery, Dani took a few steps toward the far side of the room, then stopped. Before going farther, she would test Megan.

"Is this good?" she called out.

Megan shook her head. "A bit more. I'll tell you when you get there."

Test failed.

"You're maneuvering me into a trap," she said. "I'm not moving another inch. You can stay here and burn to death—or jump down and fry yourself. Up to you."

Megan swore.

A red glow caught Dani's eye. She peered down to the level below and spotted the variable message display that had provided the clue for the Fibonacci sequence, only now it showed an odd constellation of images. Narrowing her eyes, she made out a series of hyphens and periods arranged in different patterns separated by slashes.

.- / --. / . / -. / - / ... - / . / --. / . / - / - / .... / .. / ... / .. / ... / ..- / -... / .. / . / .-- / . / -.-. / . / ..-

Minutes ago, she had heard a group of people shooting their way into the control room. Were they sending her a message? Why not spell it out like the Fibonacci clue? Why a coded message?

Coded.

Within seconds, her mind, so accustomed to recognizing patterns, detected Morse code. She had been required to memorize it as part of her military training in code breaking, and she quickly translated the dots and dashes.

A G E N T V E G A T H I S I S F B I W E C U

She pumped her fist in the air. They had found her. Their communication was obviously limited, but perhaps she could get information to them.

"You can see me," she said aloud. "But can you hear me?"

Megan whipped her head around so fast she nearly fell off the railing. "Who the hell are you talking to?"

Ignoring her, Dani waited in breathless anticipation until the screen went black again. A moment later, a fresh message glowed red.

-.-- / . / ...

YES

Unbidden, suspicion crept into her mind. Nemesis was adept at mind games. Could this be another one? Was this truly the FBI, or was the group who had been shooting sending the message from the control room? And where was Megan's father in all this? Were they working together after all? With so many questions, it was impossible to know what to believe. There had to be a test.

Following Dani's gaze, Megan figured out where she was looking. "What's on the screen down there?" she said. "Wait. Is that Morse code?"

It figured that someone smart enough to know the Fibonacci sequence would recognize one of the most famous codes in the world.

"Yes." Dani waved a dismissive hand. "Shut up and let me think."

She needed a piece of information that no one could research or hack into a database to find. Something not easily guessed and that only the people she worked with every day would know.

"What do I eat for breakfast every morning?" she said into the stillness around her.

The response came in less than thirty seconds, replacing the previous response with a new one.

-... / .-.. / .- / -.-. / -.- / -.-. / --- / ..-. / ..-. / . /

BLACKCOFFEE

Satisfied, she disregarded Megan's continued questions and wasted no time bringing them up to speed, delivering a rapid-fire explanation of her current status. She stopped in midsentence, however, when the screens went blank and flickered back on again with a fresh set of dots and dashes.

..- / .-. / .. / -. / -.. / .- / -. / --. / . / .-.

URINDANGER

"I know I'm in danger," she said, frustrated. "That's what I've been—"

The screens flickered with a new message.

. / -..- / .. / - / - ... / .-.. / --- / -.-. / -.- / . / -.. / -... /
-.-- / ..-. / .. / .-. / .

EXITBLOCKEDBYFIRE

"What does it say?" Megan asked, shrill with panic at Dani's last words.

This time, Dani translated for Megan as the next message filled the screen.

-. / --- / .-- / .- / -.-- / --- / ..- / -

NOWAYOUT

CHAPTER 65

Megan listened to Agent Vega's translation of the Morse code in growing horror. Her heart seized, then accelerated to a frenetic pulse when her worst fears were confirmed. Head swimming, she barely maintained her grip on the railing. Perhaps she should just let herself fall. Electrocution might be less painful than burning alive.

Everything she had worked for, all the plans, and the backup plans, were about to literally go up in smoke. Or, given the diesel fuel tank's location on the same level where she was now, perhaps it would be more accurate to say they were about to blow up in her face.

She looked at Vega, who stood still, apparently lost in thought, searching for options that didn't exist. Tall, stoic, and imposing, Vega was a woman she could almost admire.

If she hadn't ruined everything.

Her plan had been to lure Vega to the other side of the room, where a trapdoor in the floor would give way, sending her plummeting onto the pressure plates. Her current seat would have given her the perfect vantage point to watch the final retribution play out.

Now she would share Vega's fate. To say that it was unfair was so far past the appalling irony of the situation that she couldn't process the thought.

Vega addressed her. "My fellow agents are in the control room. Is there anything they can do from in there to put out the fire?"

"If there was, I would have told you by now," she said, not troubling to hide her disdain.

Vega spoke to the message display as if it were a video screen. "Can you find any way to stop it from spreading down to our level?"

The screen flickered again.

-. / . / --. / . / .- / - / .. / . / ...- / .

"Negative." Vega translated after a few seconds.

Megan had a question of her own. "How much time will it take for the fire to get down here?"

She held her breath and waited for the response, which came all too quickly.

..--..

Vega turned to her. "That's the symbol for a question mark."

Megan had improvised what she'd thought was the perfect plan once she realized the FBI was on the scene. Their jamming devices did not work on every frequency, and her father's elaborate systems to prevent corporate espionage had worked perfectly, giving her enough time to put her backup plan in motion.

First, she had remotely unlocked the panel covering the crawl space in the control room where she had kept her father locked for the past week so he would roll out onto the floor to find the room empty. She had already retreated to the storage closet, but not before leaving one of the loaded guns confiscated from the Colonel's team behind for dear old Dad to find on the main console.

She had previously disabled the intercom system so her father couldn't alert the Feds that he wanted to surrender. Not that he would anyway. She knew he would try to shoot his way out, using whatever controls on the panel he could to give himself the advantage. She did not deactivate the camera system. She wanted her father to see the team coming to arrest him and go on the offensive.

In short, she had set him up to die.

After putting everything in place, she'd concealed herself in the storage closet with the hidden passage and bound her wrists in front of her body with a zip tie and pulled it tight with her teeth. Next, she placed a gag in her mouth and raised her arms to knot it at the back of her head. It had taken some manual dexterity, but she'd managed it without too much trouble.

Posing as her father's prisoner would help sell her story to the FBI. She was the daughter of a madman. An innocent bystander and victim of his insane vendetta against the ones who had killed his beloved wife. He had become unbalanced after the incident, growing more paranoid over time until he began to believe his own daughter was a threat to his company. He had accused her of spying for his competition and locked her up until after the new DOD contract went through. He had probably intended to kill her at some point, but no one would ever know, because he was dead.

He was dead and she was an heiress. Most importantly, justice had been served.

She had orchestrated everything to pit her enemies against each other. She had no blood on her hands. Liars lied, cheaters cheated, and killers killed. They would be the architects of their own destruction, and she would bear witness to it all.

That had been the plan. And it had worked perfectly until Agent Daniela Vega had stepped into the picture.

When Megan had first discovered Vega's true identity, she believed the Fates had delivered a chance for perfect justice. She had reflected on the situation, judged the FBI, and found them guilty.

Who investigated financial crimes? The FBI. If they had been doing their job, Senator Sledge would never have been able to take bribes from people like her father, who funneled money through the Colonel, making all of them rich. Making them believe they could do anything they wanted.

When she and her mother had been kidnapped, who had investigated? The FBI. If they had figured out what was really going on, her mother would be alive today.

Finally, after she had been returned, who had botched the investigation and allowed everyone responsible to get away with murder? The FBI.

Someone had to pay for their incompetence, and Vega had offered herself up like the human sacrifice she was about to become. If it was the last thing Megan did—and it probably would be—she would have her revenge.

She had used everyone's personality traits against them. The senator had succumbed to greed. Arrogance had undone her father. The Colonel had fallen victim to his ruthless ambition. So what was Vega's weakness?

The newspaper articles about Vega's parents explained something Megan had not appreciated until now. How many times had she seen Vega save others in the game? Too many to count. Why would a federal agent risk her life for criminals?

Because Daniela Vega wanted to be a hero like her decorated combat veteran father to prove she was nothing like her mother.

A hero would be a sucker for a damsel in distress. Megan had already seen that when she had pretended to be locked in the storage closet. Now all she had to do was get herself into another situation where Vega would have to rescue her, then strike when she least expected it.

CHAPTER 66

Dani watched Megan edge farther forward, her body teetering on the thin railing.

"We might not make it out of here," Megan said. "And I want to say something to the FBI."

"Now you decide to make a confession?" Dani said.

"Not a confession," Megan said. "I did nothing wrong. I want to give them a clue to follow. No one should get away with murder."

"Who did you murder, Megan?"

"Like I said, no one. I'm not a killer." She narrowed her eyes. "Everyone who died brought it on themselves. They died because of what they did."

Dani turned the conversation back to the most pertinent point. "You said you might know something helpful. If it involves getting out of here, let's hear it. Then you can tell the FBI whatever you want when we're safe." She didn't add that Megan would be in handcuffs when she made her statement.

"Listen to me." Megan leaned forward, her expression filled with intensity. "If you want the truth, you've got to see what's in the mirror."

"What the hell does that have to do with anything?" Dani asked.

"You'll find out later."

Dani was heartily sick of Megan and her riddles. "This isn't a game, Megan."

"For me, it never was," Megan said, jerking a thumb at her chest. "As far as getting out of here, I—"

Megan let out a scream as she wobbled. Taking one of her hands off the railing had thrown her off balance. "Help!" She flung her arm out, trying to steady herself.

Dani realized she would reach her faster by running around the other side of the balcony. She raced along, determined to pull Megan back. Suddenly the floor disappeared beneath her, and she began to fall. Chunks of what looked like the solid concrete floor but were apparently a thin veneer of gray plaster tumbled down through a hole that had opened under her.

She had been sprinting, and her momentum carried her to the far side of the opening. She managed to grasp the edge of what she realized was a trapdoor. She kicked the air with her dangling feet, fighting to haul herself up. The loosened chunks hit the pressure plates below.

Laughter drew her attention, and she glanced up to see Megan enjoying the show.

"You're pathetic," Megan said. "Worse yet, you're predictable."

Megan had put on the exact performance necessary to draw Dani into her trap. Dani could not let her win. Not like this. She clawed at the edges of the floor, desperate to find a hold. Her fingers latched onto a piece of rebar in the concrete that had been part of the original construction. It wasn't much, but it stopped her from falling.

"Hey, what's going on?" Megan said, leaning forward to see why Dani was once again inconveniently refusing to die.

Dani wasted no energy on a response. She focused every ounce of her concentration on leveraging her body to pull herself up. She managed to get up to her elbows. Now all she had to do was swing her feet a few times until momentum carried them high enough to catch her heel on the edge.

"No!" Megan rose to get a better view. Her feet were on the bottom rail, and the backs of her thighs were pressed against the top rail. "Fine," she said. "You won't go on your own, then I'll help you."

Megan intended to come over and kick her, stomp her hands, or do whatever else was necessary to break her tenuous grip. It wouldn't take much. Dani redoubled her efforts, determined to get herself up before Megan reached her.

She checked to see how close she was and saw Megan rotate her body to swing her legs over the rail and step down onto the balcony. Megan's hurried movements telegraphed her anger and impatience to get to Dani before she could climb out of the hole.

Megan's foot slipped on the smooth railing, and Dani could tell this time she wasn't faking when she bent at the waist and threw her arms out to regain her balance. Powerless to intervene, Dani watched as Megan overcorrected, then wobbled and fell backward, arms flailing as she sailed through space. Her screams were cut short by sizzles and pops, followed by a plume of smoke that drifted up to where Dani still clung to the edge of the hole. In the space of a heartbeat, Megan's campaign of vengeance ended. Moments ago, she had claimed to have no blood on her hands. Said that everyone who died brought it on themselves. In her final moments, did she realize that she had done the same? In the end, her need for revenge had destroyed her.

The acrid smell of charred flesh reached Dani's nose, spurring her on. She would join Megan on the pressure plates if she didn't get her ass up to the balcony floor.

A few more kicks and she hooked the heel of her boot on the edge. After that, she was able to pull herself up and roll onto her back. Dragging in gulps of tainted air, she knew she had managed only a stay of execution. Flames blazed above her, coming ever closer.

CHAPTER 67

Wu heard Patel's sigh of relief when Vega finally scrambled up from the hole in the floor. He shared the sentiment but could not allow himself the luxury of celebrating the small victory. There was a much steeper mountain to climb, and he had to take a measured breath to slow his pounding heart and think clearly.

Vega was counting on him.

"I can't believe that psycho bitch was going to shove Vega into the hole," Flint said, still staring at the level-five monitor. "Only it didn't exactly work out the way she planned, did it?"

Wu had ordered everyone out, but the detective had stubbornly refused to go, insisting that two sets of eyes were better than one. When Wu pointed out that both Patel and Johnson were hooked into the system and monitoring everything that happened, Flint switched tactics. He might be needed as backup in case something happened to Wu. He could get an electrical shock from the exposed and damaged wires hanging from the control panel.

Unwilling to waste any more time arguing, Wu had allowed him to stay. Benton and his team were topside, awaiting orders and monitoring the situation on another Patel-issued laptop.

"The fire has spread down to level four," Patel said. "I'll send Vega another message in Morse code, letting her know."

"Hold off a minute," Wu said. "I don't want to give her any information that isn't useful. She knows what's going on. Why give her a blow-by-blow account of how close the flames are getting?"

"Agreed," Flint said. "We should communicate when there is some action for her to take. Otherwise we're just making things worse."

He looked at the 3D schematic again. Now that Vega was no longer in danger of imminent electrocution, there was more time to study the facility.

"Did Johnson find anything about fire regulations?" he asked Patel.

As soon as the alarms began, he had asked his chief analyst to look up emergency fire contingencies for both the original silo and after the renovations had been completed. The government would have required protocols for such a structure.

Benton had asked the local fire captain the same question after the hook-and-ladder trucks showed up a few minutes ago. Unfortunately the captain had no information about the facility. He had also directed his firefighters to stand by for the same reason Wu had ordered his personnel up to the surface. Not only was it impossible for them to get down to the lower levels to rescue Vega, but the whole structure might explode at any second.

Johnson's face appeared on the screen, crowding Patel. "I reviewed the fire regs, sir," she said. "They were relying on the blast proofing and the pressure seal in the control room to prevent a fire from causing injury."

"They never thought to have a system in place for the silo itself?" Wu said. "That's where the fuel tank is. That's where the missile goes boom to launch itself out of the ground."

"Exactly," Johnson said. "The silo was never designed to have people spending a lot of time in it. Scientists and engineers could go down and do routine maintenance and repairs, but they would stay in the control room and handle most of it remotely." She looked apologetic. "When Brinkley renovated it, they required him to add some fire extinguishers on each level, but that's it. If the fuel ignited, the original ventilation shafts were supposed to allow most of the pressure to escape."

Wu massaged his temples. "How big are those shafts?"

"Not very big at all," Johnson said. "They weren't designed for people."

"What's the diameter?" Wu pressed.

She consulted her notes. "I can't find that information."

He addressed Patel, who was watching in the background. "Send a Morse code message to Vega. Tell her there are two ventilation shafts. We need her to check and see if she can fit inside."

Patel's face replaced Johnson's, taking up the screen. "I'll send it right away, but we don't want her going toward the vent closest to the fuel tank."

An idea occurred to him. "Can you control all the display screens on the bottom level?"

"Level seven is still functional," Patel said. "But she'll probably be disoriented."

"Tell her to go down to the bottom and follow the arrows you're going to put on those screens."

"On it," Patel said, and began typing commands.

Flint stepped beside him. "What if the ventilation shafts are too small?"

He turned and gave the detective a hard stare.

Flint held his hands up in mock surrender. "Forget I asked."

CHAPTER 68

Dani glanced up at the panel to see a glowing red arrow pointing toward the end of another corridor. She had received the coded message ten minutes earlier and had followed the instructions, descending to the bottom level, where she had started the game.

She had been told that SAC Wu was guiding her, which was probably the only reason she had gone along with the idea. Every instinct she possessed screamed for her to head toward the surface, but she had to trust that her supervisor and her team knew she could make her way up through the shaft.

She reached the end of the hallway, where another wall-mounted screen awaited her.

"This screen is malfunctioning," she said into the air. "The arrow is pointing straight down. I'm on the lowest level."

The arrow flicked off. Then on. Then off. Then on.

"Okay, so it's not a mistake," she said. "But I'm not seeing anything that looks like a vent."

She peered down at a solid metal panel painted gray and screwed into the concrete walls. She gave it a rap with her knuckles, and it rang hollow.

"It's a piece of sheet metal," she said. "I guess they covered up the vents for some reason." She regarded it a moment. "This looks big enough for me to fit inside. Of course, the panel could be covering a six-inch-wide shaft."

She had meant the remark to come off lightly, but the last word stuck in her throat. She had no illusions about her situation. This was her last hope. If the shaft was too small for her, there was nothing anyone could do to save her.

"Focus on the mission, Vega," she muttered, and reached up to grasp the clip from her hair. She held it up to the camera for her team to see. "Tactical hair clip," she said. "Never leave home without it."

She stooped to put the flat head of the reinforced steel clip into the top of the screw. Painted tight. Cursing, she used the serrated edge of the clip to scrape away a thick coat of paint. After that, the screw turned easily, but she had to spend precious minutes scraping and cleaning all four screws.

She finally pried the sheet metal loose and let it clatter to the floor. "It's big enough," she said, giving a quick thumbs-up to the camera before sticking her head into the round hole in the wall.

Big enough was optimistic. The shaft could get narrower as it went up. Now that a possibility of escape existed, she considered the logistics. The silo had seven levels. She did the math.

"I'm going to have to climb more than seven stories inside a tube with smooth walls. I checked, and there are no rungs inside."

Doubt crept into her mind. Then a thought occurred to her.

"If the shaft vents out at the surface, can someone throw a rope down to me?"

She looked at the screen, waiting for a response. Apparently this involved some checking, because she waited a full minute before she saw a plus sign.

Positive. She took that as a yes.

"Okay, so I can ask yes-or-no questions." She worded her next one carefully. "Do you have enough rope to reach me?"

Minus sign.

"Will I have to push myself up more than twenty feet to reach the rope?"

Plus sign.

She blew out a sigh. "More than forty feet?"

Minus sign.

She would have to push herself up a maximum of forty feet in a tight, slippery tube. That was a hell of a lot more doable than climbing all the way out. "Is the fire close to the shaft?"

Plus sign.

Not good. The heat would be a problem.

"I'm going up the shaft now," she said, looking at the camera. "I won't be able to communicate with you any longer."

Plus sign.

Wu was green-lighting the plan. She bent and wedged herself into the tube, which traveled horizontally for several feet before turning at a ninety-degree angle and heading straight up. She had been through her share of obstacle courses, but getting her body through the sharp bend was one of the more difficult challenges she had faced. She was grateful to be wearing spandex. Nothing to catch on the welded edges as she slid herself into position.

Standing on her feet, she tipped her head back and realized she could not even see a tiny pinprick of light above her. Either she was too far down to see up to the surface, or something was blocking the shaft. Or it was full of smoke.

She braced her back against one side of the tube and lifted her boot to plant it against the opposite side. She had done this kind of maneuver before in training, but the shaft had been square. And wider.

The tightness in the space made it difficult to raise her leg and plant her foot. Twice she slid back down to the bottom after shimmying up about twenty feet.

And then she felt the heat. Failure was no longer an option. Exhausted, thirsty, and hungry, she marshaled her last vestiges of strength and pushed herself higher.

Inching up in the darkness made her claustrophobic. Her lungs seemed to compress, and she had trouble breathing. Was this what a panic attack felt like? No. Not panic. Not claustrophobia.

Smoke.

The vent was doing its job, channeling fumes and heat up from the silo toward the surface. Only she was in the way.

She began to feel light-headed. If she fell from this height, she would injure herself at best. At worst, she would tumble into a fog of toxic fumes and suffocate.

Her muscles slackened, and she knew she was slipping into unconsciousness.

CHAPTER 69

Wu stood at the top of the ventilation shaft and peered down into the fathomless darkness. He could make out no sign of Vega.

He turned and waved at the fire captain. "You got a crowbar somewhere on that hook-and-ladder truck?" he shouted.

Once Vega crawled inside the shaft, he had closed the door to the control room and activated the pressure seal, then left Patel's computer linked to the system. With the door pressure sealed and tons of earth between the silo and the control room, he felt confident Patel could continue to remotely operate the panel. With nothing left to do below ground, he and Flint had headed to the surface, where they had gotten into an argument almost as heated as the silo.

The fire captain trotted up to Wu and slapped the heavy metal bar into his outstretched hand. "I can tie the knot if you need me to," he offered.

Wu had received plenty of training tying knots when he'd been in the Atlanta HRT.

"I've got it." He gestured toward the fire truck parked in the distance. "You can wait back over there with the others."

The captain's expression told him he didn't appreciate Wu's orders any more than Flint or Benton had. When Vega had asked about a rope, Benton had responded on the com system that they had a one-hundred-foot rope in their gear. The problem was that the silo was 146 feet deep. If they had been back home in New York, they would have had one double that length, but they had traveled light.

That was when Wu had sealed off the control room and come to the surface. He'd checked out the vent for himself after the firefighters pried the cap off. The argument with Flint and Benton had started when he'd ordered everyone else to get back out of harm's way.

"The whole purpose of the shaft is to allow an escape for toxic gases, fumes, and possibly a fireball in the event of an explosion in the silo," he had told them. "Anyone standing here lowering a rope into the shaft or pulling it up will be instantly killed if that diesel tank blows."

Benton and his team had offered to do the job anyway, and he had pulled rank. "This is my op. It's my call. I'm the one who will get her out."

He pretended not to hear when Benton muttered, "Or die trying."

It was the best he could do to minimize the casualties. If everything went to shit, he and Vega would be the only ones to die. "Look," the captain said. "Our fire hose is thirty-six meters long. That's 118 feet. We can park the truck right here and reel her in like a marlin to a troller."

Wu didn't like repeating himself. "I've already given you my answer. I'm taking care of this." The hook-and-ladder truck, as well as the firefighters needed to operate it, would be well inside the blast radius if the silo exploded. They could all be burned, or the entire truck could sink into a massive crater if the silo's sealed cover imploded. Parking the truck a safe distance away would render the firehose too short for Vega to reach. He had analyzed every possibility. This was the best option.

The captain turned and started back toward his engine while Wu finished tying the knot. He tested it, then fed the heavy rope down into the shaft, trying not to think about the waves of heat that emanated up to him. If he could feel them up here, what was Vega going through down where she was?

Hoping he would get a response this time, he shouted into the shaft, "Vega!"

An obscenity came up to him from the darkness below.

She was alive.

"You okay?" he called down to her.

"A crowbar just smacked me."

He smiled. She had managed to push herself up more than forty feet. "You're supposed to grab it, Vega."

"As soon as my head stops spinning, I will."

He had sent the rope down fast. Maybe too fast. Was she concussed? Keep her talking. Keep her conscious.

"Tug on the rope when you're ready for me to pull you up."

He waited. Nothing happened. He lifted the rope experimentally. It came up easily. She wasn't holding it. The heat could be getting to her. Fear welled within him. He dropped the rope again, deliberately letting it fall free.

"Ouch."

She sounded bleary, like she was barely holding on. He reflected on everything he had learned about her over the past few days. What would her military leaders have done in this situation?

He cupped a hand around his mouth and bellowed down the hole in his best impression of a drill sergeant. "Get your ass in gear, soldier!" He paused. "Grab that fucking crowbar, Vega."

The rope grew taut, and he began lifting her up, straining with the effort. He kept in shape with regular workouts, but she was solid muscle.

"I feel dizzy."

Her words drifted up to him, quieter than before. She sounded weak.

"Are you a Ranger or not?" he called down through the shaft.

She didn't answer. She had used up all her reserves and had no energy left to respond. Was she about to pass out?

He wouldn't allow it. Not after all she had been through.

"You hold on to that bar and don't let go," he shouted. "That's an order."

She was running out of time, and he was going as fast as he could. If he lost her now, he would never forgive himself.

A pair of burly arms reached in from his right, and another pair reached in from his left. A third set grabbed him around his waist and heaved him back. Benton and his team had disobeyed a direct order. One by one, they all latched onto a section of rope and pulled. Suddenly they were jogging backward, Vega seeming weightless when ten men were tugging her to the surface.

He let go of the rope and twisted away from Flint, who apparently also couldn't follow orders and was grasping his midsection. Wordlessly he rushed to the shaft and bent down, putting his entire upper body into the tube.

Vega came rushing up, her knuckles white as she clutched the crowbar. One of her sweat-slick hands slipped off. The crowbar tipped sideways, and Vega's remaining hand began to slide toward the hooked end. If he didn't do something fast, she would plummet to her death.

"Hold my legs," he yelled over his shoulder.

An instant later, he felt strong arms wrap around his knees as he heaved himself deeper into the shaft.

The crowbar came within his reach, and he grasped the hooked end with two fingers. "Hang on," he yelled at her, desperately trying to get a better grip.

He pulled up, but her hand slid farther down. She couldn't hold on much longer.

He flung his body downward and felt the grip around his knees break. He began to fall headfirst down the shaft amid a cacophony of shouted obscenities from the men above until someone caught his ankles.

It had been enough for him to latch onto Vega's wrist. "I've got you," he said to her. "It's okay, I've got you now."

She said nothing and felt like deadweight in his grasp. More hands grabbed his legs and heaved both of them up, grunting and cursing.

When he pulled her out, she slumped in his arms, unconscious.

"We've got to get the hell out of here," Benton said. "This place is going to blow."

Wu adjusted Vega, draping her over his shoulder in the fireman's-carry position.

"I don't know whether to give you an ass-chewing or a medal," he said to Benton.

"I've had both," Benton said. "You can figure it out later. Right now we need to beat feet."

He took off at a jog, and Wu trotted beside him. They made it past the fire truck seconds before the sky erupted in a ball of fire that lit the desert below.

CHAPTER 70

Two days later, Dani stood alone in the elevator at 26 Fed. Her stomach lurched as she sped upward, the brief weightless sensation reminding her of the dizziness she had felt in the shaft. Her only clear memories of the suffocating shaft were of darkness, fatigue, pain, and nearly unbearable heat.

During her darkest moments, she had believed she would pass out, fall, and be cooked alive in an underground inferno. The only thing that kept her going was the sound of a drill sergeant ordering her to soldier on. She learned later that it had been Wu's voice barking orders at her, driving her to continue when she had no strength left.

In the end, the will to live was the only thing she had to draw from, and Wu had tapped into that final reserve. She had done all she could to help others, all she could to survive, but it had been teamwork that had saved her.

She had only a dim recollection of the ambulance ride to Tucson General Hospital, where they had insisted she stay overnight for observation. Wu had agreed, overriding her objections.

She wasn't concerned about her body, which would heal quickly. She had spent a restless night replaying scenes from inside the game, always ending in someone's death. The most painful of which had been Toro's. She was only beginning to process her feelings, which were conflicted and raw.

The elevator doors opened to reveal Wu, who was apparently waiting for her. He must have asked the security personnel to alert him when she arrived. She stepped out into the hallway slowly, muscles still stiff from her ordeal.

"How are you feeling?" Wu asked her.

"Fine," she lied.

He met the blatant falsehood with a raised brow before changing the subject. "Assistant Director Hargrave is waiting for us."

She followed when he pivoted and walked in the direction of the ADIC's spacious office. Her boss had included himself in the summons, but she was certain it had been directed at her. She had been the one who had not just broken but pulverized every rule in the book during her undercover assignment. As the sole survivor, how could she call the mission a success?

Wu opened the door without knocking, which meant the ADIC had also been made aware of her arrival in advance. She lifted her chin and strode inside, taking one of two chairs facing Hargrave's desk.

"First and foremost," Hargrave began after she and Wu settled, "I'm grateful that you're back safely. I've provided updates to Washington, and even the director himself was quite concerned about your . . . situation."

Dani squirmed in her chair. She had met Director Franklin only once. It was the day she graduated from the FBI Academy in Quantico, and she had no expectation of her name crossing his awareness again throughout her career. She had never tried for promotion in the military, and she had no desire to climb the ranks in federal law enforcement either. She preferred to be responsible for herself and those who worked closely with her rather than for a large contingent of personnel.

"You did, however, take actions that were against protocol," Hargrave went on. "The Undercover Review Committee and the Office of Professional Responsibility will conduct investigations into everything that happened during your assignment."

Her reckoning had come. They would put her under a microscope, scrutinizing every second of video Patel had salvaged from the unedited raw footage from the database before the whole system went up in smoke. Even the director, who would be too busy to devote hours to watching, would have a summary, including video clips prepared for him to view. She suppressed a shudder at the thought of him evaluating her performance.

Wu found his voice. "Agent Vega had to make tough decisions under intense pressure in there."

"We are all aware," Hargrave said. "And it will be taken into consideration."

Wu had shown her snippets of video from the dark web version of the game, and she had seen herself as Athena, fighting, strategizing, and killing.

"What about the public?" Dani asked, partly to take the attention from her own actions and partly out of sheer curiosity. "Has anyone on the dark web figured out the game was real? If this leaks out to the media—"

"No one knows," Hargrave said. "And it's going to stay that way." He appeared to consider his next words. "You will be offered counseling, Agent Vega. It's important that you process everything you've been through, and I strongly recommend you talk to someone."

"I'll do whatever is necessary," she hedged, unwilling to commit, then made her stance clear. "And I expect to return to full duty."

"After the administrative and criminal investigation into your actions," Hargrave said, "we'll consider your next assignment."

She would have to wait to find out what the future held for her. This was not the first time her actions had been investigated and her judgment questioned. The irony was that her peers and supervisors would spend months contemplating decisions she had made in less than a second. To say that it wasn't fair would be pointless. Accountability was necessary, and she believed her choices would be vindicated.

"You are dismissed, Agent Vega," Hargrave said. "Be sure you're available at all times."

She stood to leave, and Wu followed her out into the hallway. Once the door closed behind them, she laid a hand on his forearm, bringing him to a halt. Everyone had directed questions at her, but she had a few of her own.

"Did the ERT finish searching the Brinkley estate?" she asked him.

While Wu and the tactical team had been trying to rescue her from the silo, he had sent a signed search warrant to his counterpart at the San Francisco field office, requesting an Evidence Response Team to collect anything relating to the case from Oscar and Megan Brinkley's palatial home in Santa Clara.

"Come to the JOC with me," he said. "The report just came in."

Hargrave had already dismissed her, but Wu was inviting her to the briefing rather than sending her home to sit by her phone. She hoped this boded well for the upcoming OPR investigation.

When they walked into the center, Johnson rushed forward to greet her, eyes brimming. "I am so glad to see you," she said, giving her a quick hug.

Patel grasped her hand in both of his. "I've been reviewing the video," he said. "And I still can't believe what you did."

"Surprised you showed up so soon," Flint said, ambling over. "Figured you'd try to milk it for a week off."

"And let you have all the fun?" she asked him.

Wu sat in the swivel chair at the head of the conference table. "What's the latest from California?"

"They had to call in a specialist to get into both safes," Flint said.

She felt like she had missed a lot. "There was more than one safe?" she asked.

Flint tipped his head toward Johnson, who was already working, tapping her keyboard.

"Oscar had one in his office," Johnson said. "But the real prize was in Megan's bedroom. We almost missed the safe hidden behind the mirror, but then Flint recalled what Megan said before she died."

The cryptic comment came back to Dani. *"If you want the truth, you've got to see what's in the mirror,"* she quoted, then glanced at Flint. "The silo was on fire, and Megan knew she might not make it out alive. She clearly didn't want to take her secrets to the grave."

Photographs taken by the ERT appeared on the wall screen. A full-length mirror stood open at a right angle from the wall, revealing a safe.

"The only thing inside was a flash drive," Johnson said. "This was on it."

The screen switched to reveal virtual files.

Johnson began to click them, opening numerous documents.

Dani leaned forward, riveted to the screen. "Those are bank transactions."

"It's a money trail," Johnson said. "Funds were transferred from Oscar Brinkley to Colonel Xavier Treadway." She paused. "And look at the dates."

Dani narrowed her eyes. "That's ten years ago."

"Take a closer look," Flint said before Johnson could respond. "The date of the first transaction is one month to the day before Megan Brinkley and her mother were kidnapped."

Dani felt her jaw slacken. "Megan was only fifteen at the time. She didn't pay anyone to have herself and her mother abducted."

"And her mother certainly didn't pay to have herself killed," Wu said. "This is the proverbial smoking gun."

"Oscar Brinkley hired the Colonel and his team to kidnap his wife and daughter," Flint said.

"You think the son of a bitch made killing his wife part of the deal?" Dani asked.

"It was the whole deal," Flint said. "The kidnapping was a pretext for murder."

343

"But why drag his teenage daughter into it?" Dani said, unable to believe anyone could be so callous. "She'd be traumatized."

"Exactly," Flint said. "Oscar Brinkley was stone cold. He couldn't put himself in his daughter's place to understand how being kidnapped and held captive would destroy her sense of security."

"And he didn't comprehend how much losing her mother would hurt Megan," Wu added. "Imagine being raised by a father like that."

"We found evidence in one of the other folders that Brinkley wanted to divorce his wife but didn't want her to get half his fortune," Johnson said. "He stood to save more than a billion dollars by killing her."

Dani grasped the depth of Brinkley's ruthless cunning. "If she has an accident or dies under suspicious circumstances, everyone looks at him. But if she's the victim of a horrible crime—one that also harms his daughter—who would question it?"

"No one," Wu said. "Because no one would be so heartless as to have his own child abducted."

"The guy was a piece of work," Flint said. "But he was strategic. He made sure the FBI wouldn't get to the bottom of it. He didn't pay the full ransom, giving the Colonel an excuse to shoot his wife; then he sends the rest of the money without telling the case agents he was doing it."

Another piece clicked into place. "That's how he paid them for the hit," Dani said. "If anyone looked at his finances, he could explain how and why his money was transferred to an offshore account." She brought her palm down on the table. "That's how he paid the Colonel. It was right under everyone's nose."

"So why keep incriminating evidence?" Patel said. "All this documentation . . . it's a digital confession."

"I have a theory," Wu said. "People in Brinkley's position are subject to blackmail. He probably wanted to keep evidence on hand in case the Colonel—or anyone he worked with—ever decided they wanted more money for their continued silence." He lifted a shoulder. "The Colonel and his men would think twice before blackmailing someone who had evidence they'd committed murder."

Everyone paused to consider his words.

"His daughter must have stumbled onto the information," Dani said after a few moments. "She worked on the defense contract with him. He had a secure server to avoid corporate espionage, but he had to allow her access. She's clearly brilliant at codes, puzzles, and ciphers. She must have seen encrypted files and looked on it as a challenge."

"That's what we thought," Patel said. "She cracked his encrypted files, read them, and made a copy for herself on a flash drive."

Flint nodded. "And when she reads what's in the files, she goes batshit."

"How can we be sure she was the only one behind the game?" Johnson asked no one in particular.

"While I had the link to the game in the control panel, I uploaded everything that hadn't been destroyed into a quarantined server for an in-depth analysis," Patel said.

Dani braced herself for an onslaught of technobabble.

"The dark web version of the game was heavily edited," he continued. "I didn't know she referred to herself as Nemesis until I reviewed the raw footage from the internal server."

Dani tilted her head in thought. "Why would she hide a fake name?"

Patel responded with a question. "What do you think of when you think of the word *nemesis*?"

"A relentless adversary," she said. "Someone who believes you should suffer, but for a specific reason."

"You're talking about revenge," Wu said.

"*Nemesis* is the Greek goddess of revenge." Patel paused for emphasis. "That's *goddess*. Not *god*."

"Female, not male." Dani closed her eyes for a long moment. "If I had remembered that, I might have figured out who was behind this a lot sooner. I thought of the game maker as our nemesis, but Megan viewed herself as *the* Nemesis, exacting vengeance on everyone who had wronged her."

"She was brilliant, you know," Patel said quietly. "She never released them to the public, but she designed her own virtual escape room games that were filled with riddles and clues."

"I can see how she would become obsessed with escaping after being held captive when she was a teenager," Flint said. "It's sad she got warped into something dark by circumstances."

"Not circumstances," Wu said. "Circumstances imply an accidental twist of fate. Megan was twisted by her father."

Dani thought back to her first meeting with Megan. "She tried to pin it all on her father by posing as his prisoner in the silo." Another thought occurred to her. "What about Senator Sledge?" she asked. "That's how this whole thing started. How does he fit in?"

Johnson pulled up another screen. "These are more recent financial transactions."

There were records of wire transfers over the past three years going from Oscar Brinkley's account to the Colonel's, followed by copies of cryptic texts indicating that the money had reached its final destination in the Cayman Islands. Another file tied the offshore account to Senator Sledge.

"You remember the steganography in the picture of Sir Arthur Conan Doyle?" Johnson asked. When everyone nodded, she pulled up another document. "This is the information that was hidden in that image. The funds eventually ended up at an offshore account affiliated with the senator."

"Megan Brinkley had to be the original source who called the senator's chief of staff," Dani said. "But Nathan Costner told his friend the caller was an older male. How did she pull that off?"

"Figured that out this morning," Patel said as if he'd been waiting for the question. "In the process of transferring the data, I discovered whatever verbal commands I entered into the system came out in the voice of Oscar Brinkley."

"Come again?" Dani said.

"That's how Megan did it," Patel said. "Voice-cloning software embedded in the game."

Dani closed her eyes, recalling the dreaded sound of Nemesis. "Everyone heard a baritone male," she said. "Who would suspect it was a young woman talking?"

"I think that's why Megan kept her father alive as long as she did," Patel said, answering another nagging question before she posed it. "She would have used his voice to call Colonel Treadway to lure him into the trap, but she might have needed him in case the software failed or glitched. She could force him to say any random words that weren't in the database in case it was necessary."

"A backup plan," Dani said. "Insurance in case something went wrong with the software."

Once Megan killed her father, she could no longer use him to create voice commands or dialogue. Raised by a cold and calculating father, Megan had learned by example from the best.

"From the timeline, it appears the senator took bribes over the past three years but wasn't involved in the abductions a decade ago," Dani said. "What's going on with Sledge?"

Wu spoke up quickly. "You're not assigned to that part of the case, Vega."

"I get it," she said. "Need to know only."

Wu glanced at his watch. "The senator is getting some visitors right about now. There should be a breaking story on the six-o'clock news tonight."

She gave him a knowing smile. Wu had obviously orchestrated one of the FBI's signature multiple-warrant services. There would be images of raid-jacketed Feds carrying boxes of files out of the senator's many office locations throughout the state. When he finished crapping his boxers, Sledge would speed-dial every contact on his extensive list.

But this time it would do him no good.

She recalled that her boss and Flint had both been evasive during the flight back to New York. "You explained how you found me by searching through decommissioned missile silos," she said. "But how did you know where to start looking?"

"There's something you should know, and I've waited until you recovered a bit more to share it," Wu said. "Have you been in touch with your family?"

"I was planning to visit them tonight," she said, completely thrown by the non sequitur. "They know I was on an assignment, but I didn't tell them how long I would be gone. They won't miss me for another—"

"Well, I have," Wu cut in.

Icy fingers of dread crept down her spine.

"I spoke to your brother yesterday," Wu continued. "I asked him not to reach out to you until we had a chance to talk."

"How do you know Axel?" she said, heart hammering.

"I've been to your aunt's apartment in the Bronx," he said. "After he asked me to come."

"Wait . . . what?" She could not make sense of the collision of her two worlds.

"Your brother is amazing," Patel said, apparently unable to stop himself. "He broke the case."

Wu directed a glare at him, and Patel's mouth snapped shut.

Dani turned with deliberate slowness from the cybercrime analyst back to Wu. "Why is my brother involved in this case?"

"He's not involved," Wu began. "Well, he is, but not in the way you think." He lifted his hands in a calming gesture. "Let me explain."

Dani barely managed to control herself as her supervisor spent the next fifteen minutes describing how Nemesis had tried to send a Trojan horse cyberattack into her brother's computer. When he told her about the stealth virus Axel had implanted to backtrack to the game, she finally understood.

"My brother was watching the whole time," she said. "And he knew I was Athena."

Wu nodded. "We told him we would take it from there and that he should not risk his computer by accessing this game on the dark web." He shrugged. "He monitored anyway. There was no way to stop him. I think he also spent money upvoting you."

"He must have been worried sick," she said.

"I talked to him last night," Wu said. "The family knows you're safe now. They've agreed to keep the entire investigation confidential."

"My sister knows too?"

"They were all there when Detective Flint and I visited," Wu said. "But again, they know you're okay and—"

"That doesn't mean they're good with any of it," she said.

Erica and Axel had also been devastated by the death of their father and the loss of their mother, as she had. Dani had always refused to talk about her work, protecting them from further exposure to brutality and violence. And now they had watched grisly scenes play out on their computer, all the while knowing their big sister was in a battle to the death. She imagined the two of them, terrified, frantically sending money through cyberspace, hoping to keep her alive. The space closed in on her, and she realized there was only one place she wanted to be.

"I have to go see my family," she said to Wu, her throat constricting around the words.

CHAPTER 71

Forty minutes later, Dani stood on the fifth-floor landing of her *tía* Manuela's Bronx apartment. She walked to the door, then hesitated. Her sweet sister and shy brother had witnessed her in battle mode. They had watched her take human lives. When they looked at her, would they see Dani or Athena?

She knocked and waited for an eternity until Erica flung the door wide. Dani had spent the drive over rehearsing what she would say, but words failed her when she gazed into her sister's doe-brown eyes.

Erica reached out to tug her inside. "It's really you," she said, closing the door before wrapping slender arms around Dani's waist. "We were all so scared."

"Not me," Axel said from behind Erica. "In fact, I was kind of sorry for those assholes in the game with you."

Dark circles under his eyes put the lie to his words. He had been up at all hours, watching, and probably upvoting her avatar as Wu suspected.

She stretched out a hand to pull him in close. "I did what I had to do," she whispered. "Nothing more, nothing less."

How could she explain what it had been like in the game, the sound of Toro's last shuddering breaths, the acrid scent of Megan's charred body, the sight of Chopper's blood spurting from the gash in his neck, the feel of the heat burning her skin as she forced herself up the suffocating shaft.

He squirmed out from between his sisters and raised the remote in his hand. "You've got to see this."

Dani wedged herself between her siblings on the sofa. Axel pressed a button, unpausing the breaking news story on the television.

"Federal agents raided Independent US Senator Thomas Sledge's five offices around the state and in Capitol Hill in a simultaneous warrant service today," a handsome silver-haired news anchor said into the camera. "His office did not respond to repeated requests for comment." The screen switched to footage of agents wearing blue FBI raid jackets, carrying boxes to waiting vans.

Erica turned curious eyes toward Dani. "What's really going on?" she asked. "Are we going to see Sledge doing a perp walk?"

Dani grinned. "I can neither confirm nor deny—"

"Oh please," Axel said. "That dude is going down." He paused the story again. "And we know you had something to do with it."

Now they were getting to the awkward part. She glanced around. "Is Manuela here?"

Axel waved a dismissive hand. "She went to the bodega to buy lottery tickets before tonight's drawing."

"How much does everyone know?"

"It's just us," Erica said, sweeping an arm out to indicate the apartment. "We haven't told the rest of the family."

Gracias for small favors. She turned to Axel. "My boss told me you called him. I can't thank you enough, but you shouldn't have watched what happened in the game."

"Were we supposed to pretend like we didn't know you were fighting for your life?" he said. "What did you expect?"

Tears gathered in Erica's eyes. "We had to help you."

This was so much worse than she'd thought it would be. Now she understood why her father had never shared stories about his deployments.

She took one of each of their hands in hers. "Soldiers and law enforcement officers take on the enemy to keep their loved ones safe at home. The less you two know about what I do, the better."

Her heart was not pure like Erica's or kind like Axel's. Dani had the heart of a warrior, cast in hues of shadow and light. In her case, perhaps mostly shadow. As Manuela had reminded her many times, she was her mother's daughter. Her mother the killer.

Her cell phone buzzed in her pocket. She let go of Erica's and Axel's hands to slide it out. Her spine stiffened when she saw the caller ID.

She tapped the screen. "Special Agent Vega."

An efficient female voice greeted her. "Stand by for Lieutenant Colonel Harmon."

Dani reflexively shot to her feet and stood at attention, every part of her body forming a rigid line except the arm holding the cell phone to her ear.

Moments later, a man's Texas drawl addressed her. "Corporal Vega?"

"Yes, sir."

She had heard the regimental executive officer speak on several occasions at Fort Benning, where he would address the troops before key assignments. As XO, he was second-in-command of the regiment. She was well beneath his notice, and they had never had a direct conversation. She could think of no reason he would call her months after she had transitioned out of the armed forces.

"I wanted to contact you personally regarding your actions during the bombing incident," Colonel Harmon said.

A wave of dread surged through her. He didn't need to spell it out. The Army had conducted an official investigation after multiple devices had exploded in the compound, killing and wounding some of her fellow Rangers. Her conduct was deemed to fall within mission parameters, exonerating her of responsibility. In her heart, she had felt responsible anyway. Had the Army changed its conclusions?

Erica and Axel stared at her, and she realized they could overhear most of the conversation thanks to the colonel's commanding voice.

"You are to report to Fort Benning to receive a Purple Heart," Colonel Harmon said.

"Sir?"

"You sustained an injury in a combat situation," he said. "Your lieutenant submitted everyone involved in the mission for medals."

"Sir, I don't deserve—"

"The ceremony will be conducted at thirteen hundred hours next Tuesday," he went on as if she hadn't spoken. "You may bring family if you wish."

"Family?"

His tone softened a fraction. "There's a reason I'm the one who's calling you, Corporal Vega. There's also a reason for you to come to Georgia to receive your medal."

She waited.

"I served with your father."

She sucked in a breath.

"He told everyone about his little Dani." The Texas accent grew thicker as the colonel continued. "Other little girls played with Barbies, but you were GI Joe all the way. He showed everyone pictures of you in his Ranger T-shirt, snapping a salute when you were five years old."

Tears stung the back of her eyes as she remembered rummaging through her dad's closet to dig out a shirt. She had passed up her mother's high-heeled shoes to slide her small feet into her dad's combat boots, which reached her thighs.

"I wish he could see you now," the colonel said. "He'd be proud."

Erica gave her a watery smile, and Axel's cheeks flushed as they listened to the exchange.

"It would be my honor to present you with the Purple Heart at the ceremony," Colonel Harmon said quietly.

Dani found her voice. "Thank you, sir," she said. "I'll be there."

She tapped the screen with a nerveless finger, disconnecting the call.

"Can we go with you, Dani?" Erica said, gesturing to her brother.

Her gaze drifted to the wall, where a shadow box with their father's Purple Heart hung.

"He's a hero," she whispered. "I'm just a . . . a . . ."

"A hero too," Axel said.

"But I couldn't save him," Dani continued. "Couldn't save any of them." She thought of her father, of her fellow Rangers, and, finally, of Toro. "I don't deserve any special recognition."

"That's where you're wrong," Axel said. "The medal is for putting yourself in harm's way, even if it means getting hurt."

"Maybe you'll believe it when the Army makes it official," Erica said. "You have the biggest heart of anyone I know."

Dani reached out to pull her brother and sister into a tight embrace. She was her father's daughter after all.

ACKNOWLEDGMENTS

My husband, Mike, has been incredibly supportive through all my endeavors. The best partner and friend anyone could want, he is my rock.

My son, Max, brings me joy every day. How blessed I am to play a part in his journey.

So much more than an agent, Liza Fleissig shares my vision and makes miracles happen. Her advice, support, and outstanding professionalism have been life changing for me and many others.

My other agent, Ginger Harris-Dontzin, joined Liza to take me on a whirlwind tour of Lower Manhattan, the Bronx, the subway system, and other areas featured in this story, lending their insight as native New Yorkers to bring the venue to life.

Special thanks to my neighbor, friend, and private pilot Rod Kunkel, who helped me figure out how a small plane could theoretically traverse the country while eluding detection. (Don't try it!)

The men and women of the FBI work without expectation of fame or fortune. They dedicate themselves to upholding their motto, "Fidelity, Bravery, Integrity." A special thanks goes out to Ret. Special Agent Jerri Williams, who shares their stories in her award-winning *FBI Retired Case File Review* podcast.

To create a fictional story with an authentic feel, it's imperative to speak to those who were there. Former FBI executive Lauren C.

Anderson, who served in New York City, was generous with her time and considerable expertise. Any liberties taken or mistakes are my own.

Thanks also to former Marine and retired FBI Special Agent Mitch Stern, who helped keep me on track with both military and FBI facts.

Senior editor Megha Parekh, my acquiring editor with Thomas & Mercer, has been with me through every part of the process. I am grateful for her support and willingness to work with me as the story took shape.

My developmental editor, Charlotte Herscher, put her impressive talent toward making this story better. Her incisive observations and keen eye for details were invaluable.

The amazing team of marketing, editing, and artwork professionals at Thomas & Mercer is second to none. This story is particularly complex, and they worked with me tirelessly to double-check each component of the unfolding mystery. I am incredibly blessed to have such talented professionals by my side.

ABOUT THE AUTHOR

Wall Street Journal bestselling and award-winning author Isabella Maldonado wore a gun and badge in real life before turning to crime writing. A graduate of the FBI National Academy in Quantico and the first Latina to attain the rank of captain in the Fairfax County Police Department just outside DC, she retired as the commander of special investigations and forensics. During more than two decades on the force, her assignments included hostage negotiator, department spokesperson, and district station commander. She uses her law enforcement background to bring a realistic edge to her writing, which includes the bestselling FBI Special Agent Nina Guerrera series (optioned by Netflix for a feature film starring Jennifer Lopez) and the Detective Veranda Cruz series. Her books have been translated into twenty languages. For more information, visit www.isabellamaldonado.com.